Unto them he shall come
In shadow he will dwell
His hand ye shall seek
To the fires of Ferran's Hell.
One will win before it has begun.
- Author Unknown

Found in the archives of
Talaith's library

BOOKS BY TAMERI ETHERTON

*Song of the Swords**

The Prince of Dragons

The Stones of Resurrection

The Temple of Sacrifice

The Ruins of Betrayal

The Veils of Deception

The Keeper of Stars

*The Fatal Fae**

Fatal Illusion

Fatal Assassin

Fatal Legacy

Fatal Forever

Fatal Destiny

*Court of Stars**

Sunset in Shadow

*Chronicles of Eidyn**

Child of Fire

Dragon Mage

*Daring Ever Afters**

Enchant

*Books that are part of the Aetherverse: The fantastical realms of Tameri Etherton. Characters and storylines intersect within the books with magical consequences.

This book is dedicated to Abel, Carly, Rebecca, Brandon, and Lynn. Because of your faith and patience, this book made its way to the light.
And to my husband David for always believing in me.

TEACUP
DRAGON
PUBLISHING

TAMERI ETHERTON

AELINAE

WORLD MAP

N
THE WALL
THE NARTHVIER
LAN GYLLARELLE
MIDVALE
THE TELMARAN ISLANDS
PADERAU
SILDEN R.
THE ULLAN DESERT
SEA OF JADEN
JADEN FLATS
AL ROAD
LAKE OSTER
HIDDEN VALLEY
ELDERS PASS
GREAT BARREN GORGE
NES OF LDAAR
WASTES OF SLOE
JANSEN PLAIN
JANSEN STRAIT
THE EASTERN SEAS

Pendrian Wastes
Western Seas
Denk Scarbos
Spine of Ohlim
Isle of Ardyn
Caer Idris
Caer Danuri
Mount Nadrene
Danuri Provence
Gaarendahl
Celyn Eryri
Talaith
Lake Oster
Ahkae
Summerlands
Stones of Kaldaar
Sitari
Summer Seas

The Narthvier
The Weirren
Lan Gyllarelle
The Ullan Desert
Telmaran Islands
Sea of Jaden
Paderau
Jansen Strait
Wastes of Sloe
Eastern Seas

THE TWO KINGDOMS
The Wall
The Narthvier
The Ullan Desert
Sea of Jaden
The Telmaran Islands
Great Barren Gorge
Jaden Flats
Hidden Valley
Elders Pass
Jansen Strait
Jansen Plain
Wastes of Sloe
Eastern Seas

THE SUMMER SEAS
MEKIAE
SRINIVAS
THATIRAKA
MNABAIE
SCIABARRA
AHKAE
DETARRE
SUMMERLANDS
ANTHOS
NYLS
SALDANNA
MENURRA
WINE FIELDS
PIRATES COVE
SITARI
The Sea Kingdom

CHAPTER ONE

Never let fear determine your fate.

Taryn tilted her head toward the sky, eyes closed, breathing in the salt air. Sunlight warmed her cheeks. Despite the quiet around her, and the serenity of being at sea, hearing those words again caused a spike in her pulse. Nadra had whispered them to her when she'd taken Rhoane to Dal Tara for their final bonding. At the time, she'd thought nothing of them—advice given for someday. A quiver of dread tickled her spine. Taryn hoped that day wasn't today.

Are we in danger? Taryn sent the thought to Nadra. Silence answered. Never let fear determine your fate. What did it mean? Was something about to happen? Or was Nadra reminding her to enjoy the simple moments of life? Taryn kicked at the boards of the crow's nest. Pain flared from her toes to her shin, eliciting a muffled curse from between pinched lips.

The boat creaked against the gentle pull of the sea, moorings flapped on their tethers. All was as it had been since setting sail from Talaith three days hence. Calm, peaceful even. Yet something was off.

Fickle gods. Taryn was tired of the relentless guessing games they played. Warnings, riddles, all of it served only one purpose —to drive her mad. Well, they were succeeding. She was losing her mind *and* pissed off. Taking three deep breaths, she focused on the journey at hand. At the importance of this particular trip. It wouldn't do to rattle her nerves or upset her mother over nothing but suspicions.

Twenty-three of Empress Lliandra's finest vessels traveled from Talaith to Menurra. Once there, Hayden would officially ask Sabina's parents for her hand in marriage and complete the ceremony of claiming himself as hers. A chuckle tickled Taryn's gut. Poor Hayden. He continued to believe he would have to pierce an intimate part of his anatomy. It was terrible of her, she knew, but Taryn chose not to share the truth with him—the torment on his face each time she brought it up was too humorous to end.

A sharp tilt of the ship unbalanced her, and she grabbed the railing of the crow's nest to steady her legs. Tessa leaned over the weathered wood, a bit too far for Taryn's comfort. Both hands held a telescope pressed to her right eye.

"What do you see?" Taryn asked as she twirled a lock of Tessa's unruly curls around her finger. She released the slip of hair to corkscrew against the breeze. On the best of days, Tessa had a terrible time controlling her hair, but against the constant wind, it was a lost cause.

Taryn bent and enclosed her half-sister in her arms, feeling the warmth of her youthful body, the lean muscles, and emerging curves that would soon make her a woman. Too soon. Taryn had only known Tessa a short time and already she was blossoming out of her gangly childhood into an intelligent, beautiful adolescent.

"Fog." Tessa scowled beneath the heavy scope. "I lost sight of the other ships, it's so thick."

Taryn scanned the area, noting the heavy mist that rolled toward them, sucking daylight and warmth with its advance.

Rhoane, do you see the fog? Her thought met a hard wall, cutting her off from her betrothed.

Kaida? Again, the invisible barrier. Shards of dread bit deeper into her skin, cutting at her nerves. Something was definitely wrong. Her instincts had been right, and she'd ignored them.

For reasons Lliandra refused to explain, she'd forbidden the grierbas from traveling on her ship. Her mother had warmed up to Kaida in the past few months, and Lliandra's sudden decision to have Kaida bunk with Rhoane seemed spurious. The empress had argued that Taryn didn't need protection amid an armed fleet, at least, not any more than the other ladies would—with the implied reasoning being the empress could protect them all. Taryn had disagreed vehemently, but her mother refused to listen. The only reason Taryn could fathom was that she was being punished for Marissa's death. It would be just like her mother to deny Taryn any sort of comfort. Now she wished she'd argued harder to keep the grierbas with her.

Soft words drifted through the mist. Taryn cocked her head and listened. Scraps of conversation pierced her ears, heightening her sense of danger. The unnatural fog advanced quickly and within moments, a thick grey mist blocked sight more than a few paces away. An eerie half-silence descended upon them.

After a moment of stillness, shouts and cries erupted, causing a flurry of panic on the deck below.

"Tessa." Taryn faced her sister. "Stay here. Don't make a sound. No matter what you hear or see, do not, under any circumstances, leave this crow's nest. I don't care if it's for five days. You stay here. Don't try to be brave."

"I can fight as well as you." Tessa's shoulders were rigid. She stood to her full height, still a hand and a half shorter than Taryn.

"Of that, there's no doubt, my darling. But until I know what's going on, I don't want you in the scrap of things. Please, trust me on this."

Taryn pulled on her ShantiMari, not surprised when she found herself blocked.

"I can't use my power." Tessa's tone lost some of its confidence. "It's gone. How? Why?"

"Mine is as well. Do you recall how I taught you to keep a tiny bit of power in reserve? How it was like a flame in your heart you always kept lit, but never used?"

Tessa nodded, her cornflower-blue eyes huge against her tanned face.

"It's in there still. Don't let it go out. Ever." Taryn kissed her sister's forehead, inhaling her scent of peonies and a hint of perspiration. "Now, keep low so as not to be discovered. Until I can suss out what these brigands want, I need to know you're safe."

Tessa crouched against the side of the crow's nest, her legs bent to her chest, her arms wrapped protectively around them. "Will you come get me?"

"As soon as it's safe."

No sound came from beneath the crow's nest and Taryn shimmied down the rope ladder without drawing attention to herself. She darted behind a stack of crates, realizing her mistake a moment too late. Several men approached from the opposite side, where they'd extended planks from their ship to Lliandra's. Her dread spiraled into full-on terror. They all held weapons, and she saw, swirling above their heads, an inky thread of ShantiMari. Whatever that thing was, she was certain it was what blocked her power. These men weren't just pirates—they were something much more dangerous. She choked down the fear that threatened to immobilize her into inaction.

Her mind whirled with possibilities and scenarios even as her body tensed, ready for battle. Adrenaline rushed through her veins, igniting her will to fight. But first, she had to draw their attention away from Tessa.

A man taller than Baehlon, and just as wide, glanced at her.

His swift gaze took in her hair and attire. Taryn reached for her sword, but it was locked in her cabin, a floor below. Cursing, she pivoted away from the man and sprinted toward the door leading to her room. The brute gave chase, loping after her. At least Tessa was safe. For now.

Midway across the deck, the door to their cabins burst open and another brigand shoved Lliandra and Eliahnna in front of him. Taryn jerked to a halt, her breath caught in her throat. The sight of her mother wrenched her heart, searing her adrenaline into a burst of anger. Her legs shook as she fought to control the surge of fury. How dare these men disgrace the empress. How dare they attack a royal ship. Her fists clenched, but Lliandra shook her head, a subtle warning that Taryn should not act rash.

The mask Lliandra always wore was gone. In its place was the haggard face of a woman who'd spent too long wearing the cares of a kingdom. Deep wrinkles furrowed her brow and her usually bright-blue eyes were clouded with age.

Despite her sallow, jaundiced skin, there was a firmness to Lliandra's lips, a silent challenge to any who saw the reality of their empress's condition.

"Mother." The whispered word, heavy with Taryn's conflicted emotions, held a promise that the men responsible would pay for what they'd done. Concern for the woman Taryn barely knew, but had given her life, fought against a need to destroy the intruders. The intensity of her feelings frightened Taryn. This wasn't bloodlust., It was something different. Powerful, addictive.

Taryn took in the others held captive with the empress. Eliahnna stood tall, her graceful demeanor covering the terror Taryn sensed in her. Sabina shook out her long hair and stamped her foot, an indignant snarl on her lips. The ladies' maids were there, except for Saeko. Faelara was missing as well. Taryn hoped they'd managed to avoid being taken. Hoped they'd heard the commotion and got off the ship in time. Her gut told her they hadn't.

Lliandra narrowed her eyes and smoothed her skirts with trembling hands. "What is the meaning of this? You have illegally boarded my vessel and I demand to speak to your leader."

One of the men chuckled and moved aside, allowing another, shorter man, to step into the small gathering.

His countenance made her believe this was the one in charge. Hair like a raven's wing ruffled in the breeze. With eyes of green fire and skin the color of ancient parchment, he was handsome in a rugged way. In any other situation, Taryn might've been tempted to coax him into conversation, to discover what caused his lip to curl the tiniest bit, as if he knew a joke he was dying to share. His affable manner didn't fool her. Power cascaded from him, the same hue as his eyes, but tinged in black.

Unnatural, yet seductive.

She casually regarded him, assessing his posture, the arrogance of his stance. If this was indeed their leader, and she fully believed he was, then this was the man responsible for blocking her power and taking her family hostage. The only thing she wished to discuss with him was his execution.

"I am Cashiel, the new owner of this ship." He gave a nonchalant wave toward the others.

Several men brandished swords, forcing the party to the center of the deck. A faint spark lit forth from one of the crewmen.

Cashiel chuckled low. "My dear man, don't try that again, or you'll find yourself tossed overboard as a meal for the sea king."

"What do you want?" Lliandra fumed. "If it's treasure you're after, there is none on this ship. Or any of the others, if you're thinking to go one by one, looting the holds."

"No treasure?" Cashiel tilted his head to the side. "But you're mistaken."

His gaze turned toward Taryn. Heat burned from her toes to the tips of her ears. He was using his power to assess her, to take inventory of her flaws. She could feel him—his power—as it scoured her body, inside and out. The invasive probe continued until his lips widened into a grin that sent tremors of warning through her every nerve ending.

The scan had taken less than a minute, yet it had drained her and left Taryn feeling violated.

This man had not come just for her, but for something far more dangerous. He might've tamped her ShantiMari, but his thoughts he shared with abandon. He sought her darathi vorsi soul.

"Tie them up and take this one," he crooked a finger at Taryn, "to my rooms."

"You think bedding me will give you what you want?" Taryn shook her head, her voice low, filled with warning. "You think you can break my bond by sullying yourself with my body? Then you're a fool. Bed me hard, bed me for weeks on end—you'll not have what you seek."

Cashiel spun toward her, the green fire sparking from his eyes into actual flames that reached the top of his forehead. Taryn flinched and her confidence wavered.

"The last thing I want is to touch your body. This," his right hand curved as if to cup her breast, then traveled to her hips, "is sacred. I am forbidden from tainting myself with you." The last was said as an aside, more to himself than her.

A flicker of irritation crossed his features and he turned from her to speak with the brute who had chased Taryn. "Guard her." To a group of men to his right, he ordered, "Set up a frame. Make it sturdy." Cashiel returned to study her face, the flames wild, a sneer to his lips.

He reminded her of someone, but who was hidden beneath her terror.

"If you insist on making a spectacle for your family, so be it. Just remember, it was your choice."

His words vibrated through her mind. What was her choice? If he wasn't going to rape her, then what? And what was the frame for? Images of torture filled her thoughts. Her stomach rioted with spasms of anxiety. She was going to be sick. Right there, in front of this madman, she was going to lose control of her wits—and bodily functions.

Get it together, Taryn. This is what he wants. Her internal pep talk did little to ease the bile creeping up her throat, but she forced herself to keep breathing. Keep her family's safety at the forefront of her mind.

A pair of rough hands pushed her forward and she stumbled before righting herself. A quick count of his men came to eighteen. Without her sword, she'd have to fight hand-to-hand. Not good odds. Her best recourse was to let Cashiel take her prisoner without a fight. To let his plan play out until she could assess the situation fully.

She slumped her shoulders, as if accepting it was a lost cause to fight. Her jailor tugged her arms behind her back, his grip strong, sure. This was a man who understood his own strength and how much pressure to apply to keep her compliant. This was a man trained in the finer points of combat. Not a man to tussle with under the circumstances.

Cashiel's men worked with quiet efficiency. Several brought chairs from belowdecks and arranged them in neat rows. The women were seated according to rank, with Eliahnna, Sabina, and the empress in the front. Their wrists were bound, but left to rest upon their laps, while their ankles were secured to the chair legs.

Another group of men ordered the ship's captain and crew to strip to their breeches before tying them to the railing and posts. Taryn caught the captain's eye—grim determination etched his features, making him look like a stalwart cliff facing an oncoming storm.

Her gaze traveled from him to the seated women. A spark of fury lit Sabina's eyes. Her bound hands clenched and unclenched in her lap. Eliahnna watched the proceedings with her usual calm. A slight fluttering of her lashes and wobble to her lips were her only outward signs of distress. Lliandra remained impassive, giving the impression of being in control despite being restrained. Several locks of her elaborately styled hair had escaped their pins and cascaded over her shoulder. Even with the horrors unfolding around her, Lliandra maintained a defiant dignity. Her ravaged looks held a beauty Taryn admired. This woman, this strange and complicated woman, knew her own power. She wielded confidence as easily as she put on a gown in the morning.

As the men bustled around the now secure crew and ladies, they shouted commands to each other, using a cobbled lingua franca of Elennish and Danuri. Taryn followed the best she could, not having mastered the latter language, but understanding enough to know nothing good was about to happen.

She observed the subtle pecking order with keen interest. Cashiel was the leader, but beneath him were several others who the rest of the brigands obeyed without question. Cashiel rarely spoke. Instead, he leaned against a pillar, spinning an ornate dagger between his fingers.

A chill rushed down her spine. She knew that dagger. The last she'd seen of it was at the Crystal Palace when Rhoane had placed it inside a warded casket for safekeeping. Tessa had found the curious weapon amid Herbret's belongings, along with several texts that Taryn had yet to fully study. What the blasted thing was doing here—in Cashiel's hands—she couldn't fathom. And how had the bastard gotten hold of it? The answer slunk across her thoughts. Someone at the palace had to have given it to Cashiel, and Taryn had a good idea who—Marissa.

Taryn remained still, her captor's grip allowing little movement. With each rotation of Cashiel's knife, her already heightened imagination fabricated more terrors, each one worse than before.

Never let fear determine your fate.

Nadra's admonition buttressed her fleeting courage. Weaponless, powerless, and outnumbered, Taryn resolved not to let Cashiel break her. She had faith that Rhoane would find a way to free the others. She scoffed at the thought. She hated the idea of being a damsel in distress, yet that was exactly what she was. Although, she'd never needed rescuing before, and she was damned if she'd need it now. Swallowing her cowardice, she resolved to rely on herself and the others to extricate themselves from the situation. For all she knew, Rhoane was in a worse situation.

Her heartbeat quickened. What was happening with Rhoane and the others? If Cashiel hurt Rhoane, she'd flay him alive.

Taryn's arms were jerked above her head at the same time her feet were kicked apart. Rough rope was looped around her wrists and ankles, and pulled taut, then tied to posts that had been erected on the deck. One of Cashiel's men took a little too much pride in his work, tightening the rope until her wrists burned. Warmth trickled down her forearm in a crimson line. She bit hard against a grunt of pain and met Cashiel's unreadable gaze.

Taryn couldn't remember a time she'd been more terrified, but as long as she kept Cashiel's attention on her, he might spare the others. She had to buy them time.

"Something tells me you don't have the stomach for torture. Which one of these handsome fellas will do the honors?"

He sauntered over to stand in front of her, the blade of his dagger coming to rest between her breasts. Despite the thunderous pounding of her heart, she kept her face placid, her breath even. He slid the tip across her chest, lifting it only to avoid touching her pendant. He held it steady beneath her chin. Swallowing too hard would break the skin. She stared into his unnatural eyes, challenging him. The need to know him—to understand how far he would push her—drove her thoughts.

"You'll find, I have much more than a stomach for pain. I spent some time in the dungeons of Caer Idris and learned much of what I know from your father." His low voice was for her ears only. "I was his apprentice then, but I'm a Master now."

Ferran's bells, she was fucked. The short amount of time she'd spent in her father's dungeons was enough to convince her she never wanted to return. The screams of the soldiers Zakael had mutilated haunted her still.

She scanned his features, looking for any signs he might be related to Valterys. If so, perhaps this was nothing more than a play to take the throne from Zakael. Their similarities ended with onyx hair. Cashiel lacked the height and patrician features of her father. Her captor's face tended more toward fullness in the cheeks, a rounding of the forehead and chin neither Valterys nor Zakael had. Yet something tugged at familiarity.

"I'm sure he'd be ever so proud," Taryn taunted, "but he's dead."

Cashiel's eyes tightened to little slits. "They say you murdered him."

"They say a lot of things. I'll let you decide what's true."

His blade scraped along her shoulder, tearing the fabric of her thin cotton blouse. At her bound wrists, he yanked against the seam and her sleeve fell away, leaving her arm bare.

"Each time you challenge me, I'll remove another part of your clothing."

"Then strip me now, because I'll not give in to you. Ever."

A long exhale flared his nostrils, a smile curled his lips. "I heard you were irascible. I had hoped the rumors were true."

The dagger caught on the last button of her shirt and he roughly tugged upward, ripping the fabric until it dangled pathetically from her right shoulder. With a swift jerk, he tore the blouse away.

She hung from her restraints in a cotton camisole, the closest thing to a bra Margaret Tan had been able to make. Taryn shivered against the breeze.

"Your body belies your words. You're like every other woman

I've met. Once you get them unclothed, they're nothing but kittens that need petting."

Taryn's gut seized and she flinched, tightening the rope at her wrists. It was an unconscious attempt to hide from any petting he might attempt, but her restraints kept her within touching distance of his foulness. A whimper rose to her lips. This was not a time to show weakness or repulsion, no matter how much the image of him touching her made her want to vomit.

"I assure you, I'm nothing like the women you've met. You can pet me all you like. At the end of this, I'm going to cut your dick off and make you choke on it."

His hand whipped around, catching her cheek with a powerful blow. Taryn's vision danced with stars and she tasted blood.

"Stop it!" Eliahnna cried from where she sat. "What do you want with us?"

No, no, no, no. Don't attract his attention. Taryn forced the words into a thought, but the wall kept her from speaking to Eliahnna's mind. *Fuck.* She had to find a way to circumvent Cashiel's block on her power.

Ever since that day in the clearing when Zakael had attacked her and cut her off from ShantiMari, she'd practiced hiding a part of her power, but she'd not had time to perfect how to reclaim it once it was hidden.

Cashiel turned from Taryn to address the ladies. He displayed a small, almost circular disk. "I want this."

A silver darathi vorsi scale. One of hers. Taryn sucked in her breath. She hated it when she was right.

"You can't," Sabina whispered. "You'll destroy her."

Cashiel tossed a challenging glance over his shoulder. "That's entirely up to her."

How he came to possess one of her darathi vorsi scales, she had no idea. But if he meant to claim her dragon soul, he'd have to not only possess her body, but also break her bond with Rhoane.

Only two weeks had passed since Rhoane's return to Talaith and their final bonding with Ohlin. While he loved her and she him, she wasn't certain how their bond would hold against Cashiel. It was too new. Too untested. Too much had happened in the past half season for them to process fully and forgive. Even though Marissa was responsible for breaking Rhoane, he had chosen to remain apart from Taryn. That cut deeper than any betrayal her sister had devised.

Marissa's death hadn't freed Taryn from the anguish of Rhoane's breaking, nor had her father's death absolved her need for revenge. If anything, the two had fueled in her a desire to rid the world of Telraicht-Noir ShantiMari and that meant coaxing Kaldaar out of hiding.

Without their god, the Telraicht Brotherhood would cease to exist. And she might find solace in her purpose to bring balance to Aelinae. To do that, she needed Rhoane.

The silver scale caught the afternoon light, winking its brightness. Her darathi vorsi stirred within, as if waking from a long slumber. Taryn fought the urge to shift into the dragon. The need was overwhelming. Becoming a dragon would certainly break her out of the restraints—if it was even possible to do while having her power blocked. Except, transforming into a dragon might be exactly what Cashiel wanted. It would not only expose her to everyone on the ship, but set her up for capture. And if Taryn's dragon was caught, she suspected Rhoane's darathi vorsi would seek her freedom.

Whatever the bastard had in mind, Taryn vowed, she'd not let him take Rhoane from her. Ever.

CHAPTER TWO

Rhoane glared at the fog, cursing the damned thing. He'd tried to send Taryn a warning, but his thoughts were blocked. Whatever had caused the mist wasn't good, that much he knew. Beside him, Baehlon shifted, his big hand on the hilt of his sword.

They were all on edge. For two bells, they'd heard nothing from the other ship. It was as if they'd disappeared within the fog. Rhoane touched the pendant at his throat, willing his thoughts to travel through it to Taryn's cynfar. Silence mocked him as it had been doing all afternoon. Unease rippled through his belly, leaving a sour taste in his mouth. He worried for Lliandra and the others, yes, but for Taryn he feared the most. If he couldn't reach her through his power, he was willing to place a wager neither could she.

A movement at the bow of the ship caught his attention and he turned in time to see Ebus and Gian slip over the railing to the deck.

"What news?" Rhoane's voice came out harsh, concern cracking the surface.

"The ship is there, shrouded in mist. Two other ships slipped in with the fog and captured the empress's vessel. Two dozen men guard the empress and crew. Their leader has Taryn apart from the rest of the ladies."

"Did you see her? Is she hurt?"

Ebus scratched his chin, then brushed water from his face. It ran from his hair to his sleek nose, and dripped from there to his feet. His delayed reply set Rhoane further on alert. Baehlon shuffled, his movements giving away his own anxiety.

"Taryn was unhurt, but their leader does not look to be a gentle man."

Baehlon placed a steadying hand on Rhoane. "We do not yet know what they want. As Ebus said, she is still unhurt. Right now we need to keep a calm head."

Damn the man, but he was right. Despite his desire to fly off and scourge the men who held his love, he needed to remain calm, to keep his heart rate steady, his thoughts clear.

"They've secured one of the ships to *The Lady Dancer,* but we couldn't board it. Each time we tried, we were forced off." Ebus continued, eyeing the giant knight with a nod of thanks.

"By men?" Baehlon grumbled. "They saw you?"

"Nay, ShantiMari. We weren't seen." Ebus's tone conveyed his annoyance the knight would think such a thing. As the best thief in Paderau, Ebus made a nice living by not being seen.

Gian gesticulated with his hands and Ebus nodded.

Rhoane understood about a third of the lad's sign language, not enough to make out what he told Ebus. He waited for a translation, but none came. Annoyed at the man's silence, Rhoane grabbed Ebus by his collar and lifted the thief several hands in the air.

"Are you going to share what Gian said?" Rhoane jostled the thief for good measure. He was done with games. Taryn's life depended on the information Ebus could give.

"Yes and no." Ebus wheezed. "Gian thinks he recognizes the man in charge of capturing the ship. Says he was a visitor at Caer

Idris, but beyond that, I don't think you want the particulars. Suffice it to say, this man is no stranger to the finer points of torture."

Rhoane's innards twisted into a tight knot. Taryn could handle herself in a fair fight, but not against someone as brutal as her father. The other ladies would fare far worse as they were more accustomed to parlor games. He set the thief on his feet and shook out his hands. Threatening Ebus would do no good. His fingers twitched in anticipation of clenching the throat of the one who held Taryn captive.

"Is Faelara with the empress?" Baehlon worried a braid between two fingers. The small bell rattled with the constant movement.

"She was not with the ladies. Although we couldn't board the *Dancer*, we managed to board the raiders' ship. From there, we could only see the deck. Perhaps she is being held below, or escaped capture."

"Rykoto's balls." Baehlon spit the words into the breeze. "Who are these men? What do they want? And how the devil do we go about rescuing our people?"

Baehlon's rapid-fire questions were the same as Rhoane's. Except, he had an idea of what the bastards wanted—Taryn. His chest tightened and blood rushed against his sensitive hearing. He wouldn't be surprised if the attack came at the behest of Zakael, Taryn's half-brother. He'd tried—and failed—many times to seduce Taryn. Then, only a fortnight past, he'd helped Valterys kidnap Eliahnna in an effort to sacrifice her to their god. Valterys ended up losing his head—literally—for his actions, but Zakael had escaped.

After naming himself King of the West, Zakael went on a rampage through his kingdom—murdering those he believed were loyal to Valterys and imprisoning many high-ranking nobles. How much of his actions Taryn knew, Rhoane couldn't be certain, but one thing they both understood was that Zakael was more unhinged than ever and would stop at nothing to possess Taryn's powers.

Rhoane couldn't shake the feeling that whatever Zakael, or even Valterys, had failed to do at the Temple of Ardyn was tied to the events unfolding around them. Zakael needed something he'd not obtained at the temple or since. Something only Taryn could give him. But kidnapping her now? In the middle of the ocean? It didn't make sense, even for Zakael.

"I need to know what is happening on that ship. Baehlon, do you wish to accompany me?" Rhoane wiped the sweat from his palms and cracked his neck, already feeling the strength of his darathi vorsi infusing his veins.

The giant knight's mahogany skin paled several shades. "Are you suggesting what I think you are?"

"Aye, I am. It is the only way to get a grasp of the situation."

The knob in Baehlon's throat bounced with his hard swallow. "I can't let you have all the fun, can I?"

They left the others and sped to the back of the ship, where Rhoane took on his darathi vorsi form. The change was seamless and freeing. Once his wings stretched and the tips of his talons scraped against the deck, Baehlon climbed onto his back. His friend had only ridden astride the great beast once before and had hated every moment of it. But today Baehlon understood the need for stealth and kept his misgivings to himself.

Rhoane was grateful for small mercies. The gods only knew what he would find once airborne. He pushed off and caught the breeze, tilting his left wing into the turn. Baehlon's knees gripped his sides tightly, but Rhoane didn't complain. When he imagined the suffering his beloved might be going through, Baehlon's grip was nothing.

They flew above the mist, circling several times to get a feel of what had caused it. From their height, Rhoane could make out masts for three ships: *The Lady Dancer*, Empress Lliandra's vessel, but the other two were cloaked in Telraicht-Noir ShantiMari.

The dark power was almost palpable to Rhoane's heightened dragon awareness.

I can't see for shit. Can you make out anything? Baehlon's thought tickled Rhoane's mind.

Three ships. I sense Telraicht-Noir ShantiMari, and something else. It's elusive, coming from one of the raiders' crafts. Unfettered rage rippled along his scales. Who would be so bold to attempt this? Even for Zakael, this was madness. Anxiety nipped his thoughts. Had Rykoto broken loose, or Kaldaar returned? But his instincts told him this wasn't the work of gods. Perhaps the bidding of gods, but the actual attack was man made.

Baehlon shifted as he leaned to the side and Rhoane adjusted his flight.

Aye, you're right. There, just a toddle from the Dancer. *Wait, do you hear that?*

Even without the heightened dragon senses, Rhoane would've heard the low chanting coming from the third vessel. He strained to make out the words.

"*Calem, caballesi, tranctorum di dienesse valorum gentru.*"

His rage melted to horror as Rhoane pushed against the current and rose into the clouds.

What're you doing, man? We need to get closer, Baehlon grumbled, his knees pressing Rhoane's side.

That is the last thing we want. The words those men are chanting are archaic Telraicht-Noir spells. It is because of them we cannot communicate with the others. I am willing to bet they cannot call upon their ShantiMari at all.

Rhoane sped to the safety of his ship, landing on the deck with a soft thud. Baehlon scrambled from his back, his braids sticking out at wild angles, his eyes filled with righteous indignation.

"To cut off one's power, that's forbidden."

"Agreed." Rhoane shook off the last of his dragon form. "But

I fear these men do not play by the rules. They are Telraicht practitioners, I am certain of it."

"What do they want?"

If Zakael was behind the attack, Rhoane would guess he wanted Taryn's power. Yet, the timing and planning needed to capture her this far out to sea—it spoke of another, darker motivation. One he wasn't ready to admit, not even to himself.

Rhoane had to board that ship. He wouldn't fail her again.

They joined the others and filled them in on what they'd learned. Hayden leaned against a barrel, his fingers dragging through his hair hard enough Rhoane feared he would pull out every strand.

"Two ships. One with chanters, the other for what? Why two separate crafts?" Hayden's irritation echoed Rhoane's.

"Chanters?" Ebus signed something to Gian. The faerie responded with a shrug and snap of his fingers. "We heard nothing." The thief echoed Gian's shrug.

"It does not matter. They are blocking anyone on the *Dancer* from using their power. Which means, if we get too close, we will also be blocked from our ShantiMari." Rhoane surveyed the deck. "Where is Myrddin? We will need his advice to proceed."

"I haven't seen him all day. Perhaps he's in his room. I'll get him." Hayden sprinted to the stairs leading to the cabins.

"Blasted Myrddin with his tinkering. Gets as blind as a sea witch at times. Just as deaf, too." Baehlon's fingertips danced upon the hilt of his sword, tapping out a staccato beat that matched Rhoane's thumping heart.

"He's focused. That's an honorable thing for a great mage like Myrddin."

"Shut up, Ebus. What do you know about honor?" Baehlon's braids whipped across his face with the shake of his head.

"I'll have you know, gentle knight, thieves are among the most honorable of citizens." At Baehlon's snort, Ebus continued.

"At least we are honest about our dealings. How many bureaucrats can say the same?"

Sir, Gian's soft thought overrode Ebus and Baehlon's arguing. *I believe I can board the* Dancer. *Ebus was blocked from the ship, but I was not.*

Could you use your power? It was a slim hope, but Rhoane would take anything at this point.

I am weak in ShantiMari to begin with, my lord. I am afraid even my small amount of power was withheld from me.

Rhoane placed a hand on the lad's shoulder. Faeries shared the same strain of ShantiMari as the Eleri. They could commune with nature and possessed exceptional sight, hearing, and healing skills, but none of those could stop the chanters.

"Do not fear she is lost to us. I will not let that happen." Rhoane assured the faerie.

Gian stood taller, a look of grim determination on his youthful face.

"What's this young Hayden is blathering on about? Lliandra's ship is under attack?" Myrddin stomped across the deck, his clothing askew as if he'd dressed in a hurry. His grey hair protruded at odd angles and creases marked his weather-worn skin.

"Forgive us from waking you from your beauty sleep," Ebus taunted. "Up late again charting the stars? Or was it determining the currents?"

"The stars, if you must know, and yes. I didn't find my bed until early this morning. Now, will someone tell me what the devil is going on?"

Rhoane silenced the others and told Myrddin the events of the day, ending with his and Baehlon's reconnaissance of the three ships.

Myrddin stroked his whiskers, taming them somewhat with the repetitive motions. His features held no clue to his emotions. A slight narrowing of his eyes and twitch of his lips were the only signs of what he might be feeling. The others shifted in the silence, daggers were drawn and inspected, necks cracked, shoulders were straightened. Hayden paced to the rail of the ship and back, his hands no longer raking his hair, instead, they swung at his side, balled into fists. Rhoane remained impassive, giving Myrddin time to formulate an opinion.

"Seems to me," Myrddin mused, almost to himself, "what you need to do is take out the chanters. To block that much ShantiMari means there are Telraicht-Noir Masters aboard one of the ships. My guess is they have men and women, all equally as powerful as you or I, chanting ancient spells of capitulation. Those on the *Dancer* aren't blocked from their power—their ShantiMari is submitting to the Telraicht-Noir. It's semantics, really, and leads to the same end. Taryn and the others have only their wits and might to help them."

Rhoane crossed his arms across his chest, anxious for the mage to tell him something useful. He knew Taryn was alone. Knew she couldn't access her power. Knew she must be as frightened as he was.

Hayden stopped pacing, his jaw tensed. "What you're suggesting is, they can fight the submission and reclaim their power, correct?"

"It doesn't work that way." Myrddin scanned the darkening sky. "If they have a circle of thirteen aboard another ship, that's enough to keep the entire crew and passengers on the *Dancer* helpless. Even with Taryn's strength, she wouldn't be able to break through the spell. Not without serious repercussions."

Rhoane hoped like hell she wouldn't try. Myrddin was right —Taryn had vast strength, but much of it was as yet untapped. If she accidentally opened her full power…he shuddered to think of what she'd do. Not just to herself, but the others onboard.

"Dammit, man," Baehlon cut through Rhoane's thoughts, "you're speaking in riddles. You're saying thirteen people can weaken an entire ship full of people, some as powerful as you in

ShantiMari?" The big knight took up pacing where Hayden had left off, his cheeks puffed with heavy breaths.

"Tell me, how many armed men would it take to hold captive a dozen citizens?" Myrddin leaned against the ship's railing, looking for all the world like he was on a pleasure cruise.

Rhoane envied Myrddin's external calm. He was having a hard time controlling his need to return to the ship and kill the chanters and attackers—one by one, slowly and methodically.

Baehlon stopped his pacing. The bells in the knight's braids chimed with a shake of his head. "One. As long as they fear him, they won't retaliate."

"And if the others believe they're cut off from their power," Hayden said, "they won't try to fight. None of them know what life is like without ShantiMari."

"Taryn knows," Rhoane said. "She was raised without the power. Let us hope that will aid her now." He turned his face toward the thick fog. "We need eyes and ears on that ship to know what is happening, and I know just the man for the job."

He placed a sturdy hand on Gian's shoulder. The faerie nodded as he, too, studied the mist.

"If you can get him safely aboard, he might be the difference between life and death for everyone on the *Dancer.*" Myrddin's words pinched Rhoane's heart.

He pivoted to leave, but stayed his steps. "Why thirteen?"

The mage regarded Rhoane with surprise in his eyes. "I thought you of all gathered here would understand the significance."

"I do not. Please, enlighten me."

Myrddin pushed away from the railing and pointed to the sky. "Legend says there are thirteen realms in the cosmos. Thirteen points of entry from our world to the next."

"You mean veils?" Rhoane had never heard about kingdoms in the sky.

"In a sense. Thirteen is the most powerful number in the

universe. Nadra and Ohlin, they are part of the original thirteen gods who formed the worlds. Their children are pieces of the whole."

"And their children's children, etc. What does this have to do with the chanters?" The knight slammed his fist upon a nearby crate. "You're wasting time, old man."

Myrddin shrugged. "Rhoane asked a question. I thought he'd like to know the significance of the answer."

"The chanters draw their powers from the original gods, is this what you are suggesting?" Rhoane cast Baehlon a warning. Yes, they needed to move, but going off with only half the information would be as deadly as running in the pitch of night.

"Almost. Those chanters draw their strength from the realms, not gods."

Rhoane tilted his face to the sky. The vastness of space filled him with dread. Thirteen with the power of the universe at their bidding. They'd all be lucky to survive.

CHAPTER THREE

The ship lurched and Taryn braced against her restraints. Her cheek burned from where Cashiel's skin had touched hers. After his initial threats, he'd left with a promise of more fun after he inspected the other captives. While he strolled the rows of seated women, he stopped at random intervals to make sure Taryn watched his movements. He taunted her and it worked. Each time a crooked finger reached for one of the ladies' faces, her insides flipped and she struggled harder against the ropes. Each time she reacted, his grin grew larger.

Taryn knew he toyed with her. Knew that he would push her just far enough to see her strength. Knew that she was helpless to stop him from doing whatever the hell he pleased. She thanked the gods at least Faelara, Saeko, and her guard Carina didn't have to endure his disgusting touch. Their absence gave her hope. They were three capable women. Hell, they might be planning something this very moment. Bound as she was—cut off from her power—Taryn prayed to the gods for help in any form.

Thus far, Cashiel's men had behaved themselves, but the call of women would soon become too much to ignore. Most of the ladies were virgins, all young, except Lliandra and her two closest companions. Even then, they were still attractive. Cashiel's men drooled over the women as if they were roasts on a spit, each minute getting juicier and more enticing. A surge of repulsion swept up her throat, tasting of bile. She gagged trying to swallow the sickness, jarring her bruised ribs. Her head dipped to her chest. The small amount of energy she expended to stop herself from vomiting had left her exhausted. Despite being bound, hungry, and hurting, she'd not let anyone on this ship be harmed. Not while she lived.

The rough rope cut against her wrist, making deep grooves in her skin. Blood dripped from several abrasions, but she ignored the jags of pain and focused on the place inside her where she kept her ShantiMari hidden. A small flame burned, but each time she tried to coax it further, she was denied. Not blocked, exactly, but not allowed access, either.

A pair of boots came into her line of sight and she glanced up, meeting Cashiel's dark gaze. Certain he would punish her for looking away, she tensed, awaiting a beating that did not come.

"If you don't give me what I want, we will start murdering your friends." He nodded to someone behind Taryn.

The huge man strode forward, grabbed Eliahnna by the elbow, and roughly pulled her to his side. Her chair tipped, taking her with it. With a swift kick, he straightened her chair, catching the young woman's ankle in the process. A small yelp escaped Eliahnna's lips and Taryn bit back several curses.

"To what end, Cashiel? You rape them. Murder them. So what? What will you get when you have no more lives to destroy?"

The green flame burned brighter in his eyes. Sparks lit forth, landing on his cheeks.

Taryn recoiled at the sight, but she kept her face placid. "You'll never possess my *darathi vorsi*." She struggled to keep her voice calm. "Don't you understand she's not mine to give?"

A flicker of confusion overrode the flames, then disappeared.

"The secrets of dragon transformation have been the Eleri's for too long. You are Aelan, yet you have learned them. Now you'll teach me how to become one of the beasts, or I'll see you and all of your friends dead."

Taryn sighed into her chest. He would never understand. None of them would. Becoming darathi vorsi wasn't about transforming from one form to another. It was a bonding, much like she had with Rhoane, except with a spirit. The spirit chose the person, not the other way around. She hadn't fully worked out the relationship yet, nor why the darathi vorsi had left Aelinae, but they were connected.

Fading light glinted off Cashiel's dagger.

Taryn pulled her gaze back to his face. "Do your best, asshole."

He tugged on her camisole, lifting it to show the vorlock scar below her left breast. The tip of the dagger traced the jagged skin. Fire from his Noir weapon burned into her. The part of her power she'd only recently accepted stirred. Her own Telraicht-Noir ShantiMari. Rhoane had said she held the trinity of power within her, but he was wrong. Four strains of Shanti-Mari coursed through her blood: Light, Dark, Eleri, and Telraicht-Noir. It was the latter that answered the call of Cashiel's power.

Taryn strained to coax it further, begged it to be unleashed, but she felt nothing more than a gentle stirring.

Cashiel's blade made a lazy circle around her breast and moved slowly upward. He rested the tip in the little divot at the base of her throat, his eyes glazing. "I'll bet you taste as sweet as you smell."

He bent into her and inhaled near her ear. Close enough his hair tickled her cheek. Repulsed by his close proximity and wanting nothing more than to spit in his face, she held fast. It was all she could do to not jerk against the restraints. To get even a hand's width away from his wretched sneer and glowing eyes.

"Does that line ever work? I mean, seriously. We've been three days at sea. You won't convince me I smell as fresh as roses."

"Not roses, something more divine. Power. I can smell your ShantiMari."

"Okay, now that's just gross." Taryn met Eliahnna's concerned look.

Taryn slid her gaze to the man next to her sister and dipped her chin in a slow nod. The exchange with Cashiel had averted the man's attention, leaving Eliahnna safe for the moment. Her sister's eyes grew huge and filled with tears. Relief, sweet and cool, swept through her muddled nerves. Even if the calm was fleeting, Taryn didn't care. For the moment, Eliahnna was safe.

"So, tell me, Cashiel," Taryn drew her attention back to her tormentor, "are you always this touchy-feely with women on the first date? Because I gotta tell you, I find it off-putting."

"You have no idea how 'touchy-feely' we're going to get before this is over." The dagger skimmed down her chest, again avoiding her cynfar. He didn't cut her, yet the weapon left an angry red welt as it looped up her left arm, down again and across her face. The tour ended with the blade resting where it had started—at the vorlock scar. He pressed the tip into her skin.

A fresh blaze ripped through her, tearing at her nerve endings, curling against her heart. Crippling agony paralyzed her and Taryn fought hard against the scream that forced itself against her closed lips.

Quicker than a carlix, his fist slammed into her stomach, knocking the wind from her. The blows pounded against the side of her face: once, twice, and a third time. He finished with a jab to her sternum. Wheezing, blood dripping from cuts on her lips and cheeks, she steadied herself for the next assault, but Cashiel didn't strike again. Instead, he forced his hand beneath her tight leather pants and gasped.

Terror, raw and unyielding, clouded all thought. He was going to rape her there, in front of everyone. He would break her and steal her dragon. Then, a hush of reason swept through the horrific visions she conjured. He could defile her, but she would never be broken. The heartache of Rhoane's brokenness was too fresh in her memory. That could never happen to either one of them ever again.

The look of ecstasy on Cashiel's face drove a spike of dread deeper into her heart. His touch tore at her soul. She would not yield. Not to this coward who dared think he was better than an unarmed, captive woman. He was trash.

Her internal thoughts clashed as she sought to control her emotions. Even if he succeeded in physically violating her, she wouldn't let him take her darathi vorsi. Wouldn't let him worm his way into her soul. Couldn't let him destroy her from the inside out.

"I could break your bond with the Eleri right now if I wished. Here, in front of your mother and the others. Would that be 'touchy-feely' enough for you?" His fingers ground into the soft flesh of her pubis and Taryn muffled a cry. "I can and I will. Your dragon will be mine."

"The last man to make that threat regretted his words. Rumor has it, he can't get it up anymore. I would say it's a shame, but I'm fairly certain I've saved hundreds of men and women the agony of sleeping with him." Her slurred words lacked the conviction she'd hoped to convey. The effort robbed her of strength, but she didn't quit. "In fact, he once had me in a similar position. Why is it you assholes feel you have to tie me up to get anywhere with me? Are you afraid if I'm not bound I might over-power you?"

Cashiel grabbed her hair and yanked her head back until she stared at the evening sky. "Filthy cunt, you don't know who you're dealing with. I have the power of a god backing me. I could take you with or without restraints. I just happen to like it better this way."

His voice rasped with longing, as if the mere act of touching her, forbidden though he said it was, had brought him closer to his god. Taryn refused to fight. She sensed it was what he wanted. That he craved her capitulation. That he drew strength from her suffering.

The realization stole her breath and it was her turn to gasp.

Yes. This man, and his god, needed her pain, her blood. Not just hers, but the others on the ship as well. The women would be a hearty feast for this man's god. A chill swept through her veins and she embraced the sharp edges of that particular pain.

"Of course you do. Cowards always like their victims helpless. But, I'm not a victim and I'm far from helpless."

He released her hair and held her face like a vise, forcing her to look at him. "I'm going to enjoy this more than I thought I would." The dagger flashed and made one swift cut through the thick strands of her braid.

A flicker of remorse touched her thoughts, but she had no time for vanity. Hair could be regrown. Cashiel hadn't killed her yet, which meant there was still time to save the others.

Taryn shook out her short locks. "You know, I've been meaning to get a trim. Thank you."

He wrapped the braid around his fist, a slow sneer creeping up his lips. Taryn braced for the worst and Cashiel delivered. The first blow was to her temple, making stars dance behind her eyes and a ringing start in her ears. The blows continued with Cashiel making sure to smear her blood on the silver strands of her braid. Each punch was intentional, aimed at a certain body part as if he captured her agony with the beating. How long it lasted, she couldn't tell. Mere minutes or several bells, she lost count of the punches after the first several dozen. With each hit, she retreated a little more into herself, cowering in the back of her psyche where Cashiel's blows didn't hurt. Where his words didn't haunt.

From far away she heard the women's cries. They shouted at Cashiel to stop, but with each plea his fists pounded harder. It was as if their affection for her angered him. Tears squeezed from between her closed eyes.

When she hung from her restraints, unmoving, he uncoiled the braid from his hand and called to the giant beside Eliahnna. "Take this to the Eleri's ship. Tell him if he tries anything stupid, I'll send another body part."

The man took the braid and left without a word.

Cashiel gripped her face, his thumb running from her lips to her cheek. He lifted his finger to his own lips and sucked her blood. The green fire dimmed, the sparks no longer visible.

"I will own you, Taryn Rose ap Galendrin. Body and soul." A pink tongue darted out, licking at the blood stuck to his thumb. "And I will destroy everything you hold dear."

The words spoken came from Cashiel, but they weren't his voice. Taryn recognized it as the one that had been taunting her for over a season. It was the god he said backed him. But which one? Kaldaar? Rykoto? Or was there a new player on the field she didn't know?

"Bring it, motherfucker," she rasped, startled at the weakness of her voice, and stared into the emerald depths of his eyes, challenging the god to make himself known.

His dagger plunged through the vorlock scar, between her ribs, an inch below her heart. Her surprised gasp came out gurgled as she choked on blood. Fresh pain, unlike any she'd experienced, ripped through her, torching her insides. Cashiel's eyes were as wide as her own, and equally filled with shock. His hand shook as he pulled the blade free, his eyes locked to hers. There was remorse in their depths. But why? Who was this man? Why was he being used by a god and which one?

Blood oozed from her wound, staining her pants, dripping to the wooden deck, taking with it the last of her strength. The last of her life. Lliandra screamed and the other women wailed, but Taryn didn't look to them. She mustered what little energy she had left and kept her focus on the man before her.

A wicked grin crossed his face and the man Cashiel was gone. In his place was the usurper god. The flames returned to his eyes and the green sparks danced on his skin.

"Who controls you, Cashiel?" Taryn wheezed, each syllable a fresh tear upon her battered body.

His hand whipped up and seized her by the throat. "Do not speak of things you couldn't possibly understand. I am controlled by no one. I willingly pledged my soul to my god. He may use me as an instrument as he sees fit. I am honored to be of service to him."

"Then you're a fool."

He tightened his grip, then jerked his hand away. A distinct burn etched into his skin.

"You'll pay for that, witch."

How her pendant had burned him, Taryn had no idea, but she wasn't about to admit that to Cashiel. "Add it to my tab."

The green flames heightened, reaching past his eyebrows, then settled to sparks. "I shall skin you strip by strip while your mother and loved ones watch. Then, when you're whimpering and begging me to end your life, I'll have my men rape every woman on this ship while you watch."

He couldn't. Wouldn't. Yet she knew he would and he'd revel in their pain. She had to do something—anything—to stop him from going through with his threat.

"Do what you will to me, but leave them out of this. Raping them won't help your cause." Taryn's quiet voice drifted on the breeze. She didn't doubt he would rape and slaughter every single person on the ship. Her dragon strained to be unleashed, to prevent the tragedy, but that couldn't happen. Even if he had her dragon, she believed Cashiel would still harm the others. This wasn't about just power. It was about something far more sinister. She just had to sort out what.

The tip of his dagger tapped against her skin. His eyes followed the blade as it circled her belly button. He enjoyed toying with her this way, she could see it in the lust-filled glint to his eyes. Zakael's eyes had glinted like that once—when she was hiding in the dungeons of Caer Idris and happened upon him torturing prisoners. He'd sexually assaulted them as they were bound, an eerie coincidence to what Cashiel was doing to her. Taryn didn't like coincidences any more than she liked the feel of Cashiel's blade upon her skin.

He pressed the metal against the wound he'd just made. Fresh torment seared through her as the blade scraped along the cut. She bit her lips and held back tears. He wasn't just slicing into her skin. He sent his Telraicht-Noir ShantiMari into the wound, into her. Her blood bubbled and popped from the heat of his power.

Pain, raw in its savagery, robbed her of thought and blinded her for several heartbeats. Survival became an unattainable ideal, and Taryn knew the face of fear. Never before had she been this afraid. She forced images of those she loved into her mind, drawing strength from them much as Cashiel drew his strength from her agony.

The more of his power he pumped into her, the more her Noir power coiled and flexed, as if wanting to join with her torturer's. Taryn commanded it to stay hidden. Cashiel couldn't know she wielded the same power as he. Instead, she embraced his Shanti and urged it deeper. Icy shards from his power coursed along her veins, tearing her bruised tendons and muscles. But what should've destroyed her internally didn't.

After each rupture, a warm healing happened. Icy-hot sensations wracked her body, confusing her senses, befuddling her thoughts.

"What are you doing to me?" The question was directed as much to her own Telraicht-Noir power as to Cashiel.

"Have you any idea how beautiful you are right now? Writhing in pain, but fighting it. Simply stunning. I only wish I could keep you looking like this always, but I'm afraid that would kill you."

"Isn't that the plan? You want my *darathi vorsi*, and to get her, you'll have to kill me."

"I need to keep you alive, but by how much, I'm not sure."

Fresh dread wriggled down her back. She'd heard something similar from Zakael not so long ago. It was then she'd forced him to teach her to transform. An ugly thought embedded itself in her psyche.

Cashiel might not be working against her brother, but with him.

CHAPTER FOUR

Kaida sniffed the air and whined. Her claws dug into the railing as she scrambled to stay upright against the rocking of the ship. Rhoane patted her head, trying to calm the beast, and knowing it would do no good. He blamed himself for the attack on Lliandra's ship. If only he'd insisted that he and Baehlon stay with the women. It had been Sabina's idea to have the bachelors aboard one ship and the ladies aboard another. It was their last opportunity to be together before she was married and had wanted her friends all to herself.

His instinct had told him to remain with Taryn, but he'd allowed himself to be swayed by Sabina's arguments. Now his insides twisted in on themselves with impotent anxiety.

"Stupid, idiot, fool." His fingers tightened in Kaida's fur. Her low growl served as warning and he loosened his grip.

"I assume you mean yourself and not Kaida." Myrddin's jovial tone elicited a scowl from Rhoane. This was not the time for humor.

"Myself. I should never have let Taryn travel without protection."

"Let her? Since when has that woman ever allowed you to

'let' her do something? She had it in mind to fulfill her friend's wish. Nothing you or I could've done would change that." Myrddin absently stroked Kaida, his tone light, but dark clouds covered his eyes.

"She would not be in this predicament if I had been with her."

"That's rather presumptuous of you. Perhaps she would and you'd be dead. Everything that's happened to Taryn, whether you were with her or not, has been a part of her path. You being there might have been the swing of the pendulum that caused her to make a fatal mistake."

"Are you saying I am a distraction?"

Myrddin met Rhoane's scowl with his own. "I'm saying exactly that. Whatever happened to you after the Light Celebrations has affected your judgment. You don't have time to doubt yourself or Taryn."

"Aye. Yet I am selfish. I would like Taryn to be more to me and less to Aelinae."

"She is your life mate. You want more?"

Much, much more. "I wish she could be the mother of my children. The woman I grow old with and share memories of love and laughter with. I suppose I had hoped, once Aelinae is balanced, it could be so."

"That was never her path, or yours."

"I have always known that," Rhoane's voice softened, "but she does not. She believes we can have all those things. She did not grow up knowing of the prophecy, or that her life would be taken from her."

"Taken from her? The life she had before Aelinae wasn't taken from her. She chose to stay."

"And I suppose if you wish hard enough for that to be true, it will be." Rhoane patted the old man on his shoulder. "The lies we tell ourselves do not make it any easier to sleep at night, do they?"

Myrddin scrubbed a hand over his weathered face. "I suppose

not." He stared at the lingering fog, a tight pinch deepening the lines around his eyes. "Who is behind the attack and what do they want?"

"I have some suspicions, but nothing solid on which to base them. We shall have our answers soon enough."

As if on cue, a sound came from the fog and they turned in unison to see a small boat emerge. Rhoane gripped the hilt of his sword, alert to any use of power from the approaching vessel. Two men rowed while another stood behind them, a long sword held in his hands, blade tip pointed down. A fourth man, broad shouldered and too tall for such a small vessel, knelt in the bow, eyes trained on them. Neither Rhoane nor Myrddin spoke until the small party was within docking distance to their ship.

"Who goes there?" Myrddin called out.

"I have come with a message for the Eleri prince," the man in the front of the dingy said, his gaze never leaving Rhoane.

"You may board, but not the others." Rhoane held the man's stare, his nerves snapping with anticipation.

The man ascended the rope ladder thrown to him with the grace of a zaff scaling the thin trees of the Narthvier. Once he'd slid over the railing, he stood to his full height. He fished through a bag slung over his shoulder and produced a knotted mass of silver. A blaze lit within Rhoane at the sight.

"My lord bade me give you this as a token of his seriousness."

Myrddin reached for the thing, but Rhoane stopped him. Instead, he removed the braid from the man's hand and clasped it in his own. Blood streaked the silken strands of Taryn's hair. The internal blaze grew to a raging inferno. Skitters of flame danced along his forearm, followed closely by chilling pricks of ice. The need to destroy the messenger, to punish whoever had done this to his love, overrode any other thought or emotion. *Kill. Maim. Obliterate.* These words danced in his mind on repeat.

His nostrils flared as he counted backward from ten, each

numbered breath dulling the desire to cripple the bastard standing before him.

"Do you have a message for my lord?" the man asked, his expression a mask of indifference.

Rhoane had a message, but not one the messenger's lord would appreciate. In the space of several heartbeats obscene visions of what was happening to Taryn tangoed with Rhoane's need to injure those responsible. The scope of his imagined actions was vast, and far more brutal than anything he'd ever done. Just thinking of Taryn and her anguish spurred his desire of what he'd like to do to the men who'd attacked Lliandra's ship. Each more vicious than the last. His peripheral darkened until he saw little more than a black spot.

Baehlon approached with Hayden at his side and put a hand on Rhoane. The knight's presence did little to calm Rhoane, but the pressure of his grip reminded him there was little to gain by losing his temper.

"What have we here?" The strength behind Baehlon's question helped quell Rhoane's fury.

He was not alone on this ship, nor in his eagerness to rescue the others. His ire lessened enough he regained control.

"This man brought us a message. One that is most unusual." Myrddin indicated the braid.

A gasp came from Hayden and a low whistle from Baehlon.

"Who is your lord and what does he want with the empress?" Hayden demanded. A feather could've broken the tension that stretched between the men.

"He calls himself Cashiel and he wants nothing from the empress."

"Then why attack her ship? Surely he knows the punishment?" Hayden countered. His hand hovered above the hilt of his sword, as did Baehlon's, but Rhoane didn't reach for his weapon. He knew steel would do no good here. This was a time for diplomacy, as much as he hated to admit it.

"We're in open water," the messenger countered, his gaze flicking to the top of Hayden's sword. The casual tone of the messenger and relaxed stance gave the impression the man was unconcerned. He didn't have a weapon that Rhoane could see, but his muscles bulged as he crossed his arms over his chest. "Neither she nor the Summerlands king have authority over us here."

"You've studied each kingdom's laws well, friend. Tell me, what does Cashiel want?" Myrddin kept his tone light, amiable, but Rhoane saw the tightness of his lips, the slight tug of his beard.

Cashiel was a mystery to them all, one who held the lives of many in his grasp. Rhoane had never been fond of mysteries, and now even less so.

"My lord doesn't confide in me every detail. I am but a messenger."

"And I am but a cabin boy." Baehlon's harsh baritone sounded across the water. "Don't toy with us." The knight crossed his arms, mimicking the messenger, and set his feet to the deck with two hard thuds. "You are Cashiel's first man, or I'm a cur. He wouldn't send anyone else but his most trusted."

Rhoane studied the man during Baehlon's outburst. Tall. Dark hair and eyes. Could've been Geigan or Danuri. Built like Baehlon. Rhoane wouldn't have been surprised if they came from a similar region. By the way the knight's cheeks puffed and his arms flexed, Baehlon probably came to the same conclusion.

"If I am not mistaken, your mission is two-fold: deliver the princess's token, and take stock of the manpower aboard this ship. Have a good look, lad. For I've a mind to make this the last thing you'll ever see." Baehlon uncrossed his arms and stood to his full height.

The messenger cocked his head and grinned. He was only a finger span shorter than the knight. "You must be Sir Baehlon.

I've heard stories about the great knight protector. Pity you won't have anyone to protect when we're finished with your princess."

Baehlon took the bait and stepped forward, but Rhoane put out a hand to stop him. "Return to your master, messenger."

The man regarded Rhoane coolly. "Have you anything you wish for me to convey?"

What he wished to convey was the way in which he would kill Cashiel and his men—slowly, without regard to their pain. His hands shook with pent-up anger, and a quiet desire to do harm.

"*Kidaris.*" The word was little more than a whisper from Rhoane's lips. An ancient curse few would understand, and those who did, they'd recognize Rhoane's intention.

"That's it? No threats or taunts? He holds your empress and the princesses hostage and you say but one word? I expected more from you, Prince Rhoane."

"Get used to disappointment." Rhoane turned from the man and stalked away. The urge to strike him, to slice clean through his heart and jerk his sword upward, splitting his smug face, was too great. He needed fresh air and clarity. Rhoane needed Taryn returned to him unharmed, but it was too late for that.

The braid cut into his hand with each twist he gave it. The blood was Taryn's—it had to be. Otherwise, why give it to him? Cashiel wanted Rhoane to know he'd take Taryn's life if she didn't give him what he wanted. But what that was, Rhoane wasn't certain. Tiny icicles formed on his skin, only to melt a moment later. The twisting of his gut escalated the urge to confront Cashiel. He needed calm. He needed a plan. He needed his Taryn.

"I'm sorry, Rhoane. I shouldn't have let that runt get the better of me." Baehlon sidled next to Rhoane at the bow of the ship overlooking the rest of Lliandra's fleet.

The other ships sat upon still waters, their anchors keeping them from drifting away. Like sheep contained in a pen, awaiting slaughter. Would Cashiel attack each of them, going one by one to take out the nobility and soldiers of Talaith? He clutched the braid tighter. Cashiel didn't want Lliandra. The hairs pinching against his skin was proof of that. For now, the other ships were safe, but for how long?

"We must get aboard the *Dancer* and save them." Rhoane spoke more to himself than to Baehlon. He hated this feeling of helplessness. With their powers blocked from Lliandra's ship, Cashiel held all the control. Time was drifting away with Taryn's life attached at the hem.

Ebus and the ship's captain descended the stairs leading to the captain's quarters, with Gian a few paces behind. Rhoane eyed the three of them, curiosity rising the closer they came.

"What news?" Baehlon grumbled.

"We have a plan. It's risky, but should we be successful, will allow us to board the other ships." Ebus looked far too pleased with himself. Rhoane learned long ago to have caution where the thief and his plans were concerned.

"Ships? Plural?" Hayden joined the group, his attention on the wily man. "Are you suggesting we take out the chanters before we attack Cashiel and his men?"

"Cashiel?" Ebus's nose twitched, giving him a rat-like appearance.

"He is the one in charge." Rhoane held up the silver braid. "He wanted me to know Taryn is alive, but she is wounded. I believe he means to set a trap for us."

"That man's daft as a pigeon's arse if he thinks we'll take the bait." Baehlon's braids chimed with the fierce swing of his head.

"Unfortunately, that's exactly what we must do," Ebus said.

Silence surrounded them. This far out to sea, no birds cried, no waves crashed against the hull of the ship. Even the crew were quiet. Only the sounds of ropes and rigging slapping against poles—useless and inept—broke the eerie hush.

Rhoane regarded the men gathered around a shipping crate.

Their faces all showed varying degrees of concern. Even Ebus, who would have them all believe he cared for nothing but gold, showed signs of worry. They all had loved ones aboard the captured ship. Which meant they all had a stake in making sure their rescue attempt succeeded.

Ebus signaled to the captain, who unrolled a large piece of parchment. Hayden, Baehlon, and Rhoane leaned in to get a better look. Scribbled on the page were three ships: the *Dancer*, Cashiel's, and the ship with the chanters. Their close proximity to one another made it difficult to board any of them, so long as the practitioners continued their chanting.

"The key to rescuing the others is to knock out this ship." Ebus pressed a thumb upon the smallest of the three vessels.

"To do that," the captain said, "we'll need to distract the chanters long enough to cause a rift in the blackout."

"Blackout?" Baehlon asked.

"That's what we're calling the loss of ability to use their power." The captain returned to the paper and pointed to yet another scribble. "This is us. I propose we ram our ship into this one." He jabbed at the smallest ship. "The impact should jar those aboard enough to cause momentary disarray."

Seconds ticked by as they processed the plan.

Ebus tapped the page with a grubby finger. "They'll be expecting an attack, but not like this."

"It's risky, but I like it." Hayden bent closer to examine the drawings. "We should have most of our men in position to board Cashiel's ship beforehand. How many men do you think it will take to permanently halt the chanters?"

"The ship is guarded, but by only a handful of men, according to these two." The captain tipped his chin toward Ebus and Gian. "I think half a dozen strong fighters as well as Myrddin and the prince should suffice."

"I will be poised to reclaim the *Dancer,*" Rhoane stated, his eyes roving over the parchment for anything they might have missed. "Myrddin and Hayden can handle those aboard the smaller vessel." Nothing would keep Rhoane from Taryn.

Myrddin's eyes narrowed and his lips tightened, but he didn't argue. Hayden tapped the page again and nodded. His fingers traced over the lines of each ship as if memorizing them. They were crude outlines, not complete schematics, but the way Hayden studied them would have anyone believe the opposite was true.

"What is it?" Rhoane prodded when it became apparent Hayden wouldn't share his thoughts.

"If we could warn the empress and others somehow, then when the ShantiMari blackout is suspended, even if only for a moment, they'll be prepared and can react. The empress has vast stores of power. She alone could overpower Cashiel and his men, but with Taryn's strength added to hers, they're limitless."

"Which is why the bastard cut them off." Baehlon's big arms crossed against his chest, his fists balled.

"Precisely. No one would dare attack the Eirielle within a contained area unless they were certain they couldn't fail. This plan has been in place for quite some time, I'd wager. They simply waited for the opportunity." Hayden smacked the parchment and swore as voraciously as his cousin. Taryn would've been proud. "We should've been prepared, but no intelligence led us to believe there was a threat."

The captain scratched his chin. "This trip wasn't planned. As far as the empress goes, it was spontaneous, with only a few weeks' notice."

Hayden's fingers scratched over the papers, his lips tightened to a dangerous white line. "Which would suggest they were close enough to Talaith to overhear when the plans were being made."

Rhoane took a long drag of sea air and tried for the calm Taryn said deep breaths would bring. They were standing around talking when really they needed to be doing something— anything—to save the others.

Ebus met Rhoane's eye and nodded as if he'd been in the Eleri's thoughts. "We aren't dealing with highwaymen, my friends. These are trained killers with an agenda. I think it's pretty obvious what that is."

Rhoane twisted the silver braid around his knuckles. The dark thought he'd been suppressing bubbled to the surface. His words came out guarded, yet underlying fury vibrated his voice. "This is far more than a trap. I had thought Cashiel wanted Taryn for her power, but it is more sinister than that. He plans to break her until her will is not her own."

The others regarded him coolly, their expressions as guarded as Rhoane's words. Only Gian showed alarm, with animated gesticulations Rhoane couldn't follow.

It was Hayden who broke the silence. "What if he doesn't want her power, but her dragon? If he mates with Taryn as a *darathi vorsi*, her bond to you is shattered and he becomes whatever it is you are, right?"

"The *Darathi Vorsi* Prince, yes." Or, as the Aelans said, the Prince of Dragons. It was Rhoane's birthright and until this moment something he believed immutable. Bile rose to the back of his throat, almost gagging him. His firm stance buckled beneath him and Baehlon put a steadying hand on his shoulder. Rhoane took another breath before admitting, "If Cashiel succeeds, he will control all *darathi*."

"But, there are no dragons on Aelinae," Ebus protested, then stammered, "except you and the princess, that is."

Only Rhoane knew the truth about those that were exiled to another world. The great beasts he alone could rescue and return to Aelinae. He'd only come to understand his role in their future when Verdaine had placed the Crown of Awakening upon his head on Dal Tara. At the time, he'd thought nothing of it, but over the next few days, he'd studied the stones, realizing they weren't stones at all, but darathi eggs. He hadn't yet told Taryn.

Now, the future of both worlds rested on what happened in the next few bells.

The sickness in his gut roiled anew at the clarity with which he now understood the totality of Cashiel's plan. He turned to the woodland faerie and said, "Gian, get aboard that ship and warn Taryn. Cashiel is not after her *darathi*, but mine. Tell her we know it is a trap and we have a plan to free everyone on board."

Gian nodded solemnly. His fingers flew with questions and Rhoane struggled to follow them.

"Yes, warn Tessa. She can tell the others. If you can find Ynyd Eirathnacht, make sure she is close to Taryn when the fighting begins." Rhoane tapped the hilt of Claidholm Solais. His sword had been singing to him all day, but the words were jumbled and not making much sense. A fresh wave of dread washed over him. If Cashiel had Taryn's sword in his possession, he was several steps closer to owning her soul.

Rhoane reached for Gian and placed his fingertips upon the lad's temple. He infused the faerie's thoughts with one meant just for Taryn. He hoped it would give her strength to continue fighting. The braid brushed along Gian's head and he flinched.

It hurts, my lord.

Rhoane pulled away. *The braid? How?*

I feel her pain, her suffering.

Rhoane felt it, too. Through Gian's connection with the braid, Taryn's pain cut against Rhoane's heart.

Gian's eyes grew large and filled with tears.

We must save her and the others. Hurry, lad. The Darennsai depends on you.

Gian rushed off and a moment later, a splash echoed against the stillness as he entered the water.

"This plan has to succeed. Aelinae is lost if we fail," Myrddin said, his words mirroring Rhoane's thoughts. The mage stood beside Hayden, and Rhoane couldn't recall when he'd joined the group. Had he always been there, silent? Or was Rhoane finally losing the last thread of his mental capabilities? Since Taryn had been captured, coherent thoughts were difficult to capture and now his mind was playing tricks on him.

Rhoane rubbed his eyes, the silken strands of Taryn's braid slicing against his skin. Time was against them. Cashiel needed her alive, but not by much.

CHAPTER FIVE

A song played in Taryn's mind. Or was it being played aloud and only sounded like it was meant just for her? The words made no sense, yet she hummed along as if she'd known the song her whole life. Fragments lingered in her thoughts.

Save me from thee…
By the healing grace…
Time and space…
Wrapped within a protective embrace…
Sins past…
Future present…
Tamed lions rabid lambs…

Taryn's head sank further into her chest. She was losing it. Finally, the madness had come to claim her. She'd be a certifiable lunatic by midnight. Her head lolled to the side and she squinted at the sky. A blanket of stars hovered above the masts of the ship. Darkness had come and she hadn't noticed. Cashiel had left her alone for far too long. She surveyed the deck. Only a few guards were stationed near the others. *Arrogant bastard.* He'd left them poorly guarded because he knew there was nothing they could do.

Several of the ladies dozed in their chairs, their hair falling forward to cover their faces. At first, Taryn thought they were dead, but gentle snores issued from them, blowing strands of hair with regularity. Eliahnna's head dipped several times as she fought off sleep, but one last dip and her head rocked into an uncomfortable position. Lliandra sat upright, her shoulders back, a sneer on her lips. She tracked the movements of the guards, her fingers tapping out their steps. Taryn followed the pattern for several minutes. Lliandra wasn't idly passing time, she gauged how long it took each guard to walk from one end of the deck to the other.

Their eyes met and for a moment, anguish covered her mother's features. Without her mask of Mari, the strain of the day showed on her face, particularly in the deep circles under her eyes. They glowed slightly in the dim light and Taryn fervently wished that meant she could reach her ShantiMari. Her own spark remained elusive, yet she continued to coax it out of hiding. Thus far, Cashiel hadn't shut it off from her, which she hoped meant he didn't know she had Telraicht-Noir ShantiMari coursing through her veins. She wasn't sure why, but knew it would be the catalyst for either him succeeding in taking her dragon, or his death. And hers.

She no longer dared to hope she'd come out of this alive. To free the others, she would sacrifice herself. It was how it must be.

Remember me when the leaves turn gold
On a star of futures told
Where the grass does grow and memories fold
Save me from thee

Ynyd Eirathnacht. Taryn breathed deep, filling her bruised lungs with sea air. Her sword was singing and she understood the words. Finally.

Protect them, please. Protect my friends and family from whatever may come. She silently begged the weapon.

> *Nadra's tear drops upon the terrarae*
> *Marking the place where death resides*
> *Take from this what must be*
> *To save me from thee*

I don't understand. Taryn sent the thought to Ynyd Eirathnacht. It was locked in her cabin, hidden behind two layers of protective wards. Even if Cashiel found it, he wouldn't be able to touch it. *I hear the song, but I don't know what you want from me.*

The singing ceased and an unbearable silence engulfed her. Worse than death, she was left alone with her thoughts. Sadness, anger, regret—these mixed in her belly until they were blended into a single lump of guilt. She was the Darennsai. It was her job to save Aelinae. She had one job and she failed. She'd believed her own hype and thought she was stronger than all of them. Smarter, too. But she wasn't. Not stronger, not smarter, not anything. Just a girl raised far from her family, knowing nothing about her home world.

Despair weighed on her like a vorlock corpse. Brandt would be disappointed. He'd sacrificed himself for her. For nothing.

She slumped against the bonds, exhaustion and dehydration stealing her last stores of energy. Loneliness slinked through her dark thoughts, invading her mind, weakening her resolve. She was alone among strangers. Clarity came in a burst and she saw her death. For certainly she would die. Then would come blackness. Followed by a starburst. Taryn held to the final image like a life raft thrown to her in a raging storm.

Darennsai. A gentle voice whispered in her mind.

Taryn jerked, thinking it was a trick of the wind. She opened her eyes and searched for the source. Gian crouched low, hidden by a stack of boxes near the forecastle steps. *Gian! How are you able to speak to me?*

A small white grin broke the shadows of his face. *We are not bound by the constraints of ShantiMari. I have a life debt with you.*

Taryn promised herself if she survived, she would investigate the ramifications of what a faerie life debt entailed. She'd meant to since meeting the curious little man, but it never rose to the top of her priority list.

You must release the others. Cut their bindings and help them escape. Cashiel is after my darathi vorsi and is using them as bait.

The prince is coming. They will be rescued soon enough.

Taryn gave a violent shake of her head. Stars danced before her eyes and her wrists bled anew with the jostling. *He can't. Tell Rhoane to stay far from this ship. Cashiel has set a trap for him.* She glanced up to where a net made of Telraicht-Noir ShantiMari shimmered. *Can you see it?*

Gian scanned above him, then shook his head. *The prince knows it is a trap. Cashiel does not want your darathi vorsi. He wants all darathi. To claim them, he needs the prince's dragon.*

Taryn tried to follow Gian's logic, but he lost her. *What do you mean?*

The sound of footsteps came from behind and Taryn twisted to see who approached. A burly man surged forth and pushed a figure to the ground. Taryn barely recognized her guard, Carina. A knot formed in her stomach, tightening with a disturbing force. Bile swirled and splashed the back of her mouth, making her gag.

Carina's face was a purplish mass of bruises and scrapes. Blood dripped from a gash on her forehead and her hands bore evidence of a fight. She'd not surrendered peacefully. Carina took in Taryn and she winced. Sadness mixed with rage shone in her friend's eyes. However bad Carina looked, Taryn must've been worse. Her guard mouthed the words *I'm sorry* and Taryn's heart surged with love, lodging itself in her throat.

A flicker of her hidden power flared, infusing her with renewed strength. Just as quickly, it receded, leaving her weakened and confused.

"Don't touch her," Taryn rasped, shocked at the sound of her voice.

"An' who's gonna stop me? You?" The guard spat at Taryn, missing her face by a hand's width. "Some Eirielle you turned out to be. Me mam's got more power in her left tit than you do in the whole of you."

Carina stared at the wound in Taryn's side. The woman's face turned a wretched shade of lavender. "Your Highness, you've lost a lot of blood. Please, don't be concerned for me. Save your strength."

Remember me when the leaves turn gold
On a star of futures told
Where the grass does grow and memories fold
Save me from thee

The song started again and Taryn's eyes filled with tears, spilling over to drop upon the deck. He was right. She couldn't save any of them. Not bound and powerless as she was.

Never let fear determine your fate.

She blinked hard and wiped her face on her arm. The movement caused the rope to tear into her flesh and she bit back a cry. Cashiel and his men had seen enough of her weakness for one day. She met Carina's worried stare and smiled. The love she had for her guards, her friends, her family—she curled it around her, wrapping herself in its protective embrace. The Noir flame flickered anew, growing with each thought of those she cared for.

A door banged open and Cashiel burst into her view, his face a torrent of fury. "How dare you. You're not allowed." Dozens of blows rained down on her, one after the other. "You're blocked. Your power is mine now." The shrillness of his voice, the deranged wildness to his eyes terrified her. This was a man driven by something deep and profound. His hatred of her knew no bounds. This was personal. At least, it felt like it, but why, she had no idea. As far as she could recall, she'd never met Cashiel before he attacked the ship.

Taryn had nowhere to hide, no way to cover herself, no protection against the pummeling. A blow to her temple made stars spin anew. Another one to her left eye distorted her vision with a sea of red. More blows followed: to her head, her throat, her breasts, her midsection. Nowhere was spared from Cashiel's fists.

"Your power is mine. Not. Yours. Not. Ever. Again." He punctuated each word with a fresh punch.

With each hit, she drifted deeper into herself. With every smack, she grasped harder to ignite her power. When Cashiel's hands were bloodied, he resorted to his feet, kicking her between the legs, against her thighs and shins. His heavy boots landed with dull thuds against her flesh.

Her strength waned. The harder she grasped at her power, the further it escaped her. She was just a stupid girl with a fancy sword. Her hope ebbed away.

I'm sorry, Rhoane. I've failed you, my love.

"Stop it! You're killing her!" Tessa's little-girl voice shrieked from above them.

Despair washed over Taryn. *No, Tessa. Don't let them find you.* As long as her youngest sister was safe, Taryn had held onto the belief the others could be saved. But now, now Cashiel had the entire royal family under his command.

The beating stopped. The sounds of men climbing to the crow's nest were followed by Tessa's screams. A soft thud ended the ordeal. A wave of dizziness and nausea swept through her. Taryn forced herself to look, positive she would find her sister's mangled body in a heap on the deck. Instead, Tessa unfolded herself from a man's arms, her slender limbs kicking and swinging against his embrace.

She was alive. Nadra be blessed, Tessa lived.

Cashiel sauntered to where the man held Tessa, his heavy hands on her slim shoulders. If Cashiel's eyes were green flames, Tessa's were their blue counterpart. Rigid hostility shone from her features.

"Well, well, well. I had wondered where you'd hidden yourself, little one." He stroked her cheek with his bloodied fingers.

"Don't touch her," Taryn commanded.

Cashiel glanced over his shoulder and grinned.

"I'll take this one for myself." He crushed Tessa to his midsection, burying her cries in his jacket. "She and the crown princess will be the appetizers, the empress the entree, and you, my dear Eirielle, you'll be the dessert."

He licked his lips and made a grotesque smacking sound. Bile soured her tongue and Taryn fought against the bindings. Impotent fury snarled her lips. At Cashiel's nod, two men approached Eliahnna and Lliandra. The elder woman pushed her shoulders back, a haughty look in her eyes. Eliahnna regarded them with the same calm she exhibited whether playing cards or weighing a difficult decision.

Cashiel bent low, his tongue out as if to scrape along Tessa's lips. The young girl whimpered and struggled against his hold, but he easily overpowered her. He stopped his movements and turned to glare at Taryn.

"Blindfold the Eirielle."

A man approached and Taryn jerked away to avoid the inevitable. Losing her sight would be worse than seeing what Cashiel was doing. She'd imagine far worse sins. He knew her weaknesses.

A little too well.

Sturdy fabric was forced over her eyes, plunging her into

darkness. The sounds around her blurred, then settled into a discordant hum. Her breath came in shallow drags and her heart sped up to race her thoughts. This blindness would make her lose her mind. With each passing second, she sped faster into madness. The hum lengthened until her hearing became crisper, more focused. It was the Eleri in her manifesting itself. She sent a silent prayer of thanks to Verdaine.

Cashiel and his men were silent, stepping lightly on the deck.

Taryn forced herself to breathe, to take in oxygen and calm her overworked heart. Only then could she discern what was happening.

Someone near her sighed. Not Cashiel, but one of his men. It wasn't a sound of lust. Whoever he was, this man wasn't comfortable with Cashiel's handling of those captured. Another sound—the scraping of chairs assaulted her ears. She imagined the men moving the women. But why? Several ladies wept. Ellie, perhaps. Or Lorilee? Did the threat of rape break Eliahnna?

A scuffle ended with a slap, followed by Tessa's sputtered curses.

"Tessa," Taryn wheezed, "you are too brave and far too clever for these men. Save your strength. You'll need it to punish these idiots." Taryn silently begged her sister to not fight the men who were twice her height and three times her weight. They had power and strength. Although, what Tessa lacked in size, she more than made up for in cunning.

A sharp slap stunned Taryn, but only for a moment. As she'd hoped, she drew Cashiel away from her baby sister. Hopefully Gian could let Tessa know the others were on their way.

"You really need to work on your anger issues, Cashiel," Taryn taunted her captor, knowing it would cost her.

His rank breath violated her senses. His body heat seared against her flesh. The scent of perspiration—fear-fueled acridness with an underlying smell of rotting meat—sparked a memory. She grasped at it, but there was nothing left.

"You and your clever mouth." He raked his tongue over her lips and she fought off a fresh wave of nausea. "You taste divine. I wonder if your sisters will taste as sweet." Cashiel flicked his tongue against her lips again and she bit her cheek to keep from spewing hateful rage.

She'd kill him. If she survived, she'd search every hollow of every tree, every crevice of every rock and would find him. When she did, she wouldn't hesitate to ram her sword up his asshole to his skull. Then she'd roast him on a spit, delighting in the screams he'd make. The scope of her will to hurt didn't faze her in the least. This man had ignited her fury and deserved every ounce of suffering she would give.

Fresh weeping reached her ears, followed by several muffled cries. As if reading Taryn's thoughts, Cashiel whispered, "I will rip them apart from the inside. You have no one to blame but yourself."

Tears coursed over her abused cheeks and Cashiel licked them with long strokes of his disgusting tongue. If she didn't do something now, they were all dead. Cashiel was getting bolder, his desire almost frenzied in its breadth. Rhoane and the others were too late.

Taryn reached deep into herself, past where she hid her power into the Noir part of her soul. She thought of Rhoane. Of the first time she saw him in the cavern. Of when they first kissed. She remembered the night he'd told her she was his betrothed and how his words had sparked a flame in her that continued to burn. Even through Marissa's betrayal and Rhoane's brokenness, she'd held onto her love of him. Her trust that they would be united as one. She'd held onto hope.

"Cashiel." Taryn's voice was little more than a harsh rasp. The swelling of her face made it almost impossible to open her mouth. "Promise me you won't harm the others and I'll give you what you want."

His moan turned her already queasy stomach. It was all she could do not to puke on him.

"Don't tell me you still think you can save them? You're beaten, stupid girl. I've won. Your dragon soul will be mine before the night is through."

He stood close enough she could smell incense on his jacket. An odd scent, to be sure. One she recognized, but the name escaped her.

"You don't need Rhoane's *darathi vorsi*. I have the crown. I can make you what you wish to be. We'll be bound for eternity." It was a bold move, and one she wasn't entirely certain would work, but she had little else to offer.

"You'll give me a dragon soul in exchange for their safety?"

"Yes."

"No, Taryn," Tessa yelled.

"You can't. He'll betray you," Eliahnna said.

"Give us our power back," Lliandra demanded.

"All in good time," Cashiel taunted.

Taryn imagined him waving them off, impatient for her to give in to his demands.

"Say it. Say you'll let them go and none of them will be harmed."

"I give you my word, they will not be harmed."

His fingertips caressed her cheek and she had to force herself not to flinch.

"You look lovely like this. Tied up, beaten, waiting for me to take you. You won't regret this." He pushed his lips against hers.

She opened her mouth, hating Cashiel more than ever.

Rhoane, forgive me. It's the only way to save them. Ynyd Eirathnacht, protect my friends and family. Wrap them in your embrace.

She dug deep into the recesses of her core where her love, hatred, confidence, and shame resided. There, she found her Telraicht-Noir

ShantiMari. Fuck coaxing it. She grabbed it with everything she had left and dragged it forth. For certainly she would die this night, and she'd damn sure take Cashiel and his men with her.

As his tongue thrust to the back of her mouth, she did the only thing she could think of, the one thing she swore to never do—she let her power loose.

The Noir erupted and spread through her to Cashiel and out, blanketing the ship with her ShantiMari. The last sounds she heard were the splintering of wood, followed by an explosion.

Screams tore her thoughts. Pain rocketed across her body. Heat blazed from deep inside, burning her core, destroying everything in its wake. Then, icy chills turned her innards crisp and fragile. Air whooshed past her head, deafening. Her body hit something solid, yet viscous—water. The impact stole what little strength she had left and she drifted, beneath the surface, into the murky depths of death.

CHAPTER SIX

Timing be damned, Rhoane would not let this man assault his love any longer.

Rhoane, forgive me. It's the only way to save them.

Rhoane paused, unsure if he'd heard true. Taryn spoke to him in his mind. He sent a warning to her, but it was drowned out by a deafening noise. Screams erupted and the ship groaned with the impact of an explosion.

Shards of wood impaled Cashiel's men, but Lliandra's ladies, her guard, and her crew were unharmed. Rhoane raced for Taryn, but where she'd been was vacant. In fact, the entire front half of the ship was a mangled mass of wood. Fires burned in spits and starts all across the deck.

Baehlon's deep baritone shouted orders above the sounds of dying men and weeping women. Rhoane knelt and touched the decking where a scorched outline was all that remained of the scaffolding that held Taryn. Her presence vibrated against his fingertips. Her agony infused his spirit. *This wasn't where she died. She couldn't be dead.* He repeated the last again and again, willing it to be true.

Activity whirled around him, but Rhoane stood apart from

the chaos, lost. He gripped his cynfar and focused on Taryn. Empty silence answered. No songs sang in his mind. No melodies wove through his thoughts. His heart lodged in his throat as panic surged in his veins. He refused to believe Taryn was dead. She was out there—he just had to find her. He sent his thoughts out like a net, hoping to capture Taryn's essence, but again came up empty.

A sailor brushed past and Rhoane jerked to the present, where his men raced to untie the prisoners. Rhoane went to Lliandra first.

As he slashed through the knots, he asked, "Where is Taryn?"

Lliandra sniffed and tossed her hair over a shoulder. "She blew up my goddamned ship. She's probably with the sea king."

Sounds of fighting aboard the ship with the chanters echoed above the din. A surge of power flowed through him. Myrddin and the others broke through. *Verdaine be blessed.* A veil washed over Lliandra's face and her beauty shone in the night sky. For a moment, Rhoane was dazzled, but shook off the enchantment with a scowl.

"Your daughter could be dead. Do you not think you should be at least a little concerned?"

"Rhoane, this is an old dance and I'm tired. Yes, I'm worried for Taryn, but she knew what she was doing. Cashiel was going to rape all of us, right here." She indicated a table that had been brought out, a mattress placed upon it.

Rhoane shut out the awful images that tramped through his mind. His heart ached for the women who had to endure the threat.

Lliandra straightened her hair with a swirl of power and patted her skirts. "It was a show of power and Taryn stopped him. Am I relieved? Yes. No mother should have to witness that. Nor should I have had to see my daughter beaten and tortured. But these are the times we're living in. It's up to you and Taryn to stop the violence. But first, you need to make sure this ship doesn't sink."

"Worried about your jewels?"

"Don't be a fool. My jewels aren't on this ship. They're on yours." A sly smile tilted her lips.

Rhoane shouldn't have been surprised, yet he was. Lliandra was devious and cunning. He'd do well never to forget who he was dealing with. "Do you know where Taryn's sword is?"

"I've not seen it, but my guess would be in her cabin." Lliandra flexed her wrists and adjusted her shoulders as if they'd been playing cards all day. Her nonchalance irritated Rhoane.

"Where are Saeko and Faelara?"

"I don't know. They weren't brought up, so they're either hiding or dead."

Again, her chilling lack of compassion shocked him. He didn't have time to search for the women, he had to find Taryn. "Are you recovered enough to fully use your power?"

Lliandra stood and stretched her limbs. "I'm numb in places I didn't know could lose feeling, but yes. I can control the weather enough to sustain the ship."

Controlling the weather was a trick of the Light. Rhoane glanced at the retreating fog. Only someone high in the royal family should be able to command mists to obey. His first thought was to suspect Marissa, but she was dead, turned to ash by Taryn not more than a fortnight past. *Who, then?* He tucked the thought to the back of his mind and searched for Baehlon. He caught the big knight's attention and motioned him over.

"Find Faelara and Saeko. I am going to search for Taryn." Rhoane didn't give the knight time to respond; instead, he raced to the other end of the ship, where it was devoid of people.

He shook out his arms and forced himself to think of only Taryn. He fought through the cries and shouting surrounding him. *Focus. Calm. Taryn.* Yet his darathi form didn't answer. He struggled to connect with his inner dragon. Where once there had been a strong current, now there was nothing.

Panic flared anew. If Taryn was dead, did that destroy his darathi? He paced the deck, fumbling for answers to questions he hated asking. There were too many variables for why he couldn't reach his dragon. One thing kept surfacing in his thoughts—Ynyd Eirathnacht. Taryn's sword might give him answers. Mentally, he told Baehlon to meet him at Taryn's cabin and sped to the stairs leading below deck.

He raced to the sleeping quarters where he sensed Taryn had stayed. Her scent was everywhere, but he managed to separate where it was most concentrated.

Baehlon lumbered down the narrow passage. "Faelara and Saeko aren't in their rooms."

Taryn's cabin consisted of a single bed and washbasin. Typical Taryn. She'd not want anything fancy or elaborate, unlike her mother.

Rhoane searched her room for the sword, not finding it hidden in her belongings. Claidholm Solais hummed a melancholy tune and he pulled his sword from its sheath. "Lead me to your mate."

The hilt swung to the left, to a section of wall that made up the outside of the ship. A lone window gave a glimpse of the starry sky. Rhoane pressed several boards until one creaked under the pressure. Tiny flicks of heat pricked his hand. He'd found her hiding place. If not for his own sword, he wasn't sure he'd ever have located it. Even to a trained eye, it was hard to distinguish the loose boards from the others.

Rhoane used the tip of his blade to cut through Taryn's wards, speaking in Eleri to Ynyd Eirathnacht, hoping the sword understood he meant it no harm. Finally, the wards unraveled and with shaking hands, he was able to pry open the board. The Sword of Ohlin looked unremarkable tucked against the side of the ship, but Rhoane wasn't fooled. Only those Taryn allowed were able to handle the thing. He'd once placed his fingers upon the hilt to swear a secret and had no idea if he'd be able to hold it now.

A shuffling at the door alarmed him and Baehlon placed himself between the intruder and Rhoane. Gian's small frame ducked under the knight and entered Taryn's cabin.

"Bloody faerie. I should wallop you for that."

Gian motioned Rhoane to stop and he withdrew from the compartment. The faerie stepped confidently forward and gripped the hilt. He removed the sword gently, being careful not to come into contact with either Rhoane or Baehlon.

"Well, I'll be a daft sack," Baehlon murmured.

"My thoughts exactly," Rhoane said. "Tell me, Gian, will Taryn's sword help me to shift into my *darathi*?"

Baehlon's eyes widened before a deep frown creased his forehead. "Your power isn't blocked. Why…?" He left the question unspoken.

Rhoane had no answer for him all the same. There was no logical reason why he couldn't shift.

Gian's fingers flew too fast for Rhoane to keep up. He pointed to his temple. "In here, please."

It is not yet time. The Darennsai must do this alone.

She lives?

Ask Saeko.

Bloody faerie.

"He says we must find Saeko. Lliandra said she did not see her once the attack happened. I am hopeful she, and Fae, were able to hide somewhere."

The men scoured the ship, calling out to the women while trying to contact them by thought. All the while, Rhoane chafed at the time they wasted. If Gian was right, Taryn lived, but Rhoane didn't like the ominous message that she needed to do something alone. His panic thrummed just beneath his rapid heartbeats. On the lowest level of the ship, beneath where Taryn had blown a hole in the deck, they found the women.

Behind a stack of barrels, Faelara and Saeko looked like dolls slumped against the wall. A third figure lay among them. By his clothing, he wasn't one of Lliandra's men. Apprehension pricked down Rhoane's spine the closer they came to the group. His steps faltered as he imagined the worst. Baehlon removed a heavy barrel, revealing a bald head and thick neck muscles. In his outstretched hand was a dirk. One Rhoane recognized.

He knelt and checked the man for life. His pulse was low, but he lived. From his position, Rhoane reckoned he'd shielded the women from the blast. A small cauldron was tipped over, brownish liquid seeping into the straw covering the floor. An acrid smell assaulted his nostrils. It was a smell he knew all too well. Faelara loved her potions. Rhoane swiped the oily liquid with his fingertips and rubbed them together. The mixture turned ochre against his skin.

"I would wager they were making a sleeping draught." Rhoane wiped his fingers against his trousers.

"To knock out the crew. Clever ladies." Baehlon nudged at the blacksmith with his boot. The prone figure grunted and stirred. "Who's this?"

Rhoane rolled the man off the women and onto his back. Iselt blinked several times, then grinned. "You look like shit."

"Might I inquire what you are doing on this ship? With these women? The last I saw of you was in Talaith's harbor. You were supposed to be on Adesh's ship, spying for me."

"Always so formal, you Eleri." Iselt sat up, cracked his neck and shook out his arms. "We were raided and taken prisoner. The choice was simple—stay aboard as part of the crew, or be fed to King Baldev. I chose to stay. After all, you paid me to spy. I figured it didn't matter much if it was on the empress or this idiot." Iselt jerked a finger toward the upper deck.

Rhoane put out a hand to help him up. "We can discuss your findings later. First, are the women hurt?"

They had yet to stir, and Baehlon looked to be one heartbeat away from killing someone.

"When the blast hit, they were sprayed with their potion. I think it works even if you don't drink it."

Gian slipped the scabbard strap over his shoulder and bent to inspect Saeko. He lay his fingertips upon her temple and within moments she stirred. Next, he went to Faelara and repeated what he'd done. She, too, awoke. The women groggily opened their eyes and blinked into the dim light.

"I have my power back." Faelara's fingertips sparked with amber flames. "Ha-ha! I'm whole again. Thanks be to Nadra."

"Your goddess had nothing to do with returning your power to you," Iselt grumbled. "I'd wager these men did, though."

Faelara looked at Baehlon standing to the side, his fists clenched, jaw tight. She sprang forward, knocking over several bags and containers.

"I thought I'd lost you." She threw her arms around the big man and held him close.

Baehlon's look of surprise, shock, and relief filled Rhoane with an unusual sensation of joy. Bittersweet, to be sure. The others on the ship had their loved ones returned to them. For Rhoane, he only had more questions.

He helped Saeko stand. "Are you hurt?"

"I'm well, my lord. Thank you. The princess? Is she safe?"

A cloud passed over his thoughts. "She was thrown from the ship. I cannot search for her as yet. Gian believes you know why."

Saeko's face blanched at Rhoane's words. "I'm afraid I don't know—" Tears filled her eyes and she stared at a spot just beyond his shoulder. "You must find her. She's in grave danger. I sense it."

"Where? Can you see her?"

"I cannot, my lord," Saeko said, her eyes haunted. "Our danger is passed, but has just begun for the Eirielle, I fear."

Taryn had once mentioned in passing she didn't know much about her maid, but she suspected Saeko held secrets. Perhaps they were dangerous secrets. But Rhoane also recalled a time when the Shadow Assassin had almost killed Ellie, and Saeko had worked day and night to save her. Friend or foe, he had to trust Saeko.

"Tell me what you know."

Saeko closed her eyes. A soft humming came from her slightly parted lips, followed by whispered words in a voice he didn't recognize. "Two truths and one lie. Tested beyond strength. Taunted to near death. A watery grave she seeks. One you know from long past will guide her to the healing place. If the Dark One doesn't claim her first."

"Riddles? You've got to be fucking kidding me. No wonder Taryn hates dealing with the gods. They are worse than drunken Artaghs on Smelting Day," Baehlon groused, his boots shuffling against the wooden boards.

Iselt bristled and gripped his dagger tighter. Rhoane studied the man's curious reaction to Baehlon's outburst but said nothing.

"Is there more, Saeko? Is her *darathi vorsi* intact?" Rhoane prodded. He had to know what to expect when he found Taryn.

"She is wounded, the winged one. Her soul cries for her mate. If coupling does not take place within the waning moon-turn, the veil will close forever."

"What veil? Where are they? Where are the others?" Rhoane's voice rose an octave. Fear, raw and invasive, crowded any other thoughts. A veil could mean she'd gone to another world. How would he find her? Dread dripped into despair. If he didn't find Taryn soon, the darathi vorsi would be lost to him for all time. And Taryn with them.

"Easy, my friend. Let's focus on Taryn. We'll sort out the rest in time." Baehlon's big hand rested on Rhoane's shoulder.

He took a deep breath, then another. He cleared his thoughts and brought his heart rate down.

"Is Taryn on Aelinae?"

A smile twisted Saeko's lips. "For the time being, yes."

Thank the gods.

"Is she near?" Rhoane kept his tone low, his words simple. He couldn't afford miscommunication.

"Yes. And no. She is where she needs to be."

Baehlon grunted and shifted forward as if to shake Saeko, but Rhoane stopped him. He didn't like the answers either, but he needed Saeko to finish his inquiry.

"Who would use Saeko's voice?"

Behind him, Faelara gasped. Baehlon's hand flopped to his side.

Rhoane pressed on. "A name, if you please."

Saeko swayed where she stood, her closed eyelids fluttering as if in deep sleep and dreaming. "I am called many things, but you will know me by Mallaqai."

Rhoane flinched as if burned by a thousand flames.

A twisted grin bent Saeko's lips. "Ah, yes. The Eleri fear what they do not understand. I mean you no harm, *Surtentse*. You have no reason to believe me now, but in time, perhaps you will see we are allies, not enemies."

"Taryn," Rhoane gritted between clenched teeth, bringing the conversation to what he knew was real, "can you tell me where she is?"

"I already have. Look for your beloved in the depths of the sea. Only you. No others. King Baldev is not pleased with these proceedings."

"My dragon—"

"Is waiting for you where he's always been. Beneath your fear. Beyond your doubt. Look to your love."

It was true. Even then, Rhoane felt the stirrings of his darathi. A spark of hope bloomed in his heart. He would find Taryn. He would save her.

The changeling never gave without compensation. She would

demand payment for her information and Rhoane had no doubt the cost would be high.

"What do you want for your help?"

A greedy smile showed Saeko's teeth. A sibilant "Yesssss" came from the depths of the girl's throat. "Pay me what you believe my knowledge is worth."

He refused to barter with the witch. Instead, he did the last thing Mallaqai would expect. Rhoane leaned forward and placed his lips upon Saeko's. Again, a gasp sounded from behind him. "For your help, Mallaqai. I know this has cost you greatly."

Saeko swooned and licked her lips, tasting him. "Your love, so pure, so fierce. It must sustain us all, my prince. I will give this to your mate."

Icy pricks of relief swept over his inflamed skin. Thank the gods, she was pleased with his offering. If she'd rejected his payment, who knew what torment she'd conjure. Rhoane stepped back and Saeko fell into his arms. A moment later, she sprinted from his grip and vomited behind one of the barrels. Gian patted her back and held her hair away from her face.

"What happened?" she asked once she finished retching.

"You don't recall anything?" Faelara went to the maid and felt Saeko's forehead. "Does the name Mallaqai mean anything to you?"

Saeko's eyes narrowed, her face pinched. "No. Should it? One minute I was talking to you, the next, I was sick."

"Would someone like to explain who Mallaqai is, and why she possessed Saeko?" Baehlon thumped the floorboards with his heel.

"Later, my friend. Take care of the women. I need to find Taryn."

Gian handed Taryn's sword to Rhoane. After a moment's hesitation, he slung the strap over his shoulder. He then ran full out up the stairs until he was on the top deck. A lone figure stood at the railing, looking out at the clear sky.

"Did you find my daughter?" Lliandra asked without turning to him. Genuine concern laced her words.

"Not yet, but I will. Tell Myrddin to set sail for Menurra at first light. If I am not back by then, I will return once I have located Taryn."

Lliandra placed a hand on his forearm, surprising Rhoane with the strength of her grip. "Find her. Please."

"When next you see her, let her know how you feel. She needs to hear it from you."

Lliandra nodded and released her hold on him.

He strode to the side and climbed atop the railing. The dark waters stirred a suppressed terror, but he pushed it aside. He'd come to terms with his fear of water too long ago now to prevent him from doing what he had to do to find Taryn. He dove off the side and into his own kind of hell. The inky blackness of the sea swallowed him until there was no light, no dark, only him.

CHAPTER SEVEN

Taryn drifted, weightless, without sight or sound. At first, she believed she was in the void. That dark expanse of nothingness that had first brought her to Aelinae. But the longer she floated, she came to realize she was underwater. Breathing. Heart beating. Alive.

This wasn't possible. Or was it? She had no idea anymore what could or couldn't be real. She moved her hand and blinked at the paleness of her skin. Beneath the sea, she was the color of alabaster. Her short hair fanned around her face, the silver strands reflecting multi-hued shades of blue. Her body ached from Cashiel's beating. Every movement, no matter how small, caused a fissure of agony to spiral through her. The saltwater sought each cut and burrowed deep, adding to her discomfort.

A dark shape swam past and Taryn tensed. With the amount of blood she'd lost, surely she was a beacon for sharks. If Aelinae had sharks. She didn't know. There was still so much to learn about her home world.

"Darennsai," a female voice said close to Taryn.

She jerked around, regretting the movement as fresh bursts of pain shot from head to toe. Her vision blurred and she closed her eyes. When she opened them, the face of a monster filled her sight.

Long whiskers curled like tentacles in the water, reaching out, but not quite touching her. A longish snout, blunt at the end with nostrils flaring as if sniffing her, moved close enough Taryn could make out scales. Opalescent with undertones of every shade of blue imaginable, they shimmered in the scant light.

She was dead. Had to be. Dead and hallucinating. New waves of agony wracked her body and she closed her eyes once more, willing the endless pain to end. She wasn't dead. Unless this constant thrumming of misery was her own special hell. Lower she sank until even the soft illumination against her closed lids disappeared. The water temperature dropped and she shivered against the cold. Tears squeezed from beneath the corners of her eyes, adding to the salty liquid surrounding her. Where was she? Where was Rhoane? When she opened her eyes, the creature had swum away, leaving her alone in the dark.

"Come back," Taryn whispered. "Please."

A long tail passed in front of her. At its tip, a fin swished and propelled Taryn deeper. She struggled to swim, to move her arms and legs in a coordinated fashion. She could breathe, but her motor skills were damaged. Quite possibly several bones as well.

The creature reappeared, the face twice as big as Taryn's height. "Darennsai, are you ready?"

"For what?"

"Do you remember who you are?"

What was this? An acid trip down the rabbit hole? Of course she knew who she was.

"I'm Taryn Rose ap Galendrin. Second daughter to Empress Lliandra, first daughter of Overlord Valterys, Eirielle, Darennsai, shall I continue?" Talking scratched her throat, but felt good at the same time. Speaking gave her strength.

"Please." The creature echoed Taryn's plea.

"Let's see, betrothed to Rhoane, First Son of the Eleri, the

Surtentse. I'm um, a sister, friend, lover, cousin. I have Light, Dark, Eleri, and Telraicht-Noir ShantiMari coursing through my veins. I'm Keeper of the Sword, Keeper of the Stars—"

"Yessss."

Ghostly wings flared, and Taryn floated closer. She should've been terrified, but wasn't. Maybe this was what death felt like—eternal pain without fear. Curious.

"Are you darathi vorsi?" Taryn asked.

"Are you?"

Riddles. Taryn hated riddles. This had to be hell. "You're rather frustrating. That's what you are."

Bubbles floated from the creature's mouth, and Taryn would've sworn it was laughing. That's all she needed—monsters mocking her. What next? She'd wake up in London having never known Aelinae or Rhoane? A shiver of dread passed over her cuts and bruises, hurting more than anything Cashiel inflicted upon her. To not remember Aelinae or Rhoane would be tragic. A fate worse than death.

"You have many titles, but do you remember who you are?" the creature prodded, its tentacles swirling on an invisible tide.

The sad truth was, all those titles meant nothing. They didn't define her. More to the point, they constrained and confined her. The looping argument pressed upon Taryn's head, giving her a whopper of a headache. Rather than prolong the game, Taryn accepted defeat.

"No. I don't remember who I am. Or who I'm supposed to be. Or what bloody day it is. All I can remember is being tied up and in pain. Then more pain. Then you."

"But who were you before you were you?"

Memories of her life before Aelinae flashed in her mind. Bittersweet images of Brandt and a younger Taryn lingered in her heart. Understanding came slowly, but with it bloomed joy, contentment. Her heart rate slowed and the throbbing in her head lessened. "You mean before the cavern?"

The whiskers spiraled with the creature's nod.

"I was just a girl. Sometimes happy, sometimes sad. Normal. Not filled with power or fear. Not hunted. Definitely not a *darathi vorsi*."

"But you were all of those and yet you weren't. Why? Because you didn't know you existed."

The slip of understanding Taryn had formulated evaporated and she was left more confused than ever. She'd existed, surely. Hadn't she? Or was Earth all a dream?

A river of red drifted between them and the creature sniffed the water.

"You're dying, young one. I'm afraid I can't heal you and King Baldev is too far to be of much help." Consternation flickered in the dark eyes. "I must take you to *them*."

Whoever *they* were, Taryn wanted no part of it. "Take me to Rhoane. He's an excellent healer."

"Darling, he's too far away. We're near their camps. They'll know what to do with you. When you are recovered, return to me."

The creature nudged Taryn and her eyes became heavy. Her breathing slowed. "What are you doing to me? Where are we going?"

"Hush, my darling. There is much left for you to do, but you have to remember who you are."

But I don't know. I've never had the chance to choose.

Taryn drifted in the arms of the creature, safe in the knowledge no harm would come to her. For that's what Taryn's senses told her. The winged beast was female, old, and wise. Wiser perhaps than even Myrddin.

How long they swam, Taryn couldn't say. It might've been minutes, or could've been days. When she felt herself jostled and rolled onto something cold, wet, and rough, she opened her eyes and saw the scales of a serpent flash in the moonlight, then disappear beneath the waves.

"Wait," she called out, her voice a rasped scratch of nothingness. "What's your name? How do I find you?"

They call me Xianqin. You'll know where to find me. Now, sleep. You must heal.

Taryn lay on the wet sand, her head on her arm, and stared at the empty sea. The night was silent and dark. No campfires could be seen, nor city lights. *This is the end.* She would die alone, and Rhoane wouldn't know where to find her. Her fingertips stretched to touch her pendant and tears spilled from her eyes.

Rhoane. My love. My life. I will love you, always. I'm sorry for everything that's happened. I wish I could go back to that day in the cavern. I'd do everything different.

She snatched her fingers away. Would she? Would she change anything? What if doing so caused different dangers? Would Rhoane die if even one thing was altered? She couldn't bear the thought.

Her fingers clasped the cynfar once again. *No, no I wouldn't. I don't want anything to be different. Not the cavern, not Brandt's death, not Marissa nor Zakael, none of it. Without all of that, we wouldn't have right now. This isn't the end, not by a long shot. I don't know if you can hear me. I don't know where I am. By water, somewhere. I could be anywhere. But I won't give up. I won't stop fighting because I have to remember who I am.*

She was babbling, her thoughts becoming thick with fatigue and weakness. The amount of blood she'd lost was enough to kill her. Her left hand covered the wound beneath her breast and pressed hard. Pain shot through her, but she ignored it as best she could. She could heal anyone else, but not herself. It wasn't fair.

Nothing about Aelinae was fair. That much she'd learned in the past season. She flopped onto her back and gazed at the stars. A shadow passed overhead and her heart tripped several beats. Rhoane was searching for her. He had to be. The dark spot flew closer and an owl screeched before diving to hunt. It wasn't Rhoane this time. But he was out there and she'd return to him soon. First, she needed to regain her strength. She closed her eyes and fell into a misery-filled slumber.

When next she opened them, a figure stood over her. A tremor of terror spiraled in her gut. Whether friend or foe, it didn't matter—she lacked the energy to speak, much less fight. Taryn blinked against the harsh midday sun and focused on the slight form. He cocked his head, a mischievous smile showing tiny yellowed teeth. *A child? Here?* He crouched, his forearms resting on his knees and chattered to her in his language. She tried to comprehend, but it wasn't one she was familiar with. He pointed first to her, then to himself, then to somewhere in the distance. Taryn nodded and closed her eyes again.

The world shifted—right, left—then bobbed for what felt an eternity. Either the pain became bearable or she'd lost feeling in her body. What should've been excruciating wasn't. In fact, all Taryn felt was gratitude. It sustained her.

The rocking stopped and someone placed a cloth soaked in goat's milk to her mouth and she drank as much as her stomach could tolerate. Another cloth was bitter tasting and Taryn shied away from it, but her head was held in place until she drank from it, too. Then she slept. Fitfully at first, then long and deep until there was no sound or movement at all.

A howling in the distance startled her from her sleep and she tried to speak, but no words came out. She touched her lips and flinched at the cracked skin. Her fingers trailed across her jaw to her neck. The pendant was cool against her skin and she cradled it gently. Each exhale of breath came out as a soft wheeze, the pressure tearing against the rawness of her throat.

Kaida. She flung the thought outward, stretching her mind far and wide. Nothing moved in the darkness and for a moment, the cold grip of dread held her heart in a vise-like grip.

The boy had left her to die.

But she lay on soft blankets, not on sand, and she remembered goat's milk. Other things, too. Soft voices. Gentle hands.

The boy hadn't deserted her. He'd taken her to a place of safety. Hope edged her fear to the side and soothed her staccato heartbeats.

Kaida, tell Rhoane I am safe.

For the time being, she believed she was.

CHAPTER EIGHT

Kaleigh rushed through the encampment to the healer's tents. Inside, she ignored those waiting, shutting out their cries of indignation at having to wait. Her robes flapped behind her as she sprinted through the larger tents to the smallest ones in the back. She slipped through the opening of the farthest tent and stood for a moment to acclimate her eyes to the dim light.

"Why is it so dark in here?"

A small boy approached and placed his fingers to his lips while pointing with his other hand to the table. There, a figure lay still. Her chest moved with labored breaths and her stained clothing was no more than tattered scraps barely covering her mottled skin. Blood mixed with dirt, making it difficult to determine where her injuries began and ended. Kaleigh kneeled until she was eye level with the lad.

"Do you know her?" she whispered.

"No, Your Highness. I found her on the beach and brought her here."

"By yourself?" Kaleigh whistled, astonished such a small boy would travel that great a distance for an unknown woman.

He nodded, his eyes large in his youthful face. "They say you're the best healer in all the lands. Can you save her?"

"I will do my best. Can you go to the front of the tents and ask the big man to please send for Loghan? I will need him to help me."

The boy ran off before Kaleigh had a chance to ask him anything further. She shrugged out of her robes and placed her headdress on a stool in the corner. She raised her arms overhead and stretched her back muscles. It had been a tiresome night fighting with a stubborn baby who had wished to be born upside down. Eventually she'd won the battle and now mother and son were sleeping soundly. Kaleigh, however, hadn't seen her bed in almost two days. She splashed cold water on her face before turning to her mystery patient.

Long legs wrapped around themselves, the bare ankles showing signs of being restrained. She checked the wrists. They, too, were badly afflicted. She traced a finger along the seam of the woman's leather breeches, tearing them with her ShantiMari until they fell to the table. The girl was tall for an Aelan, possibly an Eleri. A quick check of her ears confirmed this was an Eleri, but the clothing was wrong. She could possibly be sheanna, her short hair was confirmation enough, but Kaleigh couldn't know for certain. The Eleri didn't approve of or appreciate the Ullan art of healing. Her heart warred with her head—if she didn't do something, the woman wouldn't survive another night.

By the time Loghan arrived, Kaleigh had the rest of the patient's clothes removed and started to wash the dirt and debris from her skin.

"What is it, Mother? I was told there is an emergency."

"There is." Kaleigh indicated the table. "I do not know who she is or what happened to her, but the boy said he found her on the beach like this."

"And he brought her here? By himself?"

"So it would seem."

Loghan took a clean cloth from the basin and cleaned the girl's legs. His movements were dispassionate and clinical. To become a healer, one had to put aside desire and focus on the patient. What they did was less about the physical act, and more about transcending flesh and bone.

Once they had her bathed, Kaleigh took stock of each cut, every bruise. "Are there any broken bones?"

"I believe her right thigh bone and possibly forearm." Loghan stretched her leg straight, eliciting a moan from the patient. When he did the same to her right arm, a pained whimper escaped her lips. "Definitely broken. This one will have to be set before we begin the healing."

"See if you can remove that necklace." Kaleigh pointed to a silver chain wrapped tight around the girl's throat.

Loghan did as asked and flinched when his fingers came into contact with the metal. "What in Rykoto's name?"

He picked up a knife before replacing it with a wooden splint. With this, he lifted the chain from her neck, working it around to the clasp.

"Odd," Loghan murmured. "There is no clasp." He bent over the girl and shifted her head to search beneath her hair. "But there is a charm."

Kaleigh squinted against the dim light and looked where Loghan pointed. A silver charm of a laurel wreath and two clear stones nestled in the girl's short hair. A memory tickled her mind. Of a king long past who wore a crown of laurel leaves. Images of something she'd read at the temple burst across her thoughts. A world between worlds. Words written in an ancient text— Verdaine's prophecy. Stars. Terrarae. Gyota. Kaleigh stepped away from the table, her hands held high.

"Do *not* touch her." She hastily covered the woman's naked body with a fur blanket. Her hands shook as she tucked the ends beneath her chin.

"Mother, what is wrong? Why can we not heal her?"

"If she is who I think she is, we are all in grave danger."

"But if we do not heal her, she will die."

"I know. She must survive, but we are not the ones to heal her. Only her life mate can do that. You must not, under any circumstances, share your body with her. She is sacred," Kaleigh implored, glancing at the erection already forming beneath his robes. "Is this understood?"

"But I can save her. You know I am strong enough. Why is she so special?"

"Fetch me the boy, Loghan. I must know exactly where he found her."

"Mother, you are trembling. Please, tell me who she is."

Kaleigh ran a hand through her short curls. Her thoughts spiraled as quickly as her heartbeat. *Of all the places in the world, she was brought here.* Tears welled in her eyes and sadness loomed over her apprehension.

"If I am not mistaken, this is the *Darennsai*. And you, my son, are half Eleri. If you mate with her, you will kill her as quick as poison."

"The *Darennsai*? As in, the destroyer of your people?" He flung the blanket from the woman's body and snatched a blade from the table. "We must kill her now."

"No!" Kaleigh grabbed his wrist and struggled to keep the razor-sharp weapon from the woman's breast. "There are two sides to the prophecy. Some say she will destroy the Eleri, others say she will save them. All I know is we are not the ones who should decide if she lives or dies. We are not gods, Loghan. I am not willing to choose the fate of Aelinae. Are you?"

He lowered the dagger and glared at the woman. A battle raged across his face until finally he stormed from the tent. Kaleigh replaced the blanket, smoothing it over the woman's broken body.

Loghan would be dealt with later. Right now, Kaleigh needed answers. Several minutes later the boy entered, pale and half-terrified. She did her best to set him at ease, asking her questions in a soft voice, but he had little information to share. He'd found the woman asleep on the shores of the Jansen Strait. From there, he traveled through the desert to their encampment. Along the way he saw several tribes, but each encouraged him to seek out Kaleigh. That they would deny the woman care irritated her. Ullans healed all—no matter race, gender, or god affiliation. It was their creed. Perhaps the tribesmen knew who the woman was and didn't want her in their camp for fear of retaliation. No matter. She was here now and was Kaleigh's responsibility. That Rhoane's life mate would end up here, after all those seasons of not hearing from him, was troubling.

She lifted her face to the sky and shook her head. *Still testing me, Verdaine? Still trying to make me your priestess?* Whether the goddess heard her or not was moot. A woman was dying and Kaleigh needed to save her.

The boy, no longer shaking, wilted into a chair. The poor thing had to be exhausted and hungry. Kaleigh sent him to the dining tents with one of her trusted ladies. If Amdi found him scrounging around, there was no telling what would happen. Her laird had been gone most of the day, but would be arriving soon. If she was going to do this, it had to be now.

With trembling hands and a pit in the base of her throat, Kaleigh turned the woman's head slightly to get a better glimpse of the cynfar and sighed. It had to be the Darennsai. Who else would wear a pendant made from Eleri metals? Taking a deep breath, she clasped the charm. When nothing happened, her knees buckled from sheer relief. She braced herself against the table. Perhaps being full Eleri protected her from harm.

Closing her eyes, she focused on a face she'd not seen in several decades. A face she once knew well and had loved as much as her laird. The memory of a brash young man, full of rage and youthful arrogance, brought tears to her eyes. They rolled over her cheeks to drip from her chin. How she'd missed him. She could only hope he'd not forgotten her in the long seasons he'd been away.

Rhoane, it is Kaleigh. I hope you can hear me. Your Darennsai is injured and needs your healing. We are three days north from the Jansen Strait, where you last stayed with us. Please hurry.

She waited several minutes for a reply. Vast amounts of power surged through the pendant to her and back again. She'd fought the urge to release the charm, to forget about calling for Rhoane's help, but this woman was her kin. It was her duty to do all she could. When no answer came, she let go of the cynfar and sat upon a stool. That small thing had exhausted her. Not just the Darennsai's power, but reaching out to someone she'd tried in vain to forget.

For a long time she stared at the stranger, contemplating her next step. If she could tap into the immense power coiled inside the woman, Kaleigh could use it to heal her. She had to at least try.

Loghan returned and brought with him a plate of food.

"You need nourishment, Mother." He handed her the plate and paced the other side of the table. "I have been thinking. If you are intent on saving her, and if she is who you say she is, we are duty bound to heal her."

"You will not touch her," Kaleigh warned.

"I can heal without sharing my body. It helps to ignite their passion, but it is not necessary. You taught me this, or have you forgotten?"

"I remember, but had to be certain you did as well. The reason Ullan healers are the best in all of Aelinae is because we use all the senses. No one else understands this is not about rutting."

It wasn't so long ago she believed the same thing. When Amdi first took her as his mate, she'd fought him about healing, believing it would break her to share her body with another. But he taught her that passions had a way of healing the mind, body, and spirit in a way that potions and tinctures never could. Since then, she'd become renowned for her skill.

"If we are going to do this, we must use extreme caution. This woman is almost a goddess. I know she does not appear that way now, but she will one day. We must treat her as such."

Loghan shrugged out of his robe. "If you say so."

"Put your clothes back on."

"I prefer to work naked. I will not touch her inappropriately, I promise. But this is how I do my best work. Unhindered."

Kaleigh chose not to bicker with him. She'd seen him naked too many times to care that he was her son. In the healer's tents, he was Loghan and she Kaleigh. Not the laird's son or wife, but healers.

She rolled the blanket off the woman until it rested at her feet. Next, she placed one hand on her breast where her heart beat strongest, and another above her pubic bone. The woman's clammy skin had turned an ashy shade. They were losing her.

Loghan positioned his hands upon her brow and midsection. His gaze focused on the patient's face. "She is weaker. There is not much time."

"When I say so, pulse your power into her, but keep it gentle. Not too much. Invite her power to join yours. Explain what we are doing with your thoughts and actions."

"You act as if I have never done this before."

"Sorry. I suppose I am nervous." She was beyond nervous. Her anxiety snapped upon every nerve. She could hardly breathe for the weight she bore upon her chest. This was not just Rhoane's beloved: this was Kaleigh's destiny. She saw it clear as the waters of Lan Gyllarelle. This moment was what her life had led up to. Verdaine didn't wish Kaleigh to be her priestess, but something more—the responsibility rested within her heart. To let this woman die would be more than a death sentence to the Eleri. It meant the extermination of her race and those they cared for. Eons of knowledge, power beyond what Kaleigh could comprehend, would be wiped out with this woman's passing.

"I can do this alone." Loghan's concern touched her. "You are crying. You know as well as I emotions have no place in the healer's tents."

"Not this time, Loghan." She didn't elaborate. Instead, she took a long drag of air and breathed out, counting to five. "Are you ready? Now."

Her ShantiMari flowed from her fingertips into the woman. She concentrated on merging her power into Loghan's and their patient's. The mix of her Light Eleri and his Dark ShantiMari was one that always startled her at first. There were subtle differences between them. His was tied to the sun and hers, the terrarae, which allowed them to combine their powers in unusual, yet effective ways.

Kaleigh coaxed the woman's power to join theirs while searching for broken bones and mending torn flesh. The wound on the woman's side had stopped bleeding, but the cut was deep, almost to her heart. Kaleigh closed her eyes and traveled with her Mari into the woman, through her muscles and tendons. A dark stain pushed against her power, burning her with its intensity. Every instinct told her to stop, but she kept her hands upon the patient's body. Searing pain ripped her thoughts to fragments as tattered as the woman's blouse. Kaleigh fought to stay focused. Fought for more than the woman's life. Fought for her people.

"Do you feel that?" Beads of sweat dotted Loghan's tattooed forehead.

"Stay away from that for now." Kaleigh was also sweating with the exertion. The woman's internal injuries were too much for her to heal in one pass. Whatever had happened to her, it had involved a brutal beating. Fresh tears stung the backs of Kaleigh's eyes and she blinked them away. What a sentimental old woman she'd become. She couldn't remember a time when she'd cried this much. Several tears dropped on the woman's abdomen. Where they landed on her skin, stars shone bright, then diminished to white spots.

"What just happened?"

"I do not know." Kaleigh wiped her eyes on her gown, not trusting what she'd seen.

Loghan's stance shifted. Through his power, she felt his indifference lessen. A snap of his Shanti against hers signaled that he concentrated his power with more precision.

A commotion in the outer tents drew their attention. In a matter of a single breath, her worst fear and greatest hope materialized before her.

CHAPTER NINE

Kaleigh, beautiful as the day he first met her, sweat rolling down her face, held her hands pressed upon Taryn's naked body. The unfettered relief he felt at finding Taryn dampened at the sight of Kaleigh healing her. *How dare she?* An unwelcome and long forgotten fury battled against his gratitude that she'd recognized the Darennsai and had the foresight to call him for help.

His appreciation of her actions soured further when he took in the handsome man opposite her. Tattoos covered his entire—naked—body. An erection strained against the table. The healer openly glared at Rhoane.

He reached for his sword, fighting hard against his desire to kill them both. "Unhand her this instant," Rhoane gritted between clenched teeth.

"Get out," the tattooed man ordered, ignoring Rhoane's demand. "We are in the midst of healing and you are hampering our efforts."

"Loghan," Kaleigh cautioned. "This is the woman's life mate. I asked him to come."

"Did you also ask if you could heal her?" Rhoane's voice

dropped to deadly quiet. "I do not recall that part of your message."

"She is dying, Rhoane. We had to do something before it was too late." She stammered, "We did not—I mean, we would not—we only used power to heal her. Neither of us shared our bodies with her."

Rhoane gripped the sword hilt tighter. If he didn't calm himself, his heart would give out. Seeing Taryn's broken body was enough to stop it beating, but then to be confronted by Kaleigh and the tattooed man in the middle of healing his betrothed, it was enough to push the gentlest man to violence. And Rhoane was no gentle man.

"She is sacred," Kaleigh whispered and knelt on one knee, her hands pressed upon her forehead. "Please forgive me. I only sought to ease her pain."

The rage washed over and away from him. He lifted Kaleigh to face him. "Your intentions may have been honorable, but he would do well to clothe himself before I rid him of his most useful tool."

Loghan stood to his full height, his shoulders pinched, his expression defiant. "I care not who you are. No one speaks to me like that."

"I care not for your tone. Cover yourself, now." Rhoane pointed the tip of his sword toward Loghan's deflating cock.

Loghan scrambled into his robe, his face losing a few shades of color.

"Still so angry? I thought when you left here, you had left your ire behind." Kaleigh adjusted her own robe, cinching it tight around her waist before she signaled Loghan to make room for Rhoane.

"Old habits die hard." He stepped around her to take Loghan's place, sheathing Claidholm Solais as he moved. How he would've loved to cut the man's appendage from his body, but right then, he focused his attention solely on Taryn. Every inch of him wanted to cover her, but he needed to see her injuries. Kaleigh was right to heal her as much as she could. Even he could see Taryn's life force was all but extinguished. Another bell would've been too late.

"She has many internal injuries. Whoever beat her was relentless." Loghan had moved to stand beside Kaleigh.

Rhoane grunted a reply. He wanted the man out of the tent, but had to admit he may have need of his healing skills before they were through.

Rhoane traced two whitish marks on her abdomen. "What is this?"

Kaleigh glanced to where he pointed and flinched. "My tears. I do not know how or why, but when they touched her skin, they left a stain."

Rhoane's hands roamed over the body he'd come to know better than his own. His fingertips skimmed the soft hairs covering her arms and legs. Only after he'd done a thorough exam did he allow himself to look at her face.

The bruises and cuts marred her beauty, making her almost unrecognizable. It took all his effort not to weep for her. Not to lash out at those responsible. To see Taryn broken and abused was almost too much to bear. He showed none of this to the others. His misery was for him alone. He kept his face serene, his feelings hidden. Rhoane leaned forward and joined his lips to Taryn's. They were cold with death and he breathed against them with his warmth.

"My love, stay with me."

"You must mate with her. It is the only way." Emotion choked Kaleigh's voice.

Mallaqai's warning teased his memory. "When is the new moon?"

Kaleigh gave him a curious look, as though he'd asked something ridiculous. "Not for two nights. Why?"

He tucked a blanket around Taryn's body, covering her with

his ShantiMari as he did. A small boy entered the tent, his filthy face streaked by recent tears. Rhoane was about to order him out when Kaleigh held a hand to the urchin.

"This is the lad who found her. He traveled a great distance to bring her here."

Rhoane's irritation melted. He went to one knee and beckoned the child closer. His fair eyes held caution, but Kaleigh urged him forward.

"We owe you our thanks," Rhoane said in Ullan.

"Can you heal her?" More tears tracked over his cheeks.

"I can, and I shall." Rhoane's words held conviction he didn't possess. He would do anything to bring Taryn back. Or die trying.

The little boy threw his arms around Rhoane, surprising him. The urchin's babbling was too fast for Rhoane to comprehend, but he understood quite clearly that this boy knew Taryn must live. The lad quieted, his face full of questions and worry. Rhoane stood and held the boy's small hand in his own.

To Kaleigh, Rhoane asked, "What exactly did you do to her?"

"We merged our power with hers to coax healing. But there was something elusive within. A dark stain that burned when we got too near. We were unable to fully integrate our healing powers before you showed up."

Rhoane knew the darkness they encountered. He and Fae had once sensed it, too. He'd have to find a way around it—or through the blot if he hoped to succeed. "How bad are her internal injuries?"

"She is bleeding. It is a good thing we did not attempt to heal her properly, or we might have killed her," Kaleigh admitted, a blush staining her cheeks, her eyes downcast.

"Your healing is not absolute. I know you believe yours is the only way, but there are other ways to heal that do not require sharing bodies. They are just as effective, if not more so."

"Agree to disagree."

Her smile tugged at his heart. It was the same argument they'd had for many seasons when he lived with the Ullans.

"What is your plan?" she asked.

Rhoane debated his options. The vier wasn't far from them, but the travel might kill Taryn. Her organs were already taxed and failing. He couldn't risk it. Staying with the Ullans was his best bet, but he loathed the idea of being dependent upon them. "Where is Amdi?"

"He is due back any time. If you are thinking he will create a fuss over your arrival, you are probably right. He misses you, as do we all."

"Misses me? I thought he would want to throttle me."

"Well, perhaps that, too."

Rhoane shifted the bundle strapped to his back and paced a few steps before turning to the table. Taryn's face was serene, showing no signs of pain or discomfort. But then, she was good at hiding her feelings lately. When she'd first arrived on Aelinae, he could read her thoughts by watching the play of emotions across her face. Now, he was lucky to know even a fraction of what went on in her mind. He stroked her cheek, being careful to avoid a nasty gash. Much of her face was damaged beyond what many would have tolerated. Cashiel might have been testing her limits, but this revolting display of power and control spoke to something else. Something Rhoane wasn't ready to accept.

Ynyd Eirathnacht sang to him a song of healing and Rhoane embraced the melody. If he allowed his thoughts to linger on Cashiel or Taryn's current condition, he'd not be able to heal her. In fact, his anger might be the thing that destroyed them all. He recalled the explosion Taryn made on Lliandra's ship and also that day long past when his mother erupted into flames. Rhoane held that power inside himself. He had to remember his training and remain dispassionate. Just like Kaleigh in the healer's tents.

Rhoane blew out his cheeks and chose the only option available. "Get a tent ready for her. Make it private, with a comfortable bed." He recalled the stiff cot he'd had to sleep on for more than three seasons and winced. "Make certain she has plenty of blankets and bring food." He pulled his attention from Taryn's injuries to meet Kaleigh's concerned grimace. "She is royalty. Do not forget that. Higher in station than me or Amdi. She is not to be touched," his gaze slid to the young man, "by anyone but myself."

Loghan's eyes narrowed, but he held his tongue.

Smart man.

"I will see to the preparations myself, Your Highness." Kaleigh's tart tone amused Rhoane.

He placed a hand on hers. "She is my life. I cannot lose her."

Tears shimmered in Kaleigh's eyes. "She is my *Darennsai* as well. You will not lose her. Not here. Not now."

"Not ever if I have anything to say about it."

Kaleigh left them and Rhoane returned to Taryn's side.

The little boy slipped his hand into Rhoane's.

"What is your name?"

"Michel, my lord." His eyes held an earnestness and longing that broke Rhoane's heart.

"Where are your people?"

"I have none."

Rhoane squeezed his hand and cleared the lump from his throat. "Call me Rhoane. This is Taryn. She will be quite pleased to meet you."

A toothy grin lit up Michel's face.

One of Kaleigh's ladies entered the tent and asked permission to take Michel for a bath and rest. The lad looked to Rhoane, who nodded he should go with the woman.

"I will find you later, once Taryn is healed."

When they were gone, Rhoane turned to regard the young man who hovered near the edge of the table. His rocking movement gave an indication of indecisiveness that intrigued Rhoane.

"Kaleigh called you Loghan." From the depths of his memories, the name stirred.

"You do not remember me." It was more a statement than a question.

The memory swirled to an image of a young boy, perhaps Michel's age, but clothed in rich fabrics. "Kaleigh is your mother? You were but a lad when I last saw you." More recollections surfaced and he shied from them. He had tried to erase all of his memories of Ulla.

"That I was," Loghan agreed. "I remember you fought bravely in the arena. I thought Father was too harsh in his treatment of you." His downcast eyes were dark like Amdi's. "I am sorry he abused you so."

"As am I, but he had his reasons. I was a rebellious adolescent who needed to be scolded. I left Ulla stronger of mind and body than when I had arrived." Thanks mostly to Kaleigh. Amdi, he only remembered as a tyrant. A bully who enjoyed seeing Rhoane battered and close to death. A man too similar to Cashiel.

The reminder sickened him almost as much as seeing what the vile coward had done to Taryn. Amdi, Rhoane had forgiven. Cashiel, he never would.

Loghan wavered as if to leave, then turned to Rhoane. "You are not my prince, and yet I feel obliged to kneel before you. Why is this?"

"Because you are half Eleri. It is that part of you that responds to my noble status. Does it hurt?" Rhoane meant the tattoos, but the question could've applied to the internal conflict Loghan was certainly experiencing. Rhoane knew all too well what it felt like to be Eleri and far from the vier. He dragged his gaze to the handsome man's face. To where tribal tattoos skirted his cheeks, up his neck to his bald head. Loghan had left his face clear of the markings, which only increased his attractiveness. The tattoos gave him a mysterious yet dangerous appeal.

"Pain is a liar. I pay no more mind to it than I do an annoying pest."

Rhoane nodded his understanding. Pain indeed was a liar. As was fear. Yet at the moment, one inflicted his beloved, and the other tortured Rhoane.

"Your Highness, if I may?" Loghan pointed to Taryn's inert form. "The body has energy stores that can help or hinder. In thought, in motion, in healing. When a person experiences passionate release, these stores are momentarily unguarded. It is then you can fully integrate your ShantiMari into her and true healing begins."

"Energy stores? Show me." Rhoane tapped his chest. "On me, not her."

Loghan shuffled around the table to stand in front of Rhoane. "Here," he pressed a thumb to Rhoane's forehead, "is where it is most difficult to open."

A humming sounded in Rhoane's ears and warmth spread over him. Loghan's power. His body fought off the intrusion, and yet he was lulled by the sensation.

"Do you feel yourself battling against me?"

"My mind is anxious to keep you from invading, but something else is welcoming your touch."

"When you share bodies, the mind and other energy locations relax. At first there is resistance, but after several bells, the body blossoms into a receptive vehicle and healing occurs."

"Several bells? You, ah, perform for several bells with no release of your own?"

Loghan's smile was disarming. "I told you, my lord, it is not about my pleasure. I am a healer. This is what I do."

"What about when it is for your pleasure?"

He stepped away from Rhoane and pulled his robe tighter.

"I do not mate for pleasure." Loghan indicated the tattoos. "When I decided to become a healer, I swore myself to the art and covered my body in these marks. They are rituals and incantations used by the ancients."

"Your commitment is admirable. I honor you." Rhoane placed a thumb to his lips, then touched his forehead and heart.

Loghan knelt and pressed his hands to his brow as his mother had. "Please, Your Highness, bless me so that I might fully embrace my Eleri ShantiMari."

Rhoane wasn't a priest, nor was he especially learned in the ways of blessing others, but he gave it a try. His hands covered Loghan's pate, the tattoos peeking between his fingers. Glamour shimmered beneath his skin, muted, but there. The black markings swirled and spiraled beneath his touch. They were, as Loghan had said, not solid lines, but words strung together in continuity. He lifted his fingers, keeping his pinkies in contact with the young man's head.

"Absolum paetenerineum gard'ath nuatha daern."

"Forever is not so long to those with faith." Loghan repeated the saying in Ullan.

Rhoane's fingers returned to Loghan's scalp and infused his ShantiMari into the tattoos. Loghan's Eleri Shanti awakened before Rhoane had uttered a word. He delved deeper, finding those energy receptors Loghan had mentioned. "Are you allowing this?"

"Yes. I thought it best if you felt for yourself what I tried to explain."

He closed his eyes and imagined each store as a lock his power could open. One by one, he traveled the length of Loghan's torso, from his forehead to his belly button, until all seven were unlocked, his power flowing through the lad and into the room.

He stepped back and a sense of wonder engulfed him. Loghan's tattoos floated above them, drifting without aid, the words forming stanzas and paragraphs of text. When he looked to Loghan for an explanation, his skin was pale and free of markings. His eyes, huge with excitement and horror.

The words danced before their eyes and Rhoane caught sight of one particularly relevant incantation. He pinched the phrase gently and lowered his hand to above Taryn's lips. He whispered the words aloud and placed his own lips upon hers, sealing the incantation between them. Warmth spread from his kiss to her cheeks and her eyelashes fluttered. He stroked her head, placing featherlight kisses along her jaw, up her cheeks, upon every cut and bruise. With each touch of his lips to her, warmth followed.

"The room is prepared," Kaleigh said from the tent entrance.

He rose to show her the miracle of the tattoos, but when Rhoane glanced at the young man, Loghan stood a pace away, his tattoos intact. The floating words had resettled into his skin.

"What is going on in here?" Kaleigh's gaze went first to Loghan, then to Rhoane. "You look as if you have seen Rykoto himself."

Rhoane cleared his throat, not wanting to explain something he didn't fully comprehend. "Lead the way."

He scooped Taryn into his arms. Her limp form, once strong and full of life, sagged against him. A hiccup of loss tore at his sternum and tears stung the backs of his eyes. Loghan reached to help, but Rhoane's quick glare told him he was capable. They'd shared something extraordinary, yes, but Rhoane couldn't trust him yet with his betrothed.

CHAPTER TEN

T he pain was almost too much to bear. Delicious torture she
didn't want to end. As long as she didn't wake up. Taryn
moaned Rhoane's name, delighting in what her dream lover was
doing to her body. His ShantiMari slid over her, into her, delving
into the dark recesses she hid even from herself. And she let him.
Let him in like she'd never done when awake. His lovemaking
just might kill her.

It would be a beautiful death, to be sure.

In that death, a rebirth.

Yet, this wasn't the time. Rhoane certainly wasn't physically
killing her. Yet there was pain mixed with the beauty of their
bodies, entwined together until she wasn't certain where she
began and Rhoane ended.

His warm breath nuzzled the spot behind her ear that made
parts of her clench, gave her a shudder of excitement, and a
promise of more to come. Another moan escaped her lips. Damn,
this dream Rhoane knew exactly where to touch her, how to coax
her to open up. The first tremors of her orgasm started low, where
Rhoane connected with her in an entirely different way. He

pushed into her again and again, a steady rocking that she met with her hips.

Even she was better at lovemaking in her dream. She could do all those things she'd wanted to try, but was too shy or thought might turn him off. Her hand snaked up and pinched her left nipple, the sensation spiraling out. She did it again, this time harder, and arched her back. Oh, gods, but this was the worst kind of dream. She panted into her orgasm, not wanting it to come, but needing it too badly to deny herself.

"Release with me, my love," Rhoane's voice whispered near her ear and she turned toward the sound. Toward her sun, her moon, her stars. Her life.

"I'm so close, it hurts." The thrusting slowed, apprehensive almost. "No, don't stop. Harder. Faster."

Her desperate pleas were lost in frustrated sobs. She wanted to let go, but something held her back. Elusive, dark, dangerous. This was the part of her nightmares she hated most. Where Zakael would appear, Rhoane's heart in his hand, blood oozing from the organ to drip upon the ground. Her half-brother would taunt her while simultaneously trying to seduce her.

No, no, no. She groaned. *Not this time. Not Zakael.* She forced her mind to focus on Rhoane. Her Rhoane. Her love. She embraced his ShantiMari, pulling it deeper into her soul. He was as much a part of her as she him. They were a team. Unstoppable. No more lies. No more hiding who she really was.

She gripped his nipple between her thumb and forefinger and pinched hard enough to elicit a cry. Rhoane's power flooded through her, more intense than she'd ever felt before. It consumed her. Devoured her inhibitions and doubts, erased her self-loathing, overcame her fear. Love, pure and sweet, lit her from inside. The Noir she'd been too afraid of acknowledging blossomed into the most stunning rose she'd ever seen. Petals made of obsidian so thin a breath might crack them. Dark as night, tiny filaments glistened from within, veins that led to a stalk devoid of thorns.

A rose with no thorns.

The thought intrigued Taryn, but her body demanded her attention. And she complied.

Rhoane's hot lips covered her nipple. His teeth clamped upon the nub. The sensation of heat and pain rocked through her.

"More," she rasped.

He nipped again and she bucked her hips, drawing him deeper. His hands stroked her body, his cock filled her womb, and his mouth teased her relentlessly, but something was missing. Her release was elusive, still. She held onto the brink, trying to coax her orgasm further, but the harder she chased, the further it retreated.

Stupid dream. It was her dream, so why couldn't she control it?

"Use your power, Taryn. Fuse your ShantiMari with mine. All of it. Even your Telraicht-Noir power."

Wait, what? Rhoane knew about the Noir growing inside her? He knew and accepted it. His ShantiMari swirled through her veins, interlocking with the Noir, not recoiling at its touch.

Slowly, she released her hold on her power. Light, Dark, Eleri: all of her ShantiMari strains were bound tightly together. Little by little, she unwound them until they floated free of each other, individual, distinct, lovely strands that she'd come to almost dread.

The obsidian rose opened, the petals stretching toward the other sources of her power. Light touched the rose first, illuminating a petal to a bright opal. Next, Dark infused the rose, turning another petal a deeper shade of midnight. Eleri infused the rose with moss green, the color of Rhoane's eyes.

The rose curled in on itself and panic pulled at her thoughts. What had she done? All of her powers would be tainted by the

Telraicht-Noir. Except when the rose opened, it was devoid of color—as clear as a polished diamond.

"I am everything and nothing," Taryn murmured. Rhoane's ShantiMari entwined with hers, turning the same sparkling clear as her power.

"You are everything to all."

"Without you, I do not exist." The words were meant for Rhoane, but could've applied to her power as well.

"Nor do I," Rhoane whispered.

"This isn't a dream, is it?"

"No, my love. Come back to me."

She opened her eyes and gazed into the face of the man she loved. "You're healing me."

"Yes."

She arched into him, longing for the touch of his skin on hers. The thrusting slowed to an agonizing pace, long and deep. Again and again until she pressed her pelvis against him, begging with her body for more.

Warm air tickled her backside and she twisted to see they hovered a meter above the bed. "What the hell?"

Rhoane's eyes became wild for a split second, then a cheeky grin tilted his lips. "It is happening, Taryn."

"Is this a good thing?"

"The best." He threw his head back and plunged fully into her. A sheen of sweat covered his brow as he worked his magic on her body.

She responded to his lovemaking with her own thrashing and cries of excitement. Tension built in her once again, building upon her desire until her thoughts were an explosion of confetti. Love and lust, glitter and rainbows, stars and suns and moons, blazed through her mind as she stared in wonder at Rhoane. The play of emotion across his face told her he felt the same as she. Bewildered, humbled, cherished.

Instead of dissipating, the orgasm continued, building to a

crescendo that rocked her hard, making her shudder violently. Rhoane called out her name and she stretched back, her head dipping close to the floor. White light lit forth from all the pores of her body. Rays of every color brightened the room, piercing Rhoane until he, too, was alight.

Their ShantiMari joined as one, uniting them until Taryn knew Rhoane's thoughts and he, hers. Images whirred past of people he knew, people who had yet to be. Memories flared and faded. Words drifted through the mist. It happened in the span of a heartbeat, but Taryn had lived a thousand lifetimes with him. For that one moment, she'd live a thousand more.

Even after their bodies stopped trembling, they stayed aloft. Taryn ran her hands over his smooth skin, delighting in the sighs and shivers her touch evoked. He was hers, this amazing man who would walk between worlds with her and slay a god to save Aelinae.

Two truths and one lie. What was true, and what was false?

Tears streamed from her eyes, trailing along her cheeks to drip to the floor.

"Are you sad?" His voice was low, husky, sexy as hell.

"No."

"Then why the tears?"

"Because I almost lost you again."

He wrapped her in his strong arms and hugged her to him so they were sitting together in mid-air. She rested her head on his shoulder and let the tears flow, not bothering to wipe them away. She was tired of hiding her emotions. Exhausted from fearing her own shadows. To cry was natural, not a sign of weakness like she'd led herself to believe.

"Nadra told me once to never let fear determine your fate. I thought I heard her say it again just before Cashiel took the ship." Taryn leaned back and placed her palm against Rhoane's. Their bonds sparked to life, white-gold illuminations in their skin. The designs shifted and changed as they always would. A new image appeared, of a crescent moon and two stars. "I can't promise to never be afraid again, but I promise I'll try not to blow up any more ships."

Rhoane's laughter was a balm to her senses. Not too long ago, she thought she'd never hear that sound ever again.

A new onslaught of tears filled her eyes. "My sisters—? Everyone on the ship—did I kill them?"

"Your family is safe." Rhoane thumbed the tears from her skin. "We had a plan, but—" His voice choked on the words. "I saw you with Cashiel before the explosion."

A tremor of guilt pressed against her heart. "I thought I was going to die. I wasn't about to let him hurt my loved ones. I thought it was the only way." Rhoane saw her kiss Cashiel. She could only hope he knew it was done out of desperation.

"I do not blame you. I am not angry, not with you." Even so, irritation infused his words. "I searched three days for you. If only I had known you were inland."

His face pinched with annoyance and she saw the glint of rage he suppressed. She'd felt it when they shared their bodies and understood it was for Cashiel, but the amount of anger he held frightened her.

"Shhhh, we're together. That's all that matters. You found me and healed me." A cheeky grin lifted the corners of her lips. "I fully expect you to teach me that healing method, by the way."

"That I will, but there is something you must see first." They lowered to the floor and she unfolded her legs from around his waist to stand. "Taryn, look at yourself." He indicated a mirror in the corner of the, well, not room exactly, but a tent, perhaps?

"Where are we?" She glanced at the rest of the space, not recognizing anything.

"We are in Ulla. You were found on the shores of the Jansen Strait."

Taryn rubbed her chin. "I don't remember anything after the

ship. Except, a boy, perhaps. With shaggy blond hair and clear blue eyes."

"He is the one who found you and brought you here. We are in the laird's encampment."

A tightening of his lips intrigued her. She knew he'd spent time in Ulla, but not the particulars. His continued silence told her she wouldn't soon be getting details about his stay. Knowing better than to poke that particular bur, she strolled to the mirror and surveyed herself.

"I look the same." She twirled a lock of hair between her fingertips. "Shorter hair, which I kind of like, but otherwise, just me."

"When I found you here, I hardly recognized you." His gaze sought hers in the mirror while his thumb made lazy circles around her nipple. "There isn't a mark upon your skin and your scar is little more than a scratch."

Flashes of Cashiel's beatings ravaged her thoughts. She relived those moments, her mind spiraling, her hands raising to cover her face. What breath she took came in short gasps. Beneath her rib cage, her heart beat quicker, pounding against the bones. With each new memory, she thought the organ might burst.

Whimpers escaped her clenched lips and she trembled uncontrollably.

"I am here." Rhoane held her against him, an anchor, solid. "You are safe."

When she looked at herself in the mirror, she saw beyond her unmarked skin to the battered and broken thing Rhoane first encountered. His anguish tore through her. He'd thought he'd lost her. For three days, he searched the coastlines of Aelinae, even confronting his own fears and swimming to the depths of the sea. Yet he hadn't found her. Guilt, horror, anxiety—all of his emotions expanded into her until she was close to bursting or collapsing in on herself.

Rhoane's memories mixed with hers. She knew them as well

as she knew her own heart. He stroked her silvery hair, his words of love calming her rapid pulse. The overinflated sensation dissipated like a balloon with a slow leak. The pounding in her head weakened and sound returned.

"Did Cashiel survive?" she whispered, half afraid by saying his name her tormentor would find her.

"We do not know, but if so, he will pay for what he has done. Later, after you are fully healed."

He was right. She needed to be completely restored before she faced him. When that day came, she would not think twice about killing him.

Rhoane slid his hand under her breast and traced the vorlock scar. A delightful tremor ran the length of her. There wasn't the slightest sensation of poison or Telraicht-Noir ShantiMari, nor was there any pain. Just a sweet feeling of being loved.

"What's this?" She indicated two white spots beneath her scar.

"Those were left by Kaleigh's tears. We do not know why or how they stained your skin." The name Kaleigh stirred in Rhoane's memories that were now hers, but it was too much to absorb. She'd find out later who the woman was, and why she was crying on Taryn. For as long as she could, she wanted to be with Rhoane and no one else.

"You're right, my scar's not ragged and angry any more. In fact, it looks like a crescent moon and Kaleigh's tears two stars." She held up her wrist for him to see the latest shadow tattoo. "Look here."

He examined his markings and there, just below the image of the great tree of the Weirren, was the same design.

"Is this what you wanted me to see?" She asked, marveling at the tattoo on her wrist and the stain on her skin.

Rhoane slowly shook his head. "No, but this is rather remarkable. I do not know what it means."

She pressed her ass into his growing erection. "Know what

else is remarkable? You. You healed me completely. What was broken is whole again."

"For both of us." His heartfelt words ignited her passion.

She turned to face him. Her knees weakened at the desire burning in his eyes. How she'd missed those moss-green orbs that always seemed to be fixed on her. His love cut through everything else she could see in their depths. Her disappearance had nearly destroyed him. She held his face between her hands and stroked his cheeks with her thumbs. The scratch of his stubble made her toes curl in all the right ways.

"First, I want to make love to you again, then I need food, and after all of that, maybe you can tell me what that light show was."

"We should get you some nourishment first."

"Not a chance. I've got you here naked—you'll leave when I say you can."

"When did you get so bossy?" Despite his words, his eyes clouded and his voice became husky. A teasing smile stretched his lips.

"When are you going to answer my questions?"

He silenced her with a kiss, but she knew his evil tricks. By the time the sun rose in the morning, she would know how she'd turned an obsidian rose clear, and how he'd managed to heal her so thoroughly. Getting answers from him would be a challenge— one she looked forward to. Whatever sex magic he'd used, she would find a way to make it work on him. Perhaps it could help her delve deeper into Rhoane's memories. She had a score to settle with Cashiel. Something told her he'd survived the explosion and it was that same instinct that made her believe Rhoane's memories were vital to her success.

From the recesses of her mind, she heard the menacing voice that had been taunting her most of the season. His slurred words were hostile in nature, not the usual condescending seduction she'd become accustomed to. Something had changed.

As Taryn lay back and watched the interplay of passion cross Rhoane's features, she knew it was his healing that had broken the hold the entity had on her. She sensed desperation from the thing. His connection to her was shaken. This was the being that controlled Cashiel.

And there, beneath the desperation, she sensed its rage—not toward Cashiel for failing, but at her for surviving.

Zakael stroked the silken strands of Kane's hair and whispered words of encouragement to his lover. Bandages covered his face, but it could've been much worse. The burns would leave him disfigured and Kane would resent having to hide, but it had to be done. If only he'd succeeded in capturing Taryn, none of this unfortunate business would have occurred.

Now, Zakael must make arrangements for Kane to stay at Gaarendahl permanently. Zakael's lips pulled against his teeth in a scorn-filled smile. With Marissa gone, that wouldn't be an issue. In fact, he could give Kane run of the castle. Let him play lord while Zakael ruled from Caer Idris. Kane would love that. Zakael would tell the man once he was done crying against Zakael's trousers.

"Really, darling. This is a temporary setback. How were we to know she'd blow up the ship?" The words were said with as much care as Zakael could afford to give. Inside, he seethed at Kane's ineptitude. The plan was simple—attack Lliandra's ship, kill the empress, and kidnap the Eirielle. He'd given Kane more than enough poison to do the trick, yet the man had improvised.

Little did Kane know Zakael was on the second vessel, the

one carrying the chanting mages. The idea had been his and, he had to admit, brilliant. Once he'd gained access to his father's archives, he'd found a treasure trove of ancient spells and incantations. He'd yet had time to read them all, but finding the chant that blocked another's power was a stroke of luck. Of course, Zakael knew how to block ShantiMari when it was one-on-one, but blocking an entire ship full of people ranging in power from the empress to a cabin boy? That was trickier.

Which was why he'd sent Kane instead of himself. If the plan failed, Kane was disposable.

"Are you angry at me?"

Ferran's bells, fuck yes I'm angry with you. "No, my darling. Not at all. We knew from the beginning this was a difficult proposition. Kane—"

"Cashiel. I hate that name. Call me Cashiel now."

"Right, Cashiel, you need your rest. The healers will be here soon."

Cashiel nodded like the good little puppy he was. "Do you think I'll be scarred?"

"Perhaps, but that will only make you more handsome. Rugged. Mysterious." Zakael slipped off the couch and placed a pillow where his lap had been.

Cashiel moaned when his damaged skin touched the fabric. Zakael had never been one for healing. He dipped his head close to his lover's and flicked his tongue over the seared lips. Cashiel's intake of breath went straight to Zakael's cock.

"I could fuck you right now, you gorgeous boy."

Cashiel's hand whipped out too fast for Zakael to stop. He rubbed the front of Zakael's trousers, eliciting a loud moan from him.

"For you, the pain would be worth it."

"You've no idea how happy that makes me. But I've a kingdom to run and can't spare the energy." He withdrew from Cashiel's grip and adjusted the front of his pants.

One of his servants stood to the side and Zakael motioned him to take care of the patient. Without saying a word, the servant went down on his knees and began untying Cashiel's breeches.

"My lord?" Cashiel's hoarse whisper sounded alarmed.

"Consider this a gift. I've been told the Ullans use rutting to heal the most grievous of wounds. Close your eyes and dream of me, my darling."

From the moans and sucking sounds coming from the servant, Zakael had no doubt Cashiel would be satisfied.

The new king hurried from the room before he changed his mind and took them both to his bed. Not that it would do any good. Ever since that night at Caer Idris when Taryn had grabbed his balls and brought him the most delirious pleasure he'd ever experienced, others were ruined for him. He could rut and play —as long as he kept Taryn far from his thoughts.

At first, he'd thought she'd meant to curse him, but he came to realize she'd only feigned it as a curse. What the clever woman had really done was attempt to promise Zakael to her, and only her. Taryn's flawed logic had served to endear her even more to Zakael.

Yes, she denied him at every step, which made her more desirable. If only she understood how much the chase thrilled him. No one had ever said no to Zakael. Surely Taryn knew this and used it to entice him further. Gods, but he loved a good hunt.

After he'd captured her in the forest glen, when she'd fought him and pretended to force him to teach her to transform, it was then he'd planned her kidnapping. Twice she could've killed him and yet she let him live. If there wasn't any other proof besides that, he would've known she wished him to be her life mate. But there had been other clues, as well. The night Valterys was killed, for one.

When Zakael plunged his sword into his father's back and

whispered in his ear, Taryn had looked on, approving. Then she'd sliced their father's head clean off. They were bound in that moment. With absolute clarity, he saw his path. It was Zakael's duty to find a way to break her bond with Rhoane. Only then could they be together. And they would be, for all eternity.

A stirring in his groin spurred him on and he all but sprinted to the gardens, where he transformed into a levon. Before his wings felt the first gust of wind, he was headed southeast, toward where Taryn had blown up the ship. He had to find her before anyone else. He was dead if he didn't.

Cashiel swore he never mentioned Zakael by name, and there was no way any of them could connect him with the event. He shouldn't be concerned, but unease settled in Zakael's thoughts.

An image of Rykoto's flames tearing his flesh as the god feasted upon his still beating heart made him falter in his flight. He spiraled west, then corrected his course with a hard bank and flapping of his wings. Unfortunately, the vision in his mind couldn't be so easily fixed. He'd witnessed too many of Rykoto's feedings not to be worried. If Rykoto didn't get what he craved, they all would perish. Rykoto had to be eliminated.

His feathers ruffled, not against the sudden gust of wind, but with suppressed anxiety. Zakael had made a bargain with the only soul possible of granting him eternal life with Taryn by his side. The cost had been Taryn's dragon. Not such a heavy expense since she wouldn't have need of her dragon ever again. She would have Zakael.

He just had to find her.

Zakael flew low, hovering near oblivious ships traveling from Menurra to Talaith or vice versa. If the princess had been found, word would have spread to the empress, but none of those onboard mentioned Taryn. Or the attack, which concerned him. Surely the fleet was in Menurra by now. Four days had passed since the explosion. Plenty of time for Lliandra to make port.

He banked north and scanned the shoreline for yet another

pass. Finally, he flew over the Ullan lands, dipping into the arid valleys and beating his wings hard to catch an updraft over the mountains. He steered clear of the encampments, all too aware of the Ullans' skill with skirths—slim, arrow-like weapons they threw with deadly accuracy. Even the worst hurl was too close to risk. Besides, the Ullans hated Aelans and would never allow Taryn on their lands.

His beak stretched in an awkward smile. His father might've discounted the value of alliance, but Zakael did not. He'd spent the better part of the past decade cultivating a relationship with Amdi Agnar. With the laird's permission, Zakael had tested many of their healers' capabilities. If only the Ullans would use their healing skills in more profitable ways.

His tiny bird brain ached from his memories, especially the ones involving several healers doing things definitely not meant to cure. The Ullans claimed to only mate to facilitate healing, but Zakael discovered there were many who copulated freely, whether there was an injury or not. One day he would have need of their skills, thus he tested them constantly in ways they couldn't suspect was his doing. Like the wildings he sent from the north.

Most of the creatures Zakael released into Ulla made their way into Amdi's arena. What a thrill it was to watch combatants try to destroy the monsters Zakael practically hand delivered to the Ullan laird. If anything, Amdi should be grateful for Zakael.

His wings ached from the extended flight and he needed rest. He vacillated whether to surprise Amdi with a visit, but it wasn't time. His manipulation of the laird was at a pivotal stage. If Zakael arrived too soon, Amdi might reject the subtle machinations Zakael had implanted into the laird's memories.

If not Ulla, then where? The Stones of Kaldaar were several leagues to the west, with Talaith a short distance beyond. The Stones would provide shelter, but neither food nor warmth. Talaith provided all three, as well as information.

He sped onward, renewed vigor in his tiny bird heart.

The city lights appeared before him, twinkling against the early evening dark. He'd flown all day without stopping, quite an achievement even for him. The increased power that came with his crown showed itself in many useful ways.

The Crystal Palace was well-lit, with guards and sentries posted atop the high towers and at the gates, despite the empress being away. It was too risky to attempt a landing there, so he dove lower until his claws scratched the tree tops. One house in particular came into view and he made a hard right, veering around the front of the dwelling. He chose a secluded spot to the side and landed softly, the transition effortless.

Within two steps, his garments reflected a man of status, but gave no hint to his royal personage. The man seated at the back door greeted him with a nod and knocked upon the ancient wood. A small window slid to the side and deep-brown eyes peered out, regarding him for several moments before disappearing. The window closed and two locks sounded in the still night. When the door finally opened, Nena appeared before him, her luscious body wrapped in scraps of lace. He skimmed her barely covered breasts, her long legs, and ample ass before returning her fetching smile.

"Lord Zakael! It has been too long since your last visit. Please tell me you are here for some fun, yes?"

Zakael stepped into the parlor and folded the madam in his embrace. His erection strained against her midsection.

Her pelvis ground against him and she giggled. "You are prepared, my darling. I am pleased."

"How can I not be with you looking as ravishing as ever?" He swiped his tongue over her earlobe, taking it between his teeth and nipping lightly. She squealed and slapped his arm playfully. "Are you available tonight? I think I would like you and perhaps a young boy. Another woman, too, if that's your desire."

Nena pulled away from him, eyes wide, innocent even. "Nena does not bed clients any longer, my lord." She clapped a hand over her mouth, eyes wide. "Your Majesty, forgive poor Nena!" She curtseyed low enough to give him a view of her glorious bosoms. "I heard of your recent elevation in status. King of the West. It is an impressive title, no?"

She rose, the lacy frill of her corset billowing. Nena was one of the few women he trusted to bring him pleasure. That she no longer entertained clients was unthinkable. Unspent cravings coiled in his gut, manifesting in irritation.

"I'll forgive the misstep this one time."

Nena placed a hand over her heart and began to thank him, but he put a finger to her lips.

"If you pleasure me tonight."

She worried her lower lip against her top teeth, her brows pinched. Whatever had made her give up whoring had to be of great importance.

"I am sorry, Your Majesty, but I cannot." She spoke around his finger and finished her refusal by sucking the pad of his fore-finger and then biting hard.

The pain shot straight to his cock.

"But, I have two lovely men and a girl—all young as you prefer—who I think will more than make up for my absence."

He stroked her cheek, then wrapped a strand of her coppery curls around the finger she'd abused. "Why must you deny me, my dove? I've only just discovered you and now you toss me aside like scraps meant for the pigs."

"Not pigs, my lord. Not you, not ever. The reasons I cannot bed you are my own and won't be shared with anyone. But trust that if I could, I would bed you gladly."

"Is there a whore named Armando here tonight? I've heard many good things about his skill and if I can't have you, perhaps he'll bring me the pleasure I seek."

"Alas, I am sorry. Armando is on leave at the moment. He and his partner are traveling with the empress to Menurra, where they're required to assist with the bride's trousseau."

The annoyance in his gut pricked against his goodwill. He cared little if Armando was available for sex. What he'd really wanted was to see the man who'd given Marissa a child. Nena provided him with more than he'd hoped to learn. She claimed to keep all her clients' secrets, but a few carefully worded phrases loosened her tongue beautifully. Something he'd have to remember in his dealings with the madam.

Unless she'd wanted him to know about Armando. In which case, he'd need to be cautious in what he gave away with his questioning.

"Your whore is also a seamstress? What an astonishing medley of skills he possesses." Zakael slipped into the smooth role of impressed admirer.

Nena giggled and sucked on the palm resting on her cheek. "He is a whore, Armando, but his partner is a tailor at the palace. He often makes garments for the Eirielle and she requested he and Armando join her for the trip. Of course, with as much as Armando works, he worried about taking time away from his clients, but it is good for him to get away and relax, no?"

"Taking time for oneself is important. I also heard he's the proud father of a newborn. Congratulations are in order, I suppose."

Nena's eyes hardened and Zakael knew he'd hit on a taboo subject. "Your spies are well informed, Your Majesty. Armando was not as careful in his work as he should have been and a client begot a child with him. He knew nothing of it until she died in childbirth, the poor lamb, and the babe was brought to Armando for raising. He is thrilled to be a papa, Zakael. That child has brought him nothing but joy and is innocent."

The use of his name was intentional, he was certain. Nena wasn't warning him to stay away from the child, she was asking as a friend. He placed his lips upon hers and swiped his tongue over their tightness until she sighed and opened herself to him. The kiss was long, deep, and overly sensual. By the time he lifted his head from hers, heat flared between them, causing an ache in his groin that wouldn't be alleviated any time soon.

"All children are born innocent, Nena. It's what happens to them later that turns their hearts. Male children have no place in some families while other Houses revere males over females. Mine included. But I've heard this child has no ShantiMari, which makes him worthless to some."

Nena's body sagged and relief spread across her features. Right then, she didn't look like a whore, but rather a loving grandmother. Jealousy pierced his heart. The devotion softening her face made him miss his own mother, who had died when he was young. She'd looked at him with the same worry and love.

"Worthless to some, greatly loved by others. Me, included. Poor Nena could never have children of her own and young Percival has filled an empty place in my heart."

Zakael forced a smile meant to disarm while shoving his feelings aside. His focus returned to seducing the madam. "Sentimental, Nena? I wouldn't have believed it." Her purr and batting of eyelashes told him his charm had worked brilliantly. She practically melted at his touch.

"Sentimental? No. But Nena loves those who are deserving."

"I would one day like to be among them," Zakael whispered close to her ear. His breathing came in rasps, same as hers.

His hand snaked from her curls to her breasts, cupping one while his thumb scraped over her nipple. Her moan for him to stop was ignored and his hand traveled further to the hem of her flimsy skirt. The softness of her skin tantalized him and he dared to be so bold as to plunge his fingers between her legs, where he was rewarded with hot wetness. Her cry of alarm excited him further. If he couldn't have her, at least he would leave her wanting him.

"I believe you promised me an evening of sordid delights, did you not? Lead the way, madam."

"Such a shame I can't join you. A damn shame indeed," she said in a haze. "Let me get my finest boys and girls."

Zakael would leave the child alone for the time being, but if he ever needed a reason, he wouldn't hesitate to kill the bastard. Or use him as leverage against Taryn. Whatever it took to own her.

CHAPTER TWELVE

Lights flickered in myriad hues from one end of the tent to the other. Rhoane blinked hard, trying to stop the constant radiance that caused his head to ache. Beside him, Taryn stretched, her naked body snuggled against his. It had taken him nearly two bells before she responded to his healing and truth be told, he could understand why Loghan said there was no passion involved with healing. Rhoane's focus had been on Taryn—her injuries, her recovery—his lovemaking morphed from something sensual to medicinal in a matter of half a bell.

Although, further truth be told, he'd loved every moment. Loved having the time to explore and memorize every freckle, all the little creases and curves, each divot of her gorgeous body.

"I believe you promised me food."

"That was quite some time ago. You have a voracious appetite for other pleasures, my love."

A sly smile crept up her lips. "And I could use a dessert if you've got anything left to give."

"You are terrible, Taryn Rose ap Galendrin. You demand I find you food, then you distract me with your lovemaking. Now you are making me choose between nourishment, which you greatly need, and ravishing you once again. I am afraid I must decline and force you to get dressed. The laird is expecting us, and unless he has changed his ways, Amdi Agnar does not like to be kept waiting."

"You've never told me about your time here. Will you? Not now, of course, because apparently food is more important than sex, but someday?"

His reasons for not sharing his past seemed silly now. He'd been afraid she would reject him if she knew the truth. A heaviness settled over his heart. It was time to put his past to rest and let Taryn fully be a part of his life. The good and bad. There were some things she needed to know. He kissed the tip of her nose. "I will tell you anything you wish to know. But as you said, not now."

Even making that small promise filled him with anxiety. Much of what he'd done was for her, but would she see it that way? Would she forgive him?

"I want to know everything about you. Everything." The solemnity of her raised brow gave him confidence she might not despise him once the truth was spoken.

They dressed in the garments provided to them, with Taryn scrunching her nose at the veil she was bade to wear. "How pissed do you think he'll be if I refuse to cover my hair and face?"

"Do you recall Lliandra's reaction to your supposed affair with Aomori?"

Taryn gnawed a cuticle, her face pinched in thought. After a short silence, she said, "Then fuck him. I won't allow anyone to dictate how I dress." She tossed the elaborately beaded sheath of gossamer onto the floor. "From now on, I decide what I wear."

She rummaged through the blankets, then tossed more Ullan clothing to the floor. She ended her search with a huff, hands on hips.

"What vexes you?"

"I make a statement of independence, then can't follow

through because it appears I don't actually have any of my clothes here." Taryn blew out a breath from the side of her mouth. "Which sucks because now I have to wear what Amdi prefers."

Rhoane stood and embraced his love. "You have the power to determine your appearance." He curled a strand of her short hair around his finger, "Even this. You are in control of you, no one else."

To prove his point, he stepped back and with a swish of his power, Rhoane's hair shortened to spikes not more than a finger's width high. Aelan clothing covered his body. The tight velvet breeches pinched against his manhood. With a snap of his fingers, the clothes became Eleri garments of varying shades of green. His tunic flowed over his broad chest. The soft trousers tucked into sturdy leather boots. His hair once again hung to the middle of his back with several braids keeping the locks off his face.

Taryn grinned at his little display. "Impressive." She toyed with the strand of hair he'd been holding. Then, with a broad smile, she mimicked his snap and the Ullan clothing she wore transformed from a long robe into a fitted jacket and breeches. Her silver tresses hung in a loose braid almost reaching her buttocks.

Amdi would have conniption fits when he saw her. Rhoane, on the other hand, approved of the way the trousers hugged her curves. An all-too familiar stirring in his loins surprised him. With all the lovemaking they'd done over the past few bells, he didn't think he had anything left. How wrong he was.

"You are stunning." He meant not only her looks, but also her command of ShantiMari.

Taryn linked her fingers with his. He'd never been more proud of the woman he loved. Let Amdi be upset. Taryn shouldn't grovel to any ruler. Together, they exited the tent. As soon as he stepped outside, an onslaught of lights blinded him.

He covered his eyes and cringed against the whizzing and snapping currents of color.

"What is it?" Taryn's voice sounded low and urgent.

"The lights are blinding."

A guard watched them with suspicion.

Taryn gently pushed Rhoane back into the tent. "Tell me what you see."

He uncovered his eyes and blinked to focus. "Every color, every hue imaginable. Some are stagnant, others are flying from one place to another."

Her laugh came from deep in her belly. Full, rich, comforting. "Remember my first day in the cavern?"

"I could never forget. The moment I saw you is etched on my heart for all time."

Her cheeks pinked with a blush, reminding him of a time when she was still innocent.

She kissed him, her power folding around them like wings. "I'll never forget it, either. You stole my heart long before the cavern, but then seeing you there, it was like I knew I was where I belonged. If only Brandt hadn't died."

Rhoane held her chin between his fingers and tilted her face to look at him. "There is nothing to be gained by wishing for things to be different."

"You're right, of course. I still miss him."

As Rhoane did his mother, but he'd not diminish her memories of Brandt with his own woes. "You were telling me about the lights."

"Oh, right. Well, when Nadra arrived in the cavern, I was almost blinded by her and you said you couldn't see anything. I think you're experiencing what I've been able to see ever since I got here."

"But how? Why now?"

"Those threads are power. It's quite helpful at times, but mostly annoying." She prodded his gut. "It must be from all that sex magic. Maybe your sexual healing transferred some of my power to you. Or maybe you're growing into your own power. I don't know."

They'd shared bodies before, but she was right—something was different since his healing. "Loghan says there are energy stores located in our bodies. To properly heal you, I had to open them." He tapped from her forehead down to her belly button.

"Sounds like *chakras*." A wistful look crossed her features. "Is Loghan Ullan?"

A shiver of jealousy slithered down Rhoane's spine. The man was a healer, but something about him didn't sit right with Rhoane. "He is an Ullan healer, yes. You will meet him at dinner, along with Kaleigh."

The tiniest of pinches pulled her lips tight. As Rhoane was not comfortable with Loghan, Taryn was jealous of Kaleigh. He would have to be gentle in his introduction of the two.

"We're already late. We should get going so the laird doesn't lose his shit. But first," she covered his eyes with her hands and her ShantiMari flowed into him. "Try your best to see beyond the lights. Squinting helps at first, but it'll take time."

When she took her hands away, he squinted and she was right, it did help. He was able to see through the lights, to separate them into individual threads, almost. They left the tent and strolled hand in hand to the dining area. Long tables, built low to the ground, stretched beneath a canopy and it appeared every Ullan ever born was seated at the tables. When they approached, the young lad Michel bolted to Taryn and threw his arms around her hips. He didn't reach much higher than her midsection.

"Whoa! What did I do to deserve such a greeting?"

The boy withdrew and smiled at her, his yellowed teeth too large for his mouth. He spoke rapidly in Ullan.

"I don't know what you're saying. Slow down."

"This is the boy who found you, Taryn. He brought you here." Rhoane patted the lad on his freshly washed head. His blond hair shone in the sunlight. Rhoane almost didn't recognize the urchin.

"Thank you." A softness entered her voice, the same softness she had when speaking to Eliahnna or Tessa.

She knelt until she was face-to-face with him. "I owe you my gratitude."

Rhoane translated for her and the boy shook his head, rambling again almost too quickly for him to keep up. "He says you owe him nothing. When he found you, he thought a star had fallen from the sky and he was just happy he could return her there."

A tear escaped and tracked down her cheek. The boy reached out and brushed it away with his thumb.

"What's your name?" She looked to Rhoane to ask in Ullan.

"His name is Michel," Rhoane answered.

Taryn pressed her forehead against the boy's. "Michel, you are my sweet angel."

His stubby little hands stroked the sides of her face and she held his head between her fingertips. For a long moment neither one spoke, but Rhoane sensed a current of energy passing between them. Before she rose, Taryn kissed him on the cheek and he returned the favor. She ruffled his sandy curls and stood, his hand firmly in hers.

"This boy is all alone, Rhoane. He has no family, no tribe to call home."

"And you think to take him to Talaith? Another misfit for your merry band?"

Taryn's eyes grew misty. "It's not a bad idea, but no. He needs to stay with his people. Gian would've been an outcast. Michel isn't."

A servant approached and bade them join the laird at his table. Michel pulled away, but Taryn held him tight. Amdi wouldn't be pleased with an urchin at his table, but Rhoane had learned long ago to pick his battles with his betrothed.

Taryn and Michel weren't led to Amdi's table, but to one on the right. Discontent pecked at Rhoane's good mood. He took a step to follow, but Taryn signaled to him that she would be fine. Indecision weighed against his thoughts until Kaleigh rose to greet Taryn, kissing both her cheeks. The three of them sat, with Michel in the middle of the women. Kaleigh should've been at Amdi's side. Her absence there perplexed Rhoane. He gave the Eleri a questioning glance, but a slight shake of her head and downcast eyes were her answer.

Amdi still believed he could manipulate anyone in his camp. Refusing to hide his ire, Rhoane joined the laird, his jaw hardened and a challenge in his eyes. Amdi ignored him, focusing instead on a young woman seated to his left. The beauty fidgeted and kept her gaze lowered, her lower lip trembling the entire time the laird spoke to her. Rhoane could guess what he was saying. The urge to pull the lecherous ruler off the woman swarmed his thinking. Amdi had gone too far.

Breathe, mi carae. Taryn's words drifted in his mind. *We are guests here.* Dammit, but she was right. His nostrils flared with the intake of breath. It took several more deep inhales for his hearing to clear, his mind to focus.

Drinks were poured and Amdi stood to address the gathered clansmen and women. "Friends, we are honored this evening to have among us one who is revered in our lands. He returns to his adopted tribe not as a prisoner as he once was, but as the ambassador to the Lady of Light."

Rhoane seethed beneath the calm façade he wore. What the hell was Amdi playing?

Amdi continued his lies, detailing Rhoane's exploits since he left Ulla. According to the laird, everything Rhoane had learned, accomplished, and became was due to his training in the desert. With each falsehood, those gathered ahhed and applauded. It turned Rhoane's stomach to hear the words, yet he didn't stop Amdi. This propaganda had a purpose—one Rhoane was keen to know. He sipped his drink, too angry to force much past his clenched jaw.

Kaleigh whispered in Taryn's ear, most likely translating Amdi's words. With each new boast, Taryn's eyes narrowed, her lips tightened. Of Taryn, Amdi said nothing.

What is the meaning of this, Rhoane demanded of Kaleigh.

He needs his people to believe you are here under his express permission. Her gaze drifted to the younger woman on Amdi's left. She sat with hands clasped in her lap, eyes downcast and brimming with tears. *Since you left us, Amdi's rule has weakened. He seeks to make stronger heirs with Ullan women.*

Rhoane glared at the laird, hating him more now than he ever had when he lived among them. To his right, Kaleigh's sons sat with legs crossed, spines straight, eyes focused on the back of the tent. A lad with the same coloring as Loghan sat in the place of honor beside Amdi. Rhoane cast through his memory for Kaleigh's firstborn's name. Gwainne came to mind, but as with Loghan, the lad had been much younger when Rhoane lived with them. This handsome man who exuded confidence was nothing like the scrappy youth Rhoane remembered.

Beside Gwainne sat Loghan, then two younger men who didn't resemble their older brothers. He scanned the line of women to Amdi's left. Three with dark hair and eyes, one with curls of crimson. Only Kaleigh had blonde hair of all the wives. The Eleri lads were fairer than their brothers, but still looked enough like Ullans. If Amdi sought to make pure Ullan heirs, there must be a reason. Later, when Amdi no longer stood before his people spouting untruths, Rhoane would uncover what was happening in the desert lands.

Amdi's speech ended, his final boasts shouted to the stars. Rhoane's head hurt and his eyes had yet to focus on any one strand of ShantiMari. It was maddening, all the threads blinding him. He narrowed his vision as Taryn had instructed and it eased the sting a little, but not by much.

How do you tolerate this? He sent the thought to his beloved.

In time, it will become a blur in the background, white noise, nothing more. A warmth spread from his temples across his scalp, tingling with Taryn's healing.

How are you doing this?

I've no idea. Want me to stop? Mirth edged her words. Truly, she was remarkable. She sat ten paces from him, yet could spread her power across the divide to heal him. Rhoane had to physically touch someone to heal.

Or, you know, we could go back to the tent and I can work some sex magic on you, Taryn teased.

A wide smile broke the tension of his clenched jaw and he winked at his betrothed. He'd love nothing more than to have her naked again.

Amdi took his seat beside Rhoane. "I see by your smile you're pleased with my introduction." Amdi said in Ullan, "When I heard you'd returned not to see me, but to claim the dhur, I admit, I was upset. But Kaleigh tells me she was beyond death and look at her now. Your healing skills are much improved, boy."

Rhoane ignored the slur against himself, but calling Taryn a dhur was not acceptable. His jaw once more ground tight. "The only thing you taught me was hatred. I returned to save my mate and, as you can see, she is very much alive. My healing skills have improved, as have all of my senses. Not from anything you gave me, but from what I took after I left your miserable lands."

"Ah, I see you're still as much an ass as you were when you first came to us. Perhaps a night in my arena will work through your issues."

Rhoane bit his cheek to keep from lashing out at the laird. It wouldn't do to start a public brawl. "Why is Kaleigh not sitting beside you as First Wife?"

Amdi shrugged, as if her presence was of no concern of his. "I'm vexed with her for attempting to heal the dhur. As I understand it, my son was about to disease himself with her before you arrived. Thank you, by the way, for preventing that abomination."

"Father." Gwainne leaned forward to catch Amdi's attention. "Who is the woman beside Mother?"

"She is the *Darennsai* of our people." Rhoane cut in before Amdi had a chance to poison his mind. "She is my life mate and beloved, Taryn ap Galendrin."

Gwainne's eyes widened and he glanced at Taryn, who was watching them with sharp interest. "She is the *Darennsai*? Truly?"

"She's a dhur, Gwainne. Don't go near her or talk to her."

An elderly woman slid beside Taryn, gesticulating wildly. She spoke too fast for Rhoane to fully follow, but three words he understood: *Mallaqai, danger,* and *vortex.*

"What's that witch doing here?" Amdi swore under his breath. "Kill her."

Several guards advanced on the women.

"Amdi." Rhoane placed a cautionary hand on the laird's forearm, but he shrugged it away.

Taryn saw the guard and rose, putting herself between them and the woman.

"If the dhur tries to stop you, kill her as well."

Kaleigh shouted a warning in Eleri to Taryn, whose eyes widened with the realization Amdi meant to kill the woman and her. Multiple lights flashed above their heads, too many for Rhoane to track. More than his mind could endure. He stood in a daze, a slight wobble to his stance. Gwainne steadied him, a firm grip at his elbow.

"We will not let her be harmed," he whispered in Rhoane's ear.

Taryn or the witch, Rhoane cared not. He had to stop Amdi before something terrible happened.

He turned in time to see the tip of a spear plunge into the elder woman's chest, a crimson stain spreading over her plain cotton gown. A scream rent the air. Taryn's? Kaleigh's? No, it was from the young woman to Amdi's left. She sprang forth, arms outstretched, but Amdi knocked her back with one blow.

A buzzing, loud enough to block sound, filled Rhoane's head. Time moved in half heartbeats. The other Ullans in the tent stayed seated, hands in laps, heads bowed. Beside the guard, only Taryn, Gwainne, and Rhoane stood. Rhoane glared at Amdi, who watched the proceedings with a glint in his eye. He wanted this. Wanted Taryn to fight back.

He sent a warning to his love, but it was too late. A blade sliced through the air, aimed at her neck.

CHAPTER THIRTEEN

Taryn flinched at the cold steel poised to slice her head from her body. The elder woman slumped behind her and she sensed the woman was gone. Had felt her Light leave her body. There was more she needed to learn from the crone, but Amdi had silenced her. Perhaps he knew what the elder had shared with Taryn. Or, he was as cruel as Kaleigh had warned.

Taryn closed her eyes. It wasn't a good day to die. Rhoane had worked too hard to save her once. She'd not let this asshole take that away.

With a deep inhale and a single thought, the blade stopped. A spasm of pain burned against her skin, and a small trickle of blood oozed down her neck. The guard fought against her power, his hands shaking with the effort to continue.

"Stop," Taryn whispered.

The guard dropped his hands, the sword clanging to the dirt.

"You don't want to hurt me. Your laird commanded this, and you're a good soldier. I forgive you." Her voice had a slight echo to it, a tinny sound that gave her pause. She was herself and yet not fully herself. It was the same strangeness that had happened when she took Percival to Armando. If she looked down, she was half afraid she'd find herself floating. The weightless feeling did nothing to steady her nerves or calm her fluttery heart.

The guard crumpled to his knees, his head bowed.

"Kill her," Amdi shrieked.

"No." The word boomed through the silent tent. Not a single person moved. Everyone stared at Rhoane, who added, "You shall not harm her."

"And who will stop me? You, boy?" Amdi spoke Ullan, but she understood. Had the crone spoken Elennish or Ullan? She couldn't recall.

"I will," Taryn said.

"You? A pathetic Aelan girl with delusions of grandeur? No one comes into my lands without my permission. Who do you think you are?"

Remember who you are. Someone had told her that. *Who? When?* The memory was hazy, yet insistent.

A chill swept down Taryn's back. She was a woman, a daughter, sister, lover, friend. She wore many crowns and had several titles, but beneath it all, she was a carbon life-form, made of stars and dust. She flexed her hands. The runes sparkled in the candlelight, ghost images swirling with her agitation. Her other hand glittered beneath the skin, Eleri Glamour, but more. Like a small galaxy contained within.

"You're right. I am a pathetic Aelan girl and I might have delusions of grandeur. After all, some call me *Eirielle*, others *Darennsai.* I've been told I'm the Daughter of the Sky, Keeper of the Stars. I am *gyota*, destroyer and savior." The words tumbled from her lips, the hidden thought nudging the back of her mind: *But who am I really?*

"You aren't welcome here, sorceress."

"Ah, now *that* I've not been called." Taryn grinned and sent a silent message to Rhoane to relax. She sensed his rapid heartbeat and worried he might have a heart attack. Or kill Amdi. Either outcome wouldn't be good for them. "I'm not a witch, or sorceress, or any of the horrible names you're thinking in your mind, but something tells me you won't believe me."

She slid between Amdi's thoughts, breaking through the wards he'd placed as if they were nothing but water.

Amdi Agnar lived in fear. Fear of losing his title, his lands, his people. She prodded further, uncovering the truth of his brother's death and Amdi's rise to power. A shadow lurked in his mind. This above all disturbed her. His ShantiMari wasn't strong, that was why he used force and intimidation to control his people. She sensed no Telraicht-Noir of his own, just a lingering shadow.

"I'm young. I've seen some of this world, but not all of it. I still have much to learn, but I know this, Amdi Agnar—your people don't respect you. They fear you, yes, but there's no loyalty within their hearts."

Amdi's face reddened and the veins of his neck bulged. "I will see you killed for this slander."

"Not slander—truth. You know it as well as I. You also know the young woman to your left doesn't wish to bed you. This young virgin will, because she's been commanded, but after you've raped her, she'll embed a dagger through her heart by the rise of the sun."

The young woman's face contorted into raw fear. She begged Amdi not to listen to Taryn.

"I also see the one who loves you most you abuse greatly and care for least. Even now she yearns to be by your side, as is her rightful place."

"She's being punished."

Taryn sighed in exasperation. This man, this tyrant, couldn't see past his own selfish needs. She glanced at Kaleigh with a reassuring smile.

"For trying to help me. Yes, I'm aware." Taryn said, her gaze returning to the laird. "She carries within her womb a child, Amdi. Did you know this? Do you realize that finally, after seven generations of your bloodline ruling these lands, there will be a daughter born to your House? And yet you toss her aside because of a whim? You're a pathetic, insolent ass."

"Kill her!" Amdi lunged toward Taryn, but Rhoane stopped him. Loghan sprang to his feet and helped Gwainne and Rhoane prevent his father from coming closer. The guard wavered between following their laird's order and rebellion.

If you fight in his arena, he will respect you. But you must win. Kaleigh's rushed warning brushed her thoughts.

Taryn had heard tales of the Ullan arena. Of the fights fought within, usually to the death. No ShantiMari, only the wits and merits of one's body were allowed. Unsure if she could trust Kaleigh—and her loyalty to Amdi—Taryn hesitated. This might be a ruse meant to goad Taryn into fighting. If she lost, Kaleigh could win favor with her laird. Conversely, if Taryn fought and won, she might be able to learn what drove his madness. There were too many unknowns about Amdi and his arena, but her instincts told her it was the right path.

"You wish me dead and I wish to be allies, Laird of the Ullans. There is nothing to be gained by being enemies. Is there anything I can do to prove myself to you? If I'm to die on Ullan soil, let it be with honor, not by the tip of a spear at your command."

"Taryn, no," Rhoane begged. The anguish she heard in his voice reflected in his gorgeous eyes. "He is not worth it."

Amdi spun with a flourish of robes. "Not worth it? This from you, boy?"

Anxiety rolled off him in waves, crashing against Taryn's ShantiMari. She'd forced his hand and he wasn't happy about it.

He paced a rough circle, rubbing his chin, scratching at the stubble of beard. "You will fight in the arena. Your opponent will be your betrothed."

She'd thought Amdi would say as much. The laird of the Ullans was simple in nature. After dealing with Lliandra for a season, Taryn could handle the likes of Amdi Agnar.

"You cannot do this, Amdi," Rhoane fumed, but Taryn held up a hand for calm.

"I'll fight Rhoane, if that's your wish," Taryn stated, ignoring Rhoane's glare, "but I don't think you feel he's much of a challenge. Nor does he wish me dead. It wouldn't be very entertaining."

"Possibly you're right. Rhoane wasn't strong in the arena, if I recall. You're nothing but a girl, hardly worth the effort of my best fighter."

"I'll only fight your best. Don't deny me this one thing, Laird Amdi."

What the hell do you think you are doing? He wants you dead and you just gave him reason to kill you. The alarm in Rhoane's thoughts tore through her mind. In them, she knew his anxiety, rage, and revulsion. Flashes of memories—of his time in the arena—bruised her heart. Amdi was cruel. A small man with a large fear.

Don't you think I know that? Amdi's an ass. But he doesn't know who I am, or what I'm capable of.

You are not strong enough. My healing is still taking effect. I can see it in your stance. You are as yet unbalanced.

Damn him for noticing. She wasn't fully healed and as good as she felt, it wouldn't take much to hurt, or possibly kill her. Still, she had to fight, not just to prove to Amdi she wasn't to be dismissed, but for reasons not yet clear. All she knew was that this was important. It was part of not just her path, but Amdi's. And Kaleigh's.

"You will fight Enghor," Amdi announced, a cruel smile turning his lips.

Murmurs spread through the tent, to the far reaches of the encampment, and Taryn breathed deep. She had been hoping he would choose Gwainne, or Loghan, knowing neither would have bloodlust for her life.

Before she or Rhoane could object, two guards approached

with caution and directed her to the back of the tent. They kept a fair distance from her as they walked past Amdi's people. Taryn watched from her periphery as people made the sign to ward off evil above their heads. It was the same figure eight she saw Lliandra's soldiers making when they'd passed Daknys's temple in Celyn Eryri. People feared that which they didn't understand.

The guards directed her toward the outer edge of the camp, every so often prodding her in the back with the sharp tip of a spear. These were Amdi's men, their loyalty to the laird, not to her. Yet they showed no true malice. Interesting.

At the arena, the rules of engagement were explained to her—no use of her power, no weapons other than those she won from her opponent, and the fight would be to the death. Against Rhoane's protests, Taryn agreed to the terms and entered the arena to trills and shouts from the Ullans. Benches stretched around the dirt pitch, five levels up like a stadium. *Or,* she thought wryly, *a theater of death.* If this was their only entertainment, these people desperately needed new hobbies.

She stood in the center of the arena, apprehensive as the master of ceremony took his place in the center of the oval and began his speech. Rhoane sat beside Kaleigh, two rows in front of Amdi and his sons. Concern etched across their faces. As she waited for the flamboyant older gentleman to finish his lengthy introductions, it occurred to her that she quite possibly might die. For all her bravado, she'd provoked Amdi just as she'd provoked Cashiel. Just as strong as that thought was, an even fiercer belief that it wasn't her time to die settled in her mind. Like dominoes, everything must happen in order. Marissa, Valterys, Cashiel—hell, even Zakael—they were put in her path to challenge her. To make her stretch beyond what was comfortable.

But why? Why did she have to strive to be better?

For them, came the answer. The Ullans were included, but not exclusive to who "they" were. Aelinae. All of the races, every individual, no matter gender or affiliation to a ruler or god. They were her people. She was their savior and destroyer. She was Taryn ap Galendrin and this was her destiny. She would not die this night.

For them.

Taryn took a deep breath and focused on the task at hand.

A hush fell over the crowd as the combatants' names were announced. Taryn searched the arena for her opponent, Enghor. Only she and the master of ceremony stood on the dirt. He finished his preamble, encouraging her to die an honorable death, and scuttled out of the arena.

The sound of a gate opening drew her attention and she turned in time to see a creature with the legs of a man, torso of an ape, and head of a ram charge toward her. In his hands, he wielded several weapons—a mace, an ax, and rope. Tucked into a wide belt at his waist were several daggers and throwing knives. Strapped to his back was a long pike. Apparently, Enghor was quite good at fighting in the arena to have so many weapons.

Holy fucking shit, she was going to die. With honor or not, the thing that stormed toward her would be her demise.

Taryn had hoped she'd be fighting a man, but this creature was twice her height. She couldn't probe his mind without breaking the rules. She'd love to take a peek at what her enemy was thinking. It skirted the terms, but then again, did allowing a monster to fight Aelans fall within the rules? Amdi might not play fair, but she would. Even if the creature had all the weapons and advantages.

Even without reading his thoughts, a muddled mass of anger, resentment, and loneliness swept across her senses. The latter surprised her, but then, she'd never seen Enghor's kind on Aelinae. If Amdi kept him as a pet fighter, he would have little interaction with the others. A drop of pity settled in her gut. This creature wasn't from this world. How he came to be on Aelinae, she had no idea. Right then, his origins were less important than staying alive. Without weapons or the use of her power, she'd have to improvise.

"Enghor, I don't wish to fight you." She held her empty hands out for him to see. "Amdi wants this, not me. And I suspect you don't want to fight, either." Something in his eyes gave her hope and she continued. "You want to be free from his tyranny, don't you?"

He rumbled toward her, a battle cry issuing from his throat. *So much for talking her way out of fighting.* Indecipherable grunts and guttural cries followed and Taryn stripped off the elaborate jacket she wore. She crouched low, timing his advance. When he was two paces away, she leapt, wrapping the jacket around the ax and using it to swing up to his shoulders. She jerked hard on the fabric, pulling the ax free from his fist.

Enghor roared and spun hard to his left, unbalancing her. She slid down his back, slicing the pike free from its leather bindings before hitting the ground. Her hair snagged on twigs and rocks as she rolled to her feet. Damn hair. She should've kept it short, but how was she to know she'd be battling a monster?

The world tilted and her stomach pinched. Aftereffects from nearly dying. If she wasn't careful, Enghor would finish what Cashiel started. She ducked to miss his mace, and rolled beneath his legs, lashing out with the ax. It caught on his thigh, making little more than a scratch. Just her luck he'd have hide tougher than leather instead of skin. At least he didn't have scales.

Taryn plunged the pike upward, into the soft folds of his buttocks, and the thing screamed.

Rhoane, do you think I could fight him as darathi vorsi? Or would that be cheating?

She chanced a glance at Rhoane, who whispered in Kaleigh's ear.

Amdi would not be pleased. Kaleigh believes he would seek to capture you for a prisoner if you do.

Yeah, that's kind of what I thought. Damn.

She twisted to avoid Enghor's mace and dodged a slice from one of the daggers. He held the mace in his closed fist, the dagger between two fingers. It was a clumsy way to fight, but he'd perfected his strikes using both weapons. This was an altogether new way of combat for her. An enemy twice her size, neither man nor woman, skin like a shell. What had possessed her to think she could win?

"Enghor," she spoke softly, "you're weary of fighting for Amdi, I can sense it. You're lonely. You must wish to return to your mate. You miss your family. Your tribe." All guesses, but she was out of options and her energy was flagging. Rhoane had been right—she wasn't ready for this kind of physical exertion.

He stumbled after her, a blade aimed at her head. "Why do you torment me, Dead One?"

"I wish to help you. I can return you to the lands from which you came."

"My life there is dead. You are dead. We are all dead."

The blade sliced toward her and she dove to avoid it. She rolled under his foot and cut a groove with the ax. Enghor roared and stomped hard, missing her by an inch.

"Let me help you. Please." Taryn stood and faced him, the pike in one hand, ax in the other. "This is pointless and you know it. Amdi doesn't control you, Enghor. Remember your pride. Remember who you were."

The words echoed in her mind. *Who was she?*

The beast pounded his chest, his horned head thrown back, a cry of rage tearing the night air.

"You will die. You are already dead." His garbled words startled her. A swipe of mace caught her in the side and she flew through the air to land in a heap on the dirt. A loud cheer went up from the crowd, followed by stomping of boards and clapping. Trills and whistles hurt her ears.

The air whooshed from her lungs and she coughed against the

dust. Pain ricocheted from her head to her toes. She knelt on all fours, her fingers grasping for the pike.

"Why do you call me Dead One?" She leveraged the pike to help her stand on unsteady legs, not ready to accept defeat.

"Because you will die." He lunged for her, daggers outstretched, mace swinging wildly.

"We all die, Enghor." She raced toward him, sliding between his legs, her ax cutting through the tendons of his calf. He stumbled and rocked backward, nearly knocking her over. She spun to miss his foot and jabbed upward with the pike, catching him between his thigh and groin. Enghor cursed and swung his right fist at her head, the dagger aimed for her neck.

Sweat dripped from her brow, blinding her. She swiped a hand across her face, surprised to see blood oozing from a wound on her arm. She hadn't even felt the blade. If she didn't end the fight soon, she'd lose all her strength and would fulfill his ominous promise. She would die. The dagger swished above her head, taking several locks of her silvery hair with it. He should've hit his mark, but missed.

"You're tired. I'm tired. Hell, I was mostly dead two bells ago and shouldn't be here. Neither should you. Enghor, please." She placed a palm on his thigh to steady herself. The moment her flesh touched his, she was seized with an overwhelming despair that wasn't of her making. "I have more yet to do with this life." Her thoughts opened and embraced his. If Amdi thought this was cheating, he could suck it. Enghor had spent too long fighting in this arena because of a false promise. Amdi had told the creature he'd earn his freedom if he fought and won, yet thirteen seasons on, and Enghor was no closer to leaving Ulla than he'd been when—Taryn shuddered at the vision her opponent thrust into her mind.

The crowd began chanting, demanding they stop dawdling and get on with the fight. Taryn had no doubt that if one of them didn't die soon, the mob would attack and finish them both.

"Please let me end your suffering. It isn't dishonorable to wish to be free from a tyrant."

"You cannot kill me. No one of flesh can." His flat tone spoke volumes to how much he'd given up believing in anything Amdi promised.

"You are in luck, my friend. You see, I'm not made of flesh. I'm made of stars." She wrapped a thought around his despair and begged him to let her end this peacefully. "Let me free you. Please."

"It must be in battle." He took two steps backward, drawing his mace up as if he meant to bash her head with it. "I am ready." The words barely touched her sensitive hearing, but it was all she needed.

Tears stung her eyes as Taryn raised the ax. With all her strength, she threw it upward. The second it left her fingertips, she sprang to his leg, then up his arm to his chest. Enghor watched as she snatched the ax from the air and sank it into the fleshy part of his neck. Blood poured forth and Enghor staggered, his hands grasping at his throat. He hit the dirt with a thud and Taryn slipped to his armpit. She scrambled atop his heaving chest and plunged the pike deep, where she hoped his heart would be.

The cheers and taunts from the crowd rose to a frenzied pitch. Taryn blocked the sounds from her mind and focused on the beast lying in the dirt beneath her. His wheezing tore her heart. A wave of nausea fought through her panting. She'd never get used to killing. Even with her life at stake, it held no glory for her. Taryn put her hand on his furry chest. "Let me take your pain. Allow me the honor of easing your passing."

He fully opened his mind and his memories flooded her own. Sights, sounds, and smells took over her senses. A world of swamps and rainforests, where his tribe swung from vines over a river of honey became as familiar to her as Aelinae. She didn't just see his homeland—she was on his home world. Enghor stood tall beside her.

"How did you come to Aelinae?" she asked, already knowing the answer, but needing to hear it from him.

He pointed to a ridge off in the distance. "A trickster came from there. He took several of us, but I alone am left."

Taryn's pulse quickened. A portal, like the one in Nadra's cavern where she'd arrived on Aelinae from Earth. The part of her being that remained in Amdi's arena hovered over Enghor's body, protecting him from the horrors of his past.

"Can you show me this man, the trickster?"

An image of Zakael assaulted her mind. It was her worst fear, realized.

"I will avenge you and your family, Enghor. Be at peace, my friend." On Enghor's home world, Taryn faced him, the spoken vow binding the pair.

The roar of the crowd drowned out the sound of his gurgled breaths, but she heard a whispered, "Leth sies, *Darennsai. Shailana ma landre." You have my grace. Tell my mate Shailana.*

It was done. She had survived.

CHAPTER FOURTEEN

Taryn slid from the beast's torso and placed a hand upon his brow. Trills rent the night air. Some of the onlookers called for her death—others praised her. Taryn tilted her head to the side, listening. A few in the crowd mourned for Enghor. It was these voices she sought and held their words. Not everyone in Amdi's tribe approved of the arena.

"Be at peace, Enghor."

His final breaths echoed off the rocks that made up one side of the fighting ring. She sent a thread of her power to his heart and another to his mind: one to stop his life, the other to ease his passing. Enghor's legs trembled with his final death throes until finally they were still. Her heart ached for him and the loss he suffered. Sadness, deep and profound, cloaked her exhaustion. She sank to her knees, spent.

"No! This cannot be!" Amdi's curses assaulted her ears. "Kill her! Kill her now!"

Three men raced into the arena, their spears held aloft, helmets covering their faces. Mustering the last of her energy stores, she grabbed one of Enghor's daggers and rose to face them. This kind of combat she knew well. Ynyd Eirathnacht sang in her mind, a song of peace for Enghor, and of redemption for her. She could call the sword to her, but she left it where it lay hidden in her tent. She'd give Amdi no reason to cast doubt upon her victory.

The first soldier approached and her stomach pinched. She could end this with her power, but that was probably what Amdi expected her to do. Even if he cheated, she wouldn't. Even though she was weakened and close to collapse, she would see this fight to the end. Cashiel hadn't killed her. Neither would Amdi.

The thought of that murderous asshole renewed her energy. Cashiel would suffer for what he did. That is, if he lived, which she sensed even now, that he was alive. Someone—and she had a good idea who—was protecting him. Once free of Amdi's pettiness, Taryn and Rhoane could leave Ulla and find Cashiel. But first, she had to deal with the approaching men.

The first soldier lifted his spear to strike. Taryn timed a well-placed punch to his sternum, knocking him to his knees. She used the butt of Enghor's dagger, which was more like a sword in her hands, to thump him on the side of his head. He slid to the dirt, unmoving. The next guard wasn't so easily dispatched and she fought hard, using her martial arts skills along with the sword to break his pike, and his will. Even though she wasn't interested in harming the soldiers, they did their best to end her. After a missed jab to her throat, she kicked the second man's sternum and he joined the first soldier in a heap at her feet. The third guard slowed his pace, uncertainty clouding his eyes.

Taryn stood still, calm in the midst of shouts and taunts coming from the stands.

Anger roiled through her blood, heating her skin. Sweat slicked her palms and she struggled to keep her mind clear. The first two soldiers had drained the last dregs of her strength. If she let her guard down for even a second, she'd be beaten. Enghor had wanted to be free of this life, but the man moving closer looked as though he craved her murder.

The cynfar resting on her skin vibrated with suppressed anxiety—Rhoane's. He, too, wanted to use his power to end the fight. It was ridiculous she had to battle Amdi's soldiers. That wasn't part of the deal, but Taryn wouldn't back down. Even if her body couldn't take much more, she wouldn't give Amdi the satisfaction of seeing her quit.

She touched the pendant and smiled as if she'd won already. She couldn't use her power, but she could draw on Rhoane's love to sustain her. Love healed all wounds. Her mind spun to earlier, when they'd been floating above the ground, her legs wrapped around Rhoane's waist. His sex magic had brought her back from near death. Not just sex—something more.

The soldier stepped closer, his pike replaced with a sword. She pushed the thought of Rhoane from her mind and concentrated on the man's movements. He swung low and she met his blow with her own. The sound of clashing metal rang out and the crowd's roars lowered. Taryn countered each swing and thrust with a block and parry of her own. She spun and attacked, aiming her strikes not to kill, but to render her opponent weaponless. He fought honorably, but without the same passion as she. His attacks were sloppy, as if he'd been too long at the feasting table and not enough in the training ring.

Several times she could have ended the fight with his death, but she chose to see how far he would go to satisfy his laird's wish. To be sure, his swordplay was meant to maim. He sought to win, of that she had no doubt. Taryn had to make certain he never got that chance.

His sword arced toward her and she spun her own blade, catching his weapon at the hilt. It spiraled through the air, landing with a puff of dust.

Dark eyes stared at her through the helmet. His hands reached forward and grabbed her throat, choking her. She pushed her arms between his and jerked hard, releasing his death grip. Her sword dropped to the ground and she fought him, hand-to-hand. His arrogance was replaced with surprise. He thought a woman couldn't defeat a man. How wrong he was.

Three quick jabs—one to the neck, the next to his gut, a third to his nose—and he crumpled to his knees. She stepped back and jumped, spinning into a roundhouse kick that connected to the side of his head. The soldier splayed to the side, his body sliding across the dirt, unmoving.

The crowd roared, cheered, and jeered, but she didn't care. Now she'd truly won. Not even Amdi could deny her this victory.

She glanced to the stands and sought Rhoane. He stood with Kaleigh, his expression a mixture of relief, pride, and awe. Her gaze traveled up to find Amdi, but he wasn't in the stands. Nor was Gwainne. Loghan sat alone, a dark scowl matching his tattoos. Confusion scrambled her already overworked mind. She searched the crowd, but couldn't find Amdi or his oldest son. If that bastard had left the arena before she finished the fight, he might declare it invalid and everything she'd left on the dirt would've been in vain. She kicked at the soil, funneling her anger into the movement.

The soldier to her right moaned and she bent to help him up. He took off his helmet and she stared at the face of the Ullan heir.

"Gwainne." She helped him stand, her anger rumbling into her confusion. With the realization she'd fought not a soldier as she'd believed, her thoughts marched toward horror. If the first soldier was Gwainne, then who were the other two?

"You do not fight like any woman I know."

"Are you hurt?" Taryn ignore the non-compliment.

"Only my pride."

Together, she and the Ullan heir strode to the next guard. He was unconscious still. A trail of blood led from his nose to his chin.

"Who is this?" Taryn placed a hand over his heart, relieved to feel it beating.

"My father's captain of the guard. Father will not be pleased."

"And the last man?" She had to ask, but feared the answer.

Gwainne crouched beside the fallen man. A trembling hand outstretched to remove the helmet and Taryn knew what she'd see before Amdi's face appeared. The arrogant laird thought he could best her. He'd gambled and lost. Her legs shook with fatigue and trepidation. Amdi would be irate when he recovered.

Kaleigh raced to her husband's side, her fingertips tapping lightly over his features. It was the same movement Taryn saw Faelara and Rhoane do on numerous occasions. Kaleigh searched for injuries unseen.

"He isn't dead," Taryn assured the woman, although part of her wished he was and for that, guilt cut at her words. "The blow stunned him, that's all."

"His brain could be damaged." Kaleigh whispered Eleri words as she pressed her hands to the laird's temples. "He needs the healing tents. Quickly."

Gwainne and several others lifted Amdi's body and disappeared into the throng of people. Rhoane fought his way through them to her side. Just as Kaleigh had inspected Amdi, Rhoane's fingers danced over her skin, his ShantiMari a welcome balm to her battered body.

"You need rest. Come." He guided her through the thinning crowd, but she turned away from her tent toward the healer's tents. "Taryn, Kaleigh and Loghan will heal Amdi. You need to take care of yourself."

"It's not Amdi I'm worried about. If Kaleigh tries to heal him, she'll lose the baby."

"You do not have the strength. I can feel your body shutting down."

"Then you'll have to loan me some." She took his hand and together they jogged after the others. His ShantiMari swirled over her skin before sinking deep into her body. With it came renewed energy. It would have to be enough to keep her upright.

The guards stationed outside held their pikes across the opening and Taryn stood facing them, hands on hips. "Really? You're going to try to stop me from entering?"

"We were given orders not to let anyone inside. This, from the heir himself."

"You mean Gwainne? The guy whose ass I just kicked? I suggest you let me through before I turn you into a lizard."

The guards exchanged glances and lifted their swords.

"Smart move, my friends," Rhoane said as they entered the darkened tent.

Voices came to them from the left and they turned in that direction. Gwainne looked up from his father's inert form. "I left instructions we were not to be disturbed."

"And I ignored those instructions." Taryn took Kaleigh's hand in hers. "My lady, do not try to heal your laird lest you lose your child." She spoke Eleri, in the hopes it would convey the importance of her words.

"How did you know? About the baby? Is it truly a girl?" Her hand spread protectively across her abdomen. "I was not even certain yet."

"I just know." Taryn couldn't tell her that she saw the child's thread of ShantiMari woven with Kaleigh's, or that she could hear the tiny heartbeat coming from within her womb. She wasn't even sure how it had happened, but there it was, like a beacon thumping in her mind.

"We must heal my father. Your kick was more powerful than you realized." Loghan emerged from the shadows, his tattooed skin gleaming in the candlelight. He wore an open tunic and breeches, his face a mixture of concern and something else—not anger, but disgust, perhaps.

"I will help." Rhoane placed his hands on Amdi's forehead.

"There is some swelling to his mind. His thoughts are chaotic with fear of dying. Of leaving his sons and his one true love."

Rhoane met Kaleigh's worried glance. Tears sparkled in her eyes. A sliver of something unpleasant curled around Taryn's heart. Jealousy. Dammit, she had no time for pettiness. Yet, Kaleigh and Rhoane shared a past, just as Rhoane and Marissa had. A past Taryn couldn't erase.

"He loves you, Kaleigh. He is ruled by fear. It casts a shadow on all he does." Rhoane reassured the Eleri woman and Taryn let her feelings of jealousy slip from her like raindrops from a leaf.

Taryn spread her hands over Amdi's torso and eased her ShantiMari into him.

"Loghan, use your healing skills to search for internal injuries. Rhoane, you as well." Kaleigh ordered. "Taryn, please be gentle with him."

"I will, my lady." Taryn gave the woman a wan smile. It was a huge risk for Kaleigh to trust Taryn with her husband's life.

Loghan's Shanti intertwined with Taryn's—fierce, powerful, full of grace. She sensed his Eleri ShantiMari and his Dark power. His strength lie in the combination of the two. Nature and the sun together. Rhoane's Shanti, as familiar to her as her own, pricked against her nerves. Odd, to be sure. Woven through Rhoane's healing, she sensed his apprehension toward Loghan. It was a thread she didn't want to pull, not then, anyway.

They searched through Amdi's veins to his cells and organs, over his muscles, past the bruises she'd given him to his heart. Nothing was broken or harmed internally. Loghan's relief swept over her. His power withdrew with reluctance.

"What did you find? Will he live?" Kaleigh's plea interrupted the silence of their healing.

"He is sound of body, but it is up to him if he will live," Loghan said. "He suffered defeat at the hands of a woman. That above all could destroy him."

Taryn placed her hands beside Rhoane's and linked her power

to his. She searched Amdi's mind until she came to the dark spot she'd sensed earlier. It was as Rhoane had said, his fear. No Noir permeated him, but this shadow was equally as binding as any oath to Kaldaar. Yet there was something else hidden deep in Amdi's fear—a subtleness that surprised her even though she'd half-expected to uncover treachery.

Do you feel this? She sent her thought to Rhoane.

I do. I cannot name it, but it is familiar.

That's because it raped you.

Marissa?

Sadness echoed in his thoughts. And guilt. So much guilt. His brokenness slammed against Taryn and she reeled with the impact.

"What is it? What have you found?" Kaleigh's worry pulled every word low.

"We know what ails him. We can rid him of this affliction, but he will have to choose to come back to you," Rhoane told the woman who carried Amdi's child.

"What have you found? I sensed nothing?" Hurt pride embittered Loghan's words.

"We can discuss the particulars later. Rhoane?" Taryn nodded toward Amdi and together they wrapped Marissa's insidious power in their own and extracted it from Amdi's memories. She was clever, Taryn's sister. But predictable.

Beneath Marissa's manipulations, they found Zakael's power lurking in Amdi's mind. Rhoane grunted and Taryn returned his disgust. Her half-siblings had done their best to infect Amdi with paranoia and fear. It was little wonder the laird considered everyone a threat. Taryn, above all others.

Amdi, come back to the light. Those who love you need you. Taryn's soothing thoughts drifted through Amdi's mind. *It is not yet time for you to leave this place. There is much to be done. Much you can learn and pass onto your sons. Your daughter will need you to guide her. She will be an Ullan princess among princes. Her place in this world is dependent upon what you can give her. Your knowledge, your courage, your faith.*

Without you, she will not survive.

Amdi's eyelids fluttered.

Kaleigh grabbed his hands. "My love, return to us. My laird, my heart. Do not leave us."

Rhoane chanted beneath his breath, an ancient Eleri song of healing. His ShantiMari swirled through the room, not green as it had always been, but clear like a diamond. Taryn could make out the threads and starbursts within his power. Roots grew from the strands to take hold in the air, forming a thicket above their heads.

Taryn answered his song, singing an older tune, one from the Great War that Daknys had sung to heal the wounded. They harmonized while Loghan, Gwainne, and Kaleigh added their power to the healing.

The amount of love these three had for their laird over-whelmed her. He was arrogant, an ass, and selfish, but they saw beyond that to the man. They knew his flaws and loved him anyway.

Amdi gasped and drew in a deep breath. His eyes blinked open and he gazed at those in the room. When his glance drifted to Taryn, a scowl crossed his features, but Kaleigh smoothed it away with a loving touch. She smothered him in kisses. Loghan and Gwainne placed a hand on their father's chest, welcoming him back.

Rhoane stepped beside Taryn and took her hand in his. "That was a kind thing you did for him. A man who would see you dead, you infused with mercy."

"I did it for them as much for us. They need him, and Amdi has a place on our paths yet to be determined. I couldn't let him die. Not yet." She swayed, her exhaustion catching up at last. "I need some of your special healing."

The room closed in on itself and she leaned into Rhoane for

support. The others needn't see her in a weakened state. They couldn't know that healing Amdi had cost more than she realized.

"Help me to our tent. I need my sword."

They left the others to care for Amdi, and Rhoane guided her through the encampment to their tent. With great care, he lay her on the thick blankets. Taryn sank into them, grateful to be off her feet, alarmed at how utterly spent she was. Her heart beat as if she'd been zapped with lightning, with stutters and stops. A sheen of sweat glistened on her clammy skin. She lay back, her vision wavy, unfocused.

Rhoane shuffled through a pile of clothing until he pulled out a crumpled blanket. Inside, her sword sang to her, soothing tones meant to calm her racing heart.

"What's happening to me? I feel strange. Like, my body isn't my own. Like it might explode into a million pieces."

"I do not know, but I can sense it in you. My power aches to be a part of yours. Not to heal, but to destroy."

Taryn sat up, alarmed. Her already skipping heart caught in her throat. "You want to kill me?"

His gorgeous eyes widened with wild horror. "No. I am sorry. That came out wrong. Not to kill you, but to release you. I cannot explain it. Something happened tonight. With Amdi, perhaps, or the song you sang—I am not sure. I do know, nothing will ever be the same."

Taryn slid Ynyd Eirathnacht from her scabbard and held the hilt against her chest. The dragons flared their wings, sending a ripple of serenity through her. "The old woman in the dining tent told me I must return to somewhere called Yawn Saine Stroot. I've never heard of this place. Have you?"

Rhoane shook his head. "There is nowhere on Aelinae with this name. Are you certain she said 'return' and not 'find'?"

"She was insistent. Yawn Saine Stroot. She kept repeating it to make sure I had it right. She even made me say it to her. She said that's where it all began, and you and I must return there.

If we don't, she warned, everything we've worked for will be lost."

So much had already been lost. Enghor, Marissa, Valterys, and so many others. In her heart, she knew more would die for Aelinae, and something told her people weren't the only thing the crone had meant. Aelinae itself was at risk of becoming no more.

Thinking made her head swarm as if a hive of bees took up residence. She rubbed a hand across her face, surprised by the tears on her cheeks. The old woman had died giving Taryn the message. She couldn't let her down.

Taryn's sword glowed in the soft torchlight and she set it at the edge of the blankets. Rhoane pulled Claidholm Solais from its covering and lay it beside her blade. She picked it up and placed it on the other side of their bedding, its tip toward their heads while Ynyd Eirathnacht's tip faced their feet.

Rhoane's head tilted left and his face scrunched as he watched. "Why place the swords just so?"

"Protection. Claidholm Solais and Ynyd Eirathnacht will not let anything or anyone harm us while we are otherwise occupied." Taryn lay back, spent.

"Do you think we need them?"

"I'm not sure, but I feel like this is important." She held out her hands and beckoned him join her on the bed. "You're right about one thing, nothing will ever be the same again because now I know about your sex magic." She pulled him to the blankets and grinned. "Come here, my Surtentse, and give me some of your special loving."

He slid up her legs to her breasts and nuzzled his lips against her skin. She would never tire of the feel of his lips against her. Ever. She needed his healing, yes, but she also needed to know he loved her.

The old woman had told her many things in the short time they had before Amdi killed her. She said Taryn and Rhoane would find the others through the vortex of Mallaqai's ruins, which Taryn had no idea what any of that meant. Also, that she and Rhoane must return to the sacred place, this Yawn Saine Stroot, and there they must make love, which Taryn thought strange, but whatever. Making love to Rhoane was no hardship for her. It was the last thing the crone had said that curdled the fear in Taryn's heart.

She said Rhoane would betray her not once, but twice.

And then he would kill her.

CHAPTER FIFTEEN

Lliandra sipped her wine as she observed the others seated at the rather large, yet modestly decorated table in Faisal's meeting hall. To her right, Eliahnna fidgeted. The poor girl was woefully unprepared for her role as Lady of Light. Lliandra would have to put more time and effort into her than she'd like, but she did what was necessary. If only Marissa hadn't been so foolish.

If only…

The stupid girl had gotten herself killed protecting Eliahnna from Taryn's father. Now Marissa's sisters lived and she, the child Lliandra had devoted decades to, was dead.

A mournful sob lodged in her throat and she took another sip of the delicious red Faisal had one of his servants bring up from his hidden vaults. It wouldn't do to let these miscreants see her emotional. Yet it had only been a fortnight since she'd lost her darling daughter. Surely they'd understand.

Perhaps she could use her grief to negotiate a deal with the king—his special reserve for something only Talaith could provide. A small smile turned the corners of her lips upward. Yes, she could use this opportunity to her personal betterment. The Summerlands made the finest wine in all of Aelinae. If only she could trade Taryn for a vault full of Faisal's wine. Then her problems would be solved.

If only…

Queen Prateeni rose and welcomed them to her home. Lliandra held back a snort. The shambles of a palace were nothing compared to the Crystal Palace in Talaith. These backwater monarchs knew nothing of truly ruling. She smiled sweetly at the elder queen and raised her glass in a silent toast to those gathered for the impromptu council.

"We're pleased you have joined our daughter on her voyage across the sea to marry Lord Valen. We had hoped to convene this council after the festivities, when the Eirielle would be present. Now that we know she is recovering with Prince Rhoane at an unspecified location, we really must carry on. Lord Darrew's been asked to return to Danuri and we couldn't wait." The queen droned on and Lliandra tuned out the patronizing drivel.

A few days ago, everyone was in a tizzy because Taryn was still missing and Rhoane, selfish as all Eleri were, dashed off to find her. Whoever had sent those madmen to Lliandra's ships would be dealt with in good time, but what the empress really longed to know was—why had they attacked her ship in the middle of the ocean? Certainly, if their goal was to kidnap Taryn, they could've done that in Talaith. Ferran's bells, hadn't the assassin tried to kill Taryn in broad daylight in Paderau? It wasn't like the girl had any care to her safety and if Taryn insisted on being a target, well, it wasn't Lliandra's job to protect her.

A grunt escaped between the twisted lips of her grimace and Lliandra coughed to conceal what others might consider rudeness. This meeting was a sham. She should be in her rooms, getting a massage by the lovely maid assigned to assist the empress during her stay. Her mind wandered to the woman's breasts and her scent, making Lliandra ache between her legs. She shifted against the hard wood of her chair and clenched against her need.

This wouldn't do. She was empress of Talaith, Lady of Light. She didn't obsess over a serving girl, no matter how tender her skin, how fragrant her quim. Lliandra swiveled her attention away from Prateeni to the others.

At the far end of the table sat a man who made Lliandra's veins chill. Goose bumps rose on her arms and the hairs on the back of her neck stiffened. This was much better. No twittering of her heart over the stranger, Lord Darrew, Chief Councilor to the Steward of Danuri.

Cloaked in black, his hood hung loose around his neck like a pool of liquid tarry. Skin the color of dusk, with eyes to match, the man hadn't spoken a word from his eggplant-tinted lips. His very presence gave her discomfort she couldn't explain. It could've been the way he studied all of them, as if he heard every conversation and marked each syllable, or it might've been the way he inclined his head when their eyes met. There was a challenge in those eyes, and not one Lliandra wanted to explore.

Never in her life had she met a man who made her womb resign so completely. It irritated her that this Lord Darrew could make her feel—she searched for the word and came up with something she'd never associated with herself—*unworthy*.

Tears pricked the backs of her eyes and Eliahnna took her hand. "If this is too much for you, I can stay on your behalf. No one would begrudge you missing a meeting."

Dear sweet, stupid Eliahnna. She would have to harden her behavior if she was ever going to be a competent ruler. "I'm fine, darling." Lliandra removed her hand from Eliahnna's before anyone saw. She blinked the tears from her eyes and smiled as if Prateeni had said the most interesting thing.

Introductions and welcomes made, Prateeni set her glass upon the table and turned her attention to Lliandra. She hadn't noticed the woman's crown earlier, but now it sparkled in the sunlight streaming through the windows. The gems caught the light and flickered, creating a colorful mosaic on the walls around them. Her smile grew. Now that Hayden was part of the family, Lliandra had access to the mines located in the Summerlands. Her treasury could use a boost, what with all the spending Marissa had been doing over the past few seasons. Not to mention now that Taryn had returned, Lliandra was forced to give her a stipend and property. Did these girls think the empress made gold coins in her sleep?

"The illegal taxation you're imposing on Summerlands and Danuri goods ends now."

Lliandra choked on her wine, a furious heat covering her cheeks. Whatever Prateeni had been rambling about before was lost to Lliandra, but she clearly heard the accusation.

"What taxes? I don't know what you're talking about." Bloody hell, as Taryn was wont to say. Where did this come from? Lliandra affected her most innocent façade.

"You've been taking a rather large sum of proceeds from our kingdom for several seasons, Empress Lliandra."

"Your Majesty, are you accusing me of stealing?"

Prateeni stood with her arms folded, her expression one of annoyance. Gone was the docile wife of King Faisal. In her place was a serpent as cunning as any Lliandra had known. She needed to tread carefully lest the asp strike at her heart.

"I am not now, nor have I ever been, placing taxes on your products above what were agreed upon by you and the king." There. That should settle it. Who would dare challenge the word of the Lady of Light?

Prateeni's narrowed eyes studied the empress. Her lips tightened, and Lord Darrew sat forward, his hands splayed flat against the table. Lliandra took in the changed postures of those in the room, the thickening of the air with suppressed tension. They all knew. They had known before entering the room what would be discussed and she, Lliandra, had been clueless. Oh, how she missed Marissa. Her daughter would've known what to expect and would've prepared Lliandra for the attack. She dared not look at Eliahnna. If her heir knew of the accusations and had said nothing to her mother, it would be too much. Her heart already fluttered with fragile life.

"Do you deny the charges? Do you honestly claim to have no knowledge of these taxes that are driving good merchants into ruin?" the queen challenged.

She had to give credit to Prateeni. The woman was fiercer than Lliandra had thought.

She could play this several ways, but opted for victim. Lliandra blinked several times, her eyes like a doe's, her lips slack. Prateeni wasn't fazed. She continued to stare down the empress with steel in her spine, a glint in her eyes. An asp measuring her kill.

With a final blink, Lliandra said in an even tone, "I tell you true. I know nothing of illegal taxes."

"The money went into your coffers. We have documents signed by your hand, Empress Lliandra." Prateeni motioned to her eldest son.

He shuffled through several sheets of parchment and handed them to his mother.

"Is this not your signature?" Prateeni asked.

Lliandra took the proffered papers and scrutinized them. How in Ferran's bells did they come to have the documents? Lliandra had been assured they were destroyed. The papers themselves weren't altogether damning—they were signed promises of increased funding for several key nobles in both the east and the west. Yet, they clearly said the monies would come from the illegal taxes. Since Lliandra couldn't pay the nobles from her own treasury, the money had to come from somewhere.

One document caught her eye and an internal tempest raged in her belly. It was the agreement she'd made with Adesh to steal goods from Danuri and the Summerlands that he would then sell on the black market. When she returned to Talaith, she'd have him strung up by his balls.

She gave a half-hearted shrug. "I agree this looks like my handwriting, but it's not. Whoever signed these edicts wanted it to appear as though I approved the taxes." She placed a palm upon them, preventing anyone from removing the papers from her possession. "Where did you get them?"

"From a reliable source," Hayden answered, but his voice lacked conviction. He wasn't certain if she told the truth or not.

Sweet, trusting Hayden.

"And who is this source?" Lliandra purred. Her seduction would be lost on him, but she knew the power of her voice, of her demeanor. If she could win over some of the others in the room, they could end this farce and she could return to her rooms and that luscious young woman. "I wish to know who provided you with these lies. I am the empress of Talaith. I will not tolerate slander."

"My lady," Lord Darrew drawled, "the documents have been verified to be authentic. If, as you say, these are forged, who would want to sully your good reputation? Of the seven kingdoms, five were approached. Three refused. I have it on good authority the Ullans are under your protection. Why would that be? And what of the cargo you hired mercenaries to guard? Can you explain everything with a simple denial?"

Fuck and fuck. If they knew Ulla was under her protection, it could only be because Marissa had told someone and Lliandra didn't have to try hard to guess who. Even in death, Valterys was a pain in her backside. And if not Valterys, then Zakael, which could be even more problematic. Lliandra had sent Marissa to Ulla to prevent exactly this situation.

"Hypothetically speaking, if the other kingdoms refused, then why are Danuri and the Summerlands being exploited? Why didn't they refuse as well?" Lliandra sat upright, her spine as straight as a sword blade. She kept calm, her voice a flutter of uncertainty despite the strength of her pose. If she could unbalance them, they would question their sources and right now, she needed them to believe her over a piece of paper.

Prateeni's eldest son Jayved leaned forward, his jaw clenched in a rigid line. "We did and were told if we didn't pay the extra taxes, our goods would be dumped in the ocean."

Lliandra hid a smile. The simpletons had thought the threat true. *What idiots.* "Who told you this? Who was the agent who contacted you? Certainly it wasn't me, was it?"

Jayved's confident sneer brightened. "It was the next best thing—your daughter."

Lliandra executed a perfectly shocked expression. "My daughter? Why, she's sitting right here. Let's ask her."

"Not Eliahnna, Your Majesty. The late crown princess, Marissa."

Hearing the name was a stab to her heart. No one in Talaith had so much as whispered Marissa's name since her death. The mourning she wore on her expression was true.

"You seek to besmirch her name when you know she can't defend herself." Lliandra sniffed and wiped a tear from her eye. "How hurtful you are. All of you. I don't know anything about these taxes and yet you claim I'm complicit with wrongdoings of my dead daughter."

"What of the illegal cargo you brought to your docks? The mercenaries guarding it were hired by you. Do you deny this as well?" Hayden, her sweet, stupid nephew spoke up.

Lliandra turned her tear streaked face to Hayden. "I know we've had our troubles in the past, and I would hate to think your heart is being swayed by these lies. You know me. I'm your mother's sister. Do you honestly believe I would smuggle contraband into my own harbor?"

Hayden met her stare with his own. "I think that's precisely what you'd do. What better excuse? Of course, no one would suspect the empress of smuggling goods into her own harbor. You're smarter than all of them, aren't you, Aunt Lliandra?"

"I don't like your tone, young man." She didn't like any of this. Politics were tedious. She'd known it was a bad idea to tax the other kingdoms, but Marissa had insisted. Said it was an insurance policy for when Taryn returned. Well, now Taryn had returned, and Lliandra was cleaning up another of Marissa's messes.

"And I don't like your lies, Empress." Faisal pressed his hands together and spread his fingertips wide. He tapped his upper lip with his forefingers, an exasperating habit she'd seen him do on several occasions. "Do you deny hiring mercenaries to guard cargo shipped to your harbor?"

Lliandra sank into her chair, a defeated sigh escaping her lips. She'd let them think they won for now. "I heard rumors of brigands raiding honest merchants and I hired mercenaries to guard my docks, not stolen goods. They were to patrol the harbor and if they found any suspicious activity, they were to report it to the captain of my guard. That's all."

"What of the weapons from Haversham?" Lord Darrew asked and all eyes turned to him. "The Artagh have purchase orders with your signature on them. Are these forged as well?"

"Of course they are." *They knew about the weapons as well?* She slumped lower, her head pounding with plans that must be made, egos soothed, tongues silenced. "I don't know how or why these taxes were put into place, but I assure you, I did not order them. What treaties must I sign to prove this? How can we conclude this terrible business and start anew?" She turned her attention to Hayden and Sabina, a warm smile reaching her eyes. "We have a joyous wedding to celebrate in a few weeks. Two great Houses will be joined for all time. Let's focus on something other than politics."

"I would like that," Sabina admitted. "This business with taxes is ever so tedious. Perhaps an audit of your treasury will appease the kingdoms?"

"If you think that will help, then of course, once we're returned to Talaith, it will be done."

"Good." Faisal leaned back in his chair, a goblet in his hands. "Because we've already sent ambassadors from the Summerlands and Danuri to do just that. They should be finished by the end of this week."

The bastards. Honestly, she didn't think they had it in them. No matter. They wouldn't find anything out of the ordinary in her treasury. She wasn't that stupid. "And how, exactly, are they to gain entrance to my ledgers?"

"Oh, they'll wait for your written authorization before combing through your accounts, Your Majesty. Right now, they're starting with—"

A door burst open and Myrddin rushed through, his robes swirling around him like a midnight tempest. "Sorry, sorry. I was distracted and lost track of the time. What have I missed?"

A swirl of hatred rose from Lliandra's depths, surprising her in its intensity. When she'd found out Myrddin was bedding Marissa, she'd ranted for near on a bell, but the old mage had ignored her outburst. They had no bond, he'd said, no vows saying he was beholden only to her. It was the truth, yet it still stung. She'd not yet forgiven him for the betrayal. He could bed anyone he wished, but not Marissa. The jealous rivalry between mother and daughter was too strong, too easily swayed by their bedmates. At least now she no longer need worry if her daughter would steal her men.

Outwardly, the empress smiled lovingly to Myrddin, who was shaking hands with the Danurian. Inwardly, she mourned the loss of his confidence and missed the warmth of his body in her bed. Since Marissa's death, when he'd felt obliged to share his illicit affair with Lliandra, he'd kept his distance and the truth was —even through her anger, Lliandra loved him more than she'd ever loved anyone.

"It seems all is in order then. Lliandra's agreed to your terms,

Danuri should be happy, the Summerlands as well. What more needs to be done?" Myrddin sat with a flourish and reached for a bottle of wine.

A servant appeared from nowhere to pour the drink into a waiting glass. The lad was naught more than ten, and his willowy arms could barely hold the bottle aloft. She peered closer at the lad, trying to discern any similarities to King Faisal. She'd heard that Faisal was steadfast in his commitment to Prateeni and never had other lovers. It was ludicrous to think a monarch would be faithful. Even more so to believe the king could have several bastards around the palace, all working for him.

Perhaps Lliandra would start a rumor that in truth he'd slept with many women, including the luscious vixen who waited in her rooms. Another pinch to her nethers made her impatient to be done with the council.

"Well, Lliandra?" Myrddin asked, a spark of mirth in his eyes.

"Well what?" She'd been daydreaming of her maid's hands and talented fingers.

"If we draw up a proclamation absolving you of the illegal taxations, will you sign a treaty attesting to the fact you will tax each kingdom fairly and the same for their goods? Also, will you send a missive to Ulla nullifying any special protection they shared with Talaith?"

If it meant she could leave the stuffy room and be naked with the woman in her rooms, she'd sign anything.

"Yes, of course. I've told you, I am innocent of these charges, but if you feel the need to make a proclamation, then do what you must. Now, if you'll excuse me, I need to lay down."

Lliandra turned to Eliahnna, who'd barely moved during the proceedings, and said, "Darling, I trust you will make sure the documents are worded in our favor?"

Startled, Eliahnna glanced up. "Yes, Mother. I'll read them carefully."

Lliandra placed a palm on Eliahnna's cheek. This girl was the dullest of all her brood. The one Lliandra thought least likely to rule. But here they were, with her third daughter now the crown princess. Where had she gone so wrong?

Before she could delve deeper into that particular wound, she smiled. "I know you will. Bring them to my rooms when they are complete and we'll sign them together."

Another startled look followed by a nod was Eliahnna's answer.

Lliandra made quick work of saying her farewells, doing her best to ignore the man at the end of the table. The Danurian had an air about him that unnerved her and she couldn't say why. Perhaps before he left, Lliandra would bed him. Men were so easily manipulated when they had their cocks to focus on. She stifled a giggle as she imagined his hardened rod the color of his lips—a lovely shade of purple that begged to be sucked.

That tantalizing pleasure would have to wait. First, she needed her own release. It had been too long since anyone excited her the way the dark-skinned Summerlands maid did. Even as she hurried down the hall, she felt herself getting wet in anticipation.

It was all she could do not to run to her rooms, and when Tarro stepped into her path, she nearly knocked him over. He mumbled an apology and she waved him off. Taryn had insisted the tailor's assistant should join them on the journey and he brought his gorgeous lover Armando with him. She'd rarely seen Armando at the palace, though, which was a shame. The whore was one of Nena's best and Lliandra had hoped he'd be working while on holiday.

The gods were good to her this morning. She glanced up to gaze into the deep brown eyes of her past lover. "Armando." She said the word as if she licked his cock. Her eyes traveled to his lower regions, only to be halted by the face of a baby. "What in Ohlin's name is that?"

Armando beamed and held the child closer. "My son, Percival."

It took all of her will not to spit at the thing. It couldn't have been more than a moonturn old. "A son? Why ever would you want one of those?"

Armando's laugh held not an ounce of bitterness. It was light and free, which confused Lliandra.

"I would've been equally as happy with a daughter, but the gods blessed me with Percival."

Lliandra snapped a glance to Tarro. "And you approve of this folly?"

Tarro took the sleeping babe in his arms and rocked him while cooing gentle words. "I do. This child is a gift."

Lliandra shook her head. She'd never understand why people chose to have children. "Then I suppose congratulations are in order." She waved to bade them farewell before they offered to let her hold the thing. It was all she could do not to shudder at the thought.

At the sight of the child, her lustful cravings had waned, but the thought of her maid reignited the fires of her womb. Lliandra hurried to her rooms and entered the darkened space. She clucked at the lack of candles. Curtains were drawn across the windows to keep the rooms cool in the insidious heat, but it didn't mean they had to live like moles beneath the ground.

A maid entered, not the wench who brought Lliandra massive pleasure, but another, unknown woman.

"Who are you? Where's the other girl?"

The maid lowered her eyes and scurried from the room, mumbling too low for the empress to hear. She searched the rooms, finding them empty, save for two of her ladies. The eldest glanced up to nod at Lliandra before continuing with reading by the flicker of a candle.

"Where is everyone?"

"Trying to stay cool, ma'am."

Lliandra insisted her ladies wear appropriate Talaithian fashions and not the skimpy pieces of fluff the Summerlands women romped about in.

"What about the maids?"

The women looked at each other before shrugging. "They're the queen's business, I suppose."

"Fetch Marissa for me."

A dual gasp came from her ladies. One of them opened her mouth to speak, but Lliandra held up a hand for silence. The words had flowed naturally past her lips before she'd had time to think.

Heartache so raw it twisted her gut moved up to her lungs. Tears stung the backs of her eyes, burning in their intensity.

She couldn't break down. Not here. Not with her ladies watching. Not in Prateeni's palace.

Lliandra spun and left the room with a swish of heavy fabric. She sped down a darkened hallway until she reached an open courtyard. Before she had time to think, she created a wind tunnel and hurled herself into the vortex. She had no idea where to go, only that her heart ached and she was tired of being alone.

Only one person in all of Aelinae could understand her anguish. With winds whipping past, she pictured the face of the one man she swore to never again beg for comfort.

CHAPTER SIXTEEN

Zakael stretched his boots upon the table, admiring his reflection. This new servant was skilled at his work in more ways than one. He rubbed his crotch until the erection became painful. Then he rubbed even harder, imagining the lad's face as he fucked him. *Yes, the new servant would do nicely,* Zakael mused to himself. *Being king definitely had its perks.*

Not that being the son to the overlord wasn't without its niceties, but as king—Zakael let the word roll across his tongue—as king, he wasn't questioned. His every demand was met with scraping and bowing. No one dared tell his father what he'd been up to because Valterys was dead. If the servants didn't like King Zakael's behavior, they were free to leave.

His hand pressed down until the ache became almost unbearable.

Of course, any servant who left Zakael's employ would find themselves locked in his dungeons. If nothing else, the new king honored loyalty—from his subjects and servants.

Just a moment more...

A flash of lightning smashed against his balcony and Zakael fell backward, tumbling out of his chair. A flagon of cider toppled, soaking papers he'd set aside to read later. A curse was on his lips as he sprang upward, murderous rage etched across his face. He knew of only one woman idiotic enough to make such an entry.

Yet the vision that materialized from the tempest wasn't Marissa.

"Lliandra?" Zakael asked, half-expecting a ghost to answer.

"Zakael." The empress threw herself at him and buried her face against his neck. Her sobs wet his skin in a not unappealing way.

He wrapped his arms around his past lover and shuttled his anger to the side. "What is it? What's caused you to come here?" *Uninvited*, he wished to say, but held back. It had been at least twenty seasons since they'd had any sort of civil discourse.

"I miss her. I miss my daughter, and I knew you were the only one who would understand." Lliandra pressed against him and found his still elongated cock. Her skirts made a soft swishing as she rocked back and forth, teasing him.

The touch of her lips at the base of his throat, the sounds of fabric scraping leather, and the scent of her arousal undid him. He should've cast her out. Should've told her to leave and never return. Should've forbidden her from mentioning Marissa ever again in his presence. Yet he did none of these things.

Zakael tilted her face to his and claimed her mouth with his own. Lliandra's sharp gasp spiked straight to his dick. Her tongued rallied to his—hot, wet, inviting. With one hand, he unfastened his breeches, while with the other he gathered her skirts. Lliandra's hands fumbled with his and in a matter of moments, his cock was free. She gripped it like a levon its prey and for one mad second, he envisioned him the mouse and she the bird.

"Not likely," he growled and shoved her backward until her spine met the wall.

A surprised "Oof," and widened eyes gave her an innocence

she didn't deserve. Still, those gorgeous blue orbs of hers watched him with a wariness he quite enjoyed.

Lliandra had never liked it rough. At least, not as rough as Zakael craved. He could've taken her a multitude of ways, each one more violent than the first, but he didn't. Out of sentiment perhaps, he lifted her gently until her hips were even with his own. She wrapped her legs around his waist, a wildness playing across her features.

Features she used her power to mask into youthful beauty.

He guided his cock into her a finger's width at a time. He wouldn't be violent, but he could still be cruel. A snarl twisted his lips. He'd make her beg, like she'd done to him all those seasons ago—when she'd lost the baby and blamed him. Then demanded they try again too soon and told the court he'd beaten her senseless.

Zakael thrust into her. Lliandra's head knocked against the wall and she whimpered. His snarl snaked into a smile. She could pretend innocence all she liked. He knew her heart was made of pitch.

Again, he slammed hard. Again and again until he was panting as heavy as she. No further whimpers came from her lips, only cries of delight. He pulled out, only leaving the tip touching her soft, womanly lips.

"More, Zakael. More."

"More what, my lady?" The last two words were said with venom, but the empress didn't notice, or ignored him.

"Please. Dear gods above, release me."

"Beg for it." Zakael nudged her vaginal walls with his cock.

"Yes, please. Please Zakael. Fuck me. Now." Her eyes darted from his face to his chest and back, the wildness full of pleading.

He could leave her there, pinned to his wall, on the cusp of her release. He could call his new servant and force Lliandra to stay still while Zakael took his pleasure. It would please him immensely to watch her face as he fucked another man. The image brought to mind a night not so long ago when he'd made Marissa observe him with Eiric. At the memory, he almost lost control of himself.

Zakael slid into Lliandra, the night of fucking he'd had with his sweet Eiric fresh in his mind. The cries and sobs from Marissa playing like a melody in his ears. He'd loved her that night. As much as he could love anyone, that night he'd given her something special.

His thoughts skittered dangerously close to thinking of his one true love. He careened his attention back to the moment, where Lliandra was gasping, her hands clawing at his hair, his chest, his buttocks.

"Yes, yes. Harder. Hurt me, Zakael."

His shaft throbbed with an ache to be released. *Not yet.*

He liked this side of Lliandra. Liked hearing her call his name. Liked being in control.

Zakael snaked a hand up to her neck and stretched his fingertips around the delicate skin. For the briefest of moments, Lliandra's eyes held terror. He shushed her and shoved his tongue into her hot mouth. She gasped and sucked him farther into her warmth. When he sensed she was about to crest, he gave her throat a vicious squeeze that sent Lliandra over the edge.

She cried out loud enough to wake the entire castle and shuddered against the wall. Her head banged again and again as she thrashed, pushing her pelvis into him, locking her legs tighter around his waist. Zakael reached beneath her skirts and shoved three fingers inside her pulsating vagina. The feel of his slick cock, and the sensations of her vibrations undid him. His seed streamed into her womb.

An awkward silence engulfed them. Zakael withdrew from the empress and adjusted his flaccid dick into his breeches while she straightened her skirts first, then hair.

"Thank you." Lliandra placed a hand on his forearm, her look earnest.

A smart quip came to his lips, but he bit it back. "You're welcome."

It was the most kind they'd ever been to each other. Perhaps it was a start.

"Can I offer you some wine? Are you hungry?"

She shook her head, her eyes scanning the room. "I see you've redecorated."

"It's been four decades since you were here with Valterys. A lot has changed."

A wry smile wound its way up her lips. "I suppose so." Lliandra reclined on a sofa and put a hand over her eyes. "Everything is changing and there's nothing we can do to stop it, is there?"

Zakael's snort was followed by a low chuckle. "You and I both know you're doing everything in your power to stop her." He still couldn't say Taryn's name. Not yet. Not this soon after rutting with the empress.

"I don't know what you mean." Her hand hadn't moved, but Zakael felt the pierce of her glare.

For a moment, he studied her—from the forced casual posture to the way her slipper-clad toes flitted back and forth.

"Let's not play games, Lliandra." Despite her refusal, he poured her a glass of wine. He could call for food, but that would mean his new servant would see the empress in his rooms, and despite his fetish, that was a complication he didn't need. "Here, you'll feel better."

She eyed the wine before gripping the goblet in both hands. "This isn't some of your father's wretched stock, is it?"

His father's tastes ran a bit too organic for Zakael. "I assure you, it's not."

Lliandra took a tentative sip, then another. "Not bad. You've improved much over the last few seasons."

He ignored the slight. She had no idea how much he'd improved, and in areas she'd never begin to guess.

"Do you miss her?"

Zakael knew who Lliandra meant, but his thoughts went to her other daughter. To Taryn.

He struggled to find something kind to say about Marissa. "Do I miss her deceptions? No. Do I miss her body wrapped around mine? At times." Lliandra's lips pursed and he continued, "Don't pretend you know nothing of what your daughter was up to." Zakael indicated the lavish room that once belonged to his father. "She manipulated all of us. Her plans didn't stop at ruling."

Tears shimmered in Lliandra's eyes and Zakael stopped himself from saying more. His heart beat triple time and his jaw tensed. Remembering Marissa was dangerous.

"I refuse to believe she manipulated you. From what I heard, you were equally as keen to be rid of the abomination."

"Is that what she told you? That I wanted to kill Taryn?" His laugh tore through the tension in the room. "You honestly have no idea, do you?" A sliver of compassion wormed its way into his heart. The expression Lliandra wore was genuine confusion.

"What are you talking about? I know you and Valterys were planning to muster an army and attack Talaith. I know you lured my daughter to your bed to get revenge on me."

Zakael held his breath for fear of blowing fire. Marissa had twisted everything to her favor. It shouldn't have surprised him, yet it did.

"I know you were planning to usurp my agreement with the Ullans—most likely to attack either Paderau, or the Narthvier."

The last was a guess. Zakael's need for the Ullans had nothing to do with attacking other kingdoms.

"Please, continue, what else do you know?"

Lliandra lay back, a hand once more covering her eyes. "Please, Zakael. This is tedious business and I've had a difficult day. What will it take to be your ally once more?"

"Allies? Is that what you thought we were? I used you, Lliandra. Just as Valterys did. Just as Marissa would keep doing if she hadn't gotten herself killed."

Lliandra sat up so quickly, she spilled wine on her gown. He knew she was angry by the fact that she ignored the stain on the expensive fabric.

"Marissa died saving Eliahnna. Don't you ever besmirch her again."

His laugh echoed off the paintings and tapestries hanging on the walls. The sound was oddly satisfying.

"Is that what they told you?" He poured himself a goblet of wine and drank it all before refilling the vessel. Lliandra said nothing, but kept a close watch on his movements. "Marissa wasn't trying to save anyone but herself. *She's* the reason Eliahnna was at the temple in the first place."

A crack of lightning struck the balcony outside his open windows. The sound of stone falling reverberated with each tumble. Zakael's gaze went from the ruined balcony to the empress. She really didn't know. His sparse compassion had run its course.

"You'll pay for that, Empress. And before you decide to destroy any more of my castle, remember, I am the King of the West now. My powers are equal to your own."

Lliandra stood and paced the room. Sparks lit from her fingertips and Zakael pulled his ShantiMari close like a protective shield.

"You always were a troublesome cur. Bedding Marissa after your time with me. Did you think you could make another Eirielle? Is that it?"

"After you?" Zakael's laughter grew until he had to set down his goblet for fear of spilling the wine. When he'd collected himself, he looked to Lliandra with pity in his eyes. "I've been rutting with Marissa since the night after Taryn's birth. She was seventeen seasons, if I'm not mistaken. It was you who came after."

"You lie."

"You didn't know your daughter at all, did you?" He picked up his goblet and emptied it in one long gulp. His thoughts muddied with the amount of spirits he'd had, but still he refilled his cup. *Damn Lliandra, coming to his home and bringing up memories he'd tried for a quarter century to bury.*

"I suppose you're going to tell me Marissa ordered the attack on my ships." Lliandra, hands on hips, challenged him like a fishwife asking after her husband's whereabouts.

"No," Zakael intoned, already growing bored with the discussion. "I did."

Her hands dropped to her sides. She stared at him like he'd grown a vorlock head in place of his own.

"You? Why?" Her pacing resumed, as did the sparks from her fingertips.

He could've told her all manner of falsehoods. Instead, he opted for the truth. "I had to break Taryn's bond with Rhoane. It's the only way to defeat her. Marissa tried at Gaarendahl—"

"What do you mean, she tried?" The sparks subsided and Lliandra's features took on a look of interest.

Zakael situated himself at his desk, his legs outstretched. If Lliandra truly wished to know, this would take some time. He downed the rest of his wine and refilled the goblet before offering more to Lliandra. She held up a hand and motioned for him to continue.

"It was Marissa's idea to lure Rhoane to Gaarendahl. There, she seduced him—while under the guise of Taryn. Unfortunately, his betrothed walked in on them, shall we say, before the deed was done."

"She raped Rhoane?"

"That's such a vulgar way of putting it. He didn't seem to mind. In fact, he finished the job even after Taryn discovered them."

"That's why they went to the Narthvier. And why they were

both so angry afterwards." Lliandra spoke in a hushed tone, as if the ghost of Marissa might hear and be displeased. "She should've told me."

The puzzle pieces were falling into place for Zakael. "She couldn't tell you because she was with child."

Lliandra's eyes flashed and the sparks returned to her fingertips. "Impossible. I would've known."

This time his laughter was forced mockery. "I've already told you—there is more you don't know about your favorite daughter than what you do." He set his goblet down and stood to face her. In his rooms, she looked small, easily beaten. Yet he knew not to underestimate the empress. His fingertips stroked the edge of her chin. His thumb pulled at her lower lip.

"Stop it."

"Why? Because you want me again? Or because you don't like hearing the truth?"

Her eyes became flecks of blue granite. "I don't appreciate being lied to. If Marissa was with child, where is the baby now?"

It would be nothing for him to tell the empress the child lived in Talaith, but he would keep the information to himself. He might need the leverage someday and if Lliandra got to the child first, he'd be left with nothing.

"Died. At the temple the same night as Marissa."

"My granddaughter...dead?"

"Grandson." He could at least give her that much comfort. Lliandra would've rejected a grandson.

Relief eased the tension of her brows. "You said it was Marissa's idea to take Eliahnna to the temple. Why?"

He flicked his tongue over her lips, tasting wine and salty remnants of her tears. "To sacrifice her to Rykoto. He was almost strong enough to be released."

A shiver of excitement danced over his skin as he recalled the way Taryn had looked that night. Sword held high, her face serene as she made the fatal stroke that beheaded Valterys. His cock jumped and a moan escaped his lips.

Zakael cleared his throat and stepped away from Lliandra. Being near her scent overwhelmed his better judgment. "Taryn stopped the sacrifice and killed Valterys. Marissa arrived right after. The shock of seeing her lover murdered was too much. She miscarried and died from a broken heart, I suppose." It sounded romantic when phrased that way, but Zakael knew the gritty details about the child's birth.

"Was—" Lliandra choked on the words. "Was the child Valterys's?"

"Does it matter?" His palm rubbed against his pelvis. "They're all dead. The child, Valterys, Marissa. We can mourn them all our lives, but it won't bring them back. Or," he stepped close enough to nip the lobe of her ear, "we can forge new alliances."

"Stop it." She pushed him hard enough he stumbled backward three steps. "Stop this madness, Zakael. I know you're lying. You must be. Marissa would never betray me."

Another flash of lightning crossed the clear sky. Zakael looked from it to Lliandra.

"Am I lying when I tell you Marissa was scheming with not just myself, but with my father, and also Rykoto? She had agreements with all three of us, and none of them included you. She was a grasping, power-hungry bitch."

The slap from Lliandra's open palm stung his cheek and rattled his teeth. Thunderstorms rolled over the castle and a moment later, a deluge poured through his open windows.

Zakael called on his power and wrapped a thread of Shanti-Mari around the empress, tightening the cord until her eyes bulged and her mouth popped open and closed like a fish. It was only a portion of the power allotted to him since taking the crown. In her struggles against his dark Shanti, he felt her waning strength. His threads held her paralyzed and blocked what little Mari she had left.

"You're fading, Lliandra. We both know it. I saw you on the ship, when your power was blocked and you couldn't wear your mask of youthful beauty." He scraped a finger down her cheek, delighting in the tiny whimpers that came from her useless mouth.

"How. Dare. You."

"Shhhh. Now, now. Does anyone know you're here? Hmm?" At the widening of her eyes, he chuckled. "I thought not." His thumb traced her lips. "I could throw you into my dungeons and no one would ever be the wiser. Or," he stepped behind her, out of her sight, "I could kill you and feed you to Rykoto."

"Please. No." The animosity had left her voice.

"He hungers for your bloodline. Eliahnna was to be his final meal as a prisoner. Just think what you could do for my god."

A dark stain hovered near the window and Zakael turned to see what made the odd shadow. The hazy outline of a man floated several feet from the floor.

"What in Ferran's be—" Zakael started, but silence swept over him. Something forced his words to still.

The thing hovered closer until inky tentacles of mist reached Zakael. He tried to step back, but couldn't move. A compulsion to obey, to kneel before the blot fought against his need to dominate. The blot moved closer, undoing the threads of ShantiMari that held Lliandra prisoner.

She sputtered and spun to heap curses upon Zakael, but froze at the sight of the hazy figure. A moment later, she knelt on the floor, her hands cupped over her face. Zakael heard her sobs, but was useless to do anything—comforting or otherwise. The thing had him as paralyzed as he'd made Lliandra only moments before.

He struggled against the compulsion, denying the blot. A battle raged inside his mind—to do as the thing suggested, and to break free of the hold and murder it. Surely his power was greater than a puff of mist? Yet, he couldn't grasp his power. Not that he was blocked from it, but more like his ShantiMari was coated in grease and kept slipping from his fingertips.

A frustrated groan ground out of his throat through his clenched lips and he twisted where he stood, trying in vain to break free.

A hiss came from the misty blot, then it split open, elongating to an enormous mouth. A shrill scream came from Lliandra, followed by a curse from Zakael.

The thing expanded until it enveloped them both and there was nothing—no sound, no light, no life.

When Zakael came to a few minutes later, revulsion churned in his gut and panic darted across his nerves.

He was alone in his rooms.

The black spot was nowhere to be seen. Neither was Lliandra. He wiggled his fingers, surprised and relieved to have control of his senses again. With a trembling heart, he searched the area, finding no signs of the empress, but scattered across the floor were tiny flecks of black glitter. Zakael bent and touched the sparkling dust with his fingertips. Anxiety crippled his thoughts and his head throbbed.

The substance wasn't new to him. He'd seen it twice before— once on Marissa's lady-in-waiting Celia, and once on Marissa. She'd laughed it off as nothing more than a fashion accessory, yet he'd always wondered. Finding traces of glitter in his rooms, on the same night Lliandra arrived uninvited and begged him to take her, made him more than wary.

Of the blot, his mind scrambled to find an answer. Once, in passing, Marissa had mentioned a phantom. As Zakael stood on his ruined balcony and searched the night sky, his hands shook uncontrollably. Few entities could command that much control over another. Zakael turned his attention to the north, where Rykoto was imprisoned.

The blot had appeared when Zakael threatened to feed Lliandra to the god.

His heart thudded against his ribs. The throbbing in his head worsened and blurred his vision.

He leaned against the balustrade and stared into the distance, not seeing the ocean or stars before him. Whatever the presence might be, it was gone, and it took Lliandra with it. She was no longer his problem.

Yet, he feared, his problems were just beginning.

CHAPTER SEVENTEEN

Taryn's screams woke Rhoane and he bolted upright, Claidholm Solais in his fist. He scanned the tent, using more than his senses to detect movement, but nothing stirred in the night. Taryn kicked at an unseen opponent, her face contorted in pain. Rhoane stroked her hair and whispered soothing words, but the nightmare continued. Sweat beaded on her brow and several tears squeezed between her tightly closed lids.

These were the nights he hated most. The times when he held her, comforted her, and yet still couldn't ease her troubled mind. He feared for the times he wasn't near. How terrible was the torment for her then?

"Taryn, wake up, mi carae. You are having a night fright." His lips trailed along hers. He tasted tears. "Whatever it is, tell me so your demons become mine."

She stirred, a small smile curling her lips.

"That is my girl. Do not let the terrors of darkness take you from me. Wake up to the light." He nuzzled her neck, inhaling the oil she'd applied before bed. Caerleon from the Narthvier. A mix of honeysuckle and gardenia. "You smell like Dal Tara."

"And you're getting sappy in your old age."

Relief surged through him like rain after a long drought. "What was it this time? Cashiel again?"

Taryn snuggled into his embrace and kissed beneath his jaw. "I wish. Those dreams at least I can fight back. This was something else. Elusive, but all-consuming. Like a disease spreading through Aelinae unseen until it's too late. I can't explain it, but what it did to you—" She finished the sentence with a violent shudder. Her fingers wound around his long hair and she rested her head on his chest. "That creature I fought tonight, he wasn't from Aelinae."

"How do you know?" There were many creatures that lived in the northern wastelands, and the jungles of the southwest. He could've been one of them, but Rhoane had never seen his kind.

"He let me into his mind. He was lonely, Rhoane. I think he let me kill him so he could be free of Amdi's abuse."

Rhoane let her words rest upon his thoughts before he replied. "If this is true, that means someone else has access to the portals." It was a fear he rarely acknowledged, but was always present.

"He wasn't from where I came, that's for sure." She propped her chin on her fist. Her steady gaze bore into him. "We need to find all the portals and either close them, or search them. What if someone's been bopping from here to there, hiding seals, stealing artifacts, and what if they've brought over other beasts? What if whoever it is has been gathering an army on another world?"

Fresh tears tracked over her smooth cheek. He brushed them away with his thumb. If only he could remove the threats facing them just as easily.

"Perhaps that is the unseen terror you dreamt of. We now have four mysteries to solve. How did Enghor come to be in Aelinae, what Yawn Saine Stroot is or means, what did the old crone mean about Mallaqai and a vortex, and Cashiel. Who is he, what does he truly want?"

"Five. We have a new mystery. Hayden tells me Lliandra denies any knowledge of the illegal taxes. For the record, I don't believe her, but whatever, and he says Ulla is under the protection of the Lady of Light."

"When did you speak with Hayden?" A strange tickle started in his belly, one of anxiety that he was coming to know well. She'd not been out of his sight since he'd arrived in Ulla.

A lovely rose bloomed across her cheekbones and she grinned. "I can see him sometimes. Like, I'm with him, but not. I know it doesn't make sense and please don't ask me how I do it, because I don't know. It's only happened a few times."

The tickle turned fuzzy and warm. "You have the gift of the ancients. You can project yourself over far distances without leaving where your physical body rests." The warmth grew to encompass all of him. This was part of her process.

"Well, whatever this gift is, it allowed me to talk to Hayden. They had a council in the Summerlands with some guy from the Danuri Province who swears Lliandra orchestrated the illegal taxes. What I'm more concerned about is, I doubt Lliandra would come to Ulla to make a deal with Amdi, so who did? I have my suspicions, of course."

"Marissa?" The warmth turned to spiky chills. How could he have been so blind to Marissa's machinations?

"Even in death she's a pain in the ass. You sensed her in Amdi's mind same as I did. She's been here, in Ulla. But what's her ultimate goal?" Taryn thumped Rhoane on the chest with her fingertips. "Tomorrow, we're going to have a showdown with Amdi."

Rhoane rolled her onto her back and covered her body with his. He stroked the sides of her face, smoothing away her tears. "That is not for many hours yet and you need sleep."

"Then why are you on top of me?" A cheeky grin lit up her face. "More of your sexual healing? A girl could get spoiled with all this attention, you know."

His knee nudged her legs apart and she obliged without hesitation. Her beauty took his breath—silver hair fanned over the pillow, her pale cheeks warming with a pink glow. He bent to take her lips between his at the same time he entered her. A soft moan filled his mouth—hers, mingling with his own. The pace he set was languid, more for pleasure than healing, but he made certain his ShantiMari infused her, healed her beyond flesh-and-bone injuries.

Taryn's hips bucked to meet his and she pulled his head close to hers. The heated kiss she gave him fueled the flame burning just below his sternum. He pumped faster, a sheen of perspiration covering his skin. Her power mingled with his, her body became his. They were one.

Darath nocht nardem. Ta'ay aken solven tirrn all daen holsvletten absolm. A dreamy expression came over her face. "We are one, my love. We are all."

The tent expanded until there was no tent, no Ullan encampment. They floated on a sea of stars, their bodies connected, yet as indistinct as a cloud. Below them, the terrarae gleamed golden in the moonlight. Jewels of blue and green glinted where the seas and oceans embraced the land. This was their fate.

"What is happening?" Fate or not, floating several leagues above the terrarae wasn't natural and he wasn't certain he liked it.

"I'm not sure. This happened to me the first time we made love. I think we're communing with the universe."

They drifted and she blended with the stars. She was his Taryn, but where flesh and bone should've been, he saw galaxies and other worlds. When he looked at his own hand, roots grew instead of veins. Where skin should've covered bone, leaves that looked like scales overlapped.

"When you commune with the universe, what does it tell you?"

"Everything and nothing." Her smile was a nebula of peachy-plum shades. "It still kind of freaks me out."

"I can see why." Rhoane gazed at the terrarae, at the waterfalls that showered into space. He could see the entirety of Aelinae from where they floated. "Are you not afraid of falling?"

She shook her head and stardust spread around them. Silvery motes of glitter lit up the space where they lingered. "I feel at peace here." She reached a fingertip toward one of the sparkles. "Someday, this might be a planet where new creatures live. Or this one, or this. I love the possibility that surrounds us."

Not for the first time, his heart beat with awe for this woman who'd come to Aelinae unprepared, but had better understood what the world needed than any of them.

"You are remarkable, my Darennsai."

"We are remarkable." She tapped the tip of his nose with her fingertip and the speck of glitter winked upon his skin.

They drifted down until they rested atop the many blankets laid out for their bed in the Ullan tent.

"I don't understand how I do it, but damn, it feels good."

"Agreed."

She flipped them over until she straddled him, her breasts teasingly close to his lips. He groaned and struggled to keep his ShantiMari firmly in place. Taryn knew full well how to please him most. His tongue lashed out and flicked a nipple, garnering a gasp from her. He met her fevered pace thrust for thrust, his hands gripping her breasts. Every so often, his thumb would drag across her hardened nub and she'd reward him with a moan and slight grinding of her hips into his pelvis.

They came undone together in a sea of sparks with Light and Dark, Eleri and Telraicht-Noir ShantiMari cascading over his senses. He sucked it in, held onto her power like a greedy child to a bit of candy.

She collapsed on his chest, her own heaving with labored breaths. "I'm out of shape. That was like running a marathon."

"You have had a busy few days. Sleep now. You need rest." He settled her beside him, her head cradled in the crook of his neck.

Within moments, she was sleeping peacefully, her soft breath tickling him.

Rhoane lay awake long after she slept, his thoughts as tangled as the roots of a vine. Taryn's presence was expanding beyond her physical body. He'd hoped they'd have more time together before she made the final changes, but with how quickly she was adapting, he feared times like this would be lost too soon.

He kissed the top of her head, breathing in her scent. It would have to be enough. This scant amount of time he'd have with her—it would have to sustain him for the remainder of his mortal life.

Yet, Verdaine called him Surtentse, and he'd drifted through the stars with Taryn.

Rhoane shook the thought from his mind. He was never meant to become a god. That was Taryn's fate, and hers alone.

He held up a hand and studied his skin in the dim light. Unremarkable. No roots traveled where veins should be. No buds sprouted from his fingertips. No leaf-like scales covered his arms. Rhoane closed his eyes and drifted in an uneasy sleep. Images of Aelinae past, present, and future settled in his mind. Rhoane's past, present, and future became one with Aelinae's.

Taryn was Darennsai, daughter of the sky and he was Surtentse, son of the terrarae. Two parts of the same whole. Without him, she would fail.

Rhoane curled around her body, taking her warmth into his chilled skin.

Without her, he would cease to exist.

With that realization, Rhoane understood their purpose. Together, they were the sun and moon and stars. They were the soil and water and lifeforms of the terrarae. They were life.

In his hazy dream state, Rhoane reflected to Amdi's speech in the tent when he rattled off Rhoane's accomplishments since he'd lived with the laird. Panic struck like an asp and he flopped to his back. He stared at the top of the tent, his mind whirling. Much of what Amdi had said were outright lies or exaggerations of the truth. It was the latter that startled Rhoane awake. Only someone with intimate knowledge of his life could've given the laird that information.

His chest heaved with renewed fury. To what end did Marissa lie and deceive? Surely not for the crown, then what? The shadowy form of the phantom came to mind and Rhoane shivered against the memory of seeing Taryn blast it into tiny fragments. They'd all thought the phantom was defeated after the events at the Stones. Rhoane's nerves vibrated and the hairs on his arms stood to attention with a radical notion.

In the morning, he'd speak with Taryn about it. He rolled to his side and wrapped Taryn protectively in his arms. If his misgivings held even a sliver of truth, it could change everything.

Just after daybreak, his plans were thwarted when they were woken by one of Amdi's servants informing them the laird requested their presence for breakfast. Taryn rolled out of the blankets in no hurry to appease the man, but Rhoane dressed with purpose. The sooner they had their answers from Amdi, the sooner they could leave Ulla. Rhoane didn't want to address his midnight suspicions while under the laird's watch.

The servant led them to a tent filled with golden candelabra flickering with hundreds of candles. Dishes of gold and silver shone on every surface. Wooden chests, stained a rich mahogany, lined the walls of his tent, a testament to Amdi's wealth and prestige. Food was laid out on a low table where Kaleigh, her two sons, and Amdi awaited their arrival. At their approach, Kaleigh stood while the men remained seated. Only after Taryn took her place did the Eleri woman resume her seat.

They made small talk while breaking their fast and Rhoane hid his impatience to be away from the laird. Finally, after nearly a bell and several courses, a thick black drink was poured and Amdi sat back, inhaling the bitter scent.

"Have you tried this? It is new, from the west. A Danurian

merchant brought it to us not more than three seasons past. He said he found it north of the province in a small town. The villagers there had discovered it by accident."

Taryn sniffed the drink, and her nose crinkled. She took a small sip and set the cup down.

"You do not like it?"

"Not really. Do you have any sugar and milk to add to it? That might make it more palatable."

"Most guests would be honored to dine with me in my tent. They would drink horse piss if I served it to them. Yet you turn your nose at my offering."

Taryn faced the laird and Rhoane braced for conflict.

"In case you haven't noticed, I'm not most people. If you served me horse piss, I would think you're trying to offend me and I would neither drink it, nor feel honored. I'd be pissed. No pun intended."

Amdi barked out a laugh, startling his wife and sons. "I want to despise you, but I find I cannot. You aren't what I was told to expect."

Rhoane and Taryn shared a glance. He saw the rose flush creep up her neck, the tightness of her lips.

"What were you told, and by whom?" Rhoane asked.

Amdi dragged his gaze from Taryn to answer. "I was warned an Aelan girl, a false prophet, would one day show up in my kingdom and she would be the ruin of all that is Ullan."

"Care to share who gave you this news?" Rhoane had his suspicions. He hated that his friendship with Marissa had blinded him for too long.

Amdi fidgeted against his pillows and took a long drag of his drink, stalling. Rhoane sipped the dark liquid and grimaced. It would indeed be better with milk and sugar. The acrid bitterness settled on his tongue with unwelcome permanence.

"Let me guess. It was the crown princess of Talaith, wasn't it?" Taryn snorted at the hostile glare Amdi shot her. "Whatever story she told you, you believed in its entirety. Don't be ashamed. Marissa was very good at deceiving people."

A pit formed in Rhoane's gut. The same seed of disgust and guilt he nurtured every time Taryn mentioned Marissa's name. Except now it had more resonance. Now he understood how far Marissa would go to achieve her ambitions. Rhoane slipped a thread of ShantiMari into Amdi's thoughts. He knew the laird would never give him the truth and needed to know the extent of Marissa's deceit.

Taryn's gaze slid over the two young men and Rhoane swallowed his anxiety. He knew what she would say next.

"I'll bet she loved you." Taryn pointed to the tattooed Loghan. "What did she tell you? She was injured on her travels? Or did you even need an excuse to bed her?"

Loghan's ears turned pink and his jaw clenched.

Beside him, Gwainne steamed. "You bedded her? You took an oath."

"It was before I made my final vows." Loghan fidgeted with his robes, his gaze refusing to meet Gwainne's. "It was not for pleasure. There were internal issues that needed addressing."

"Don't blame yourselves. Marissa was an expert at seducing men. With or without their permission." Taryn waved a hand as if batting their blame aside.

A wave of sadness crashed against Rhoane's guilt. It came from his betrothed. As much as she tried to forget what Marissa had done, it would never truly be forgotten. The pit of self-loathing threatened to enlarge and swallow him whole if he let it. Instead, he reached his fingers to enclose hers within. She gave a slight squeeze and kept them in his grasp.

If she could forgive him, perhaps one day he could forgive himself as well.

"Did you also bed the crown princess?" Kaleigh asked, her eyes downcast.

She didn't name Amdi, didn't need to. Everyone knew who she meant.

"No, he did not." Rhoane answered for the laird. "She tried, but he denied her."

Rhoane stole the memory from the laird. It hadn't been easy for him to refuse Marissa, but Rhoane wouldn't tell Kaleigh how close Amdi had come to succumbing. It was Marissa's Aelan taint that had prevented him from soiling himself with her. His hatred of Aelans went deeper than Rhoane had ever guessed. He pressed further into the laird's mind to uncover the reason why.

Kaleigh glanced up, relief in her sad eyes. "Is this true?"

"It is." Amdi turned his ire to Rhoane. "I'll thank you to stay out of my thoughts."

Rhoane scrubbed a hand over his face, exhausted from constantly being on edge around the laird. "We need answers and I am hoping you will be honest with us. We know Ulla is under the Lady of Light's protection. What did Marissa promise you?"

"You might as well tell us everything." Taryn gave a half shrug. "I'll pull it from your mind if you don't. And I won't be gentle."

Rhoane felt Taryn's ShantiMari snuggle up to his. She'd been in the laird's mind as well. He hid a smile while his heart bloomed with pride.

"You allow your woman to speak to me like this? You've brought dishonor to your Ullan family, Rhoane ap Glennwoods."

"Taryn speaks her mind because she is a free woman. She is not mine, any more than Kaleigh is yours. You do not own women, Amdi. They are not trinkets to be played with and tossed aside when you tire of them. If only you would see their value, you would be a much better ruler."

Amdi's face puffed and reddened until Rhoane thought he might actually explode. Spittle formed at the corners of his lips. Kaleigh reached across the table to hold his hands, but he swatted her away.

Taryn heaved a frustrated sigh and Rhoane stood to go. "This is pointless. He is not going to tell us anything we do not already know. We do not have time for this. If he wants to ruin the Ullans, that is his problem."

"Sit down, boy." Amdi was frothing now, his anger all-consuming. He sat with legs crossed, their vibrations strong enough to shake the table. "You'll go nowhere until I say you can leave."

"You are not my laird. Ferran's bells, you are barely their laird." Rhoane pointed to Amdi's sons and wife, then toward the rest of the encampment. "I know why you are so angry. It is because you are fading. Your power is lessening and you are frightened. But that does not give you the right to force yourself on virgins or hold people against their will."

"You watch your words, boy. I am a great leader. My name will be remembered for generations to come."

"For what? Being the biggest jerk in the world?" Taryn stood beside Rhoane, her arms folded across her chest.

Amdi sprang to his feet and faced them. "I have done a great many things during my reign. I have—"

"Name three," Rhoane challenged. He was tired of Amdi's baseless claims.

Kaleigh covered a cough with her drink. A smile hid behind the mug.

Amdi stammered and bellowed, spouting insignificant achievements he'd made. It was nothing more than any tyrant would do to protect his crown. Ulla needed drastic change and either Amdi would rise to the challenge, or let his kingdom fall. A terrible realization sprang to Rhoane's mind.

The empress was hoping Amdi would fail. Counted on it, even. That's why Ulla was under her protection. Amdi would never accept his fade, in fact he would fight it and deny it long after he should step down and allow Gwainne to rule. Ulla would descend into chaos and that's when Lliandra would step in to clean up the mess. Now with Marissa gone and Lliandra fading, Rhoane had little doubt Zakael would be only too happy to make Amdi his puppet ruler in the east. It was time Ulla made a stand for itself and to do that, the kingdom needed strong leadership.

Rhoane held up a hand to stop Amdi's rambling. "Have you bettered the Ullans' lives? Have you given them anything to hope for? A future worth fighting for? You live in tents, Amdi. You travel over the desert not to survive, but because that's how it has always been. Long ago, the Ullans were nomadic to follow the herds and crops. Times have changed. Build cities. Educate your people. Train them to use their ShantiMari for more than healing."

Taryn gripped Rhoane's hand and her power thrummed with his. These were the words he'd longed to tell Amdi all those seasons ago when he'd suffered at the laird's behest.

"Amdi," Taryn began, her voice low, full of concern. "Just because it's how you've always done something doesn't mean it's right."

"The crown princess was right—you wish to destroy the Ullans. I was wise to accept her protection."

"You were a fool, but I do not blame you." Rhoane turned to Taryn. "There is no more to discuss here. He will not listen to reason."

Taryn pivoted to leave. "You're right. This is a waste of time."

Rhoane faced Gwainne and Kaleigh. "Will you at least consider what I have said? Ulla could be a great kingdom with a flourishing trade spanning all the way to the west. You have much more than horses to barter. You always have." He hoped his meaning was not lost on Kaleigh.

Neither answered, but then, he hadn't expected them to.

"What happened to the boy who lived with us for three seasons?" Amdi wavered on shaky legs, the spittle on his lips dripping over his chin. "That boy was full of fire and never backed from a fight. You've become complacent, Rhoane. Letting this dhur fight your battles, it's repugnant."

Taryn opened her mouth to speak, but Rhoane shook his head and her lips snapped shut. She was upset, he could feel it in his cynfar, but this was not her argument to win.

"The only thing repugnant here is you. That boy, as you call him, matured. I traveled Aelinae and learned from truly great leaders which battles are important enough to fight and which ones are petty irritants that can be let go. As for Taryn, I will fight any battle I must to protect her, and she will do the same for me. We have a love built on trust and respect. It is something you should seek with your First Wife."

"You'll not get horses from me," Amdi bellowed. "Try getting more than a few leagues without a ride. You'll return, begging for my help."

"No," Rhoane said with sadness, "I fear it will be you who will be asking for help. I hope it will not be too late."

Rhoane spread his hand against Taryn's lower back, propelling her forward. She wore a rough cotton tunic and loose-fitting breeches, not the silk gown Kaleigh had left for her the night before. The male attire must've driven Amdi mad, knowing Taryn had a dress made for royalty and yet she chose to wear peasant's clothing.

"I feel bad for him." Taryn said once they were out of earshot from Amdi's guards. "He's actually quite frail, as you saw last night. Kaleigh is still young and beautiful, which worries him. He's afraid she'll leave him for someone less volatile." Taryn sighed into Rhoane and wrapped an arm around his waist. "You can't fix stupid."

"No, you cannot." Rhoane chuckled at her eccentric speech. "Perhaps we have given him something to think about, though. There is always hope."

"Hope, yes, but not much time. The lies Marissa planted into his memories wreaked havoc on his psyche. You were right that he's fading, but it's much more insidious than that."

Taryn slid her eyes to take in the guards lounging against nearby poles. They looked relaxed, but Rhoane took in the way their stance allowed easy access to weapons.

"We can discuss what we discovered later." Rhoane hurried her to their tent. He too had found the implanted memories. Marissa was gifted in the power. If only she'd used her strength for bettering her people instead of destroying anyone in her path.

They had no luggage to pack, only their swords to gather. Rhoane wrapped both of their swords in a blanket and was about to secure them to his back when Taryn stopped him.

"I don't think we should fly from here. Something tells me if Amdi knew what we could do, he'd exploit that and I've had enough of being hunted." She unraveled the swords and gripped them both between her clenched hands. "I can get us to Paderau, I think. If it doesn't work, then we'll be bits of goo from here to the palace."

"What are you saying? How?"

"It's a Dark thing. I'll teach you another time." Her eyes took on a wildness he didn't often see in her and for a moment, his heart stopped beating. Something frightened her, but she gave him no time to question motives or feelings. "I don't know about you, but I'm ready to ditch this place for a hot shower, warm meal, and heavenly bed." She placed his hands over hers. "Whatever you do, don't let go."

A rush of her ShantiMari enveloped them both, then air and sound dissipated into a whir of nothingness. Their hair flew into their faces and the swords trembled in their hands. A moment later, they stood at the foot of Taryn's bed in Paderau.

"It worked. Rhoane, it worked." Abject relief flooded her features. She puffed out her cheeks and smiled so brightly she lit up the room. "It worked. Thank the gods."

His stomach roiled with the sudden stop and his head spun.

He touched her face, then his, then his chest. Satisfied everything was intact, he shook his head and grinned. "I would like to learn how you took us from Ulla to here."

"And I'd like to teach you, but first, a shower." She placed their swords on the bed and led him to the strange stall in her bathing room. After she fiddled with the knobs, she stripped off her clothes and stepped inside. "Join me."

He sloughed off his dusty clothing and took her proffered hand. Questions, so many questions raced through his mind, but as she grinned up at him, water streaming over her face, her freckles giving her an innocence he'd all but forgotten, he dismissed the questions and let the stream of hot water wash away his cares. Later, there would be time for answers.

CHAPTER EIGHTEEN

Voices sounded from inside the tent and Loghan raced to where Taryn and Rhoane were staying. He pulled the flap open in time to see the pair vanish. One moment, they were there; the next, gone. He stepped into the warm space and sniffed the air. His ShantiMari spiraled out, searching every nook and cranny. A fire burned in the brazier, blankets were tumbled where the two had slept, but there was no sign of them. No sense of their presence at all.

Loghan bent and retrieved the gown his mother had given Taryn to wear. His fingertips brushed a fur blanket and her aura filled him, suffocating him until he struggled to breathe. Her image danced in his mind, her smile brighter than a summer's day, and eyes the color of darkest sapphire. Her silver hair tormented his thoughts, teasing him to reach out and stroke the silken strands. This woman, the Darennsai of his mother's people, affected him as no other had. As no one should.

He'd taken an oath. His vow was sacred to his healing. Despite what Gwainne might believe, Loghan had not shared a bed with the crown princess out of lust. She'd come to him for healing—she'd not been able to conceive and Loghan had helped her release what blocked her from bearing children. It had been a simple thing, and yes, Marissa had tried to lure him to her bed several times after, but he'd refrained. The memory of their time together was not pleasant for Loghan. He'd had a feeling of being used. Now, seeing how upset Taryn had been at the mention of the crown princess, shame embedded itself in his heart.

Loghan threw the blanket upon the ground and pivoted away from the spot where Taryn had disappeared. He would forget the woman. Put her out of his mind forever.

"Are they gone?" His mother's voice startled him.

"Yes."

She picked up the dress he'd dropped and smoothed the fragile fabric. "This would have been lovely on her."

Loghan didn't answer. He couldn't trust himself to keep his voice calm.

"She is not wrong, you know. We are a weakened people because of Amdi's superstitions. I did not want him to make concessions with the crown princess, but he thought her protection would help our people. We must look to Gwainne to restore our power."

"Those are traitorous words, Mother." He snuck a look to the doorway where one of his mother's guards kept watch. That he agreed with her was enough to get them both killed.

"These are dangerous times, my son. If we are weak, we will be easily controlled. Have you never wondered why the princess sought us out? Our lands border the Narthvier and there is little love between Talaith and the Weirren."

"Mother," Gwainne slipped into the tent, "have they left so soon?"

"It appears so." Kaleigh's fingertips traced a string of beaded pearls on the gown.

"I am sorry for that," Gwainne said, "but there are wounded. We need you in the tents. You as well, Loghan."

Kaleigh swirled her robes and rushed from the tent, with her sons following.

A frown creased Gwainne's forehead as he jogged to keep pace with their mother. "I was hoping to speak to the prince. He said something to me last night I did not fully understand."

"What was that?" Loghan increased his stride, anxious to see the injured.

"He asked if Fayngaar had a son. Who is Fayngaar?"

Their mother chortled, her face growing soft. "That is his horse. He has had Fayngaar many seasons. Perhaps he is looking to replace his faithful stallion."

"Perhaps," Gwainne mused. "He also asked if I have ever witnessed the reflection of the twin moons in Lan Gyllarelle. Is this in the Narthvier, Mother?"

Kaleigh's steps slowed, her breathing labored. Loghan skidded to prevent himself running into his mother. The gaiety of a moment earlier left her face and Loghan's nerves tightened.

"Why would he ask this of you?" She shook her head. "He cannot mean that you—" She cut off her words with another violent shake of her head. "No, I will not. Cannot. You are Ullan. You. Are. Ullan."

As if to prove her point, she jabbed Gwainne's chest with each word.

"I do not understand."

"Nor will you, if I have a say in the matter. Now, go sit with your father. We must focus our healing."

Gwainne hesitated a moment, as if he would question their mother more, but then departed without a word, leaving Loghan and Kaleigh to rush into the tents. Whatever Rhoane had meant, and what it would mean for Gwainne, would have to wait.

Three patients lay atop the tables, their clothes stripped from their bodies. Two had several long lacerations on both arms and legs. One would not survive. His throat had been ripped out.

Even as they assessed him, his life force drained away, leaving his skin sallow, his breathing a rattled death toll.

"Give him ransthip. These two, bath their wounds," Kaleigh ordered as she began the process of disseminating her ShantiMari over the patients.

A servant scuttled around the room, making preparations. Loghan stood quietly in the corner to calm his mind. Yet his mother's response to Gwainne's inquiry chased his serenity. Why would the Eleri ask Gwainne to travel to the Narthvier? And would Taryn be there if he did?

"Loghan. Now." His mother snapped her fingers.

He disrobed, his erection fully extended. She pointed to the female whose arm bent at an irregular angle, obviously broken. Her leg also protruded against the natural curve of her body. What the hell had done this?

Kaleigh issued orders to two other healers who had entered the tent. The dying man was taken away, leaving his mother to concentrate on the other patient, a man of middle age with a large gash on his head. Her robes dropped to the floor and Loghan turned his focus to the woman laying before him.

She was pretty, perhaps a season or two older than him. Long blonde hair gathered on the pillow, mud and blood turning it an ugly shade of ochre. Her face had sustained few injuries. Her eyelids remained closed, the eyes behind the lids darting furiously from side to side. She moaned and grasped at the air with her hands.

"Shhh." Loghan soothed her brow while whispering healing words.

She had little ShantiMari of her own, which always made healing more difficult. Sometimes sharing his body didn't need to occur, but this woman would need all of his power and more if she were to survive.

His fingertips traced the line between energy stores while his ShantiMari probed the woman's mind and body. A flurry of images assaulted him, of a great beast, fangs the size of a grown man's leg, fur like shimmering midnight. Her fear overrode his mind and he pulled his thoughts from the woman. Whatever the beast had been, Loghan had not seen its kind before. A shudder of revulsion marred his healing and he drew a deep breath to force calm.

The woman needed his complete focus. With another cleansing breath, he centered his attention on the first store just beneath her belly button. His mother tended to the other man, her whispers a welcome comfort. They worked apart, yet in tandem. A synchronized unit of healing that had grown organically over the seasons. Her presence strengthened him, as his did her. In the healing tents, they weren't mother and son, but healers. Period.

Some didn't understand how he could work beside his mother. They couldn't comprehend the difference between healing and coupling. There was no exchange of passion between him and his patient. Male or female, he sought only to use his power to heal, not to release his desire. He'd been trained to have no desire. To be devoid of wants and needs.

He slipped his hand between the woman's legs, his fingers working to coax her own power to assist in his healing. A low moan came from her lips, an encouraging sign to have a reaction so early in the process. Loghan bent and swiped his lips over the patient's little bud, his fingers entering her warm channel. The more internal stimulation he could give, the better the healing.

His tongue stimulated the woman, his power slipping deeper into her energy stores the more she became aroused. The first energy store opened, and he doubled his efforts. The next two complied with little resistance, but the fourth and fifth took more concentration, more effort on his part. At the sixth energy store, he hit a wall. His fingers and tongue brought her release with a shuddering convulsion, and then her body shut down. This happened sometimes, not often, but enough not to concern Loghan.

The other healers bustled around the room, bathing the patients, setting bones, stimulating breasts or lips when necessary, but otherwise didn't disturb him in his work. He rose from between her legs and ran his hands up her thighs to her belly. The soft skin reminded him of Taryn.

His thoughts wandered to the beauty, her silver hair framing a battered face. Even in death, she had glistened with the brightness of stars. For she had been dead, he was sure of it. Not for long, but there was a period of several minutes where he sensed nothing from her. No life. No thought. Nothing. A vast void that had beckoned.

He stroked his patient's thighs and angled her to better accommodate his cock. She moaned again, her hips tilting toward him.

"Rance," she whispered, her head drooping to the side.

Loghan motioned for one of the helpers to suckle her breast, hoping the added stimulation would be enough to unblock the last two energy stores.

Perspiration dotted his marked skin as he worked his healing. His body joined with hers and his power infused her veins. He fought hard to weaken her barriers. She was tough, like Taryn. In the little time he'd lain hands upon her, he sensed her strength. Then, in the arena when she battled not just the creature, but his father and brother, he saw a warrior. For a brief moment, after she'd defeated his father, she stood tall and he saw the ghostly shape of dragon wings flare behind her. He'd been mesmerized by the sight. She was Darennsai. His mother's people thought she would destroy them, but Loghan didn't believe so. She was meant for greatness, Taryn ap Galendrin.

The last of the patient's energy stores popped open, flooding him with her energy. His thoughts lingered on Taryn's eyes, her lips, her breasts. The Eleri prince had healed her so completely no marks remained on her body. What had he told Loghan? *Love.* Love had healed her.

Love was foreign to Loghan. A curse word to his kind. Yes, he loved his family, but a man or woman? Never.

Stars burst in his mind; a cacophony of voices murmured. His body trembled from the exertion. This was new, unexpected.

Forbidden.

"Loghan, what have you done?"

He opened his eyes to find his mother glaring at him, a look of disgust marring her pretty features.

The healer who'd been assisting him grinned from where he crouched over the woman's breasts. Color infused her cheeks. Her body took on a warmth it had previously lacked. Confused by his mother's ire, he glanced down, noticing his flaccid cock. He'd released his desire.

Shame snaked between his lustful thoughts and wound around his heart.

"Clean her up, make certain no seed remains, then come see me in my tent." Kaleigh stormed from the room.

A thousand needles pierced his heart. He'd disappointed his mother, and himself. Guilt slid beneath his shame. Never before had he been careless. Why this woman?

It wasn't the patient who had caused this disaster, but his feelings for Taryn. He desired her. It could not be. He would be banished from the Ullans if his father found out. Loghan shrugged into his robe, aware of his nakedness and uncomfortable. They bathed the woman, cleaning her womb of his seed. After transferring her to a recovery tent, he did as told and joined his mother.

She sat at a table scribbling on a piece of parchment. Gwainne rested on a sofa, his long legs dangling over the side. For a quarter bell, no one said anything. Loghan paced the luxurious tents, going from one to another, his anxiety making him too restless to sit. Finally, when he thought his blood would burst from his heart, his mother stopped writing and turned to face them.

"The world is changing and we must convince your father to change with it. I have decided I will venture forth to discover what has become of Aelinae since last our borders were open."

"You cannot. Mother, you are with child." Gwainne sat up, his eyes alert.

"One of us has to, and Loghan cannot be trusted. Not after what happened today."

"What did you do?"

Loghan glared at his brother, hating his mother for confessing his truth. "I became distracted while healing and released."

Gwainne's laughter surprised him, but their mother's lips spread to a thin line.

"That is all? Mother, that is no crime. Hell, I would gladly be a healer with all the coupling you do."

"We do not heal to couple. It is completely different," Loghan ground out between clenched jaws.

"Then why the fuss?"

Their mother tapped a quill upon the table, her eyes narrowed. "Loghan is an Ullan prince. If he gets a woman with child, they can lay claim to your throne. You already have several half-brothers only too anxious for your demise."

"And what kingdom do I have to rule? The Darennsai was right. We are weak, not just because of the deal Father made with the crown princess. Our strength has been diminishing for several seasons. Father is mad, Mother. His choices are harmful to our people. His commands and edicts are limiting economically as well as socially."

Loghan was taken aback that Gwainne had cared enough to notice. He'd always thought his brother too lax in his responsibilities as heir. He reclined on a sofa and studied the crown prince with renewed interest.

"It is true," Kaleigh admitted, her features softening. "I do what I can, but his madness is beyond healing. What do you suggest?"

"Let me go into the world. I will see for myself what has become of Aelinae in our exile. If, as Taryn said, the crown princess wishes us harm, I will uncover this truth for myself. We have too long depended on the information of others. It is time we think for ourselves."

Their mother chewed on a thumbnail and paced a circle. "I do not know what to do."

Loghan had never seen his mother this perplexed. In the healing tents, she was a calming strength, and beside their father, she always held herself with dignified composure, no matter the abuse he heaped upon his wife. A buzz started in his gut, one that promised to unhinge all of his nerves.

"What can we do to help?" Loghan stopped her pacing and took her hands in his own. "We are here for you, Mother."

Gwainne joined them, his callused hands rough against Loghan's. *What opposite lives they'd led*, Loghan thought. Gwainne always at the side of their father, while Loghan stayed with their mother.

"Thank you both," Kaleigh said. "You are my sons, and you are Ullan, but I must ask you for the moment to remember you are also half Eleri."

Loghan shared a glance with Gwainne. This was unlike their mother. Hadn't she just a few bells earlier told Gwainne with no uncertain terms he was Ullan?

Kaleigh folded to her knees, her hands clasped together and resting against her forehead. "Great Lady, hear me now in my moment of greatest need. I seek your guidance, your wisdom, your forgiveness." She rambled on in Eleri, pleading with this unknown Great Lady.

Tears streamed down her face and Loghan bent to comfort her. Rarely did his mother cry.

A bright light shimmered in the tent, casting a rainbow across every surface. The form of a woman, skin as pale as the moon, hair spiraling in streaks of rust, gold, and green, appeared. Her evergreen gown draped from her shoulders to the floor, puddling around her bare feet.

Loghan gaped at the woman. She was even more beautiful than Taryn ap Galendrin.

"You are kind to think so, my son."

Loghan blinked. *He hadn't spoken the words aloud, had he?*

"Rise, Kaleigh of Clan Dantura, wife of Amdi Agnar, novice of Verdaine."

Kaleigh rose on unsteady legs and Loghan supported her. Gwainne stepped to her other side and wrapped an arm around her waist.

The woman reached out to stroke their mother's cheek, sadness shadowing her tri-colored eyes. She took a short curl between her fingers and sighed. "I have missed you."

A sob came from Kaleigh and she nodded quickly. "As I you, Great Lady. Can you forgive me for abusing your grace?"

"Abuse? There was nothing of the sort. You fell in love. It happens. And sometimes that love becomes an obsession." The lady's gaze flicked to Loghan.

He swallowed hard. How she knew of his feelings for Taryn, he shuddered to guess. To be safe, he pushed all thoughts of Taryn low, deep into the recesses of his mind and heart.

"It is not so easy to forget your first love." The woman smoothed Kaleigh's hair away from her face. "You have more than served out your sheanna. Grow your hair, reclaim your pride."

"I cannot." Kaleigh's hand flew to her curls. "The king has not released me, nor have I been purified."

"I am Verdaine, your goddess, Kaleigh. Do you not think it in my power to absolve you? Or do you think the king has more power than I?"

Gwainne openly gasped and Loghan's belly buzzed faster. This woman claimed to be a goddess their father swore didn't exist.

His palms slicked with sweat and his heart beat close to his throat.

"No. Never, my lady. I never thought I would return to the Narthvier, therefore I would always be sheanna."

"Verdaine?" Gwainne whispered, his expression a curious mix of horror and fascination. "I thought you were a myth."

"As I am sure your father would like you to believe. The Ullans are godless, but that does not mean there are no gods."

"Can you help us?" Kaleigh asked.

Verdaine closed her eyes and a rushing sound filled the tent. "I can advise, but not offer assistance. What is it you would like to know?"

"Can Father be saved?" Gwainne blurted before the others could speak.

"No, he cannot. His madness is natural and therefore, must run its course."

"Was the crown princess right?" Loghan rushed to ask. "Is Taryn a false prophet? Have we been deceived?"

"No, no, and yes. Marissa was a schemer who desired what her half-sister Taryn has—both Light and Dark ShantiMari. Taryn is the Eirielle your father fears. Many fear her. Some, love her." Again, her gaze slid to Loghan. Yet the expected shame didn't surface. Instead, a warm tingling infused his head.

"Taryn is the daughter of the empress?" Gwainne asked in a hush. "Marissa would have me kill her own sister?"

Their mother gaped at Gwainne. "You did not tell me the crown princess wished you to commit murder of her own kin."

Gwainne slowly shook his head. "She told me many things, and now I see they were lies. I have been deceived and for that, I am ashamed."

"As Taryn said, it is not entirely your fault. Marissa was skilled at manipulation and deception. She feasted upon others' fears and insecurities. Even Taryn's."

"Where is she now?" Loghan fidgeted, half-ready to saddle a horse and ride after Taryn.

"Your feelings betray you, Loghan Agnar. Taryn was never meant for any other except Prince Rhoane, First Son of the Eleri and her betrothed. Tuck your love away. It can help better your skills at healing, but will only harm Taryn if left unchecked." Verdaine's tri-colored eyes grew misty. Sadness fell around them like physical blows. "There are too many who wish her death already. She needs allies, not adversaries."

The suspended shame wrapped him in its grip. He was being selfish, he knew, but that didn't mean he knew how to stop himself from loving a woman who could never be his.

"Besides the crown princess, who else wishes her dead?" Gwainne's tone held a hint of disbelief. He hadn't seen Taryn when she first arrived—only later when she appeared healthy in the dining tent.

Loghan clenched his fists to keep from punching the man in his stupid mouth.

"Within three moonturns, Zakael will visit you. Once heir to the Obsidian Throne, he now wears the crown and calls himself king. He is Taryn's half-brother and desires her for himself. He will stop at nothing to claim her." Verdaine motioned toward the sea, a league or so to the south. "He was responsible for the attack on Taryn and her family."

"He did that to her?" The image of Taryn's battered body lodged itself in Loghan's mind and his veins ignited with unbound fury.

"Calm yourself, Healer," Verdaine warned. "Your anger will not do anyone any good. Zakael did not directly harm Taryn. The young king has many agents and just as many allies. He will try to continue Marissa's work now that she is no more."

"The crown princess is dead?" Kaleigh whispered the same thought Loghan had.

"She perished little more than a fortnight past." Verdaine

wavered, as if to say more, but then turned to Gwainne and touched his cheek.

A tiny sprout of jealousy took hold in Loghan's heart.

"You must go at once to the Narthvier. Taryn and Rhoane travel there now to seek answers to a riddle one of your people set into her mind. She wishes to know the legend of the Jansen Strait."

"But I do not know the legend."

"No, but you will discover it all the same. You must be the one, Gwainne. What you learn in the Narthvier will be the difference of life and death for the Darennsai. From there, you will travel south to Paderau. You may stay at the palace, but make certain to visit the marketplace. Ask questions. Talk to the people. The duke is not in residence, but others in Paderau can help you. Listen well, and learn all you can. When finished in Paderau, travel to Talaith. There, seek out those with ties to the Telraicht Brotherhood."

"You purposefully send my son to his death?" His mother stepped in front of Gwainne as if to protect him from Verdaine's words.

"Not all practitioners of the Telraicht Arts are sworn killers. They seek salvation by another path, is all." A softness entered Verdaine's tone, one meant to impart understanding.

"Do I tell people who I am? That I am an Ullan prince?"

The goddess tilted her head, a small grin on her lips. "Tell them what you will. They will believe what they want to believe."

"Riddles?" Gwainne groaned like a child told to perform a chore. "And you wonder why Ullans are godless."

"Gwainne!" their mother scolded. "Show some respect."

Gwainne mumbled an apology, neither heartfelt nor memorable. Loghan understood his brother's enmity. A goddess they didn't believe in half a bell earlier tells him he must leave his people—even though Loghan would leave Ulla this second if it meant being near Taryn. It wasn't fair to ask Gwainne to desert his people for a prophecy they didn't acknowledge.

Loghan glanced to Verdaine, then Gwainne, and finally his mother. Reverence shone on her features and for a brief second, he saw her as one of Verdaine's disciples. She believed in not only the prophecy concerning Taryn, but in what being Darennsai meant for Aelinae. And, in that brief moment, so did he.

He shook himself to clear the visions lurking in his mind, yet they remained. Verdaine studied him, her grin elongating into a smile that could brighten the dreariest of days. In that light, he witnessed the importance of Gwainne's journey to the Narthvier.

A heartbeat later, with a subtle pop, the vision was gone and he stood with the others as if no time had passed. But what he saw in Verdaine's radiance was a lifetime of possibilities for not just Taryn, but all those he loved. He staggered beneath the weight of responsibility the Darennsai carried.

"When will he leave?" His mother scanned the room, her eyes darting over the many chests and cupboards. "We must make preparations."

"There is no time. The Darennsai will be at my temple within a day. Gwainne must ride now if he is to intercept them."

"But, the veils? Surely he cannot lift them." Concern tugged at Kaleigh's words.

"He is Eleri. He will know how when the time comes."

Loghan envied his brother this mission. He'd never traveled far in his father's kingdom, staying away from the borders, and avoiding the vast openness of the shores. There was safety in staying close to the encampments, yet now he wondered how much he'd missed by keeping himself sheltered. Amdi had the Ullans believing they didn't need outsiders. As Loghan watched his brother leave the tent with an air of excitement, a grain of doubt planted itself in his long-held beliefs.

Within the span of two days, all that he'd held true had been questioned.

Verdaine took Kaleigh aside and bent her head close to his mother's. A subtle light shone from them both, illuminating the tent with a soft glow. Its warmth enveloped Loghan and he despaired of ever feeling the full impact of Verdaine's grace.

You have my grace within you already, my son.

His head jerked up, his gaze intent upon the goddess. She continued to whisper to his mother, as if nothing untoward had occurred.

Your healing skills are a gift. Do not squander them on one girl. Taryn will need you before the end. Need your healing and your friendship. Your loyalty will be tested. When the time comes, do not fail her.

The words Verdaine spoke in his mind settled like a feather drifting upon a breeze.

Taryn is strong, but as of yet, is only flesh and bone. Love her with all your heart, but never with your body.

The former Loghan would do until his last breath. The latter would be torment, but he would heed his mother's goddess.

And Rhoane. Loghan inquired, *Must I love him as well?* The image of him kneeling before Rhoane, of the words from his tattoos swirling in the air, came to the front of his mind. He loved the man. Not as a brother or a patient, but as his prince. Yet he hated him for having Taryn.

Verdaine's gaze swept from Kaleigh to him. *Him you must love above all.*

Gwainne returned with two bags packed to overflowing. "I am ready. Tell Father I love him. I will return within three moon-turns. If the one called Zakael should arrive before me, do not let Father give him any concessions."

Hugs and farewells were said, tears shed, last-minute details discussed, and then Gwainne was gone. Not as immediate as Taryn and Rhoane's disappearance, but just as awful for Loghan. They were brothers and while they'd grown apart over the last few seasons, they'd always been confidants. Loghan said a silent blessing for his brother, his heart weary, his nerves a tangle of anxiety for Gwainne.

Verdaine drifted to where Loghan stood staring at the empty tent opening.

"I will watch over him. You both have a role to play in Aelinae's future. Gwainne is riding north to discover his. And you," she turned him to face her, "will soon discover yours."

He puffed up his chest and jutted his chin a little too far forward. "I am a healer. That is my purpose."

Her gaze shifted to his mother's flat stomach.

"Your skills will be needed in the coming moonturns. This child must live, Loghan Agnar." She pressed her hand against his skin where his heart beat wildly in his chest. Verdaine leaned forward, keeping her hand where it was, and touched her mouth to his. Soft as rose petals, her lips tasted like honey.

You could be the greatest healer Aelinae has ever witnessed, but to do so, you must learn to trust yourself.

Her hand slipped down his robe to stroke his cock. It began to stir, to quicken for healing.

Not with this. Her hand traveled back to his chest. *But this. Trust, my love. Believe.*

She released their kiss and drifted away. The room spun and his woozy thoughts scattered into incoherent ramblings.

Kaleigh looked away from the empty tent opening as if the kiss had never happened, as if she hadn't noticed her goddess fondling him. "You promise you will keep Gwainne safe? Both of my sons? You will protect them?"

Verdaine stretched a hand over his mother's womb. "I will protect all of your children. Be light, my daughter." She rested her forehead against Kaleigh's. "When next we meet, may it be in sweetness and not sorrow."

"When next we meet," Kaleigh finished.

Verdaine faded to nothingness, taking some of the light with her. Loghan slipped his hand around his mother's. Something momentous had happened, but he wasn't sure what. Wasn't sure he'd ever fully know how to explain what he'd seen, felt, heard. Too much to process all at once. A goddess had blessed him. A goddess his father refused to admit existed. A goddess he would die protecting.

I am not the only one. Verdaine's voice drifted on a breath of a whisper.

No, she wasn't the only one. There was another.

CHAPTER NINETEEN

Rhoane's heartbeat thrummed beneath Taryn's ear, strong and steady. He was her rock. He'd saved her in Ulla. She snuggled closer to her love, wrapping an arm over his chest and pulling him close. Rhoane stirred and she turned to kiss the warm skin of his neck. Those in the palace were waking and soon they'd have to leave, but for a few more minutes, she wanted Rhoane all to herself.

Laying in a comfortable cocoon of blankets, a soft mattress, and relative privacy, she luxuriated in quiet serenity. No one knew they were there and she hoped to keep it that way.

"That shower is a gift from the gods, you know."

Taryn smiled at his morning greeting. He'd been unimpressed when her uncle had first showed her the renovated bathroom, but she'd promised he would love it—and he did. For near on a bell, he'd stood under the cascading hot water, letting it work out the Ullan dust, and the tension in his muscles. They'd soaped each other's backs, washed their hair, and lingered as long as they dared in the heavenly enclosure.

If she never set foot in Ulla again, it would be too soon. Dust and dirt everywhere.

She hoped Michel would be safe there with Kaleigh. The laird's wife had promised to take him in as one of her own, but Taryn didn't trust her completely. Something had stayed the woman's tongue on more than one occasion and her thoughts were blocked from Taryn.

"When shall we leave for the Narthvier?" Rhoane stroked her long hair.

She settled onto his chest. "I know I said I wanted to go there to discover the meaning of the old woman's words, but that's being selfish. We're needed in Menurra. Verdaine's temple can wait."

His chest raised with a deep breath, then slowly lowered. "I was hoping this would be your choice."

She raised her head to look him in the eye. "If you didn't think we should go, you should've said something."

"This was a decision you had to make on your own."

She narrowed her eyes, not sure if he was joking or not. "What's so important about this decision and not the hundreds we've made together up to now?"

His hands trailed along her arm, leaving sparks of heat in their wake. "I cannot say. Only, it was a feeling I had that this should be your choice."

"If it wasn't my choice, where would you have us go?"

"Menurra. Your family and friends are worried for you."

Guilt tumbled through her serenity. "Oh shit. I forgot—the last they saw of me, I blew up Mother's ship. I bet she's pissed."

"She was not happy to lose her ship, but she was grateful to not lose her daughters."

Taryn stretched until she could reach his lips with her own. "You're sweet to say so, but you and I both know she'd be happier if I wasn't around. I'm a threat to everything she is, was, will be, what she does, what she doesn't admit to doing—everything. I'm her own personal abomination."

"Do not speak of these things. They are not true."

"For a supposed assassin, you're pretty bad at lying."

Rhoane stilled. His heartbeat increased and she smelled a faint acrid scent. *Anxiety.*

"Why would you say this? Who told you I am an assassin?"

Bollocks. Her heart raced to match Rhoane's. She had ruined their perfect moment. Had brought reality into their quiet.

"Amdi." Agitation edged her words. "In his thoughts, actually. He believes he pushed you hard in the arena so that you would become hardened enough to bear what was to come. He meant me, didn't he?"

Rhoane nodded, but added nothing else to accept or deny what she'd said.

"Why does he think you're an assassin? His thoughts were fairly cemented on the idea."

His heart continued to thrum with the rapidity of a drumline, but she sensed him forcing his muscles to relax. His fingers took up their casual stroking of her hair and skin.

"When I was a lad, I swore an oath to Verdaine. I was young and did not know what the words truly meant, but I was honored she chose me. Later, I rejected my oath. I was not kind about it and my resistance caused my mother's death."

Taryn listened as Rhoane's story spilled from his lips. Of how his mother had burst into flames, something he feared would happen to him if he didn't control his emotions. Then, he told her of his seasons in Ulla. Of fighting in Amdi's arena, of his close relationship with Kaleigh. A tiny crack of jealousy wedged itself in Taryn's thoughts each time he mentioned the Eleri woman's name. Perhaps this was what she'd tried to hide from Taryn. They had loved each other, but not shared their bodies. Kaleigh saw to that, but Rhoane had been tempted.

The brittle trust she'd been building since Marissa's betrayal frayed at the edges. She'd loved only Rhoane, for all of her life, just him. Yet he'd loved others. It was a truth she'd have to accept.

She snuggled closer, not wanting the ghosts of his past to

chase off the promise of their future. His fingertips stroked her naked skin as he spoke. This was the story of his life before she existed. The chapters she'd always wondered about, but never had the courage to ask.

After three seasons with the Ullans, he'd learned what he could from them and left the desert for Talaith. There, he met the empress, who had tried to seduce him into her bed.

This didn't surprise Taryn at all. Still, a knot formed in her gut. Gods, but Lliandra was pathetic. Thinking every man on Aelinae was born to be her bedmate. Knowing her own mother had tried to bed Rhoane made bile rise up her throat. She gave a disgusted grunt and Rhoane's heartrate increased. This wasn't easy for him to admit. In his quickened breaths and heavy strokes of her hair, she felt his distress.

"What happened after Talaith?" Taryn asked when the silence stretched.

"I went to Menurra, where Faelara and I assisted the queen with the birth of her first child."

He paused and Taryn suspected there was more to the story. Half afraid he might admit he'd loved Queen Prateeni, she remained silent, but tension coiled around them, ready to snap any moment.

"The king and I became friends during my stay. It was he who suggested I learn the ways of espionage." He sighed, as if that was the end of his confession. "I had many strange occurrences in my travels, and yes, Faisal taught me what it is to kill without remorse. I serve no ruler, only my heart."

He meant her. He may have loved others, but she was his only mate. His love. His heart. As he was hers.

"This is a Rhoane I don't know." She traced his lips with a fingertip. "Why haven't you told me any of this before?"

"I was afraid you would reject me. I have done things I am not proud of, killed innocent people if needed, and manipulated situations. I saw your reaction to Marissa and feared you would see me as no better than her."

"Those people you killed, and situations you manipulated, were they to serve your own purposes, or for something greater than either you or I?"

His breath lingered between them, the moment frozen, as if his next words could collapse everything they'd built, all that she loved in him.

"For Aelinae. Never for myself."

All of the unease she'd been gathering since he started his tale drained from her, leaving her exhausted.

"Then you have nothing to be ashamed of. We'll all have to do things that are difficult before this is over."

He will betray you twice.

Then he will kill you.

The words sent a shudder throughout her body. Rhoane tightened his grip and touched his lips to hers. They were like ice upon an already frozen surface.

It was her turn to confess.

She propped herself on an elbow and met his steady gaze. "After I blew up Mother's ship, I was drowning. Something saved me. I don't know who or what, but I didn't wash upon the shore of the Jansen Strait. I was put there."

"Could have been the gods. They have a special fondness for you."

It wasn't a god. At least, her heart told her that wasn't the answer. Rhoane's eyes tightened and his nostrils flared. He knew what it was, but didn't want to say.

"My memories are hazy, but I remember feeling safe." She studied his face, noted the twitching of his lips. "Not just safe, but loved. She, he, whatever it was, could've killed me, but instead chose to help. I won't forget that kindness. Someday, I'd like to go back and see if we can find whoever it was."

"Shall I pencil it in?"

Taryn's laughter rocketed from her. "I said that to you a long time ago and you said I was weird."

"No, I said you say the most curious things."

A tentative knock at the door startled them. Rhoane put a finger to his lips and slid from the bed. Naked as the day he was born, he crept to where Claidholm Solais was propped against a wall. Taryn held in a giggle as he unsheathed his sword and stood to the side of the door.

"Who is it?" Taryn called out, cackling at the look of horror that crossed Rhoane's face.

"'Tis Mayla, miss. I, erm, I came to check your rooms." After a brief pause, she added, "I was not expecting you."

Rhoane hopped over their discarded clothes to the bed and wrapped a sheet around his waist.

"Give us a minute," Taryn said between fits of giggles. "No, wait. Can you bring us some food?" She rattled off several items for her maid before dissolving into full-out belly laughs.

Gods, but it felt good to laugh. To let go of the stress and strain the past few weeks had rained upon her. She'd killed, and almost been killed. She could no more hold Rhoane on a pedestal than herself. They did what had to be done. Did she like it? Not at all, but it was their fate.

The laughter slowed and she pulled Rhoane to her. "Whatever you've done, whoever you've loved, all of those experiences brought you to here, right now."

"You are remarkable, Taryn ap Galendrin. If only we could stay here forever and not be interrupted, I should like to show you my gratitude." A playful smile teased his lips, but he held something back. She saw it in the depths of his eyes.

Instead of pulling that particular thread, she forced herself to get up and dress. Mayla would return in a few minutes, then they'd be off to Menurra, where the others waited. As much as she wished to linger in bed, they had obligations.

Mayla returned with food and tea just as they finished dressing. With Carga gone, no one in the kitchens knew how to make grhom. Tea would have to do, but Taryn longed for a taste of Rhoane's homeland.

Taryn hugged her maid, squeezing a little too tightly. "I've missed you. Promise you'll tell no one you've seen us? We'll be leaving after we eat and don't want a fuss."

"You have my word, miss. Do you know when you'll be returning to Paderau?" The girl's eyes sparkled with unshed tears.

"Not for quite some time, I fear. We have the wedding to get through, then who knows where my travels will take me. The world is a curious place right now. Are you continuing your lessons with the sword master?"

"I am. Although, I don't understand why."

Taryn held her chin between thumb and forefinger. "Because I couldn't bear to lose you and someone needs to protect these ridiculous courtiers."

Mayla laughed, a hearty sound that warmed the room. "Best you be off before too many others are awake."

"We'll be discreet. Thank you, Mayla."

She curtseyed low to Rhoane, a blush staining her cheeks. "Be well on your travels." Mayla left them alone to finish their meal.

Taryn watched the girl's retreating back and hoped they'd return soon to Paderau. Of all the places she'd been on Aelinae, this palace was more home to her than anywhere else. It was the only place she felt she belonged. She surveyed her surroundings, spying several threads of her uncle's ShantiMari. Anje and Hayden waited for her on Menurra. It was time to go.

Taryn and Rhoane slipped through the palace unseen and made their way on foot to the outskirts of town, where they transformed into great beasts. Their darathi vorsi spiraled into the early morning sky and banked south, toward the Summerlands. As happened each time she left Paderau, a sense of sadness, as if part of her was missing, touched her heart. She turned her snout away from the city and sloughed off the melancholy. Some day she could settle down, but that day was far off into the future.

They flew high above the clouds to keep out of sight, only drifting lower once they were over the Summer Seas. They skirted the area where her ship had been attacked, but all signs of Cashiel, his men, or debris from Lliandra's ship had long since disappeared. A pang of disappointment sucked at her gut. She'd been hoping to find something, anything, to help her discover who Cashiel was.

He'd known far too much about her for him to be a casual mercenary. And the mention of Valterys had piqued her interest. The past few days had been a flurry of saving her life and then dealing with Amdi, but now Taryn had to focus on this new threat. Something about the man's attack on her, yet the way he refused to touch her intimately, then his rough handling of her privates, confused the hell out of her. Why beat the crap out of someone, but not rape them? Wasn't rape the ultimate "taking" for a man? His best way of showing control?

Perhaps Cashiel didn't want control. She struggled to recall his words, all of them, but only had fragments. Frustrated, she snorted a burst of flame.

What is it, mi carae?

I can't remember the attack. Parts of it are clear, like the beating, but why Cashiel attacked, or what he wanted, I don't recall any of that. Perhaps Mother and the others will know.

The tip of Rhoane's dragon wing touched hers, the talon scraping along her scales. A flutter of ease rippled along her back. This man loved her. He'd killed for her. Another shudder vibrated her scales. Someday he'd kill her, as well.

No, Taryn forced the thought to her heart. Rhoane would not betray her a second time and he would not kill her. They were in charge of their fate, not the gods, nor prophecies. She snorted fresh flames and grinned. She and Rhoane, they would decide their paths. Together.

They flew on, Taryn scanning the depths of the ocean with her enhanced darathi vorsi vision. Nothing stood out as strange or beckoned her attention. Several times they rose higher in the sky to avoid ships, but other than a few vessels, the sea was empty. Just a vast expanse of blue. After several bells, a speck dotted the endless sapphire, a golden pearl within the ocean's embrace. The closer they flew, one island became several. Lush forests covered parts of the main island, with mountains to the north.

Taryn's heart sped up with excitement. Soon, she would see her friends—would be among those she loved and who loved her. *Sabina's home is gorgeous.*

Tomorrow, I will take you to a special place I found when I first arrived in Menurra. I think you will like it.

If you're with me, I know I will. A bloom of emotion overwhelmed her senses—of loving Rhoane, of being alive, of knowing she was where she needed to be and with a man who loved her so completely he would die protecting her.

They dipped low, flying away from the harbor to land unseen in a densely forested area a bell's walk from the capital. Their talons touched the ground and they sloughed off their dragon forms. It was always bittersweet to return to her Aelan form. She took Rhoane's hand and followed him into the green lushness.

The vines and moss-covered trees reminded her of Enghor's memories. But this place was different. Not a rainforest, per se— it was too arid—but something about the area was off. She scanned the ground, stepping around a circle of mushrooms, and studied the curve of the trees they passed. Where the Narthvier grew flowers of every color imaginable, this forest was all varying shades of green. Not a single blossom disturbed the scenery.

"Something's not right here. There's life, but I also sense decay."

"I sense it as well." Rhoane's pace was steady, but he walked with one hand gripping the hilt of his sword. "When last I was here, flowers were in abundance. Now, there is only death beneath the overgrowth."

"That's what I was thinking. What happened here?"

"I do not know." He stooped to press his palm upon a tree trunk, his eyes closed. "The tree lives, just. Memory is twisted with something elusive. A desire to see the old ones, a fear of the new ones. I do not know what it means."

The air thickened deep into the forest and a quiver of apprehension tickled her belly.

Rhoane wiped his hand on the front of his pants. "We would do well to leave this place. The plants do not know friend from foe."

A vine whipped across Taryn's cheek, leaving a thick gash. She yelped and drew her sword, slashing at the vines.

"Do not fight it. We must hurry." He jogged down the path, with Taryn close behind.

The faster they ran, the more agitated the forest became. Vines ensnared their feet, tripping them. When they hit the ground, leaves would rise up to cover them. At first, they used only their feet and hands to escape the verdant prison, but with each new attack, they had to resort to weapons.

Rhoane sliced through a thicket of briars, his leather pants shredding from the thorns. Blood oozed down his legs and arms. His face was a hopscotch of small cuts. They fought their way through the horrors of the jungle-like forest, cutting limbs from trees, chopping their way through poisonous ferns. Their skin bubbled and hissed, a yellowish pus dripping from the hideous rashes the ferns left.

"You know, if I wasn't so pissed at these things, I might be excited you get to heal me again." Taryn sliced at a wicked-looking vine. Blood-stained thorns aimed for her face, a mouth of sorts with hundreds of tiny pointed fangs opening to engulf her whole. "What the bloody hell is that?"

She swung her sword wide, catching the vine just below the

bud. It landed with a plop on the damp soil, then inched its way toward her boot. A scream rose in her throat, but she bit her cheek to keep from giving it a voice.

Rhoane's sword split the thing in two, then made minced meat of it. "I do not know, nor care to find out. Run, Taryn."

They sprinted through the jungle, avoiding vines, slashing at angry plants. A tendril caught Taryn's hair and she spun around, her sword slashing through the silvery locks with a soft whoosh. With one final push, they broke free of the wretched place.

Stars twinkled in the sky above them. Air as pure and fresh as she'd ever known filled her lungs.

She panted, hands on knees, the wounds a constant burn. "That sucked."

Rhoane bent as well, his chest heaving with the exertion. "Agreed."

The tip of a spear came into focus and Taryn rose slowly. A dozen guards, wearing a dark tunic with the logo of King Faisal on the front, held swords and spears aloft.

"Put down your weapons." One of the guards, a tallish man with jet-black hair and matching eyes, stood a pace in front of the others. He held no weapon, but Taryn saw the faintest glimmer of ShantiMari glistening in a frenzied loop around his body.

"I…" Taryn heaved, not yet having caught her breath. "I am Taryn ap Galendrin, daughter of Empress Lliandra, and this is Prince Rhoane of the Eleri. We're expected at your lord's palace."

"Taryn ap Galendrin is dead."

"Says who?" Rhoane demanded. He faced the weaponless guard, his expression full of fury.

"The Lady of Light herself."

Taryn stared at the guard. Several arguments tumbled through her mind, but none that she cared to utter. The look on his face, and those of the other men, told her he believed the empress and nothing they said would change their minds. A soldier to his left poked a spear at her midsection and ordered her to walk.

Another guard reached to take her sword and snatched his hand back when Ynyd Eirathnacht burned him. Rhoane's half shrug conveyed little sympathy. A grin tilted his lips in the way that made Taryn's knees quiver. She asked one of the guards for his tunic and wrapped their swords in the fabric before handing them to him.

He took the bundle with trepidation and Taryn stifled a laugh. She was too tired and far too annoyed to argue with these dimwits. If they chose to believe she was dead, she'd at least be courteous. After all, dead girls had nothing to lose.

CHAPTER TWENTY

The group marched onto the palace grounds with Taryn and Rhoane bound with leather shackles, a ring of ShantiMari added for more security. They passed under a huge arch, the walls supporting it at least ten feet thick. Guards stood at the entrance, with another four placed inside the archway. Taryn took in the soldiers and buildings, hiding her surprise. She'd expected Sabina's home to be light and airy, but the palace of Menurra was a three-story squat structure. In truth, Taryn thought it quite ugly.

"Not much to write home about, is it?" Taryn mused to no one in particular.

A spear tip jabbed into her back and she winced against the pain that shot across her skin. If that man poked her one more time, she would shove that spear straight up his ass.

Best to not encourage him. Rhoane's thought was edged with mirth.

Laugh now, pay later, Taryn promised.

The path turned to the left and a huge courtyard opened before them. A columned walkway clung to the sides of the structure with an elaborate fountain gracing the center. The group kept to the walkway and entered the palace through a side door. Several buildings enclosed another courtyard, this one with a reflecting pool. Not quite deep enough to swim in, but enough to tempt her to rip off her shackles and dive in.

Sap and nettles from the forest jungle clung to Taryn's hair and clothing, causing discomfort, but the heat had soaked through to her core, leaving her dehydrated, tired, and grumpy.

They passed several corridors, some with high arches and decorative columns stretching down to lush gardens. This was how she'd imagined the palace. The inside definitely didn't match the exterior.

"Taryn!" A familiar voice called out and a swell of love constricted Taryn's chest.

A shrill gasp came from one of the guards. Taryn glanced around her captors. Kaida and Tessa emerged from a pool and dripped water as they rushed to the group.

"What are you doing?" Tessa's little hands fisted onto her hips and she glared at the soldiers. "Don't you know who this is?"

"She claims to be Taryn ap Galendrin," the soldier who'd poked Taryn with the spear said, his confidence less than it had been. "But the empress of Talaith says she's dead."

"Mother said you're dead? Why?" Tessa looked from Taryn to Rhoane.

Something ails the empress. I cannot decipher what it is. But I know it is not natural. Kaida's growl was a comfort to Taryn. She'd missed her grierbas friend. She reached her cuffed hands to pet the grierbas. The touch of Kaida's fur sent waves of calm through Taryn's shattered nerves.

Rhoane explained about their capture outside the forest, and the confusion.

I am glad to see you well. Taryn sent the thought to Kaida. *But confused by your attire.*

Kaida wore a bandana around her neck, an eyepatch over one ear, and had a belt complete with dirk hanging from her waist.

Your sister required a distraction. The events on the ship upset her immensely.

Tears stung Taryn's eyes. She hadn't allowed herself to think of how the ordeal would've affected her friends and family. First to see her beaten repeatedly, then the last they saw of her was in an explosion. She'd been selfish in not wanting to know their torment, but now she had to face it.

Tessa sidled next to Taryn, her hand stretched to clasp her sister's.

Thank you, my friend. I owe you a debt of gratitude for taking care of my sister.

How is it you are healed?

Rhoane. Taryn kept her grin discreet. Who knew if grierbas understood the ways of Ullan healing?

Kaida nudged Rhoane's hand and he scratched behind her ears.

"Certainly you can release them. I vouch for their identities." Tessa addressed the weaponless guard.

"I take my orders from King Faisal."

Taryn squeezed Tessa's hand and shrugged. It wasn't worth the argument. The guards would soon understand they'd made a mistake. She didn't envy them the ribbing they'd get tonight.

They walked through several more corridors until finally they stopped outside a set of closed doors. The weaponless guard paused before opening them. In that pause, Taryn sensed his reluctance and determination. Accepting his fate, he gripped the iron handle and pushed both of the huge doors open. Taryn and Rhoane were prodded forward, but with the butt of a spear now, not the sharp tip. Tessa cast a scowl over her shoulder to the indifferent soldiers.

A handsome man with deep-chestnut hair, and Sabina's eyes, jerked his head to see who had disrupted his evening. He wore no crown, unlike the woman who sat to his right. Ebony waves cascaded over bare shoulders. Her turquoise shift sparkled with gems, but it was the aura of serenity surrounding the woman that took Taryn's breath away.

Dark hair, with equally dark eyes, skin the color of a copper penny, she watched the group approach with a smile tugging her lips. Her elaborate headdress jingled when she turned her head toward Taryn. The slightest of nods was the only sign indicating she knew who entered her throne room.

Taryn returned the gesture, feeling at once unworthy and awed by the woman. Beautiful not just in her physical appearance, the queen radiated compassion.

"Your Majesties, these two were caught trying to infiltrate your lands. We found them on the outskirts of the Hben Firn."

"The Hben Firn?" The king's brows rose and surprise flickered across his features. "What in Julieta's name were you doing there?"

"We meant to arrive unseen, but did not realize your firn would try to kill us," Rhoane supplied before the guard could reply.

"Kill you? How so?" Bells chimed with the queen's movements. Her headdress caught the light and sent reflections skittering across the walls.

"Are you saying these two are who they say they are? This one claims to be the dead daughter of Empress Lliandra." The soldier angled his chin toward Taryn.

The king's glance swept to Taryn and she curtseyed low.

"This is the Eirielle?" Laughter boomed from his lips and those in the room twittered with indecision. "I had imagined you quite different, my girl."

"Well, it was my hope to present myself to you a little cleaner. And without an audience." Taryn's gaze swept the guards and onlookers who had gathered in the corridor.

"Release them," the queen commanded.

A soldier stepped toward her and Taryn broke the restraints in half, dissolving the ShantiMari as she did.

"Thanks, but I've got it." She snapped her finger.

Ynyd Eirathnacht appeared in her hand. The soldier who'd been carrying their swords gasped, his face turning a light shade of ash.

Another bout of laughter came from the king.

"I like her," he said to his wife.

"Welcome." The woman stood and stretched her arms wide. "I am Prateeni, Queen of the Summerlands, and this is my husband, King Faisal. We are honored to have you in our home."

A screeching from the entrance drew their attention. Taryn turned, her grip firm on the sword's hilt. Sabina sprinted through the crowd toward her and she braced for the impact of Sabina's embrace. Tears stung her eyes and she didn't care. She hugged her friend in the tightest embrace she could muster. Sabina's tears mingled with hers as they laughed and cried. Taryn felt Tessa's little arms wrap around her midsection and she reached an arm to include her sister in the hug.

"I thought you dead, you mad, mad woman. Don't you ever, EVER do that again," Sabina said once they'd dried their eyes and had a chance to catch their breath.

"Which part? Getting beaten up or blowing up my mother's ship?"

"All of it. Any of it. I'll gladly suffer the pains of brigands to know you're alive." Sabina pressed her lips against Taryn's, her ShantiMari a wobbly intrusion against her skin. "I'll never be able to thank you for what you endured. I am forever in your debt."

"As we all are." The sound of her cousin's voice almost unraveled the minuscule amount of self-control Taryn had left.

Taryn reached out to him, fresh tears spilling over her cheeks. Hayden's grin widened as he sidled closer and whispered, "Please try to be more careful. Your mother is most upset you nearly destroyed her ship."

Taryn chuckled and held him tighter. Her uncle, his pale

cheeks wet with his own tears, shook his head and beamed. She understood. There were no words to say how relieved and happy she felt in that moment. Baehlon's baritone sounded in the hall, followed by Eliahnna's astonished gasp, and a moment later he, Faelara, and Eliahnna wrapped their arms around the group. Baehlon's big hand patted her head. Somewhere in there, Kaida and Rhoane had squeezed in, making it the best, biggest, and most tear-filled embrace in history. At least to Taryn.

"Where is she? Where is my daughter?" Lliandra's fragile voice called from behind the thrones. "Is it true? She lives?"

Taryn unwound herself from the group and stepped to the side. "Yes, Mother. I'm alive."

Lliandra eyed her skeptically. "You look different."

"I'm a little bruised from some vicious plants, but I'm still me. Still Taryn."

Lliandra enclosed her with a painful squeeze and sobbed against her chest. "You stupid, stupid girl. You could've been killed. Why? Why, Taryn?"

"Why what?" Taryn refused to allow herself to distrust Lliandra's display of emotion. Yet it was there, the doubt and hesitation.

Lliandra sniffed and looked Taryn in the eye. Her mask of ShantiMari held on by a few threads. "Why did you take the abuse?"

"To protect you, Mother," Eliahnna said. "To protect all of us."

Taryn stroked her mother's face, pulling the threads of Lliandra's power tight and securing them with a single thread of her power and a silent wish. Her mother was fading, but whatever had taken hold of her mind oozed Telraicht-Noir ShantiMari. Taryn dared not try to draw it out. Not here. Not yet.

Lliandra's hands in turn traced the lines of Taryn's face as if she were seeing her daughter for the first time. "You've been gone so long. I was told you were dead."

Eliahnna started to answer, but Taryn held up a hand to stop her. "I didn't mean to be gone so long. I'm here now and desperately in need of a bath."

"Yes, you stink, my love."

Several gasps echoed in the room. Taryn took in the wisps of hair around Lliandra's face, the way her gown hung off her collarbone. The empress had lost weight in the few days Taryn had been in Ulla. It might be part of her fade, or stress, but whatever it was, Taryn would do what she could for her mother.

"Go bathe. After, we'll dine together and you can tell me of your adventures since last we met." Lliandra indicated to Taryn that she leave. Her elation turned to sorrow at the realization Lliandra might not know she was in the Summerlands, and not her throne room in Talaith. The coincidence of two rulers fading and losing their memories was not lost on Taryn.

The soldiers had slunk away, leaving Taryn and her friends in the center of the throne room. She glanced at each face, memorizing them as her mother had done to her. These were cherished ones. Her family. Each had tears in their eyes, a look of relief on their faces.

Her sorrow soured to guilt. She would die to protect each and every one of them. Had died, actually, but how many more times could she abandon them without a word to her whereabouts or wellbeing? Tears shimmered in Tessa's eyes and Taryn's heart wrenched. They all knew Taryn would one day die for good and as much as they accepted it, none of them wished for it.

A worm of regret wriggled into her marrow. This wasn't the life she'd choose for herself, or for any of them, but it was the life they were given. It was up to them to make the most of it while they could.

Taryn turned back to the king and queen, catching a glimpse of Lliandra's expression as she did. Behind the mask Taryn secured to her face, Lliandra's features twisted in disgust.

Despite Lliandra's flowery words and pretty show of affection —her mother had wanted her to die on that ship.

CHAPTER TWENTY-ONE

Faelara didn't believe Taryn purposefully wanted to get her into trouble, but if the empress found out they'd snuck away from the palace for a swim, Lliandra would be furious. More so than she already was. Since Taryn's return two days hence, Faelara was impotent to curb Lliandra's irritations—everything from the heat to the tea served at breakfast offended the Lady of Light.

Faelara fidgeted with the heavy skirts she wore. Lliandra forbade any of her ladies from wearing anything other than Talaithian fashions. The poor women could find no relief in the palace, and going outside was even worse. Except when a certain princess had ideas to alleviate the stifling heat.

"I don't know how you ladies do it. I'd be sweating like a pig in those skirts." Taryn swished her midsection and giggled at the string of beads that swayed to and fro. If Lliandra had commanded her daughter to dress appropriately for a princess of Talaith, Taryn had ignored her.

"You're going to get me into trouble again, I fear." Faelara kept herself from plucking her blouse away from her sticky skin.

"Probably."

Due in part to Faelara's dress, a large group was headed to a secluded beach south of Menurra's harbor. Taryn, her sisters, Sabina, Hayden, Rhoane, and Baehlon of course, were closely followed by several soldiers who'd been sworn to secrecy. Lliandra would have a litter of carlix if she ever found out.

Faelara opened the front of her velvet robe to allow some air flow. She'd have to speak with Lliandra about the dress code—this was ridiculous. She would faint of heatstroke within the bell.

"What happened in the jungle?" Faelara changed the subject because she was overheated and talking about her heavy skirts did little to alleviate her discomfort, and also because she'd been curious ever since Taryn and Rhoane returned. Their ragged appearance in the throne room, with scrapes marking their extremities, and twigs stuck to their clothing, was shocking.

Rhoane slowed his step to answer. "Something ails the plant life. We were not welcome there, which is not how I remember the Hben Firn."

"It was terrifying. The plants tried to kill us. Whatever's going on, it's not good." Taryn shuddered and wiped at her arm as if remembering a vine curling against her skin.

Faelara's nose scrunched with her pout. "I was hoping to visit and perhaps study some of the fauna."

"Not on my life," Baehlon grumbled. "You saw the state of these two when they entered the palace, and they're trained swordsmen. How do you think you'd fare?"

"I can handle myself with a weapon, thankyouverymuch." *The cheek!* She was more than capable of protecting herself. She'd been doing a rather fine job of it all her life. Without the help of a man, she might add.

Baehlon stepped beside Faelara and said low enough only she could hear, "Aye, lass, you can. Don't be getting any ideas, now. If you're thinking of seeing the forest, I'm coming with you."

"Why, Sir Baehlon, are you worried about me?"

He placed a hand on her lower back and leaned in, the bells in his braids tinkling with the movement. "You have no idea."

Those four words made her heart gallop and stop and start again. Since the attack on Lliandra's ship, Baehlon had made certain he was close. Always hovering nearby, but never actually interacting with her. It was the same dance they'd practiced since they'd met. Neither one brave enough to admit their affection, neither willing to risk the pain rejection would bring. Their history was steeped in missteps and missed opportunities.

It was time to end the games and take a leap of faith.

With his head bent toward hers, his lips so tantalizingly close, all she had to do was turn her face upward, yet she hesitated. It wouldn't be proper to force herself upon him. She bit her lip and glanced up the slightest bit, just enough to see if he still watched her.

Baehlon jostled and suddenly, she was in his arms, her feet slipping out from under her. His great paws held her fast, his face a study in concern.

"Are you hurt?" he asked.

"No, confused. What happened?"

He set her upright, his arm wrapped around her shoulder. "I believe the Eirielle tripped."

Taryn held her side, her face swollen with suppressed laughter.

"Did you push him into me?"

"Me? What? Why would you say such a slanderous thing? I never!" Taryn's fists pounded against her hips, her face set in indignation.

Rhoane's laughter burst forth and soon Faelara and Baehlon joined in.

"Hayden, do you understand the madness of your cousin?" Sabina's voice came from behind them.

"Not a whit. But you know, she is rather good at matchmaking."

Faelara ignored the taunt. They were outnumbered, it seemed. Baehlon kept his arm around her shoulder as they continued to the beach. She didn't need his support, but she craved the warmth his body heat gave off. It was definitely past time for new beginnings.

They rounded the corner and the sea spread out before them. Faelara sucked in a breath. The glittering water never ceased to enchant her. Whether it was the shores of Talaith, or the Summerlands, something about the blue-green depths called to her, awakened a yearning she didn't quite understand, nor ever satisfied.

Tessa was already splashing in the water when they arrived and Taryn made short work of stripping to her swimming garments. Faelara busied herself setting up their blankets and shades while Rhoane and Baehlon patrolled the area with several soldiers. Sabina raced for the water, leaving Hayden and Eliahnna to help Faelara. They each grabbed a blanket, neither speaking as they spread the fabric over sand. Eliahnna then unpacked a basket of food, placing each item with care.

Hayden caught Faelara's eye and motioned to his cousin. Faelara shook her head and shrugged.

"Eliahnna, you seem melancholy today. Is there anything I can do to help ease your burdens?" Faelara settled on a blanket near the crown princess.

"It's nothing. Thank you for your concern, though."

"I helped bring you into this world. I've watched you grow into a lovely young woman. I know when something is bothering you." She took Eliahnna's hand in her own and traced the lines of her palm. "What troubles you, my sweet?"

Eliahnna sighed and slumped into herself. "Look at them." She pointed to the waves, where the group was splashing each other. "Even the guards are having a good time. Do you know what Mother said to me this morning? 'Don't do anything to besmirch my crown, Daughter.' It's always about her. Her kingdom, her crown, her throne. Yet I'm not allowed to enjoy any of it, or even behave like them because someday it will be *my* crown." Her huge blue-green eyes searched Faelara's features. "I never thought to inherit, even though Taryn tried to warn me on several occasions. I had a far different future planned."

"Does that future involve a certain Eleri lad?"

A look of panic crossed her pale face. "What do you mean?"

"Come now, your secret is safe with me." Faelara tapped the girl's chest where the wooden pendant hung. "Eoghan made this for you, didn't he?" At Eliahnna's brief nod, Faelara continued. "I know the two of you correspond often."

"Do you think Mother is aware?"

"I would assume so. When you're the empress of Talaith, you may reign however you see fit. You don't have to continue the tradition of bedding hordes of men to beget heirs. You could rally a new era for the Crystal Throne. Take Eoghan as your consort or marry him and proclaim him emperor. It's your crown and your kingdom. The only thing you must do, without fail, is care for your subjects. They should be your priority, not your sleeping arrangements."

"Are you going to sit here all day gossiping?" Hayden grabbed Eliahnna's hand and dragged her to the water, both of them laughing.

Faelara sat on the uncomfortable sand, her many layers of clothing doing nothing to ease her annoyance. The call of the ocean reached her ears and she struggled to shut it out. It was a mistake to come here, to this cove, of all places.

She twisted to avoid seeing the water, but her ears picked up every sound. Waves rolling against the shore, critters above and beneath the surf chattering—she tried in vain to shut it out.

Then, overriding the ocean sounds, she heard singing.

For several long breaths, she listened, her head cocked at an angle, her eyes closed. Yes, singing. Many voices harmonized a song meant just for her.

She rose, her irritation with the heat forgotten, and stumbled toward the water. Long ago, when she wasn't much older than Taryn, Faelara lived in Menurra with the queen and king. She'd loved her life in the Summerlands and spent many happy days at this very cove.

Her toe stubbed on a pebble and she faltered, shaking the memory from her mind. No, she wouldn't go into the warm depths of the sea, not ever again. *Not since—*

The singing rose in tempo and volume, drowning out Tessa's giggles and Kaida's barks. They beckoned her—*join them*, the song said. *Join them and be free.*

With no small amount of effort, she shifted one foot and then the next. Her heart yearned to return to the sea, but her body refused to operate correctly. It was as if she'd forgotten how to walk. She shuffled closer to the waves, her heart beating harder than it should. Her vision blurred and focused to a narrow path. She wore no blinkers, yet anything outside of her peripheral was lost to hazy greyness.

The more she propelled herself forward, the easier walking became.

The song surrounded her. The words pinched against her skin.

Water lapped at her ankles, soaking the boots she wore. The hem of her skirts dragged with the pull of the surf returning to the sea.

Long ago, she would spend entire days at the cove with the little princes and princesses. Each year, she would compete in their races, often winning.

She loved the water—loved to swim. Until that day so long ago.

A wave crashed against her waist, knocking her back a step, but she plowed ahead, her face set with determination.

Long ago, she loved to swim.

Then one day she went beyond the swells and shore break.

Her lungs expanded with each intake of air, her arms powerful in their strokes. She trusted the water back then. Before she knew there was something to fear beneath the surface.

Faelara hesitated.

That day, so long ago the memory should've been lost to time, she'd found herself too far from shore to call for help. Exhausted, frightened, and alone, she'd tried frantically to swim back to the safety of land, but each kick sent her farther away from the cove.

The singing continued, lulling her with its sweet melody. She continued into the surf until she could no longer feel the sandy bottom beneath her feet.

Yes, she thought. *Yes, I've missed this.*

We've missed you, Lady Faelara, the singing answered.

A surge of joy encompassed her and she let go of her anxiety. Let the waves take her fear like a butler would take a cloak.

Down she went, into the depths. Above her, the sun reflected on the surface, but the farther she sank, the smaller the spot of golden starburst became.

She held her breath and floated. Her clothing drifted around her in a cloud of burgundies and greens. So much fabric. Velvets and cottons, too heavy for the Summerlands heat.

There was no burning sun here in the expanse of deepest blue.

The song heightened and Faelara turned toward the sound. There, not more than an arm's length from where she floated, was a face she'd only ever seen once before.

Long ago, Faelara loved to swim.

Then one day she found herself too far from shore.

She panicked and kicked with all the energy she had remaining, but it was too little too late.

Then something joined her as she struggled to return to shore.

Not a creature nor a beast, but a woman.

A woman with auburn hair and eyes the color of a forest. Not just one green, but many. Her milk white skin shimmered like scales when she swam.

Faelara stared into the face of the woman who had saved her on that day so long ago.

Her chest heaved and she swallowed the air she'd been holding. The woman's face crumbled with worry. Another, stronger, pump from her heart and Faelara released the air in her lungs. Water rushed through her mouth to her lungs.

She jerked against the intrusion, her body shaking with the loss of breathing.

The woman's encouraging smile frightened Faelara. A slim hand reached out to take Faelara's and she was pulled lower, away from the surface and life-giving oxygen.

Baehlon.

The thought settled in her heart as the final light from the sun blinked out and she was surrounded by silence.

CHAPTER TWENTY-TWO

Rhoane noticed Faelara's absence first. He scanned the shore, then the waves, catching a hint of auburn as it slipped beneath the water. For twenty breaths, he counted, waiting for her to reemerge. When she didn't, he edged closer to the shore, his eyes locked on the spot he saw her go under.

Another twenty breaths passed.

Rhoane sprinted to the waves and dove beneath them.

Terror gripped his nerves and he faltered, flailing wildly in the water.

Faelara, he chided himself. She's in danger. He swallowed his fear and stilled his movements. Fae was a good swimmer. Although, a nagging thought tugged at his mind, he hadn't seen her go into the water for quite some time. Long ago, she'd swum in this very cove, but not for several seasons.

A roar of sea creatures deafened him and he fought to tone down their ramblings. Unlike on the terrarae, sounds beneath the water vibrated and echoed, a constant murmuring in his head. Rhoane understood about half of the chattering.

He kicked hard and swam farther under the water, to beyond the breakers where the depths were calmer. Dozens of fish swam past, their tails swishing against the current he created with his movements. From far away, he thought he heard singing. A chill cast through his bloodstream, despite the warmth of the water. He'd heard similar sounds from those who'd come to him in a dream long ago.

The mythical merfolk, yes, but it was the other that vexed him most. On a deserted beach a short ride from where they were now, he'd dreamt of a darathi eneari. She had shown him many wonderful things, but she'd also warned him he'd betray Taryn not once, but twice, and then he would kill her.

Rhoane never forgot those words, whispered in his mind to burrow further into his spirit until it became part of his life force. Her snouted face became the source of nightmares. Season after season he'd tried to ignore the warning. No matter how hard he tried, it was there, just beneath the surface of everything he did. And now, it was coming true.

He'd already betrayed Taryn once, and almost broke his spirit in the process. Another betrayal would destroy him. He couldn't let that happen.

A motion to his right caught his attention and he turned toward it, half horrified it would be the creature. Baehlon thrashed against the steady current, his cheeks puffed out, eyes wild. He shook his head and pointed to the surface before kicking upward.

Rhoane touched his lips, the ones the darathi eneari had placed her own upon all those seasons ago. He could breathe under water. Confusion scoured his mind. It had been a dream, one deriving from a day spent in the sun without food or water. A hallucination. Had to have been.

In the shadowy depths, he swam until his chest ached. The singing grew louder and he propelled himself faster. There, in the near blackness, he saw Faelara's lifeless form floating behind a woman with hair like a sunset.

Rhoane kicked hard to catch up and grasped Fae's wrist. She

blinked, startling him. Her gaze went from his hand to the woman's, then back to Rhoane.

"Where am I?" Her words were slurred beneath the water, but he clearly heard her.

"Please," Rhoane said to the woman, "let her go. She is not a water breather."

"You know not of what you speak, Prince Rhoane of the Eleri." The woman tugged on Faelara's other wrist and jerked her away from Rhoane.

He doubled his grip and held fast. Fae's grunt came out as a large bubble from her open lips.

The woman swished and a moment later, she was an inch from Rhoane's face. Her multi-hued green eyes regarded him with hostility. "She is mine. You've had her long enough."

Three things rammed through Rhoane's brain simultaneously: the woman was not a woman, but a mermaid. She knew who he was and had called him by name. She wasn't going to give up Faelara without a fight.

"Who are you?" Fae asked, her head tilted to see the mermaid's face. "I feel like I know you."

The mermaid hissed and bared her fanged teeth at Rhoane. He instinctively backed away, lessening his grip on Faelara. With a grin that showed none of the fangs, only pearly white, straight teeth, she beat her tail and swam off with Faelara trailing behind.

"No," Rhoane shouted and sent a spiral of his ShantiMari to ensnare both the mermaid and Faelara.

The water spirit fought against his power with her own. A new song started, its tempo faster, no longer lulling. Rhoane's heart beat in time to the tune. His muscles strained to counteract the strength of the mermaid. They were locked in a stalemate, with Fae at the center of the battle. With each parry from either Rhoane or the mermaid, Fae was tossed and jostled. Her many skirts fluttered in wide circles around her shimmering body. A tickle of anxiety started at the base of his neck.

Faelara had spoken to him. Under water. That wasn't possible.

He gathered a massive ball of energy, using the ocean's flux for increased power, and aimed it at the mermaid. As he wrenched his arm back to throw, horror crossed the woman's features and she released her hold on Faelara.

A swish of fin was all he saw before the singing stopped and he was left holding his unspent ShantiMari.

Rhoane dared not look behind him to the thing that frightened the mermaid away, but he had to—had to see for himself the face from his nightmares. A long tendril snaked its way toward him and his stomach clenched. It wasn't possible. Yet every part of him screamed that it was true. It hadn't been a dream.

The creature came into focus and the cramp in his gut spun outward to paralyze his movements. He couldn't breathe as he watched the darathi eneari swim closer to Fae. His lungs burned and his heart pumped faster, but he remained frozen.

"Breathe, my prince." The water dragon glanced in his direction. "It is not yet your time."

His body wilted as he took in a huge gulp of water. What should have killed him, didn't.

"Not my time for what?"

A warbled smile lifted her lips. "You will know when it is time."

Riddles. Rhoane hated them as much as Taryn did.

Taryn.

Fresh panic raced through his veins. Something had saved her after the explosion. He peered closer at the darathi eneari, who was cradling Faelara in her whisker-like tendrils. It was a simple thing to ask, but then he'd know and Rhoane didn't want this creature anywhere near his beloved. What she'd told him so many seasons past would destroy Taryn if she knew Rhoane would betray her once more.

Then he would kill her.

No. No, she could never know about the darathi. Whatever saved her was a mermaid, most likely.

Rhoane silently applauded the ease with which he manipulated his belief system. He'd distract Taryn if she ever mentioned the water folk again. He couldn't lie to her—they'd both done too much of that already—but he could avoid the topic.

"Are you finished?" The water dragon's huge eyes regarded him with mischief lurking in their depths.

Rhoane opened his mouth to speak, then shut it. Then opened it again to say, "Taryn can never know. Please. What you told me once, when I thought I was dreaming, she can never know. It will destroy her."

The darathi swam toward the surface, Fae safely in her hold. "She is stronger than you give her credit."

Annoyance throbbed in his brain. He knew plenty well how strong Taryn was.

Several strokes before the water break, she stopped her forward momentum and turned to face him. Her tendrils unfurled and Fae drifted in the space between him and the water dragon.

"Not all deaths are in vain." Then she was gone.

A current from her long tail launched them toward the water's surface and Rhoane grabbed Fae around the waist. A wave carried them to shore, where Baehlon rushed to take Faelara into his arms. He raced up the sand to their blankets and lay Fae on the closest one.

"Breathe for me, please." Baehlon turned Faelara to her side and patted her back. "Breathe, damn you."

Rhoane followed close behind and skidded to a stop at the blanket's edge before kneeling to assess Fae's condition. Taryn sprinted over and knelt on the other side of the stricken woman. He felt Taryn's power combine with his as she examined their friend's vital organs. Her brows dipped to a V, her lips pulled taut. She felt it, too. Water clogged Fae's lungs and her heart had stopped beating.

"Breathe, Faelara," Taryn cooed. "Breathe, sweetness."

"Turn her a little more, so she faces the sand," Rhoane instructed Baehlon.

He pushed his power into her lungs, expelling sea water as a thread of Taryn's ShantiMari closed around her heart and massaged it. They worked in tandem, him forcing air where it didn't want to be, and she valiantly mimicking a heartbeat.

Faelara jerked as if shocked, then her mouth opened and closed as if gasping for air. Taryn's sharp intake of breath caused a spike of alarm to slash through his thoughts.

"Again," Taryn said, sweat dripping from her nose. "Force her to expel the water."

He pushed his power deeper, and shoved upward. He wasn't sure if he heard or felt a pop, but then Faelara coughed and gagged, spewing sea water onto the blankets and he didn't care. The life-stealing water had been removed. The others gathered close and Taryn asked for space. Faelara choked several times before she raised a hand to her throat. Her eyes widened until they almost bugged. Her face turned several shades of red before darkening to a sickening purple.

"What's happening? What did you do to her?" Baehlon's frantic expression matched Rhoane's thoughts.

Faelara's heart now beat, weak, but steady. She should've been breathing air, but instead was suffocating. Taryn bent low to place her mouth over Fae's and blew air from herself to her friend. Rhoane studied her as if in a daze. He saw and heard the others, but he was apart from them.

Something the darathi eneari said tickled his memory.

"Get me a cup of sea water," Rhoane told Baehlon. At his bellow, he cut him short. "Just do it. Now."

Taryn turned from Fae's unmoving body to stare at him. "Are you mad?"

"I hope not." Her eyes narrowed and he told her, "It is a gut instinct." She of all people couldn't argue with him about instinct. The amount of times she'd asked to be trusted without any assurances was too many to count on two hands.

Baehlon plopped on the blanket and handed Rhoane a wineskin. "You won't harm her?" Baehlon's concern spilled past his words. He smoothed Faelara's hair while watching Rhoane.

Taryn moved aside and Rhoane tipped the wineskin to Fae's lips. Seawater poured over them to run down the sides of her face.

Someone behind him cried and another comforted, but Rhoane couldn't give them thought or energy. He focused everything on Faelara.

His fingertips shook as he held her wrist. A faint fluttering beneath her skin quickened his own heart rate. There, under the milky white of her flesh, he thought he saw a flash of something shimmering. Like scales.

Again, he streamed seawater from the bag.

Faelara gasped and sputtered the water, making several people behind him jump and cry out. He held firm to her wrist, noting the striations of color that vibrated up and down her forearm.

Not darathi vorsi scales, but something else.

Her lips stretched and she opened her mouth to take in more. She gulped and swallowed until the entire skin was empty. With each drag of water, her heartbeat strengthened and her breathing evened out.

Concern clouded his relief. When he looked again at her arm, it was nothing more than pallid flesh beneath layers of burgundy velvet.

Baehlon propped her against his chest where she rested her head against the giant knight. Her unfocused eyes swiveled from one face to the next, a smile growing larger with each.

"What happened?" Her voice came out scratchy and barely audible.

"You went for a swim, ye daft girl." Baehlon continued to stroke her hair, an air of tempered happiness about him.

"In my clothes?" Faelara shook her head against the knight's shoulder. "What a remarkable thing to do."

Rhoane put a hand to Fae's cheek and blew out a breath at the warmth coming from her skin. "We thought we might lose you to King Baldev." The look he gave her was steeped in meaning.

"I don't like swimming." Fae's words didn't hold conviction.

"Then I suggest you do not go into the water fully clothed." Rhoane motioned for Eliahnna to bring a blanket to place over Faelara's wet garments.

He leaned back and met Taryn's curious gaze. Her deep, almost midnight-blue eyes reminded him of the sea where twice now he'd met the water dragon.

She is stronger than you give her credit.

The words echoed alongside her warning of the betrayals, and finally, the ominous *Not all deaths are in vain.*

Rhoane took Taryn's hand in his own and kissed her palm. She tilted her head and grinned, but didn't ask the questions swirling in the depths of her eyes. They'd saved Fae, and somehow, he'd save them as well. Despite the darathi's words, he'd never kill Taryn.

CHAPTER TWENTY-THREE

Taryn stayed with Faelara long after she'd insisted she was fine and ordered the others to enjoy their day. Baehlon didn't leave Fae's side. He doted on her and for the time being, Fae allowed it. Taryn swallowed more than a few chuckles as she watched the pair dance around each other's feelings.

What they needed was a chance to be together without court speculation or interference from Lliandra. Or herself, if she was honest. An idea formed in her mind—a scandalous one that would have her mother pitching a fit. She rested Faelara's hand in her own and grinned with the wickedness of her mind.

"It makes me nervous when you smile like that," Baehlon groused. "It usually means I'll be in trouble soon enough."

"Funny, that's what Faelara said earlier. Are you two plotting against me?"

They shared a look—one that couples who have been together for a long time share and Taryn's grin grew even larger.

"Don't encourage her." Faelara's fingertips curled around Taryn's.

Kaida loped up the beach and snuggled beside Taryn with a languid huff.

Done for the day? Taryn pet the grierbas's wet fur, untangling snarls the waves had caused.

The child is exhausting. But she is much happier now that you have returned.

Taryn sighed, the grin slipping from her face. *We'll be leaving soon enough. I fear she won't be happy to see us off.*

Where will we be traveling?

Taryn leaned her head close to the animal's. *I'm not sure. It depends on which answer I seek to find first. Who is Cashiel, what is Mallaqai's vortex, or what's happening in Ulla? I'm missing something crucial for all of the riddles and it's pissing me off.*

Kaida's nose snuffled her hand. *You are not alone, Darennsai. There are others just as capable of solving puzzles.*

Taryn snuck a glance at her knight protector and Faelara. Kaida was right. Her friends were more than capable.

The others straggled to the blankets in pairs. All of them dripped water except Rhoane. He'd spent much of the last bell staring at the horizon. He was hiding something from her, she could tell. Faelara, too. Something had happened beneath the waves that neither wanted to speak of. Whatever it was, Taryn told herself, she needn't worry. If it was important, they would share it in their own time.

They packed up their supplies and shuffled up the hill with less energy than they'd descended it that morning. By now, Lliandra was bound to know Taryn had taken the princesses out of the palace and would be livid.

"Sister," Tessa said quietly as she slipped her hand into Taryn's. "When we were on the ship and that man beat you, why did you let him?"

Taryn drew her baby sister in close, with a fierce sense of protectiveness. "I thought if I could keep him focused on me, he wouldn't harm you."

"But he would have anyway. Surely you know this," Eliahnna argued.

"I didn't know for sure, and I had to prevent him from hurting you. Any of you. All of you." Simple words, but they were at the heart of her burden. How could she protect them all?

You cannot, Darennsai. You must trust them and let go of your need to be everything to all things. Kaida's thought touched her own.

Easier said than done, my friend. Taryn stroked Kaida with her free hand. *I love them too much to see them suffer.*

"He said the most dreadful thing." Tessa curled her arm around Taryn's waist and rested her head against her ribs. "When he held me, I could hardly breathe. He said, 'I shall take you and your sisters hard, with no compassion or thought to your pleasure, then I'll slit your throats and watch you die. Whatever would Mother do then?' and he laughed a little, like it would be the most splendid thing ever. I've never been so frightened. Not for me, but you."

Taryn's step faltered and she tasted sickness in her throat. A pounding started at the sides of her head and a roar rushed through her hearing. "He was a terrible man and I'm going to find him." She kept her words even, her tone serious, but not dramatic.

"But he's dead," Tessa stated.

"I don't believe so. Something tells me he survived the explosion."

A tremble rocked her little sister and Taryn regretted her words. "Do you think he'll come for me?" Tessa tightened her grip on Taryn's waist.

"No, I think he's off somewhere licking his wounds. Whoever sent him won't be pleased he didn't get what he came for."

"I think, after a nice bath and some refreshments, we should all play a game of chantain. Father has a wonderful set in his library. Perhaps we can persuade him to let us use it?" Sabina tactfully changed the subject and Taryn mouthed a silent *Thank you.* "I do adore the beach, but the sand I'm really not fond of."

"It gets everywhere," Baehlon agreed. "And chafes places that ought not to be chafed."

A crimson stain covered Faelara's cheeks and she held her fan close to hide the blush. But Taryn guessed her friend was thinking of ways she could alleviate Baehlon's discomfort. Her plan was brilliant, but she'd have to get Lliandra to agree.

Myrddin. Taryn sent the thought toward the palace, hoping the mage wasn't busy.

Yes, Taryn?

We're heading back from the beach. Can you meet me in Mother's rooms in a quarter bell?

She's not pleased you took Eliahnna out of the palace.

Seriously, Myrddin, when is she ever pleased?

"Tessa." Taryn bent low to whisper in her little sister's ear. "When you get to the palace, go straight to your rooms for a bath. If Mother sends guards to escort you to her apartment, ignore them. Have everyone meet in my suite in one bell. Do you understand?"

"What's going on? Is Mother upset?" Tessa stage-whispered so everyone could hear.

"Not as much as she will be." Taryn kissed Tessa's forehead. "Promise you'll bring everyone?"

"Yes, of course, but why?"

"You'll see." Taryn sprinted up the hill, calling back to her friends she would meet with them soon.

Once in her rooms, she did something she rarely did and used her power to transform her ragged, salt-stained beach attire into something her mother would approve of. Nowhere near as nice as a hot shower, but her ShantiMari cleaned her skin and warped her hair into draping tendrils. Within five minutes, she strode to her mother's rooms, no one the wiser. Even her maids had missed the show. They were with Darius for their afternoon sword lessons.

A guard stood sentry outside the empress's luxe apartment, only allowing Taryn entrance once Myrddin had opened the door and gave his approval. It was a tired, tedious game, but one her mother insisted upon. Those tiny displays of power annoyed Taryn beyond reason, but they were also what had given her the idea to confront her mother before the others returned from the beach.

Myrddin folded Taryn into an embrace.

"Please don't disappear like that again. We're still not recovered from the events on the ship." Myrddin's voice was full of concern. "I thought I'd lost you. Thought we all had. You were very brave." His whispered words stabbed her gut.

"And foolish," Taryn admitted. Guilt laced those two words.

"You're returned to us. It's a miracle." He held her at arm's length, a frown pulling his brows to a dangerous point. "The princesses said you were beaten nearly to death. How is it you're here, alive?" She'd not had time to speak privately with Myrddin since her return, which caused another slice of guilt.

"It's a long story. And we have an audience." Taryn indicated the two guards standing at the open door.

The door closed of its own volition and he held her tighter.

"Yes, yes, I understand." Myrddin's warm lips pressed against her forehead. His tears dripped onto her cheek. "Forgive my unseemly show of affection."

Taryn wrapped her arms around him and held off her own tears. "Thanks for worrying about me."

"We all worry, my dear." His look penetrated through her doubts. She didn't have to ask who he meant.

He led her into an open room flowing with gauzy draperies. Diamond-studded chandeliers hung from the ceiling in several places, casting a warm glow around the lavishly decorated room. Pillows in rich shades of purple, orange, and teal spilled from sofas onto the floor, where some of Lliandra's ladies sat, fanning themselves.

"Taryn, to what do I owe this unscheduled visit?" Lliandra drawled from where she lounged near an open window.

Taryn had to bend at an odd angle and stretch her arms to embrace her mother. "I've missed you. Is it so terrible for a daughter to want to see her mother?"

"Of course not, darling. Sit." Lliandra indicated a chair and Taryn plopped onto the overstuffed cushion.

One of the servants Taryn recognized from Talaith brought them drinks. She hoped it wasn't that disgusting trisp her mother adored. Thankfully, it was one of Faisal's rich wines. She sipped slowly, enjoying the notes of chocolate that slipped down her throat.

"Why is it you're truly here?" Lliandra eyed her above her own goblet. "We both know you were missing from the palace all day, with Tessa and Eliahnna, I've been told. I'm most vexed you didn't come to me for permission. Is that why you're here now? To ask forgiveness?"

Damn, her mother was good. But this time, she was wrong.

Taryn decided to begin with diplomacy. Even though she'd rather be anywhere else but in her mother's rooms, she needed the empress's blessing for her plan to succeed.

"I know I should've asked first, but you have too short a leash on those girls. They need to experience the world, to see not only their kingdom, but all the others as well." Taryn drew in a ragged breath. "They need to live a little outside the confines of your palace."

"And do they also need to be taken prisoner and almost raped by a madman?" The chill in Lliandra's voice was a warning.

It was a fair point, but Taryn ignored the question. Any answer she gave would be countered with another claim of putting her sisters at risk.

"Are you any closer to discovering how Cashiel was able to

cut off the entire ship from ShantiMari?" Taryn took another sip of her wine, regretting not eating more for lunch. Her stomach swirled with the alcohol. She placed the goblet on the table until her thoughts settled.

"He used a circle of thirteen powerful Telraicht mages." Myrddin took a seat in a chair centered between the two women. His hands splayed over his thighs. "I've been making inquiries here in Menurra, and have sent men to both Talaith and the west to find clues as to his identity and where he came from."

"At least we won't be bothered by him again. But there will be others." Lliandra stared at Taryn. "Which is why I can't allow you to take your sisters away from my protection."

"With all due respect, Mother, you were on that ship as well. Your protection was useless. That's why those girls need to be strong of mind, body, and the power. You can't keep pretending life is how it was before I returned. Everything's changed."

The mask Taryn had secured to her mother's face held fast, giving the empress a youthful, healthy appearance. Beneath it, Taryn saw Lliandra's lips snarl and her eyes tighten.

Her mother's fingertips danced along her jaw, then up to her temple. "I feel you here, you know. Your strength, your compassion, your love. Some days, I don't believe I deserve any of those things. Not from you."

The words sucker-punched Taryn. When she thought her mother might rail and hurl abuse, she almost complimented her daughter. Almost. If Taryn weren't exhausted and hungry and tired of the drama, she might've asked Lliandra what she meant. It was too late in the day for her to worry over a phrase. Still, it rankled.

"Today is a new day, Mother. You have a choice right here, right now, to change or continue on as you have. The world is evolving. For better or worse, things are happening out of our control. It's how we react to those changes that will determine our future."

Lliandra's unsteady gaze slid to Myrddin. "I'm tired, my love. I think I should like to rest."

A swear word sprang to Taryn's lips, along with a whole slew of unkind terms. She was tired of being pushed aside, but as she watched her mother's hand shake hard enough to spill her wine, she swallowed her ire.

"Are you ill?" Taryn knelt in front of the empress and took her wrist. Lliandra's pulse fluttered beneath the skin. "Is this part of her fade?"

"I'm afraid it is. The ordeal on the ship took many seasons from her. The fade is advancing." Unabashed love and worry wove through the creases of Myrddin's brow. "I do what I can for her, but you cannot stop the process once it's begun."

Guilt tore through her thoughts. She'd caused this. She'd stolen unknown seasons from her mother and for what? "What can I do? There must be something."

Lliandra smoothed a curl from Taryn's face. "Continue to be as brave and reckless as you are, my daughter. It's in your spirit to fight, and I fear there is war coming to these once peaceful lands."

The gentleness unsettled Taryn's nerves. This kinder Lliandra was what she'd always hoped for, but not if it meant she'd lose her mother sooner. "Not if I can help it." Taryn bore meaning into her steady gaze. "I won't let anyone tear this world apart."

"I believe you. Finally, I see what you were meant to do." A tear streaked over Lliandra's smooth cheek. "I once wanted you dead and I'm sorry for that. I feared you. Your power, your youth, your beauty. I thought if I could eliminate you, nothing would change, but I see now I was wrong."

Taryn had always suspected, but to hear the words spoken so plainly, she reeled with the admission. The wine in her empty stomach soured and tears pricked her eyes. No daughter wanted to hear their mother say they wanted them dead. Even if Lliandra were to declare to all of Aelinae she loved Taryn, something had been lost. The last thread of hope Taryn held onto frayed and dissipated. Lliandra could never be the mother Taryn had always longed for—would never see her as a woman and not the Eirielle.

Her mother wasn't comfortable with the amount of Shanti-Mari Taryn could wield, fine. But to admit she'd wanted Taryn dead? Tears threatened to spill over and she blinked them away. The last thing she wanted was to show Lliandra weakness.

"What else have you been wrong about, Mother?" Taryn used her anger to burn away the pain Lliandra's admission caused. "Do you know anything about the illegal taxes, or what that money was used for?"

The empress shook her head. "Truly, I don't. I have signed papers stating this, and I have promised to keep a watch over all trade in my kingdom."

Whether she was lying or not, Taryn didn't really care. She needed to know something far more important and that question had served to focus her emotions and distract Lliandra. "What about Cashiel? Did you recognize him?"

"W-w-w-hy, of course not. Are you implying I had anything to do with the attack? That's low, Taryn." Her mother stuttered the answer.

It *was* low. Taryn was using Lliandra's tactics against her. Taryn softened her tone. "It's just, he behaved strangely toward you and said something peculiar to Tessa."

Myrddin leaned forward, his blue eyes intent. The care he'd worn on his aging face doubled. "What are you suggesting?"

Taryn bit her nail, unsure of her misgivings. "Where are your sons, Mother? Do you keep in contact with them?"

The empress blinked at the direct question. "With their fathers, I would imagine. Once they leave the palace, we have no further communication."

Harsh, but that was her mother. Compassion was a blight in her world.

"Do you believe Cashiel is one of Lliandra's sons?" Myrddin crossed an ankle over his bent knee and leaned into the soft cushions of his chair. His fingers stroked his short beard, tugging the ends hard enough to pull the skin.

Myrddin had put into words an idea she'd been considering. His astute observation eased some of the tension she'd been holding.

"I never got a look at him," Myrddin admitted. "Lliandra, was there anything about him that would indicate he's your son?"

"Of course not. I hardly paid him any attention. I suppose any of the men on Aelinae could be my sons and I wouldn't recognize them. Males, as you know, are of no use to me."

Taryn choked on the sip of wine she'd drunk. The irony of her mother's statement was lost on the empress, however. Without her gaggle of adoring men, there wouldn't be any heirs to inherit the Light Throne.

"How many are there?" A bitter seed of grief settled in her gut. She'd never thought to ask about them. They were as much her brothers as Zakael. Considering the way he treated her and her sisters, it might've been for the best she never sought out Lliandra's sons. Although, now she might need to.

"Three, originally, but the firstborn died about ten seasons past. Kane and Gren are living still," Myrddin said. "I have, from time to time, paid a visit to the villages where they were raised. The last was, oh, about six seasons past. Good lads. Quiet, intelligent. They didn't strike me as someone who would beat a woman near to death."

Taryn pulled her gaze from her mother to look Myrddin in the eye. "I've learned that people are rarely what they appear to be."

She'd also learned over the course of the past season that her gut was often right. In this instance, she hoped it was dreadfully wrong. What better way to exact revenge on a mother who cast you out than to slaughter her daughters? If Taryn, Eliahnna, and Tessa died, there would be no one left to inherit the Light Throne.

A tremor ran the length of her. Unless Cashiel didn't truly want to kill his sisters. He might've been saying that to frighten Tessa. Cashiel had wanted Taryn's darathi vorsi, not to control the most powerful women on Aelinae, but to control all dragons. Why? Taryn worked through possible motivations her brothers might have. Or, did Cashiel think by capturing her dragon he would have control of the empress? With Zakael in the west, and Cashiel in the east, they could rule as they saw fit, without much opposition from the other kingdoms.

The weapons Marissa had smuggled from Haversham, Taryn realized with a burning dread in her belly, weren't for Lliandra. Hell, her mother might have told the truth about the taxes. Taryn's mind spun with each new revelation. The Haversham weapons were for Zakael. And that creature in Amdi's arena, Enghor—he was a test.

Her belly buzzed with horrified anxiety. Somehow, Zakael had found a way to travel to other worlds. His schemes reached far beyond what Aelinae could offer. And somehow, she was the linchpin to everything.

CHAPTER TWENTY-FOUR

By the time Taryn returned to her rooms, the others were waiting. Faelara reclined on a sofa, Baehlon attentive at her side. Sabina, Hayden, and Rhoane stood to one side, their heads bent in conversation. Tessa sat near Faelara, her feet swinging beneath her seat. Eliahnna hovered close to the balcony windows, a pensive expression on her face. Scattered plates, some with remnants of a meal growing cold, were nestled among half-empty glasses. Rhoane and Hayden held crystal tumblers full of amber liquid. At first glance, it looked like a dinner party rather than the strategic planning session it would soon become.

Rhoane noticed her entry before the others. Always attuned to her location, he was like a sun orbiting a planet. Or was it she was the sun, and he her world? Their gazes met and a frown creased his usually smooth brow. In two steps, he was there, beside her, his hand at her elbow. Even that small amount of touch set off spasms through her nerves. *He'd be the death of her.*

At the thought, her breath stilled.

The old Ullan crone's warning settled in her heart anew. Rhoane would betray her twice, then he would kill her.

Bring it. She'd already died once after she blew up Lliandra's ship; she was certain of it. That was why Enghor had called her Dead One. He smelled the pall of death on her. What would be another death? And by Rhoane's hand? As long as it involved his sex magic, she wouldn't care.

"What troubles you?" Rhoane's silky voice came just behind her ear. His warm breath tickled the hairs on her neck.

"Just accepting what the gods throw at me, I guess." She turned and brushed his cheek with her lips. "Nothing you ever do will make me not love you. Always remember."

His eyes clouded. "I will remember. As you should keep in your heart the knowledge you are my life, Taryn ap Galendrin. I would never knowingly hurt you."

"I know." She held his gaze, unease rippling down her back. The turn of phrase, and the stress he put upon the words—she would have to keep tighter control of her thoughts. It wouldn't do if he plucked the old crone's warning from her memories. She never wanted him to know what she'd been told in Ulla. It would only hurt him, and they'd been through too much already.

"Would you like us to leave?" Hayden snorted. "If you need privacy, please, say the word. Otherwise, if it's not too inconvenient, would you care to tell us why we've been assembled?"

"I have news." Taryn scanned their faces and scrambled for the best way to present her hypothesis.

"Well, what is it?" Tessa asked.

"I believe I know who our mysterious pirate is, and why he chose to attack Mother's ship when he did."

Their voices rose in unison. Question upon question was hurled at her, and she withered under the scrutiny. It was a working theory, nothing more, but they wanted details.

Taryn gave them a complete account of her conversation with Myrddin and Lliandra, including her misgivings about her half-brother Zakael. They listened intently, not even stopping her to ask questions. All the while, Eliahnna took notes in the huge leather binder she brought to all their meetings. She wrote in an obscure language only she understood, afraid if the notebook fell into the hands of their mother, everyone in the room would be executed for treason. Taryn didn't blame her for being cautious.

"So, you believe this Cashiel fellow is really Lliandra's first son?" Hayden set down his drink and took Sabina's hand in his own.

Faelara shook her head. "Second son, Kane, I would guess. The firstborn male died some seasons back. I attended him until the last breath."

"I wasn't aware you were in contact with any of the surviving males." Baehlon puffed his chest, his arms folded across them like great logs gathered for firewood.

"Only the first. The other two went to the west and I never heard from them again."

Taryn tucked Faelara's information into the index in her brain. She eyed the half-eaten plates of food. She hadn't been offered anything to eat in her mother's rooms and the wine made her light-headed.

Rhoane disappeared into an adjoining room, leaving Taryn flummoxed. She pulled her attention from her missing betrothed and stammered, "Myrddin said he kept tabs on them, but lost contact about six seasons ago."

Hayden ran a hand through his sandy curls, his eyes narrowed. "Marissa was just a wee thing when her brother Kane was born. He's the only full-blood sibling of all Lliandra's children."

Most people, Taryn assumed, upon discovering they had siblings, would seek them out. Perhaps share family photos, or recipes, or stories. Not her family. They'd try to kill her. Hers was probably top five in the most messed up, dysfunctional, crazy families of all time.

Rhoane slipped beside Taryn, a cheeky grin on his handsome face. She gave him a questioning glance, but he looked ahead and kept that ridiculous smile on his lips.

Taryn pulled her gaze from Rhoane and blurted, "I've convinced Mother to send Baehlon and Faelara to Ulla on the pretext she's there to study their healing, and Baehlon is her guardian." *Well, shit. So much for easing into the topic.*

Faelara spit the drink she'd been sipping, a look of chagrin on her face. "Guardian? But I'm so much older than him."

For his part, Baehlon beamed as if he'd won first prize at the county fair. "Five seasons is not *so much*."

A knock at her door startled everyone. Saeko quietly answered it and a moment later, her maid returned, carrying a wax-sealed envelope for Baehlon. With a sheepish expression, he opened the letter and read the contents. No one spoke until he'd finished and looked up.

"It seems my brother is in Menurra. Adesh and Amanda have gone missing." He held up a finger to silence any questions and re-read the letter. "He says he became aware of our situation at sea from a mutual friend, and no, before you ask, he doesn't say who. Hearing of our troubles, he sought out Adesh, but his tents were empty, his storeroom bare. Denzil then went to Amanda's house, and was met with a rather hostile old man who said he'd been living there for twenty seasons."

"We've been played." Taryn slumped into a chair.

Rhoane sat beside her and took her hand in his. "We put our trust in a man who did not deserve it."

"They had to have been working with Cashiel," Taryn said. "I feel like such an idiot. We practically gave them Mother's ship. Fuck."

"Don't blame yourself. I was as much, if not more, to blame." Hayden slammed a fist on the desk where Eliahnna sat. She jumped and held her binder close. "Hell, I practically forced you to trust them."

"Denzil tried to warn me, back in Celyn Eryri. But I didn't listen." Gods, but why hadn't she paid more attention? Taryn ran through a string of curses meant for her alone.

"Iselt," Sabina said. "He survived the attack on Adesh's ship, and the explosion. Do you think he's in league with them?"

"No." Taryn gave a firm shake of her head. "I would know if he's betraying me. Us."

Rhoane's grip tightened and a surge of jealousy spun through her cynfar. He was jealous of Iselt, but why?

"We don't know what happened on Adesh's ship. It might've been staged for all we know, and Adesh made it look like Iselt survived to draw our sympathy. Darius," Taryn commanded, "find Iselt and bring him here. If you see Denzil, have him join us as well."

Sabina rubbed a finger along her jaw, her face pensive. "Is that wise? Bringing two questionable characters into the palace?"

"Iselt is already here," Hayden said. "He's staying with the soldiers, but he has been inside the palace often. I believe Taryn is right. If he wished us harm, we would know."

"Or he's spying on us for Cashiel." Tessa sneered. "I can't stomach traitors."

"We don't know who's a traitor right now, and until we do, we'll keep our guard up. Be wary, not hasty or rash in judgment," Taryn cautioned the group, but kept her gaze firmly on Tessa. Her sister could be impulsive and they didn't need a scene. Lliandra would have Taryn's sisters on the first boat back to Talaith in moments.

"You sound like my father." Tears glistened in Faelara's eyes. "He would be so proud of you."

"Thank you." Taryn took her friend's hand. "Besides, I asked Ynyd Eirathnacht to protect my friends and family before the ship exploded. If Iselt wished me harm, he'd be fish food right about now."

"Friends and family?" Eliahnna whispered. "Then—"

"You saved Cashiel's life," Tessa finished for her sister.

"If he's your brother, that is," Ellie added.

Everyone turned to look at her. It was rare Taryn's maids

spoke aloud in these clandestine meetings. With the attention drawn to her, Ellie shuffled backward a few steps, her head bowed.

"Ellie's right. If he's our brother, then my wish would've saved him." When Taryn had requested her sword protect the others, she didn't think she'd have to specify only those she actually knew, trusted, and cared for, but a blanket statement left room for interpretation. In the future, she'd be careful about word choice.

While they waited for Darius to return with the blacksmith turned spy, they made plans. Rhoane and Baehlon would investigate the market, ask a few questions of key merchants to determine if Amanda and Adesh had come to the Summerlands. Since his father, Hanan, was a well-respected businessman, they doubted it, but after the surprise of learning Adesh had betrayed them, they weren't giving him the benefit of the doubt.

Another knock interrupted their discussions, but it was only a servant bringing Taryn dinner. Rhoane took the tray from him and ordered her to sit at the table and eat while the others continued their conversations. He sat opposite her and watched each morsel she put into her mouth.

"You need to eat to regain your full strength." Rhoane handed her a chilled glass of water and she took it gratefully.

Oranges and lemons flavored the plain liquid. At least, they tasted like oranges and lemons; she had no idea what the Summerlanders called them.

When Darius returned half a bell later, Iselt slunk into Taryn's rooms behind his son, apprehension clear in his features. At the many faces who greeted him, his eyes turned stormy, but he said nothing. He sought out Taryn and she gave him a reassuring smile.

"Iselt," Taryn began, keeping her tone light. "We've asked you here because we have some questions about Cashiel's attack on the ship you were on before rendezvousing with the empress's fleet." She chose her words with care, not trying to implicate him in Cashiel's schemes, but letting him know they required absolute truth of the events.

Iselt rubbed a hand over his bald pate, his head tilted. "There isn't much to tell. I was on Adesh's ship as they commanded." He indicated Hayden and Rhoane. "We were sailing for Menurra when a dense fog covered the ship. Much like Cashiel used for his attack on the *Dancer*. I was on the top deck, setting some sails, when all hell broke loose. Armed men swarmed onto the ship, surprising us. We were unarmed and, as he did to you, our power was blocked. Everyone was brought to the upper deck, where we were sorted into two groups—Adesh's crew and men like me, who were hired on in Talaith."

The string of sentences were more words than Taryn had ever heard him speak in one setting. He fidgeted from one foot to the next, clearly uncomfortable in this setting.

"What about the women?" Baehlon leaned forward, his gaze intent. "You were on a pleasure vessel. What did Cashiel do with them?"

"They were sorted with Adesh's crew."

"But we found no women on either of Cashiel's ships. Other than the mages used to block our ShantiMari," Rhoane argued.

Taryn sensed his irritation at having Iselt in her rooms and she placed a reassuring hand over his forearm.

"Your Highness, I tell you true, there were women on board. A dozen or more." A sly smile slanted his lips.

Taryn guessed they were, indeed, women of pleasure. "Did Adesh ever join you on the ship?"

Iselt turned his gaze on her. They were like ice chips, his eyes. She'd never noticed them before, probably because she'd only met him a few times in his forge, where it was dark. But here, in her rooms, they startled her with their clarity. "Not that I noticed. As far as I knew, he stayed in Talaith. And if you're set to ask me about that waif, Amanda, I only saw her a few times. She wasn't with the other women, but stayed close to the captain."

"She and Adesh are missing. Her mother, if she even is such, as well." Anger dripped from Hayden's words. "Taryn was warned Adesh had ties to the Telraicht Brotherhood, but we, I, was blind to a setup."

"Don't blame yourself, lad. We all fell for their scheme." Baehlon patted her cousin's shoulder, his big hand covering part of Hayden's back.

"What else can you tell us?" Taryn trusted Iselt, but if he knew anything else, now was the time to speak.

Iselt glanced nervously at Darius. They looked nothing alike, Iselt and his son, yet there was an unmistakable resemblance in the way they held themselves. A certain stance of their feet planted to the ground, their hands fisted at their hips. The black-smith's gaze tracked to each face as if memorizing them.

"After Cashiel took over our ship, we were led to the holds, stripped, bound, and forced to sit in our own piss and shit. A dozen armed men kept watch over us. Adesh's men and the women were separated from us. We could hear the women above our heads, pleasuring Cashiel's crew." Iselt paused, his face a brewing storm cloud. "A few of the men objected since the women had refused to service them. Those who spoke out were cut down. Right there, beside us. The bastards left the bodies to rot, never bothering to remove them."

"No better threat than a pool of blood and a warm corpse." Baehlon shook his head and the tiny bells added solemn chiming to the grisly moment.

"Too right, m'lord." Iselt nodded to Baehlon. No one corrected him on the improper use of the title. "After several days, the stench became too much. Even the thugs guarding us couldn't stand it. I figured Cashiel was testing us. Humiliation first, followed by the clear threat of death if we didn't do as asked. We weren't beaten, but the constant threat existed. I suppose at some point we were deemed trustworthy. We were given back our clothes and instructed on what we'd be expected to do once we reached the empress's ship."

"Did you know it was Lliandra's ship you were attacking?" Hayden leveraged a glare at the man.

Taryn wavered between wanting to comfort her cousin, and assure Iselt they didn't blame him. The animosity from both men, for the same, yet different reason, was draining. Her head pounded with a headache that promised to keep her from a good night's sleep.

Iselt regarded Hayden a moment before shaking his head. "We were naked, cold, and starving. We barely knew our names. If Cashiel had ordered us to kill our own mams, we would've. By the time we were brought up from the hold, the women were gone, as were Adesh's crew. All we were told was that we'd be expected to loot the ship and kill anyone not loyal to Cashiel. It's devastating what the promise of a warm meal will do to a man."

Hayden stood with his fists planted on the table. His breath came in shallow drags. "Adesh could've been trailing his ship the entire time, waiting until Cashiel's men were finished with the women, then sidled up to them, taken on the women and his crew, then sailed away without anyone the wiser." Suppressed anger dripped from each word.

Poor Hayden. This betrayal stung. Taryn rose and wrapped her arms around her cousin's waist.

"We'll deal with Adesh later." Taryn tried to ease his frustration. "Right now, we need to find Cashiel."

"But I thought you killed him." Surprise lit Iselt's weathered face.

Guilt lodged in her sternum. "I didn't. For the same reason you're alive, so is my half-brother."

Iselt's mouth dropped open. His eyes grew large. "Cashiel is Zakael?"

"Different half-brother. Cashiel is Kane, we think," Faelara explained. "He's Taryn's older brother by twelve seasons, thereabout."

"But he knows Zakael. Intimately, if I'm not mistaken." Taryn recalled the lust in Cashiel's eyes when he spoke of living at Caer Idris. She'd mistaken it for his zeal of torture, but on further examination, he was the perfect lover for Zakael. Young, beautiful, full of desire for revenge. Zakael would've taken this man's anger and wrapped it neatly around his little finger. And Kane, or Cashiel, would've been only too happy to please the young lord. A chill swept down her spine. Cashiel might've been at the castle while she was there. He might've been one of the courtiers she'd ignored during her brief stay.

What is it, my love? Rhoane's hand slipped around hers, warm and comforting.

I might've met Cashiel at Caer Idris and not even known.

Do not blame yourself for not knowing the future.

Easier said than done.

They made plans and sketched ideas, Eliahnna scribbling notes the whole time. Everyone had their roles to play, even Taryn's sisters. They would spy on Lliandra. If their mother were truly fading, Eliahnna must be prepared to take up the mantle of empress. If, however, something else ailed Lliandra, they needed to know what or who had infected the Lady of Light.

"What about you, Taryn? Where will you go?" Tessa's sweet face tore at Taryn's heart. She'd not enjoy leaving them so soon after being reunited.

"What do you think, Rhoane? Do we chase Cashiel or Adesh?"

"If Cashiel lives, he is probably well guarded. I should like answers from Adesh first."

Taryn nodded her agreement. If Zakael had sent Cashiel, and he lived, he'd most likely be at Gaarendahl and Taryn had no wish to return to her brother's castle. The horrors of her last trip there were too fresh.

She tapped her lip with a forefinger. "If you had a ship full of women you didn't want to be found, where would you dump them?"

The room quieted in thought, then Tessa's face brightened. "The Sitari!"

The wind knocked from Taryn's lungs. Of course that's where Adesh would hide. "Crap, I think you're right."

The fabled warrior women were the last people Taryn wanted to ask for help, but if that's where they'd find answers, she had no choice. They might even provide answers to the Mallaqai conundrum. After all, the Sitari were cursed by Mallaqai. If anyone knew of a vortex or what she'd intended by sending the darathi vorsi off Aelinae, it would be them.

"Rhoane and I will sail for their island the day after Hayden and Sabina are wed." Taryn said, hoping her words held the confidence she lacked.

In the corner, hidden by shadows, Ebus shifted and Taryn saw the devious little man rub his hands in anticipation. Naturally, the men would want to visit the Sitari's island. All of them except Baehlon and Rhoane. At her side, Rhoane stiffened, his eyes like hard granite. Baehlon stood equally formidable. Taryn understood their concern. The Sitari's reputation of using men for breeding was legendary, but they were equally renowned for their fighting skills and distrust of outsiders. Taryn would be walking into a hornet's nest.

Despite her need of them, the Sitari believed the Eirielle an abomination. At the very least, they wanted to kill her.

CHAPTER TWENTY-FIVE

Gwainne reached the border of the Narthvier five days after setting out from their encampment. He rode at a leisurely pace, uncertain why he obeyed a goddess he didn't worship, or believe in. Yes, he saw her with his own eyes, but it was easy to play tricks with ShantiMari. For all he knew, this was Loghan's idea of a great farce. And he, the butt of the joke.

Well, if this trip turned out to be a waste of time, he'd have words with Loghan when he returned. Whenever that would be. Verdaine had said to seek out her temple, then travel south to Paderau and from there to Talaith. For what purpose, she wouldn't say, only that he could tell his true identity if he wished. What did that mean? Why wouldn't he present himself as an Ullan prince? It was as if she wished to insult his noble blood. Goddess or not, he didn't favor being treated as unworthy.

His horse sidestepped a fallen branch and Gwainne pulled his attention to the forest on his right. Huge trees stretched to the sky. Brambles and shrubs blocked entrance into the forest and so he carried on, keeping the trees to his right, the desert kingdom to his left. Another two bells of riding and he was no closer to finding a pathway into the Narthvier. Verdaine had said he'd know how to lift the veils when the time came, but he had no idea how to accomplish that once he found an opening.

He kicked his horse to a canter and trudged along, scanning the trees for an opening. Twice he thought he saw movement, a flash of color among the dense greenery, but then it was gone. He neared the Ullan border and slowed to a walk. Once past the invisible line, he'd have traveled farther than any other time in his whole life. He'd be truly on his own, without the protection of the desert.

His heart beat in his chest, a rapid staccato of fear and excitement. Could he do this? Could he leave his homeland on the whim of a make-believe deity?

Another flash of color to his right drew his attention. He definitely saw something. The flank of a horse, perhaps? Or another woodland creature. The staccato tripped into a wild thumping. What sort of animals lived in the Narthvier? He'd heard rumors, but like most things not involving the Ullans, he'd ignored them. What a fool he'd been. Perhaps this was what Taryn had warned them about. Living in isolation had made them ignorant of the rest of the world. Would he allow his lack of knowledge to hold him back now? Or would he face the dangers as a prince of Ullan blood?

He spurred his horse on, crossing from the desert to a meadow that stretched to eternity, it seemed. The rocky sand gave way to soft grass and flowers that swayed in a gentle breeze. He glanced over his shoulder to his homeland, the dusty reds stark against the blue sky. This was another world, here beyond his border. He'd never guessed there was such beauty past the harsh sands and sculpted cliffs of Ulla. He threw his head back and laughed at the sheer ridiculousness of his ignorance.

A sound to his right cut short his glee. Yes, there it was again. The clomp of horses' hooves. He turned his stallion toward the forest and stared hard into the depths. The harder he stared, the more a wavering opening revealed itself to him. A gasp escaped his lips. Was he doing this? His horse nudged forward, toward the trees. A pace or so from the entrance, he panicked. Unsure if his safety was guaranteed once through the veil, he paused.

The sound of voices came to him and he leaned forward. Mistaking his movement for a command, his horse stepped into the Narthvier.

Gwainne breathed in the loamy scent of leaves and moss. The strangely familiar smell brought calm to his racing heart. Tension coiled in him like a snake ready to strike, but nothing untoward happened. No spears whipped through the trees to impale him, no nets scooped him up to dangle precariously until such a time a beast might like to snack upon him.

His imagination ran wild with scenarios of death, yet none came to fruition. A light laugh sounded through the trees. His, which surprised him.

"By the grace of Verdaine," he mumbled, "I am here."

Cold steel snugged against his neck, just beneath his chin.

"By the grace of Verdaine," a deep, menacing voice said, "you will die."

Gwainne slid his gaze to the left. An Eleri of immense beauty glared at him. His white-gold hair hung down his back—several braids kept it from his face—and his eyes, deep set emeralds that glistened with unabashed distrust, never left Gwainne.

The blade cut into Gwainne's throat, a stinging pain he valiantly tried to ignore lest he swallow and encourage the steel to meet bone.

"I was bade to seek out Verdaine's temple by the goddess herself." He said with care and held his hands up, to show he had no weapon hidden in his palms.

Another man reached over to place his fingertips on the sword at his throat. "Bressal, hear him out."

Equally as handsome, this Eleri had long chestnut hair, but his eyes captivated Gwainne. Three shades of blue, from light to dark, they sparkled with hidden mischief and promised truth-fulness.

The sword stayed where it was, despite the Eleri's request. "Why would Verdaine send you to her temple? You are not Eleri, your ears are not tipped, and you wear your hair short."

Behind the men, an Eleri woman sat on her horse, her gaze roving Gwainne until he felt naked beneath her scrutiny. His confidence faltered in the midst of his half brethren.

"I am Gwainne Agnar, First Son of the Ullan laird Amdi Agnar, son to Kaleigh, his Eleri wife."

The one called Bressal sucked in his breath. "An abom-ination."

"An Eleri," the more sensible one said. He placed his hand over his heart and bent his head. "I am Eoghan, Third Son to King Stephan, ruler of the Narthvier. Welcome, kinsman." Eoghan tugged the sword from Gwainne's neck, ignoring the glare the other Eleri gave him. "Please forgive my brother. He does not easily trust outsiders. Come, we will take you to Father."

"But I am to seek out Verdaine's temple," Gwainne muttered, not at all sure he wanted to meet the king.

"Father will know the importance of your quest and, if he thinks you worthy, will offer aid." Eoghan shrugged as if it was of no consequence.

"And if he does not?" The question came forth before he could stop it.

"You will be returned to your Ullan laird." Bressel's ominous glower did little to instill confidence.

They turned their horses and led Gwainne through the forest. Every so often they stopped to lift a veil and with each one, a rush of murmuring touched his thoughts. The woman warrior rode beside him, a smirk plastered to her lips. She wore a short leather top and leather breeches, showing far too much skin. As much as Gwainne tried to avert his gaze, it continued to slip to his left to spy her lovely features.

"Careful," Eoghan warned in a low voice. "She is promised to Bressal."

Gwainne glanced at the young prince.

"See the gold chain at her waist? That is her betrothal vow."

Gwainne had to force himself to keep his head facing forward to keep from ogling the gorgeous woman. "Are all Eleri as attractive as this?"

Eoghan's deep laugh frightened several birds from their nests. "I suppose so. To me, we look the same."

They rode on and Gwainne snuck a peek at the woman's waist. As Eoghan had said, there rested a slim gold chain. It bounced with her horse's movements, teasing him to reach out and touch it.

Gods, but he had a death wish. He dragged his gaze away, only to meet her curious stare. The smirk grew to a full-fledged grin and he suddenly felt foolish, like a boy among adults, not quite understanding the conversation, but desiring to be part of the action.

After several bells, exactly how many was hard to tell with the sun blocked by so many trees, they arrived at a clearing and Gwainne gaped. Before him, stretching to either side, was a huge tree. Its branches drooped with walkways and staircases. Delicate structures with arching spirals and lace-like balustrades were built into the branches. He could only wonder what they were for. Houses, markets—they could be anything. It stole his breath to see them integrated into the forest as they were.

An image of his homeland burst into his mind, of the arching rocks and cliffs, of a whole society living within them, like the Eleri did in the trees. The idea startled him. Never had the Ullans settled in one place, but what if they had? Would it be as lovely as this?

"Welcome to the Weirren," Eoghan said. "This is the seat of our rulers, as it has been since the first seed of this tree was planted."

They slowed to a stop outside a set of huge double doors. Just as they were dismounting, the doors opened and a group of Eleri stepped onto the small entryway. Gwainne knew at once who was king. Not because he wore a crown, he didn't, but by the imposing stance he took. The quiet authority he held over the group. His eyes skimmed the other riders, settling on Gwainne with an air of mistrust. He swallowed hard and reminded himself he was a prince in his own right. He wouldn't be intimidated by this king any more than he was his own father.

"What is an Ullan doing in my forest?" The king stayed where he was on the top step, giving him the advantage of height.

Gwainne tread forward with caution. At the base of the steps he knelt, placing his hand over his heart as Eoghan had done to him. "Your majesty, I am Gwainne Agnar, First Son of Amdi Agnar, laird of the Ullans, and Kaleigh, his Eleri wife."

With his head bowed, he couldn't see the king, but clearly heard the grunt of disgust.

"Kaleigh is sheanna. Her bastards are not welcome here."

Gwainne rose slowly, his hands clenched at his side. "My mother is no longer sheanna, by the deed of Verdaine. Nor am I a bastard. You do not have to accept me, Your Majesty, but I will continue my quest as set forth by your goddess Verdaine."

At this, the king's brows rose. "Verdaine sent you? What is it you seek?"

"She asked me to travel to her temple so that I might uncover the mystery of the Jansen Strait. I am to meet Their Highnesses, Taryn and Rhoane, at the temple." At the mention of the names, King Stephan jerked his attention to Bressal.

"Have you seen them? Are they in the Narthvier?" The king closed his eyes and lifted his face to the sky.

The murmuring became louder, a soft female voice standing out from the others. Gwainne struggled to make out the words, but they eluded him.

"They are not here." His penetrating glare fell to Gwainne. "Do you dare lie to me?"

"No, I swear it. Verdaine sent me, but I might have taken too long, or they are delayed. I am not sure. If there is a way to contact the goddess, you could ask her. I am telling the truth, Your Majesty."

The king turned, a swirl of crimson fabric flowing in his wake. Gwainne wasn't sure if he should follow or get on his horse and ride for home. Eoghan touched his arm and indicated the stairs.

"Might as well find you a room. Father will pretend you do not exist until Verdaine confirms your claim. He has been vexed with nightmares of late. Did you truly see Taryn and Rhoane?"

Gwainne nodded, unsure how much to confess. "They stayed in Ulla a few days."

Tears shimmered in Eoghan's strange-colored eyes. "I saw her death. Is she well, my deific sister?"

"She was when she left us, but not upon her arrival."

He told Eoghan what he knew of the attack and Taryn's injuries. By the time they reached a grand staircase that wound up the interior of the tree, a small group had gathered close to him, listening. Among them, the warrior woman and Bressal. He'd forgotten Rhoane was First Son and, technically, heir to the Weirren Throne.

Eoghan led him to a room on the fourth level of the massive tree and he was surprised to see it furnished with fittings similar to what he'd find in his father's tents. Much of the furniture was even grander, more ornate than his father owned. He'd half-expected to find rough wood walls and beds made of leaves. The Eleri continued to surprise him.

He was left to refresh himself after the long ride, and after a short time, two small boys entered to run him a bath and prepare him for dinner. They spoke Eleri, and by their conversation, weren't aware Gwainne was fluent in the language. They joked about the Ullan false prince and his audacity at arriving in the Narthvier claiming he was a guest of Verdaine. Gwainne listened without comment, gleaning as much information as he could from them. If they knew he understood them, they would fawn over him, bowing and scraping like good servants. It was refreshing to hear the truth for once.

After they dressed him, and made several inappropriate comments about his manhood, they left him alone. Apparently, the Ullan custom of snipping the tip from one's cock wasn't practiced in the Narthvier, but his little servants believed this deformity would cause not only speculation among the Eleri women, but a desire to sample him to determine if it made a difference in his lovemaking skills.

He'd also discovered they weren't boys, but full-grown men. At half his height, they looked like children, but they were woodland faeries. The first Gwainne had ever met. Or heard of, for that matter. Once again, he was reminded how much he didn't know about the world outside his border.

Eoghan arrived a short time later to escort him to dinner. He grinned the entire way, as if he held some great secret he didn't wish to share. Just before they reached a huge door with ornate carvings along the edges and interior, Eoghan turned to Gwainne.

"I once escorted the Darennsai to this room. She, too, was thought unworthy of being in our presence. I hope you prove my father wrong, as did she."

"Thank you, Eoghan. For your kindness and support." Gwainne squeezed the man's shoulder, humbled by his belief.

The door opened and Eoghan motioned for him to stay where he was while he entered the quiet room. Gwainne watched until Eoghan took a seat to his father's left. The filled room twittered with hushed comments he could neither make out, nor tried to understand. His nerves already made it difficult. He didn't need to know what was being said about him. At a guard's signal, he entered the hall. Every head turned toward him, expectant.

Gwainne stepped forward until the king stood and beckoned him to stop.

"This Ullan has trespassed on our lands. He claims he is of Eleri birth through his mother, Kaleigh, a disgraced novice of Verdaine, and sheanna in our eyes. His quest, he says, is to seek out my son and the Darennsai, who are not presently in the Narthvier, yet he believes they should be. Among his lies, he tells us Verdaine herself commanded him to come into our midst. For no other reason than to investigate a legend surrounding the Jansen Strait."

Mumbling and chattering filled the room.

"Silence," Bressal shouted.

The room quieted.

"Since the Jansen Strait is on the southern shores of Ulla, we have to ask ourselves, why would he come here to discover a legend on his own land? Is he a spy? Does he wish us harm? He claims to have seen the Darennsai, yet where is his proof? Is there anyone here who can speak for this man?"

Gwainne opened his mouth, but Eoghan gave a quick shake of his head. If he wasn't allowed to defend himself, how would he convince the king he wasn't lying? No one in the room knew him, nor did they know that Verdaine had asked him to travel to the Narthvier. To them, he was as the king suggested—an interloper, and possibly meant to cause them harm.

"No one? Not one Eleri can vouch for you, Gwainne Agnar. You—"

"I can." A delicate voice interrupted the king.

Stephan scowled toward the back of the room, his face turning an awful shade of purple.

Gwainne turned slowly to see who had spoken on his behalf. There, half hidden by the others, was the most beautiful woman he'd ever seen. More lovely even than the warrior Eleri. Dark-brown hair cascaded over her shoulders as she stepped lightly toward him. A gossamer gown of pale-green silk floated around her, setting off her moss-flecked eyes that danced with merriment. An odd expression, considering her life was in peril. A smile broke across her heart-shaped face and she reached toward him with both hands.

"I will vouch for him, Father."

Father? This girl was the king's daughter? Gwainne's heart sank and fluttered at the same time. He hoped this wasn't a case of her attempting to rebel against a parent. He had no desire to be caught in the middle of a family squabble.

"Carga." The king inclined his head, the color draining from his face. "How is it you know this young man?"

"I do not know him, but I know the quest of which he speaks. Verdaine sent me here to convey her apologies. Taryn and Rhoane are in the Summerlands and will not be able to meet you as believed." Her warm hands gripped his with a tight squeeze. "Taryn is nearly healed from her injuries. She has your mother to thank for saving her life."

"An Ullan healed her?" The deathly pall spread over the king's body, turning him an even more terrible shade of grey.

"Of course not." Carga chuckled and it sounded like the fall of rain upon his tent. Comforting, soothing. "Kaleigh realized who she was and called for Rhoane. He healed her." Carga's gaze slid back to Gwainne. "This one is not a healer, but his brother is. One of the best, as is Kaleigh. Their fates are tied to ours, Father."

King Stephan sat with a huff, his hands dragging over his face, which thankfully had regained some of its pigmentation. The gathered Eleri took a collective breath as if they'd all been waiting for the outcome of the situation. Gwainne stood still, his hands in Carga's, unsure what to do.

She led him up several stairs to the right of the king's massive chair. At Stephan's scowl, she said, "He is a prince, Father. You must at least show him the courtesy his title demands."

The king motioned to a chair and Carga sat, indicating Gwainne do the same.

She leaned toward him and whispered, "I have opened the door for you. It is up to you to step through."

"I do not know how to thank you, my lady. I am Gwainne—"

"I know who you are, Gwainne Agnar ap Briarwood. Son of Kaleigh, one of the few who can control time, and novice to Verdaine. Your mother is a legend at the temple." A playful smile tugged at the corners of her mouth.

He wanted to kiss her there to steal the mirth hidden within.

Control time? He didn't know this about his mother. What other secrets might he discover while in the Narthvier? About his mother, yes, and possibly the pretty girl to his left, but also about himself?

The marketplace was crowded this morning, which made it easier for Rhoane and Baehlon to blend in. Although, the big knight almost always drew attention. It wasn't just his height, but the tiny bells he wore in his braids and the longsword strapped across his back. Baehlon didn't know stealth, had never learned the finer points of espionage. Rhoane had learned all of those and more. He knew how to become a shadow if necessary.

A dark thought brushed his mind. Of a day in Lliandra's orchard when Ebus had seemed to disappear, and Taryn had done the same a few minutes after. She'd promised to show him how it was done, claiming it was a trick of the Dark, but that promise was as yet unfulfilled. How long ago had that been? Certainly not more than a season. Of course it couldn't have been. Hadn't Taryn returned to Aelinae only a season ago since her birthing day? To Rhoane, it felt like she'd been here forever.

Yet it also felt she'd been gone forever as well. And now, he sensed he was losing her again, not to another world, but to her destiny. All he could do was be with her for as long as the gods allowed. Then he would have to let her go.

He scanned the shoppers and merchants in the bustling area,

noting each face, every flinch of a hand. Their talk with Hanan the spice merchant hadn't gone well. His old friend hadn't seen his son Adesh for over five seasons. When told Adesh was missing, Hanan had shrugged and said he had other sons. Soon enough he'd send one to Talaith to sell his wares. Nearing his one hundred fourth season, Hanan was too old and tired to worry about a rebellious child. He did, however, exhibit a burst of energy when told the illegal taxing of his goods would cease.

In fact, letters were being drawn, alerting his other sons in towns as far away as Paderau and Danuri of the good news. At least Rhoane was able to spread cheer to a few people today. A pall had settled over him that he couldn't shake. Of a darkness he couldn't name, nor see nor sense. Yet it was there, pinching the back of his neck like a scremp meant to suck his blood.

Perhaps it was his upcoming journey with Taryn that had set his mood so foul. After Hayden's wedding, they would sail for the Sitari. What awaited them there, he dreaded to even ponder. Of all the places on Aelinae, the warrior women's islands were avoided at every cost. They were known to kidnap men for breeding—then, if rumor were to be believed, they feasted upon their corpses. Rhoane wasn't one for listening to gossip, but he understood caution and an island full of barbarian women wasn't his idea of fun.

Verdaine had said he would know only one woman, yet Marissa had raped him, and it was her abuse of his body that had broken him so completely. Believing he'd let his goddess and Taryn down, he'd closed in upon himself, refusing to forgive his actions. Except, he hadn't known Marissa's body. She'd seduced him in the visage of his beloved, and even after, when she'd shown her true face, when his rage had poured into her, spilling his seed, he hadn't known her. In fact, he'd never known Marissa. Not in body, mind, or character. She'd been a farce since the moment they met.

It wasn't until he healed Taryn in Ulla that he fully comprehended the fact he hadn't disgraced his oath to Verdaine. The only woman he'd ever known was Taryn. And she knew him better than he knew himself. Never once had she blamed him for Marissa's betrayal. Instead, she'd fought to bring him from his despair.

Now, she wished to take him to the Sitari, where he would be one man among many women. He knew how to dissuade the attentions of females, but dear gods, a whole island of them? He'd keep his vow to Taryn or die trying. If the Sitari had any ideas about mating with him, they would be sorely disappointed.

"Mayhaps we should've brought the ladies with us? We're but two gents in a sea of women." Baehlon indicated the market, but could just as easily have been reading his thoughts.

"We have one lady with us." Rhoane stroked Kaida's head.

She nuzzled his hand, her tongue lolling to the side of her mouth.

"The others are too busy preparing Sabina for her wedding."

Baehlon chuckled, a deep rumble in his chest. "Aye, and young Hayden gets his piercing soon, I've been told."

"Surely a custom thought up by a woman." Rhoane flexed his hand where the ghost markings shimmered beneath his skin. Certainly they were more of a marriage vow than any piercing could convey.

"If the man gets a piercing, what does the woman do to show she's taken?"

Rhoane grinned. Unlike the Summerlands men, the women didn't get a piercing, but rather, a small tattoo on the underside of their right wrist. The design would be chosen by the bride and applied the morning of her nuptials. The male, however, had to pierce a part of his anatomy. As much as Taryn loved to tease her cousin, making him believe he must pierce his distinctly male appendage, he didn't have to. An ear, an eyebrow, a nipple—all would suffice. It just had to be somewhere on the body. The location was up to the groom.

"Unless," Baehlon drawled before Rhoane answered, "they both have their nethers pierced. Wouldn't that be something? Do you think it heightens the experience?"

"I would not know. You should ask." Rhoane shuddered at the idea. Heightened experience or not, unless Taryn specifically requested it, he'd never let a needle near his cock.

"Faelara is looking forward to the trip to Ulla. Do you think she wishes to participate in their healing rituals?"

From his friend's tone, Rhoane sensed the big knight was worried about what Faelara might discover in the desert kingdom.

"It is possible, and knowing Kaleigh, she would be allowed. But if she does, there is nothing to concern you. The Ullans use their bodies for healing, not pleasure." As he said the words, his gut roiled at the memory of Loghan standing naked beside Taryn's inert form. He'd been close to violating her. Too close.

He was being a hypocrite, but the thought of another man, or woman, touching Taryn sent jealous fury spiraling through his veins. His face screwed into a snarl and his fists clenched.

"You might want to control your temper, lad. You're scaring the children." Baehlon nudged Rhoane's shoulder. "Is there something you're not telling me about the Ullans?"

His anger rolled off in waves with each thud of his boot to the dirt, indeed affecting those around them. Women cowered as they passed, hiding their offspring between their skirts. Rhoane smoothed his features, shook off thoughts of Loghan and his perfect body. Tried to forget the way the Ullan's gaze had rarely left Taryn, a look of desire haunting him.

"There is nothing to fear from the Ullans except their laird, Amdi. He might insist you fight in his arena. Avoid this at all costs. Amdi is cruel and going mad. He trusts no one, not even his wife and sons."

Without warning, a vision seared his thoughts. A dark figure crouched in the corner of a room, his body nothing more than an outline of shadow, his eyes two dots of white. Yet he sneered. A slim arm reached forward, one long claw extended as if to strike. Rhoane was overwhelmed as he sensed Taryn's fear of the creature. She'd seen him. But where? When? The thing hissed and slipped into the shadows. Next, an image of a tree, dark as pitch with thorns along the trunk, stood solitary upon a cliff. The cloud-strewn sky behind it churned with shades of grey. Sap dripped from the tree, between grooves of bark. No, it wasn't sap, but blood.

"Rhoane, look at me." Baehlon's big hands held his shoulders. Rhoane blinked to focus.

"Are you well?"

Rhoane was on one knee, his breath coming in short gasps. His stomach spun and pitched, his fisted palms slicked with sweat. A roaring like the buzz of insects infested his ears. Kaida sat beside him, her paw on his bent leg. Her golden eyes regarded him with the same concern as in Baehlon's gaze.

"I am well. I saw the strangest thing, although I am not sure what it was. A door, then a figure, like from a drawing, and a tree. Evil. That is what I saw. Pure, raw, evil here on Aelinae."

Baehlon helped him stand and he took several long breaths to clear his thoughts. Kaida nudged his hand with her muzzle and he sank his fingertips into her fur.

"Taryn saw it, too. At least, I sensed her fear." Rhoane paced in front of the fruit stand where he'd been kneeling a moment earlier.

The merchant scowled at them, but Rhoane ignored him. Images, thoughts, memories flooded through his mind. He knew the tree. Had glimpsed it in his dreams. But where?

Before he had a chance to process further, Kaida barked and lunged away from them. He and Baehlon gave chase, skirting around the shoppers. Kaida was a streak of white amid the bright colors and burnished skins of the Summerlands people. He tracked her as best he could, nearly tripping over a small child. The mother cursed him and he apologized as he sprinted onward. Toward what, he wasn't sure.

They cleared the market and raced down one street and the next. Baehlon huffed beside Rhoane, his face dripping from the exertion. Rhoane's clothes clung to him as they chased Kaida through the back alleys and narrow walkways of Menurra. Rhoane's legs burned with the effort, but he pressed on, despite his heart pumping like it might explode.

At the far end of the city, where the buildings were nothing more than short dun-colored shacks piled together, Kaida growled.

Baehlon skidded to a stop and bent at the waist, wheezing. Rhoane paced a small circle, taking in deep breaths to calm his blood, lower his heartrate. Kaida whined and he directed Baehlon toward the sound, drawing his sword as they moved cautiously through the narrow avenue. Whatever had spooked Kaida wasn't a friend. Rhoane's apprehension lingered beneath his seasons of training. He tightened his grip on the sword hilt.

The grierbas sat in front of an unmarked door, her steady gaze on the window to her left. Baehlon crept near, his arm outstretched to push open the door. Rhoane guarded his flank, scanning up and down the street, checking neighboring buildings for movement. These ramshackle homes were a warren of walkways and tunnels. Their quarry could be in any one of them by now.

The door swung open with a slight creak and they entered the sparsely furnished room. Remnants of a meal scattered across a table—bread and cheese, a cooking knife embedded into a thick loaf. A mug of something dark sat beside the food. Rhoane tread lightly to the table and felt the still-warm mug. He pocketed the knife and signaled to Baehlon. The pounding in his ears increased as they moved forward, to the only other room in the house.

A strangled cry came from behind the closed door and Baehlon burst through, splintering the old wood. A blade sliced toward his friend, leveled at his chest. For an average man, it would've hit at the neck, cleaving the head from body. But Baehlon was ready for an attack. He swatted the sword away with a gauntleted forearm. With his other hand, he grabbed the attacker's cloak and shoved him against the wall with a hard thud.

A stream of ShantiMari flooded over them, meant to paralyze their movements, but it was weak and clumsy. Kaida slithered between their legs and snarled at the hooded figure in Baehlon's grasp. Even before he entered the room, Rhoane knew who they'd been chasing. Had suspected it the moment Kaida leapt from their sides. A shiver of disgust raked down his spine. He needed all of his strength to keep a cool head, yet the struggle to lash out was strong.

A middle-aged man crouched in the corner, shaking from the ordeal. Rhoane motioned for him to leave and he bolted through the bedroom door without a word. His bare feet slapped the hard dirt and then drifted away. Rhoane took a deep, calming breath and turned to face the Shadow Assassin.

"Well, my friend. It appears we meet again." Rhoane wrapped his power around the man, delving into his mind with a savagery few knew he possessed. This man, this *thing*, had hunted Taryn far too long for him to leave anything to chance. He whispered a few words in the ancient dialect the assassin had used in Celyn Eryri, enjoying the scream of agony the man made.

"Settle down, you filthy whelp." Baehlon held him tighter against the wall with one hand, his blade in the other, at the man's throat. "One wrong twist and you'll end your life."

"Careful, Baehlon. I think that is precisely what he might wish for at the moment." Rhoane came in close to the man and jerked his hood away from his face. Chilling, emotionless eyes the color of ice cliffs regarded him with the same detachment he remembered from before. Truly this man was a cipher, as Taryn had said. He searched his thoughts, finding no memories, nothing to aid in their search for his master. Then, unbidden, Rhoane saw the tree once more. Saw the creature in the corner of the room. Saw Kaldaar.

CHAPTER TWENTY-SEVEN

The palace at Menurra didn't have a dungeon, at least nothing Rhoane would consider appropriate for a prisoner. He surveyed the rounded walls of the outbuilding, eyeing the colorful mosaics that stretched to the domed ceiling. Sturdy wooden beams intersected across their heads. From one, a rope had been fastened to hold the assassin. His feet dangled near the ground, yet there were no markings on his wrist where the rope cut into his skin, no blood oozing down his forearm.

"Comfortable?" Rhoane patrolled around the prisoner.

He'd had the man in a similar position, once. For a sennight, he'd been able to study him, but then he and Taryn had left Celyn Eryri and someone had helped the cur escape. Rhoane's jaw tightened and his nostrils flared. Not this time. He would get answers from the demon or kill him for his silence.

Unlike in Celyn Eryri, Rhoane had forbidden anyone from using their power to contain the Shadow Assassin. It was a hunch, but Rhoane suspected having no power of his own, the assassin stole from others what he couldn't gain for himself. If he were living, he might have been powerful, but who could say? As it was, a Shadow Assassin was neither alive nor dead, but subsisting in-between.

"Where is Kaldaar?" Rhoane asked in Elennish. If he could end the thing's existence right then, he would've. But they needed answers. Taryn needed answers. As much as it annoyed him to let the assassin draw air, he had to keep his own desires far from what must be done.

The assassin kept his head lowered, a snarl on his lips. A guard of six men had shown up at the house where Baehlon and Rhoane caught the assassin, followed closely by the owner of the residence. Together, they'd brought the demon through back streets and alleyways to the palace, not wanting to draw attention or cause alarm in the city.

Once here, the outbuilding was declared the safest place to interrogate him. Faisal had cells, certainly, but they were full of thieves and pirates. The king hadn't wanted to risk the assassin influencing them or vice versa. And so Rhoane found himself with several guards, questioning someone who didn't wish to be found, let alone confess his sins.

A commotion at the front of the building drew Baehlon's attention, but Rhoane stayed focused on the prisoner. He lifted his head slightly, a gleam entering his starkly blue eyes. A moment later, Taryn burst through the doorway with Myrddin a step behind. It was subtle, but Rhoane sensed a shift in the man. As if he'd been waiting for her all along.

"Why wasn't I told he'd been caught?" Taryn demanded.

Rhoane tore his gaze from the assassin to explain, but the words lodged in his throat.

Instead of her usual leather breeches, blouse, and vest, she wore a Summerlands half top adorned with swags of beads. They jangled and jostled with each of her movements, swaying across her flat stomach in a fetching way. A semi-sheer skirt, also embellished with beading, barely covered her legs. Dark kohl rimmed her eyes, giving them a mysterious appeal.

"By the gods," he stammered, "you look lovely."

"Sabina is making us have a dress rehearsal for the wedding. I feel like an idiot." Taryn waved him off, her sheepish reply in stark opposition to her tone of a moment earlier.

"You look anything but." Her presence in the chamber upset the composure Rhoane had donned. Of course she would wish to see the assassin, but Rhoane would've liked to save her the torment.

Taryn's gaze drifted past him to the bound prisoner. "Where did you find him?"

Rhoane blew out a long breath and refitted his indifference into place. "In the marketplace. Kaida sensed him before I did."

Taryn scratched the grierbas and lavished praise on the beast.

"If only we had the same ability to sniff him out as she does." She straightened and approached the assassin. "Just can't keep away, can you?"

Why isn't he guarded with ShantiMari? Taryn asked Rhoane in his mind.

I believe he steals from others what he does not have.

Makes sense.

There was much he needed to tell Taryn, but not here. Not with the Shadow Assassin so near.

She brushed hair from the assassin's forehead and Rhoane's jaw twitched. He hated Taryn being near the thing, hated even more that she touched him. The demon was too close, too clever. Rhoane's fingernails dug into his palms as he struggled against his need to harm the assassin.

"Are you sad you didn't get to slice up one of my friends this time? I was upset you'd escaped," Taryn taunted, her tone a sweet contrast to the words she spoke.

The assassin regarded her with the same disinterest he'd shown Rhoane. Despite a minuscule hitch to his sneer, he gave no reply.

Rhoane slipped his mind into the cur's, hoping to avoid the

image of the tree and Kaldaar. At first, he encountered a blank wall. Then, to his surprise, Taryn's memories, of her childhood, her life with Brandt, and her time on Aelinae flashed in Rhoane's thoughts. Alarmed, he sent a warning to his love.

He is stealing your memories, your thoughts.

I know. I'm allowing him access. It seemed important to him for some reason.

The unease in Rhoane's gut expanded to infect all his organs. Breathing stalled, his heart slowed. A nagging suspicion he'd had since Celyn Eryri tugged at his sanity.

Taryn kept her fingers on the cur's face, her eyes trained on his. Another commotion at the door drew Rhoane's attention. The empress sashayed into the dimly lit room. With her came a burst of air and brightness that nearly blinded those gathered.

"So, you're still skulking around, I see. Is your Master here? Hmm? I should like to have a word with him, if he'd be so kind to accept my invitation." Despite the cordiality of Lliandra's words, there was venom in each syllable.

The empress stood beside Taryn, glaring at the assassin as if daring him to reply. To see the three of them, together, ripped a new dimension into Rhoane's reality.

At his side, Baehlon swore.

You see it as well, my friend? Rhoane asked the knight.

Julieta's left tit, how can it be? In Baehlon's thought, Rhoane heard utter disbelief. He'd drawn the same conclusion.

I do not know.

Yet Taryn and her mother were oblivious as they faced the assassin.

The empress huffed and stomped a slippered foot on the tiled floor. "This silence really is tedious. I've a mind to end you now. What say you to that? Would you like to be released from this hell you're made to live each day? With nothing to do but hunt my daughter? No thoughts. No memories. No one to love. You're not even allowed the pleasures of life, are you? No food, or human company. Tell me, does it hurt?"

A thin thread of Lliandra's ShantiMari snaked around the prisoner. Rhoane was too late to warn her off and a visible shudder ran the length of the assassin. The assassin took her power into himself. Taryn, who had kept her touch light upon his cheek, saw it too, for she drew her mother's power into herself before the Shadow Assassin had a chance to assimilate it. Rhoane wavered between ending Taryn's contact with the demon and letting her continue. The urge to protect, to keep her from what was to come, battled with what he accepted must happen. Taryn had to discover the assassin's identity on her own.

If the demon so much as uttered a single syllable to harm Taryn, Rhoane would cut him down. Paths be damned, he wouldn't lose her to the Telraicht-Noir.

For a long time, no one spoke. Lliandra paced around the prisoner, her power swirling in a tempest, but she didn't use it against him again. Taryn remained where she was, standing still in front of the assassin, her gaze glued to his, her hand upon his cheek. She claimed she was filling him with her life memories, to show him what goodness meant. Baehlon and Myrddin talked quietly beneath one of the many columned windows that circled the room. Rhoane stayed at Taryn's side, his hand on the hilt of his sword.

Finally, Taryn released her touch on the demon and turned to Rhoane. "There's nothing for him to tell. I don't think he knows who his master is. Or rather, he only knows of the man who cares for him, but to him, he's like a father. He has no name, none that he's shared with our mysterious prisoner. It's a hunch, but the caretaker isn't his master." Taryn cricked her head from side to side and shook out her hands, flexing her fingers.

"He told you this?" Rhoane took her hand in his, needing to feel her touch. The jealousy he'd had over her contact with the assassin wormed through his being.

"No." She grinned. "My memories did. He clung to certain ones, and in the grasping of those, new ones were imprinted. His, not mine. What Mother said rattled him. He never knew what he'd been denied until I showed him."

Rhoane studied the prisoner. Yes, there was a slight softening of his shoulders, a sadness to his features. But they'd been fooled by him before. He wouldn't let an afternoon of daydreaming convince anyone that the prisoner was no longer dangerous.

A dozen guards were stationed inside the building, and another dozen outside. Two huge men with axes and a mace positioned themselves at the entrance. Even so, it wouldn't be enough to keep out Kaldaar should he desire to rescue his pet. Rhoane suspected not a Master or mage controlled the assassin, but the banished god himself.

He'd have to tell her. Not only about Kaldaar, but about the assassin as well. Any hope of keeping her from discovering the truth was futile. She needed to know, but he dreaded it all the same.

The empress left, taking Myrddin and Taryn with her, and Rhoane breathed as if for the first time since she'd entered the chamber. His reprieve didn't last long when his beloved returned a short time later wearing her usual garb, kohl still rimming her eyes. His body warmed at the sight of her, but the joy her presence brought was tempered by the sense of foreboding he couldn't quiet. Every moment she spent with the assassin was one closer to her discovering the truth.

Rhoane shared a look with Baehlon and the knight lifted his chin in acknowledgement. They'd agreed not to say anything to Taryn until absolutely necessary. It was risky, but Rhoane had a hunch about the demon and his master.

Taryn brought a tray of food with her and fought with the elaborate curls and braids that hung down her back to the tops of her buttocks. Instead of cutting her hair as she'd threatened to do in Ulla, she'd lengthened it. Most likely to please Sabina. Taryn always seemed to know what others needed to calm or soothe their frazzled nerves. It was her healing skill. It was what made her, her.

She set the tray on a wobbly table. "You need to eat. Both of you." Taryn pierced Rhoane and Baehlon with a look that defied argument.

The soldiers guarding the prisoner rotated in and out, but he and Baehlon had been there from the start. His stomach gave an appreciative growl and he picked at the contents on the plate, not wanting to give too much attention to the food and not enough to the prisoner.

Dusk turned to night. No more visitors came. Their conversations were stilted, as if none of them wanted to give voice to their fears. Before daybreak, Rhoane had had enough of the insufferable waiting. The assassin wasn't going to confess, even under torture. They'd tried that in Celyn Eryri and nothing had happened.

Rhoane hadn't been waiting for a confession, however. He'd hoped Kaldaar would come to claim his weapon. If not Kaldaar, then the Master at the very least. Yet, nothing stirred in the chamber except the dust where they paced.

Taryn leaned against the colorful tiles, her eyes drooping.

Rhoane touched her arm. "Come, let us get some sleep."

"No, I need to be here. What if he says something? What if—"

"He will not escape this time. We will make certain of it," Rhoane assured her.

Baehlon nudged her shoulder toward the door. "Go on, lass. I'll guard him while you rest."

Taryn wavered. Rhoane took her elbow and led her to the door. They left the squat building and shuffled toward the palace. They were halfway to the entrance when she stopped him.

"I don't want to go inside. I'm too keyed up." She glanced at the still dark sky. "Niko and Fayngaar have been cooped up too long. Let's take them for a ride."

"Now? Before daybreak?"

She was already headed toward the stables. Rhoane instructed a page to bring them food and jogged after her.

They saddled their horses in silence. The words to tell Taryn about Kaldaar and the assassin stung his lips. Each time he opened his mouth to speak, a riot of anxiety choked his speech. Kaida padded into the stables, stretching to nuzzle both horses before sitting on her haunches. Rhoane petted Kaida, whispering in her ear to keep watch over Taryn. He knew the signs of her melancholy and hoped to keep her from further spiraling down a hole of darkness.

"Ready?" Taryn's voice jerked him from his musings. "Kaida, stay here. Watch the assassin. Make sure nothing happens to the men guarding the prisoner."

Kaida whimpered, but Taryn pointed to the outbuilding. The grierbas slunk off with a low growl and Taryn looked away. He sensed her guilt and shared in it. Kaida needed to get out, too. He made a mental promise to take her for a long run once the assassin business was complete.

The page trotted toward the stables, a heavy pouch in his hands. Rhoane took it from him with thanks and tied it to Fayngaar's saddle. The twin moons waned over the eastern seas, giving scant light by which to see as they rode west. They rode from the palace at a slow pace, not wanting to risk injury to their horses. Rhoane led them without thinking of his destination, but when they crested a bluff leading to a hidden cove, he reached for Taryn's hand and smiled for what felt like the first time in days.

It was the same beach he'd come to when he first arrived in Menurra.

They unsaddled their horses and let them roam free along the shore. Niko snorted and bucked with the energy of youth while

Fayngaar stayed close, munching on the tall grass that grew at the base of the cliff.

The sun started its rise, an orange haze emanating from the horizon. A few scattered clouds glowed pink with the coming sunrise and Taryn stood at the water's edge, her face turned upward, arms outstretched.

Rhoane sat heavily on the sand and untied the laces of his boots.

"Let's go for a swim." She beckoned him forth at the same time she unbuttoned the leather vest she wore.

It snugged over her breasts to her slim hips, the tightness accentuating her small waist. She'd lost too much weight in the past few moonturns. Whereas before she was muscular and toned, now she was wiry and too thin. To see her withered weighed him down with sadness. He hated knowing his brokenness had something to do with her decline in health.

"We should eat first." He held the bag of provisions the page had given him.

"After." The vest flew to the sand beside him, followed by her blouse. Next came her Eleri boots, and finally, her leather breeches and smallclothes. In a matter of minutes, she stood before him, completely naked.

Thin or not, she was sexy as hell. Desire warmed his blood and his cock twitched with anticipation.

"Well? Will you join me?" Taryn teased, her hand outstretched.

Her eyes—as blue as the deepest sea—sparkled with mischief. Her long, silvery hair floated on the breeze. Her body glittered with stars, as if beneath her skin the sky existed. She laughed, and it was the sweetest sound he'd ever heard. Full of hope and promises.

"The sea is calling, my love. We should answer it."

"And what is there you hope to find?" A tremor sounded in his voice.

He recalled his dream from that morning so long ago, when Taryn had appeared to him exactly as she was now. Then he'd dreamt of the darathi eneari. But it wasn't a dream. The water dragon had told him he would betray Taryn not once, but twice, and then he would kill her.

Taryn laughed again, silken chords taken by the sea. He swallowed the despair that threatened to drown them both. He couldn't lose her. *Not again. Not ever.*

A flitter of indecision crossed those lovely eyes, then she smiled and it was like the sun parting storm clouds. "I don't know what we'll find. That's why we have to explore. Always be curious," she said. "Never accept that what you see is all there is."

A shudder racked his spirit. He knew what she would say before the words were spoken. Knew it from his vision of that day...

"Take risks, make mistakes, and get messy. Be brave, and do what frightens you most, but always, always have hope, my beloved." She bent to caress his cheek, and a warm current swept over his skin. Her lips sought his with surprising force.

He shook from her touch, from the realization he'd had the gift of foresight that day. A gift he'd mistaken as a dream.

"Who are you?" He breathed the words, awestruck by the power of his love for her.

She laughed once more and stepped back. "I am yours, mi carae. Forever."

He half-expected Lucitan to gallop through her image, like he had that day, but Lucitan was long gone and this time Taryn wasn't a vision—she was real. She stood not more than a pace from him, fingers outstretched to take his hand. Dream or vision of the future, whatever he'd witnessed on this beach all those seasons ago, this right now was his life. He was in control. He determined his destiny.

Rhoane rose slowly, stripping first his jerkin, then tunic over his head. Taryn's eyes darkened as she stared at his torso. He knew that look well. Her passion flowed to touch his skin, igniting in him his desire. He removed his boots and pants with haste, wanting nothing more than to be naked with his love.

A moment after he kicked his clothes to the side, she was on him, her mouth claiming his, her hands frenzied in their exploration. This was new, her manic excitement, but not unwelcome. She wrapped his long hair around her fist, while scratching his back with the other. Thrill after thrill cascaded down his spine with each touch of her fingertips.

He returned her passionate kiss, tangling his tongue in her mouth, his arms enclosing her shoulders and lower back. Taryn hitched a leg over his hip and angled herself onto his erection, sliding onto it with ease. Their coupling was hard and fast, not at all what he'd become accustomed to. There was no gentleness, no healing this time. Raw, carnal desire flooded through them and he thrust hard into her, faster and, selfishly, to his own rhythm. She cried out with her release and he followed suit, growling as his seed shot forth, filling her.

"Taryn—" He started to apologize for the coarseness of their lovemaking, but she put a finger to his lips.

"Shh. This is what I need, my love. You, here, now. Just this." Her lips sought his and he kissed her long and deep, his hands stroking her hair, her smooth skin, her ass. She curled her fingers in his hair and moaned into his mouth.

Time and space meant nothing as he held her. His world, his reason for being, for the moment was serene.

She ended their kiss and stepped back, a sly grin on her face. "I could use a cooldown. How about you?"

Rhoane hesitated and searched the rolling waves. The darathi eneari might be out there. He couldn't risk meeting her with Taryn.

The sun had crested above the horizon, its rays stretched across the blue sky. Its soft glow illuminated the stars beneath her skin. A gentle flurry lifted her hair and it reminded him of a nebula in the night sky.

"Perhaps we should head back." Indecision rocked his words.

"We will, but a quick dip won't hurt." Taryn took his hand and sprinted toward the waves. Before they'd taken more than a few steps, she stopped and grabbed her head.

"What is it?" He held her face between his hands and searched her eyes. Pain sliced through him and he clearly heard Gian's voice screaming through his mind as if he were being tortured.

"Get dressed," Taryn rasped. "We need to return to the palace."

They threw on their clothes, not caring if a button was out of place, or a lace was missing on their boots.

"I will gather the horses," Rhoane offered, but Taryn shook her head.

"There's no time. We'll come back for them later." She gripped his hand tight in hers. "Don't let go."

As if he ever could.

Then darkness suffocated everything around them.

CHAPTER TWENTY-EIGHT

Rhoane and Taryn appeared in the stables, where there was less likely to be many people to see their return. Her legs wobbled after using so much ShantiMari, but Rhoane's strong hold gave her strength. As they raced to the outbuilding, she unsheathed Ynyd Eirathnacht. Gian's tortured cries lingered in her mind, her imagination bringing forth visuals that made her stomach churn.

The outer guards remained at their posts as if nothing untoward had occurred. She slowed in her step, uncertainty clouding her thoughts. It could be a trap. Most likely was and if she ran in there half-cocked, she'd be dead within a pace. Rhoane put out a hand to slow her further, a finger at his lips. The guards nodded and stepped aside to allow them entrance.

She and Rhoane sent tendrils of their power into the room, scouting for danger. Several times her thread was scalded by something she couldn't visualize. With each flinch of Rhoane's features, she guessed he also sensed the presence. Her head throbbed and her empty stomach spun quicker than the winds of a hurricane. They paused at the door, listening.

Low voices came from inside, muffled to Aelans, but with their heightened senses, clear to her and Rhoane.

"What did you tell them, my son?"

Kaldaar.

Holy shit. Fuck, Kaldaar was here.

Rhoane's eyes widened, then narrowed to dangerous slits.

You know who that is, don't you? Taryn asked in his mind.

Kaldaar. The single word cut through her brain.

What do we do? He's a god. Fighting Rykoto while he's locked in his prison was one thing. This guy's right fucking there.

"Join us, my children," the voice on the other side of the door said. "I have been waiting for you."

Taryn's knees wobbled and she clenched her fist around Ynyd Eirathnacht, begging the sword to give her strength. Her confidence floated around her like a tattered window dressing. This was the god responsible for Julieta's rape, and had almost succeeded in doing the same thing to Sabina. He was desperate, and Taryn knew enough of the world to know when someone had nothing to lose, they gambled everything.

With shaking fingers, she turned the latch and entered the small, round building. The guards were plastered against the wall, arms and legs splayed as if they'd been thrown there and stuck. They almost looked like comic characters, or crime scene cutouts. They didn't move, and for a moment she feared them dead, but then one of the men blinked. She took a deep breath to calm her jackhammering heart. Next, her focus darted to the shadows, where the faint outlines of Ebus and Gian could barely be seen. A wave of relief swept over her and tears teased her eyes. Then she saw Baehlon pinned next to the door, rage clear in his dark eyes. Next to him, Kaida stood mid-growl.

"Taryn, come here, my darling." It was the rasping voice she'd heard in her mind for the past season. The one that taunted her, tormented her. She'd always thought it was Rykoto, but it belonged to his brother, Kaldaar.

He stood in front of the Shadow Assassin, blocking him from her view. A bony hand protruded from the long sleeves of Kaldaar's hooded cloak. His face, if he had one, was hidden in the deep recesses of fabric.

"No." She forced the word out. "I'm not your darling and I won't obey you."

But there was a strong compulsion to do exactly that. Just like she'd felt when she was in Marissa's rooms and had spied on her sister fornicating with an invisible lover.

"Oh, but you will. You must."

"What do you want, Kaldaar?" Rhoane stepped next to her, his sword drawn.

The creature hissed, his attention swiveling to Rhoane.

"Betrayer." He spat. "You have spoiled what is mine. Always mine."

Rhoane held his sword loose in his grip, but he was poised to strike. Behind Kaldaar, the assassin moaned and blood oozed from several cuts on his face. But how? He wasn't alive.

"Your memories, my sweet. They gave him just enough life to feel a heartbeat. You thought you could seduce his memories from him. All you did was incite agony. He now feels what you Aelans feel. Humanity, you might even call it, right, Taryn?"

"Don't say my name, you worthless piece of shit. I was never yours and if this thing can feel, good. I'm glad I did that to him."

Every time Kaldaar spoke, her resolve cracked the tiniest bit. His compulsion was hard to resist. She didn't want to go to him, but *needed* to. It was as if her life depended on his touch. At her side, Rhoane swayed. Kaldaar must have been using the same force on him.

"What's going on in there? Let me in this instant!" Lliandra's shrill voice demanded from the other side of the door.

"Taryn, are you in there?" Myrddin asked. "Open this door. What's happening?"

No, no, no, Taryn thought. *Not her mother. Not Myrddin.* She desperately wanted them to stay away. *But why?*

Her thoughts tumbled and heart cartwheeled.

She didn't want them to stay away—Kaldaar did. She fought off his compulsion and called out, "Mother, I'm here. We need your help."

Kaldaar hissed, his hands snaking into his long sleeves.

The hooded figure leaned forward to whisper in her ear, "On her wedding night, I will have the *Sabinth Aarendhi.* Even now she is primed to carry the seed of Dark and Light. She will be my vessel for all future followers. Her children will be even more powerful than you."

More shouts and pounding sounded from outside and Taryn gripped Ynyd Eirathnacht between clenched fists.

Kaldaar sucked in a breath, then blew it out. Rank heat burned her cheek. Her movements froze. She couldn't move, couldn't speak.

"I will be restored, my darling, and you shall sit at my feet as my slave."

"No," Taryn fought his control and said through gritted teeth. "Never."

Calling on every ounce of power she had, she sliced her sword upward, into his chest. A hollow laugh escaped the cloak as it drifted to the dirt, empty. Her hands shook, setting off a tremble that coursed through her entire body.

Lliandra and Myrddin burst through the door at the same time those pinned to the walls plummeted to the floor. They gasped and rubbed where Kaldaar had bound them. Kaida leapt, but landed on nothing. A low growl, more of a whimper, came from her throat as she positioned herself at Taryn's side.

A sick gurgling drew her attention from the others and she stared at the Shadow Assassin. His light-blue eyes shone in the early morning light. They filled with something she never thought she'd see from him—relief. Her gaze traveled to the blood bubbling from his mouth. His lips moved to speak, but no words came out. Then her gaze moved to the sword impaled through his chest. Her sword.

The blade glowed bright blue and pulsed with an energy that frightened her. Remorse, regret, death: those emotions swirled through her mind. Then, with absolute clarity, she saw the assassin for the first time. Not as he was now, a prisoner hanging from a rope in this round chamber, dying from the wound she inflicted, but as he could've been. A man in his own right. Powerful, with both Light and Dark ShantiMari. The Eirielle of the prophecies.

Savior. Betrayer. Destroyer.

He was all of those and none of them. Just as she was all of those and none of them.

He was her. She was him.

The truth burned her innards, scalding her blood cells, singeing her memories. A violent shaking started in her core and she struggled to keep her grip on the hilt.

He was her twin.

"What have I done?" Tears coursed over her cheeks. She pulled her sword free and tossed it to the side. It clanged with hollow resentment.

"Taryn," the assassin said, "thank you."

"No." She placed her hand over the wound on his chest. "No, you can't die."

This was her brother. Her twin. It didn't matter what he was before this moment—she could save him. Could give him the life she stole from him. Her manic thoughts were drowned out by her sobs as she cupped the blood pouring from his injury.

Rhoane's hand covered hers and his power flowed over them both, to the Shadow Assassin. "Taryn, he cannot die. This is only a release. He was never truly here. Please, let him go."

Emotions roiled across the assassin's features. His gaze slid to Lliandra and he whispered, "I'm sorry."

Confusion clouded Lliandra's startling blue eyes as she took in Taryn and the assassin. Heartbreak nearly cracked the mask of Mari she wore, but then her aloof composure fitted back into place. Only a brief nod gave any indication she understood what took place.

"End this, please," he whispered. "Let me be at peace."

Taryn stood on tiptoe to touch her lips to his. The blood tasted like a rotting corpse and she gagged, but held firm. Her thoughts mingled with his. Memories flooded into her—all of them centered around him being taught to fight, to hunt, actually. His purpose was to kill her, yet each time he'd had the chance, he hadn't taken it. And there had been many chances, she now realized. He'd been denied memories or thought or compassion, yet he'd somehow found a pinprick of sentience for Taryn. All of the loathing she'd once had for him twisted and reshaped as gratitude, even love. Her heart swelled with affection, blotting out everything else. Her lips trembled upon his.

From the very start of her journey on Aelinae, he'd been attuned to her presence. He'd trailed her from the cavern to Ravenwood, then to Paderau, and everywhere else she'd ventured. Only when she flew as a dragon did he lose her. He'd even been on one of Lliandra's ships the entire time. He saw the explosion and had hoped she'd died so he wouldn't have to be the one to kill her. There was a tiny slice of regret for what he'd done to Ellie.

The assassin had plenty of opportunities to kill her. Yet he'd chosen to defy his Master and let her live. Which was why he'd been allowed to be captured. Somehow Kaldaar knew she'd end up killing her own brother. He'd planned it this way.

Taryn placed her palm against the wound on his chest. There was no heartbeat, nothing to indicate life.

How do I release you?

Forgive me.

I do. I forgive you, my brother. A new memory seized her, of being in the womb with him, their tiny hands clasped together. He'd started to leave her and she feared being alone. Then their umbilical cords had wrapped around her neck, cutting off her air. Before he disappeared from her sight, he'd sent his power into her, loosening the cords' grip, allowing her to live.

You gave your life for me.

You were meant to be the Eirielle, not me. It was never meant to be me.

"Taryn." Rhoane's gentle voice rocked her back to reality. "He needs to go."

Taryn infused her brother with all of her power until they both glowed—he as bright as the sun, she a star. Light and Dark. Sun and Moon. He had given her his power, his Dark ShantiMari.

It was a gift I freely gave. You must stop Kaldaar…my sister.

Then he was gone. Nothing of his body remained. The rope hung empty from the rafters and a hush settled in the room. Emptiness filled her soul. A longing she never knew she had sat heavy upon her heart, yet there was lightness, too. He was free. Her twin would never suffer again.

"What was his name?" Taryn asked her mother.

"Who?" Bafflement edged the word.

"My brother. The twin who died the night I was born. What was his name?"

Tears shimmered in Lliandra's eyes. "Gavyn."

Taryn nodded then and scooped her sword from the floor. Gavyn. She hoped he would be at peace, finally. For thirty-six seasons, he'd lived in torment. She exited the outbuilding and stared at the sky. Perhaps he was with Brandt in Dal Tara. Somehow, she doubted it, but just in case, she asked her grandfather to watch over him. It wasn't Gavyn's fault. It was Kaldaar's. A terrible thread of anxiety broke through her grief.

That bastard had promised to take Sabina on her wedding night.

Over Taryn's dead body.

She spun on her heel and headed toward the harbor.

"Where are you going?" Rhoane asked.

"To find Julieta. I'm sick of that asshole being in control. We need the strength of a goddess if we're going to stop him."

Taryn, a voice whispered, *you have the power within you.*

It wasn't Kaldaar's voice, or even Rykoto's. It was Nadra who whispered in her heart what her mind refused to accept.

She ran faster, trying to outpace her internal demons. Kaida joined her, easily keeping pace as Taryn's legs pumped harder and she sprinted down the road leading to the city. The hill was too steep, or she was too tired, but her legs couldn't keep up the pace and she stumbled, hands splayed on the dirt. The sharp sting of skin tearing brought tears to her eyes, but they weren't for the wounds.

Rhoane reached her and knelt low, his soothing voice in her ear, his strong arms around her shoulders. He turned her to face him and raw fear was rampant in his eyes.

"He's going to rape her, Rhoane. On her wedding night, Kaldaar swore to take Sabina as his vessel. We can't let that happen."

His face crumpled and reddened, his jaw tightened. Rage, powerful and sustained, coursed from him to her cynfar.

"We will not allow it."

"But he's a god, Rhoane. You felt it in there, the compulsion he places over you. How can we fight that? How do we destroy a god?"

He shook his head, braids swinging wildly with the movement. "I do not know, but we must try."

Taryn leaned into him, breathing the scent of forest and mint. It calmed and soothed her broken spirits. How he managed to always smell like the Narthvier, no matter where they were in the world, amazed her. She clung to him and he sat on the ground right there in the middle of the road, not caring if anyone walked past. He wrapped his legs around her, enfolding her in a full-body embrace. Kaida lay beside them, her tail draped over Taryn's legs. For a long time, she stayed curled into Rhoane's tunic, one hand clutching the grierbas. Soft sobs came from deep inside of her. For Sabina, for Gavyn, for everyone she couldn't protect.

"He took my dead twin and turned him into a weapon."

"Yes."

"Did you know the assassin was my brother?"

Rhoane hesitated and she braced herself for a truth she wasn't prepared to hear.

"Not until yesterday when I saw you and your mother standing beside him. The resemblance was too much to ignore."

"You should have told me."

"Aye, and I wanted to, but would you have believed me?"

She searched her heart for the answer and admitted he was right. If he'd said the Shadow Assassin was her dead twin, she would have thought him mad.

"But, how?" Taryn couldn't comprehend how someone would be so cruel. "I mean, he was an infant. How did Kaldaar make him grow?"

"A Shadow Assassin can be raised from any age, even a newborn. They are fed on fear and death. Kaldaar supplied no shortage of each."

"I killed him. I killed my brother." A fresh wave of sobs left her breathless and trembling. "Not just him." She buried her face in his tunic, too afraid to meet his gaze. Too afraid he would loathe her as much as she hated herself. "I killed Marissa, too."

"I know. I do not blame you for what you did."

She tore herself from the safety of his embrace and stared into his eyes. Those same moss-green orbs she'd dreamed of all those years on Earth, the ones she first saw in the cavern and knew he was someone special in her life. The same eyes that looked at her with reverence and love. The words stalled on her lips. *Would he hate her now? After her confession?*

"I could've saved her in the temple, but there was too much darkness inside. She wouldn't stop hurting us. I murdered her instead of saving her."

Rhoane brushed a lock of hair from Taryn's forehead and placed his lips upon her skin. His warmth eased some of the chill from her heart.

"She raped me, used a child that was not mine to manipulate me, then she arranged for Zakael to take your sister Eliahnna to the temple to be sacrificed to Rykoto. If you had not killed her, I would have myself." His powerful arms tightened around her. "She deserved nothing less."

"We're not gods. It's not our decision to decide who lives and dies."

"Is that what you think gods do? Make life-and-death decisions? I would wager if you asked Nadra if this were true, she would say no. Gods are there to observe, not determine our fate. That is our decision and ours alone."

"It doesn't feel that way sometimes. Most of the time, actually." A troubling thought wiggled its way through her mind. "Did Kaldaar seem solid to you? Like, there was a body under the cloak?"

He pulled her closer and rested his chin atop her head. "I am not sure. Why?"

"He's supposed to be between worlds, in the great nothingness or something like that, right? What if…he's found a way to sort of be here, not quite physically, but enough that he seems real even though he's still trapped between worlds?" She was rambling, but didn't care. This was important. She had to know. Had to understand.

"I saw only a hand."

"Yes, corpse-like and gross. It wasn't very substantial, was it?"

She disentangled herself from his hold, regretting every movement that took her away from his warmth. He stood and helped her to her feet. For a long moment, he remained still, his unwavering gaze seeking hers. Her questions had unsettled him as much as they unsettled her.

"If he has not yet found a way to return to our world, he can still be defeated," Rhoane said at last.

Taryn's nerves trembled beneath her skin. "That's just it. I think he's found a way."

Rhoane quirked an eyebrow.

A carriage led by two sturdy horses trundled up the street and they moved out of the way, to a sheltered corner off the main square. Taryn paced a path in the dirt, her mind working, her teeth nibbling at a cuticle on her thumb. Kaida sat beside Rhoane, who leaned against a stone wall, his gaze fixed to her. He appeared calm, but Taryn sensed his apprehension.

"Kaldaar said he'd claim Sabina for his vessel, but to do that, he needs a body, right? I mean, if he's not fully flesh and bones, he needs a proxy."

Rhoane eased from the wall, his eyes lit from within. "He does not want Sabina."

"No," Taryn agreed. "He's after my cousin."

Taryn wavered between seeking out Julieta and returning to the palace to find Hayden. Exhaustion rumbled through her and she swayed against Rhoane. He gripped her hand and turned them away from the harbor, making the decision for her. The walk up the hill burned through her energy stores, more than it should've. It was a short hike, nothing too taxing, yet her legs stumbled every few steps. Rhoane kept an arm wrapped around her waist, half dragging her into the palace.

Myrddin came to assist, taking Taryn's arm and slinging it over his shoulder. They brought her to her rooms and she collapsed on her bed, half asleep. Kaida leapt onto the bed to snuggle beside her. The men spoke quietly and then Rhoane kissed her forehead before leaving to go somewhere. Had he told her? She couldn't remember.

Myrddin sat next to her bed and held her hand in his. They were warm and comforting.

"Stay with me awhile, please?"

The mage's eyes twinkled like they always did. Like tiny stars dotted a velvety denim sky.

"I'll watch over you as I always have, my dear."

"Thank you," she murmured and snuggled into her blanket. She gripped Myrddin's hand tighter as she drifted to sleep. Kaldaar had shown himself at last. Now she knew the face of her enemy. Well, almost. A bony hand did not a face make, but he'd come out of the shadows to confront her. He'd made himself known.

Why? The muddy thought fought through her fatigue. *Why now?*

CHAPTER TWENTY-NINE

Rain pelted the windows of Caer Idris, irritating the king more than he already was. He wore a path in the carpet with his incessant pacing, his fists clenching and releasing in perfect rhythm to his heavy breathing. *Where the hell was the Eirielle?* No one had seen her since the explosion. At least, none of his spies had caught wind of her whereabouts or whether she was alive.

Yet, he knew she wasn't dead. He paused at the balcony of his lavish rooms, those that used to be his father's, and took a deep breath of sea air. His hand went to his chest and he felt his own heartbeat beneath his summer tunic. In there, he sensed his half-sister's existence. He was bound to her by blood. He would know if she were dead and his heart told him she lived. There was still time to claim her as his own. Still time to seize both thrones and rule Aelinae with her as his queen.

Wind whipped his hair across his face and ocean spray misted his skin. Soon. Soon he would have her. Soon she would come to him of her own free will. But how? The longer she stayed with that piece of Eleri trash, the more in love with him she fancied herself. Glennwoods had some sort of hold over her. He'd hoped

Marissa's seduction of the prince would break Taryn's bond with Rhoane. But it had only made it stronger.

He strode to his mirror as if waiting for a message from his dead lover, but none came. Marissa would never again send her thoughts to him through the scrying bowl. The time for delighting in the sensuous pleasure of her flesh was past.

"Ho now, getting melancholy, are we?" His reflection stared dully back at him. Yes, this was what ailed him. He was lonely. Kane, er, Cashiel was still recovering at Gaarendahl, which left him without a playmate. Even his father had deserted Zakael at his hour of greatest need.

Before he knew what he was doing, he stormed out of his rooms to the queen's chambers a short distance down the hall. Several servants darted out of his way, but he ignored them. The doors to the queen's rooms were locked, but with a flick of his wrist they opened to him. Only to him. No others were allowed in these sacred rooms. Not after *she* had stayed there.

The huge bed remained untouched since her last visit and Zakael crawled beneath the covers, searching for the sweet jasmine scent that Taryn had left on the linens when she stayed at Caer Idris little more than a moonturn hence. Only a faint lingering remained. The passing of time had stolen her scent. A catch in his throat surprised him and he coughed it away. It wouldn't do to shed a tear. Not here. Not ever. Taryn would be his. She would.

A familiar hiss came to his ears and he trembled against the sound. He burrowed deeper under the covers, blotting out the intruder. He didn't wish to be disturbed. This was his time alone with his memories and there was no room in his thoughts for the capricious god who sought to control Zakael.

Words whispered into his mind despite him covering his ears and keeping his eyes firmly shut. If he opened them, he'd see the phrases scrolling across the ceiling, floating on air. But not today. No, he wouldn't listen, wouldn't turn his head ever so slightly to see the figure crouching in the corner of the room, watching. Couldn't. Not today. Not again.

The hiss grew louder and Zakael suppressed a tremble. He breathed deep to capture Taryn's scent, hoping it would offset the terror the creature brought on.

"Look at me," it commanded.

Zakael shook his head, eyes shut so hard they hurt.

"You cannot escape me, young king. I own you."

The compulsion he couldn't deny overwhelmed him and Zakael rolled to his side, his eyes blinking open against his will. The shadow from the corner elongated and drew near. At first, it was nothing more than a streak of pitch, but as it came closer, it took the shape of a man. Faceless, featureless, but altogether terrifying, it leaned toward him, its mouth a gaping maw.

Zakael's mind screamed for him to recoil, but there was no escaping the thing. His insides watered and clenched. He swallowed a sob and waited for the inevitable.

The maw grew to encompass him fully, taking his body into the darkness until he saw nothing, felt nothing.

In a flash, he stood in front of the runyon tree at the farthest end of the castle grounds. It sat upon a high cliff with the ocean stretching far below. No one but Zakael ever came to see the tree, which meant there was no one nearby to help. Calling out would be useless as the creature would silence him swiftly and painfully.

"Show your respect." An inky tendril pushed him forward.

Zakael approached the tree with apprehension.

Thick barbs dotted the trunk, slick with an oily substance. Crimson in color, Zakael had often thought it resembled blood. He reached forward and tried to control the shaking of his hand as he pressed his palm against the trunk, onto one of the barbs. Pain shot from where the thorn's tip pierced his skin straight up his arm, ending with a dizzying snap at the base of his neck. His blood oozed from the cut, mingling with the oil until he was as much a part of the tree as the creature.

Since the night Lliandra had visited him, the thing had come to Zakael, promising to make his desires reality, but only if Zakael would pay. He'd laughed in the creature's face—well, what he thought was his face—and told him to fuck off. Ever since, he'd been compelled to visit the queen's rooms, where the creature stayed hidden in the decorative paintings near the ceiling. Every day, the creature had made him come to the runyon tree and offer his blood as tribute.

"What do you want from me?" Zakael forced himself not to suck blood from his throbbing palm. Stinging pain radiated from the tiny wound.

"Your offspring." The shadowy figure swayed as if a breeze might tear through its fragile existence.

"I don't have any children, you buffoon."

A flick of the demon's shadow cut across his cheek and he bit the inside of his mouth to keep from blurting out something even fouler. He valued his life too much.

"You must find a woman of Light and get her with child. Do it with force. You cannot be gentle with her. This child must never know kindness."

"The Eirielle?" His heart skipped a beat in anticipation of the answer.

The inky shadow wavered a moment, then hissed. "She is far too powerful and has made the change too quickly. She will not conceive children by you or anyone."

Taryn couldn't have children? Ever? A part of him mourned the loss of any future heirs he'd planned to have with her.

"She must be of the Light, and powerful, this surrogate."

"Why?"

Another wavering silence. "I have lost my assassin and need a new agent to carry out my plans."

His assassin? So this thing, this inky darkness without a form was responsible for the Shadow Assassin sent to kill Taryn? "Why would I supply you with something you'll only use against

Taryn? I don't wish her dead. I need her alive to become my queen."

A second lash sliced his other cheek and Zakael flinched.

"You stupid boy. She was never meant to be your queen. You will ruin everything with your daydreams."

Zakael wiped the blood pooling along his cheek and slowly put the finger in his mouth, sucking it clean. "You will not speak to me so. I am King of the West, and you are nothing but a shadow."

A bellowing laugh followed his statement, but Zakael stood firm. He was tired of this thing bullying him.

"I am much more than that, you ignorant whelp. Can you not recognize your true god? Do you only play at practicing the Telraicht Arts? Or have you fully taken my teachings into your heart? I thought you smarter than your father, but I was wrong."

"Kaldaar?" His breath left him in a gasping whoosh. "But… you're banished. To the edge of nothingness, between the worlds. How is this possible?" He bent to one knee, apologies flowing from his tongue like a river he was unable to stop.

"Get up. You are an embarrassment."

Zakael stood, searching for a hand he might grasp, a ring he might kiss. This was his god. The reason the Telraicht Brotherhood existed. And he'd been a fool to insult him.

"The Eirielle has placed powerful seals on Rykoto's tomb, preventing me from reaching him. Without my brother, and with my Shadow Assassin vanquished, my power on Aelinae is limited. He was never meant to kill Taryn. Quite the opposite, in fact. His sole purpose was to serve me, to act as an anchor in this world. Without him, my power would fade. The attempts on the Eirielle's life were merely meant to serve as a warning. To scare her, keep her unbalanced."

"How did he perish?" There was more to this than Kaldaar was admitting.

"It is not important. His tasks were completed and now, I need another agent to act as an anchor."

"Forgive me, but that doesn't seem well-thought-out. Why not have another assassin ready before you destroy the first?"

"There can only be one at a time. I had hoped to use the crown princess's child once born, but as you know, it is of no use to me."

"Take me, my lord." The words were out before he could stop them. Kaldaar was his god, but acting as his vessel wasn't something he relished.

"You're far too alive to be of much help. And I have further need of you to afford your disposal at this time."

He should've been relieved, but the matter-of-fact way Kaldaar said it alarmed Zakael. If he wished, Kaldaar could strike him down at any moment.

"Yes," Kaldaar's shadow said as if reading his thoughts, "you shall serve me until I no longer have a use for you. Be certain that time never comes."

"I will. You have my word." Zakael's oath warbled with his lie.

The shadow snorted and a puff of smoke came from the general area of where a face would be. "When has that ever amounted to much?"

This wasn't going well. He had to do something to gain Kaldaar's favor. "This anchor of which you speak, it must be of a powerful house of Light and Dark, yes? A baby is too small and you have great need of an anchor now. What about Marissa?"

The shadow wavered as if Kaldaar entertained the thought. "Intriguing suggestion, but the Eirielle made certain we couldn't use her. There is no body to claim."

"No body? But how? Why?" An injection of sorrow filled his spirit. Knowing Marissa's body lay in the crypt of Talaith had soothed him. He'd even gone to the crypt alone once to pay his respects.

"Perhaps she foresaw exactly this moment. I do not know. But shortly after the crown princess's burial, the Eirielle went to the crypt and destroyed the body through flame and ice. There is nothing left but an image constructed of ShantiMari meant to fool those who would seek to gaze upon the dead princess."

Humiliation scorched his sorrow. He'd believed the artifice. "How do you know this?"

"I traveled to Talaith before I lost my assassin. I thought to raise her even as you have suggested, but it was too late."

Kaldaar wavered and a slimy, grizzled hand snuck from the black fog, grasping Zakael with a force stronger than any he'd known. Despite himself, he let out a frantic gasp, but didn't disgrace himself further by yanking his hand away.

"You must secure my anchor," Kaldaar ordered. "Or it shall be your doom."

Zakael stood at the edge of the cliff and gazed over the calm sea. He didn't like leaving his fate to chance, but had to do as Kaldaar commanded. Once Zakael found a surrogate assassin, he would be released from the god's hold and once more able to fulfill his destiny. Kaldaar be damned, Taryn would be his.

The shadow enveloped Zakael, sliding over his skin like a lover's caress. His breath caught and his heart beat furiously in his chest, but he didn't move. Instead, he allowed the thing to cover him completely, let the dark tendrils of nothingness sneak beneath his clothing to seek out his most private places. One by one, his orifices filled with the god's insubstantial mist. There was pain, yes, yet it was akin to the most exquisite lovemaking he'd ever known. His body tingled with hopeful expectation, every nerve alive to the shadow's touch. He moaned into the darkness, as Kaldaar's magnificence fucked him delirious.

The last he heard before he lost himself to lust was, "Bring me my anchor. Do it with violence, my son. Make him scream as he dies."

Zakael curled into the blankets and bucked his hips with his release. His seed spread across the front of his breeches, making a dark stain upon the fabric. The shadow creature slunk into the corner as the words settled into the ceiling and doubt crept into his thoughts.

They no longer stood on the cliff near the runyon tree. Kaldaar no longer invaded his body. After a moment, Zakael was alone in the room, as if nothing had happened. Perhaps nothing had. He could've had a nightmare.

No amount of deception would convince Zakael he hadn't been visited by a god. Every orifice of his body ached as if someone had abused him.

He traced the markings on the ceiling and slid his gaze to the corner. Abuse or no, it was the best fuck he'd ever had. If Kaldaar wanted him to find an anchor, he would. With a final inhale of Taryn's fading scent, he rose from the bed and straightened his aching cock.

The release Kaldaar had given him only served to incite his desire. He knew exactly how to slake this particular thirst and left the queen's chambers, impatient to be at Gaarendahl. The need to find Kaldaar's assassin shuttled to the back of his mind. A worry for another day.

He needed a release and despite Cashiel still needing to heal, the man would give Zakael what he needed. The thought thumped against his mind—Cashiel hated Taryn's family and had never known kindness, exactly the qualities Kaldaar required. He would make an excellent assassin, but Zakael was selfish. He needed Cashiel's anger to pursue his own ambitions.

Zakael's pace slowed even as his heart raced. What if, a small warning said in the back of his mind, Cashiel had used Zakael for his own vengeance? His arms trembled with suppressed violence. How could Zakael have been so blind? He had believed Cashiel loved him, and wanted to see him raised above all others, yet Cashiel—no, Kane was his proper name and would still be called

—Kane had used Zakael to get revenge on a mother who had discarded him.

Kane cared little for Zakael's plans for immortality. He saw it all clearly now. The plot to kidnap Taryn had been Kane's. The suggestion to use Adesh's pleasure ships, also Kane's. The brutality he'd heaped upon Taryn on the ship—that puzzle eluded Zakael. Unless it was Kane's desire to watch his mother suffer while Taryn died.

Revenge did indeed taste sweet, and by the time Zakael was done with Kane, he'd have feasted on the delicacy.

CHAPTER THIRTY

The forest rose around them in lush shades of green Gwainne had never imagined. His was a world of beiges. The Narthvier, something from a dream. After only one night at the Weirren with the stern Eleri king and his sons, Gwainne had asked permission to continue his travels to Verdaine's temple. To his utter delight, Carga had offered to act as his escort. By the time they reached the sanctuary, he was already half in love with her. She was charming, intelligent, and more beautiful than any woman he'd ever seen, including the mysteriously ethereal Darennsai.

Ulla didn't have temples, nor did they believe in Aelinae's gods, but meeting the one prophesied to destroy his mother's people, and then seeing Verdaine, Gwainne had to admit that perhaps his father's beliefs were misguided. For how could the Ullans deny their existence, when Gwainne had met a goddess? Well, he couldn't deny their existence any longer. Convincing his father's people would be another issue entirely.

The forest opened to a small clearing and Gwainne sucked in a breath. Verdaine's temple, or the sanctuary as Carga called it, nestled between massive trees much like the Weirren had, but where the Weirren was large and imposing, the temple was light, almost like it was made of silken webs. No, that wasn't it. Gwainne shook his head and tried to think of exactly the right word to describe what he saw before him. *Gossamer.*

The temple looked as frail as a thread of gossamer, like the wings of a butterfly stretched between great trunks with ivy stitching the two together.

"You are gaping, my lord."

Carga's gentle voice pulled him from the trance the structure had put him in. Surely he was bewitched by the beauty of the place.

"There is nothing comparable to this magnificence."

"You speak truly, for there is not."

He followed her under a bridge spun from light and shadows, drops of dew making diamonds of the late afternoon sun. A groom rushed out to take their mounts and Gwainne reminded himself he was a prince, and his gaping belied his station.

A gaggle of young women dressed in simple cotton gowns gathered at the temple entrance. They wore their hair loose, hanging in long sheaths around lovely young faces. These were the Eleri novices of the goddess Verdaine. His mother had once been among their flock.

Carga shooed them away with soft scolding. The entire time, a smile played at the corners of her lips. "I am afraid, my lord, they are not accustomed to seeing men here."

"But the groom who took our horses, if I am not mistaken, he was a man."

"He is a woodland faerie."

If Gwainne was supposed to understand the meaning of this, he didn't.

"And a eunuch."

An involuntary flinch caused him to cross his nether regions with his palm. "Is that necessary? Certainly extreme measures are not essential to keep the novices from seeking his bed?"

"He chose to be castrated. We do not require it of him."

But why? Why would anyone voluntarily do such a thing? He thought of his brother Loghan and chuckled. If ever there was a contradiction of ideals, he and the groom were it.

"Something amuses you?"

"If you knew my brother, you would understand."

Her green eyes darkened to something he couldn't quite decipher. "He is the healer, yes?"

Gwainne gave a slight nod, his mouth going suddenly dry.

"I would like to meet him someday." She cocked her head to the side.

A flurry of jealousy swept through him. He'd raise a demon before letting his brother touch this divine specimen.

"Verdaine's priestesses are known for their healing skills, but we cannot compare to the legend of the Ullan healers."

"He is very good at what he does." Normally Gwainne was proud of his brother. A stroke of shame pierced him. Carga was a high priestess as well as an Eleri princess. There was no future for her in his life. "My mother often speaks of the healing ways she was taught while a novice here."

That damned smile played at the corners of her lips and he wished he could brush it away. With his lips.

"Your mother's skill is well-known. Even here, hidden deep in the forest, we have heard of Kaleigh's successes."

This surprised him. He'd not thought anyone from the Narthvier would remember his mother. She'd left in scandal, an outcast.

Carga led them from one room to another, the whole time keeping him in her periphery, even while greeting those they passed. Twice he thought he saw a male, but it could've been a trick of the light. Even Eleri men wore their hair long, and were almost as beautiful as their women. Finally, she turned down a corridor of spun silk and stopped before a door that resembled a leaf.

"This will be your room while you stay with us. I have made arrangements for you to meet with one of our scholars in the library. She will be able to help you with your riddle."

"You will not be assisting me?" Panic edged his words and he cursed his infantile crush.

"I am afraid not. I am needed elsewhere, but it has been my pleasure meeting you, Prince Gwainne."

He thought he detected a note of sadness in her voice. At least, he hoped so.

A dozen questions sprang to mind, but he asked none of them. On their ride to the temple, Carga had been entertaining and jovial, but shared little of her life with him. Even the simple questions he'd asked seemed to cause her distress, so he'd kept the conversation to topics other than the Darennsai or Rhoane. Only once, when he'd mentioned the name Zakael, had she shown anger. It was quickly hidden, but there was something about the man that troubled her and Gwainne had wanted to protect her from any harm Zakael might cause.

"Then I will say goodbye, Princess Carga. It has been my pleasure traveling with you this past day."

She gave him a full smile then, not the coy, teasing grin she'd had all day, but one that lit up her face and showed her teeth. "I am sure this is not goodbye, but rather until we meet again. I have a sense our paths will cross soon enough."

"I look forward to it."

She left him and returned in the direction they'd come. He watched her until she was out of sight, then he retired to his room. It was even more enchanting than he'd dared believe. A cocoon of sorts, the room glowed with pale light, the floor and walls made of the same silken gossamer strands as the rest of the temple. He'd assumed it would be cold, yet it was remarkably warm. A small fire burned in a hearth near a great bed made of tree branches and draped in leaves.

Two servants arrived and bathed him in a copper tub with hot, scented water. After he was clean, they dressed him in his court attire and left. The entire time, they'd said less than a dozen words. Idly, he wondered if they were eunuchs as well. He imagined so. Being around all these lovely young maidens would be difficult for any man, even a woodland faerie. Whatever that meant.

A soft knock at his door surprised him and for a heartbeat, he hoped it was Carga come to favor him with her presence. It wasn't Carga at his door, but another young lass. As fair of face as Carga, but pale blonde where the other Eleri was dark. And she wore her hair short, quite short, actually. Blue eyes, as deep as the night sky, stared at him beneath a fringe of dark lashes.

"Lady Carga asked me to escort you to the library. I understand you wish to do some research." Her brusque tone and forthright manner was an abrupt change from the more amenable princess.

"I am Gwainne," he said, bowing low.

"Khrystina." She turned on her heel and strode down the corridor.

He hurried after her petite frame, his long legs making quick work of the distance. From his height, he saw several streaks of color hidden beneath her blonde wisps. "Are you a faerie?"

Her grunt should've been answer enough. "Why? Because I am not as tall as the others? No, to answer your question. I am full Eleri, despite my lack of stature."

"I did not mean offense." He strolled beside her. "My mother is about your height and she is also full Eleri."

She glared at him.

He chuckled. "She also has a fierce scowl like you. I wonder if we are related."

"I doubt that, my lord."

The extra emphasis she put on the last two words made him wonder what she had against nobility.

"I have heard of your mother's exploits."

She didn't elaborate, but Gwainne got the distinct impression she wasn't as forgiving as Carga. "You wear your hair short. Are you sheanna?"

A gasp escaped her full lips.

"Not at all. I choose to wear my hair short." She pointed toward a notch in the tree. "Be careful here. The stairs are steep."

Before he had a chance to reply, she had skipped down the stairwell, if one could call it that, and out of sight.

The stairs weren't just steep, but treacherous. They rounded a sturdy tree trunk, about a man's circumference, and continued down, down, down, until Gwainne was certain they were beneath the leaf-strewn terrarae. No doors or windows banked off the stairwell, making him slightly claustrophobic. When finally his feet touched dirt, he breathed out the half breath he'd been holding.

Dizzy with lack of oxygen, it took him a moment for his eyes to adjust. When he could see clearly, he blinked again to be sure his eyes weren't playing tricks on him.

All around him, scrolls were stacked in cubbies from floor to ceiling. Small desks dotted the cavernous space, with little reading nooks carved out of tree roots. Bulbs of drossfire were set at even intervals along the walls, and across the arching ceiling. They were indeed underground, but the warmth and coziness belied the fact. Only the appearance of gnarled roots gave away their location. But what truly astonished him was the great lake in the middle of the library.

He could have stood there the rest of the day and marveled at it, but his host's voice prevented him from loitering.

"Come on, Your Highness." Khrystina's sigh was enough to tell him she didn't fancy being his helper, but it was the way she cocked her hip out and arched her brow that really settled her opinion of him.

"How is this possible?" He stumbled after her, stealing quick glances to his left where glittering crystals protruded from the dirt walls.

"You have never seen a cavern before?" She half snorted. "Ullans."

"Why do you say it with such disdain? Have you ever been to the desert?"

"No, and I do not wish to see it. I have everything I need here. So, Prince Gwainne, what is it you seek?" She stopped abruptly and turned to face him.

The change of pace and subject unbalanced him. He stared at her a moment, lost in the fathomless depths of her eyes. With a start, he remembered himself. "I seek information about the Jansen Strait."

She tapped a finger to her lips, her eyes narrowed.

"That will be in the east quarter, I believe. Come." And she was off again.

She led him to a dark section of the library where no others mingled. On their way through the strange building, he saw at least a dozen other women, some with scrolls bundled in their arms, others lounging on thick cushions, sipping a mug of something dark and spicy. But here, in the east quarter, it was only him and Khrystina. She rummaged through stacks and stacks of parchment, tugging on scrolls until they popped free, or shuffling a sheath of papers into a neat pile before setting them on a desk. Gwainne offered to help several times, with each being met with a muttered rebuff.

Once the desk was covered to overflowing, Khrystina nodded. "I think that is everything. When you are done with something, put it here." She indicated an empty basket. "Please do not try to put it away. It will take me an age to restore order if you do."

"Are you leaving me, then?"

"What? You thought I would do your work for you? Not hardly. I have my own work to complete." She strode away, her short hair bobbing playfully with each step.

Gwainne took a deep breath and glared at the stacks of papers before him. He didn't know what he was looking for, or where to begin. He retrieved a scroll off the top of the pile and unfurled it, ready to begin his search. For two bells, he read myths, legends, and sometimes completely fabricated tales about the Jansen Strait. He scribbled notes on some blank parchment he found nearby, and came up with a semi-respectable sorting system.

Any scroll or book with a new variation of the strait's origin went into one pile. Similar myths went into a separate pile. All legends bearing what he considered a mark of truth, he placed in yet another pile. Those stories too ridiculous to believe, he tossed in the basket for Khrystina to re-shelve.

He was deep into a text on yet another variation of the strait when a shadow fell across his lap. A soft scent of lily drifted to him and he smiled.

"Change your mind about helping me?" he asked, without glancing up.

"Not at all. I brought you something to eat. Carga said you might be down here for days and I do not favor the idea of finding a corpse mixed in with the books."

Khrystina set down a tray overflowing with pastries, fruit, cheese, and a mug filled with a curiously dark liquid. He sniffed at the contents, frowning against the spices that tickled his nose.

"What is this?"

"Grhom. And if you do not drink it, Carga will take it personally. It is her private recipe."

"The princess made this for me?"

"She is a wonderful cook."

Khrystina turned to leave, but he put out a hand, inadvertently grazing her hip. "Please stay. There is more food here than I could possibly finish and I would love the company."

Indecision crossed her face and she bit her lower lip. "I have so much work to do. The elders will be upset if I leave my station untidy."

"Just for a few minutes. Then you can scamper off to the secret corners of this bizarre library and do whatever it is you do."

"Scamper? Am I a mouse, then?"

He cocked his head to the side and grinned. "A mouse? Hardly. Something tells me despite your tiny frame, you are quite the warrior. I should not wish to cross you in battle. Of words or weapons."

She sat with a huff, her bottom lip working feverishly between her top teeth. "I do not know if you are jesting or not. You unsettle me, Prince Gwainne. I always thought the Ullans to be barbaric and uncivilized."

"Yet here I am, sipping grhom like a gentleman."

Khrystina snatched a pastry off the tray and shredded it with her fingertips. Every so often, she would scoop the crumbs into a pile and pinch them between her fingers, then she'd plop the mess into her mouth. Gwainne watched, transfixed as she debated whether to stay or leave him alone in the dank mustiness of the library.

"If I stay—only for a short time, mind you—will you share what you have found?" Intelligence burned in her eyes alongside a hunger for knowledge.

"I will do that and more." He explained his system for filing the stories and showed her his notes, which were pitifully few.

She listened without offering much in the way of approval or disapproval, merely nodding and grunting from time to time. Gwainne sorely wished to know what she thought, but she offered no clues. He was no scholar and this was out of his comfort zone. He'd been sent to find clues to help Taryn, but why and to what purpose, he didn't know.

What if he found something that would destroy the Darenn-sai, not save her? He'd taken on Verdaine's task without fully thinking it through. He was an Ullan laird's son.

And an Eleri healer's daughter.

When Gwainne finished recounting what he'd learned, he sat quietly, waiting. Khrystina ate another pastry and eyed his grhom before asking if she might have a sip. He indicated she could, curious at her lack of propriety. Surely the Eleri didn't eat from the same plates and drink from a communal mug? Hadn't he witnessed those gathered in Stephan's great hall dining like civilized people? No one threw bones on the floor; there was no loud belching or pounding of tables. Yet here was an Eleri girl, asking to share his cup.

He shook his head and chastised himself for thinking ill of all Eleri. It was he who had invited her to eat from his plate. He'd been too long with the Ullans, had grown overly suspicious of anyone outside of their clan. Besides, it was the Ullans who were thought to be the less civilized of the two races, and it was true, they ate with their fingers and shared a common cup. A bitter swell of shame passed over him. Perhaps they were as uncouth as the other races believed.

Hadn't his father slain a woman during their evening meal just a sennight past? Her only crime was speaking to the Darenn-sai. And then Amdi had all but forced Taryn to fight in the arena, even knowing she had been near to death only bells earlier. He was mad, Gwainne's father. The sickness took over his mind and controlled his bad decisions. Gwainne glanced at the stack of papers left on the table for him to sort. Why was he here, in the Narthvier chasing riddles, when his place was at his father's side? He should return home immediately. Despite Verdaine's wishes, he couldn't continue this folly. Ulla needed him.

"So, those in the basket you have given no credence to at all, am I right?"

Khrystina's voice drew him out of his reticence. He'd all but forgotten she was there. Mentally, he'd already packed his bags and raced through the forest to his homeland.

"Yes, that is true."

"Then we should start with those."

"But I just said—"

"If there is one thing I have learned in my scant seasons on this terrarae, it is that the thing least likely to be important is of the greatest magnitude."

He waved his hand dismissively toward the basket.

"They are nonsense. This," he held up the scroll he'd been reading when she returned, "tells of King Jansen, and how he named this particular body of water the Strait as a way to keep sailors from crashing on the rocks. Over time, it became known as King Jansen's Strait, then eventually, just the Jansen Strait. That is much more sensible than those other tales."

"I see," she tore the crust off a sausage stuffed roll, "and you want it to make sense, yes? What did Verdaine send you here to do, exactly? Corroborate legends that make sense to you? Or understand a clue that might help the Darennsai?"

Gwainne fumed in time to fifty heartbeats. His breath came in short gasps, his nostrils flared, and his fists curled. How dare she? He was a prince, and not accustomed to being called an idiot. Not that she actually did, but the implication was there. Of course he wasn't there to corroborate what he already knew. His fingers thrummed on the desk, above the notes he'd taken. And yet, that was what he'd done. He skimmed his writings and sighed.

Gods, but she was right. He had been repeating the same legend in his mind and on paper. The myths he deemed ridiculous were about a man who grew from the terrarae and a woman who had fallen from the stars to be with him. And one disturbing account of the strait being a great wound in the fabric of the world. Evil had once oozed from the waters of the strait, squelching upon the shore to take root in the hearts of all those who dwelled on Aelinae. Gwainne had openly chuckled at that one.

He crumpled the sheet of notes he'd already taken and pulled the basket toward them. If she insisted he was so wrong, he'd make her stay and prove she was right.

CHAPTER THIRTY-ONE

Taryn listened again to the message Carga had sent wrapped within a single golden band. Gwainne was in the Narthvier, studying myths of the Jansen Strait. How foolish she'd been not to recognize Yawn Saine Stroot as Jansen Strait. The crone had spoken in the old tongue and Taryn missed the subtle inflections.

Gwainne had only been at the temple a few days, but was making progress. Taryn kissed the golden band and placed it on her right ring finger. It shimmered like a wedding band.

Rhoane took her fingers and kissed the slim ring. "I will send word to Carga and my father to let them know we are well."

"Thank you," Taryn said, distracted by an unease she couldn't name. "Ask Carga to let us know how Gwainne gets on with his research."

"Are you well?" Rhoane turned her face to him, a look of deep concern in his eyes.

"I think so." She stood and shook out her arms and legs. "I think I'll train. It's been too long and I'm restless."

Rhoane stood as well. "I will let Flik know to expect us."

"You need to reply to Carga. Her message sounded like

they're worried about you. That's your priority." She turned to Darius, who positioned himself at her balcony. "Come on." She strode from her room with Kaida by her side, Darius a step behind.

The man Rhoane called Flik was in the farthest courtyard of the palace training a group of youngsters, maybe seven or eight seasons in age. Rather than disturb him and the young recruits, Taryn and Darius found a vacant yard where they could train.

Taryn unsheathed her sword and motioned for Darius to take his place in front of her. "I've been lax in your training. Let's see how you've fared in my absence."

A dark irritation clouded her thinking this morning and she hoped training would rid her of the rawness.

She stretched slowly, letting her muscles warm up. Darius practiced with a straw dummy, but she could see his attacks were half-hearted. It wasn't yet mid-morning and the air was cool enough. There was no reason they should be sluggish, even though they both obviously were.

Taryn cracked her neck and flexed her arms, before shaking out her legs. A workout would be good. She could sweat out her annoyance. She swished her blade a few times, getting a feel for the hilt in her hand.

With each swipe, she pictured Gavyn's expression as he pleaded with her to end his suffering.

Was she an angel, or a murderer?

Darius took up his place in front of her and held his sword in the customary pre-training position—with both hands wrapped around the hilt, blade tip pointing upward.

She nodded they could begin and tension coiled in her gut.

Zakael had once told her she was responsible for Brandt's death. She hadn't believed him, but what if it was true? What if she'd killed her grandfather?

Her blows came swift and strong, her strength returning through the use of her sword. Darius defended himself from her attack, but only just. His timidness in attacking her showed, and this only infuriated her more. Again and again she went on the offensive, targeting him high, then low, then using the hilt as a battering ram. She was relentless in her attack.

It wasn't Darius Taryn saw before her, but Zakael. A grin on his smug face, blood smeared across his teeth. Then she saw Rykoto in his temple, tearing the flesh from Eliahnna as he consumed her heart. Next, Marissa haunted her. Taryn's eldest sister taunted her with slurs against Rhoane.

Taryn swung at her adversaries, each cut meant to slice the memory from her mind. At one point, she heard the fabric of the thin garment she wore tear and beads scattered across the packed dirt. Sabina would be furious Taryn had ruined one of the expensive outfits she'd had made for Taryn, but she didn't care. Nothing mattered except winning.

Kaida barked from somewhere in the distance and Taryn thought she heard Ellie scream, but bloodlust had taken over. Her vision clouded red as she sought Darius's defeat. His sword work wasn't up to the challenge, and he spent most of his energy dodging her blows. Frustrated, denied a victory, she lashed out with her power and threw him against a wall. He hit with an awful crack and slid to the ground, unconscious.

From the back of her mind, she recalled that day long ago, in the cavern, when Zakael had fought Brandt and she saw him fly through the air much the same way as Darius had. Her stomach roiled and pitched. No, she argued, it wasn't her who had killed Brandt—it had been Zakael. Zakael killed everything she loved. Zakael was the enemy, not Darius.

Her focus narrowed to a pinpoint of black and Taryn lifted her sword to advance on the slumped figure, her confused mind believing him to be Zakael. Kaida barked louder and tugged on her pants, ripping them. She lifted the blade higher, seeing Zakael's sneering face in place of Darius's. Zakael and Marissa. They'd known who she was from the very beginning and had sought to destroy her at every turn. She had killed Marissa—now she'd end Zakael and be free of them for good. First Marissa, then Zakael. Next she would seek Rykoto's death, and finally, Kaldaar's. They would all die by her hand. It was her path.

Darennsai, stop! Kaida's harsh command sounded in Taryn's mind.

Taryn hesitated and blinked hard, focusing on the huddled form in front of her.

"Never raise a weapon in anger." A blade pressed along her throat, barely touching her skin, and Taryn froze. "First rule of fighting and you've failed."

Taryn slid her glance to the right, where a grizzled old man held his blade with both hands. "Do it. I beg of you."

"By the looks of you, I'd say you're the Eirielle everyone's so keen on, but by the unschooled way you handled your weapon, I'd say you're nothing but a spoiled brat." The man spat on the ground as if to underscore his words.

"You know nothing about me."

"I know you'd attack an unconscious man for what? What did he do to you?"

The bloodlust drained from her body, leaving her weak and confused. Darius hadn't done anything to her. This man was right. She'd attacked out of anger. She knew better.

"That's more like it." He released his sword from her neck, but just as quickly, brought the flat of the blade against the backs of her knees.

She went down hard, pain spiraling to the base of her spine. She bit her tongue and tasted blood. Anger surged anew and she elbowed his crotch, enjoying the yelp of pain he uttered as he bent over.

She kicked at his legs, knocking him off-balance. From there, it was nothing to push him onto his back, her sword tip at the base of his neck.

"Not bad," he wheezed, "but still sloppy and undignified.

Not to mention, you left yourself open to this." He knocked the sword tip aside and rolled into her. She wobbled, but didn't fall, which was what he had expected, she realized too late. Using her unsteady weight as a fulcrum, he launched himself at her like a jaguar pouncing on its prey. Before she knew it, he'd taken the offensive and was attacking her with the same gusto she'd had with Darius.

Her moves were purely defensive, with little time to think of how to get the upper hand. His swift cuts and jabs interspersed with broad strokes, keeping her guessing the whole time.

She'd hoped he would tire, but with each step, he gained more control, more strength. She studied him for ShantiMari, but couldn't see any threads.

If what she didn't see was true, he used only his strength against her. She'd been cocky to think his age would make him weaker than her.

Obviously, this man had been studying fighting techniques far longer than she and he knew her weaknesses like no opponent she'd ever faced. Despite herself, she was intrigued by him, even if she wished he'd stop trying to kill her.

"Enough!" Rhoane's sharp tone rang out across the yard and the man halted the fight immediately. He bowed low to Rhoane and sheathed his sword.

Taryn stared at Rhoane, then the man. Her reality hadn't yet fully settled.

"Flik, see to Darius. You," his tempered tone was leveled at Taryn, "come with me."

Before she knew what was happening, he lifted into the air, transforming into his dragon and dragging her with him. She clung to his talon with one hand, her sword gripped between white knuckles in the other. The palace shrunk the higher they rose and irrational fear gripped her. If she fell, she'd die.

I will never let you fall, Rhoane's gentle voice said in her mind.

CHAPTER THIRTY-TWO

Rhoane set them down on the soft sand of the deserted beach he'd taken Taryn to just a few days earlier. Too much had changed since then. Taryn's outburst was a surprise, to be sure, but his own anger had taken him aback as well. They'd had to deal with too much in too little time.

Taryn lay curled on his back, her tears slipping between the scales of his dragon. Each one burned fiercer than the one before. Each one reminded him how much he had to learn about Taryn, himself, and their future. He wasn't like most men. His was a life lived under constant scrutiny, as much as hers. He'd brought Taryn here so they could talk in private, without court spies hearing every word.

He shifted to a man, cradling Taryn in his arms as he did. She blinked at him in surprise, then glanced at their surroundings.

"Did I kill Darius?" She buried her face in his chest and he held her tighter.

"No, my love. You stunned him, nothing more. There is no permanent damage."

Her breath tickled his skin. "Thank the gods. I was worried."

He set her on the sand, being careful not to jostle her too

much. She was fragile today, more so than he could ever recall. He'd do whatever it took to alleviate her sorrow.

"I saw him as Zakael." Taryn stretched her long legs in front of her and grabbed handfuls of sand, letting the grains run through her fingertips. "A long time ago, Zakael accused me of killing Brandt, and I saw it. I saw how I could've been responsible for his death."

"No, Taryn, you did not kill Brandt. Zakael did."

She shook her head, tears spilling over her cheeks. "In the cavern, when they were fighting, Brandt took my hand and when he attacked Zakael, I added my power to it. I didn't know I had power at the time, but I'm sure it was that force that stopped Brandt's heart. It was too much for anyone to bear."

It was possible she had killed Brandt. "It was his time, Taryn. Whether by your hand or not, I think Brandt knew he would not be joining you on your path once you returned to Aelinae."

She blinked up at him, her eyes red from crying, tears making stars in her dark lashes. "I'm lost, Rhoane. I keep thinking I've got it together, then something happens and I lose my shit."

He sat behind her, his legs alongside hers, his arms wrapped around her waist. She sighed and leaned into him, her head resting below his chin. "If you are lost, let us find a way. Together."

"This wasn't just about Zakael. I sought vengeance on Marissa, too," Taryn admitted. Her body thrummed beneath his touch. He felt her rage through his cynfar. "I hate that she took something private and perfect from us. I hate her for doing that to you. But I also hate you a little for letting her. And then when you were broken and wouldn't talk to me, I thought I'd lost you for good."

"You did not deserve that, Taryn. Any of it. I am sorry it ever happened. I should have been there for you, but I was selfish to think I was protecting you while I was broken."

"We haven't had a chance to deal with it. So much has

happened. I have to trust you, Rhoane. But, there's this thing between us and I don't know how to deal with it."

"If you had been conscious, would you have let Loghan heal you?"

"What kind of question is that? Of course not." She shifted and glared at him. "Please don't tell me you're going to make that my fault." Heat came off her in waves and he knew he was treading on fragile ice.

"I do not blame you, nor would I if you did desire him."

"You're jealous of Loghan?"

A hornet's nest buzzed in his belly. "Of course. He almost shared his body with you. Just thinking about it tears me up inside." The realization of his words hit him with a force that took his breath. "Is this what you feel when you think of that day at Gaarendahl?"

Taryn stiffened in his arms and he braced himself for a verbal attack. "Yes." The word came out barely a hush. Her body began trembling and he tightened his hold on her.

"You never had a choice who to choose as your mate. There are days I do not believe it would be me if ever that choice was given to you."

"You weren't given a choice, either."

"No, but I had opportunity. I chose to follow my path. I chose you."

She twisted further until she faced him, her legs draped over his and wrapped around his back. The tattered clothes she wore barely concealed her private parts, but she seemed not to notice. It was so very like her to be unconcerned with how she looked, or what she wore. His desire for her stirred, but he held himself in check.

"I always had a choice, Rhoane. Before I knew you were mine, there were plenty of men I could've picked. Hayden, Tinsley, Aomori, Baehlon, any number of the soldiers and guards I trained with. Don't think I've never noticed the way men look at me. I choose not to see their hungry eyes, or the way they lick their lips like I'm some prize slab of beef. It's actually kind of gross, but I can't stop it. The only one I care about is you. As long as you look at me with desire, I'm content."

"I do not want you to be content. I want you to be fulfilled."

"I am. Trust me, you fulfill me in ways I never thought possible. And I'm not just talking about sex. Although, that's pretty damn good." Her brows knit together and her lips tilted toward the ground. "I don't really know what happened today."

"How do you mean?"

"I was consumed by hatred. For Zakael and Marissa, mostly, and everything they've done to us. There was so much hate. I couldn't control it."

"Bloodlust. It happens to even the best soldiers, Taryn. It is difficult to control."

She shook her head, her eyes searching the sand for answers. "It was and it wasn't. I almost felt like someone else was forcing me to attack Darius. If I had to guess, I'd say Kaldaar is still close and doing his best to upset the balance of things here in the Summerlands. He did threaten to impregnate Sabina tomorrow night." Fresh tears sparkled in her eyes as she glanced at him. "I never told Hayden."

Neither had Rhoane. Every chance he had, he'd lost his nerve.

"There is one way to prevent Kaldaar from claiming Sabina. I could pretend to be her after the wedding." Taryn's words lacked conviction and Rhoane sensed the apprehension she was feeling.

Rhoane wrapped his arms around her, pulling her against him, and gazed out over the ocean. They'd need the strength of gods if they were to protect Hayden and Sabina from Kaldaar.

"Tell me, what did you call that tree from your nightmare?"

Her breathing deepened and her heart rate increased. "The runyon tree. It's at Caer Idris. I saw it when I was there. Why?"

"I have seen this tree in my dreams as well. And a shadow

creature who lurks nearby. I believe that tree is where Kaldaar is getting his strength."

"Do you think my father was in league with Kaldaar?"

"I do not know, but if he was, certainly Zakael is now his minion."

"Which makes him even more unpredictable. Tomorrow we'll sort out Zakael's next move." She placed her lips over his, her tongue seeking entry to his mouth, which he happily granted.

His desire flooded through him, yet he held back, letting Taryn set the pace. If she wished for only a kiss, he wouldn't press for more, but by the way her hands tangled in his hair, by turns pulling and smoothing his braids, he knew she wanted more. Much more.

Without breaking their kiss, she rose, taking him with her, and untied his breeches. He fumbled with the skimpy pants she wore, making light work of ridding her of them. They broke apart long enough to strip off the rest of their clothing, throwing it in a pile on the sand.

Taryn led him into the waves and he followed without question or fear. The warm water wrapped seductively around his ankles, then calves, and up to his waist the farther they waded. When they were beyond the waves, treading water, Taryn returned to him, her mouth seeking his. Then, his all-too familiar panic raced up his spine as they sank below the surface, their bodies locked in an embrace.

Breathe, Rhoane, Taryn's sweet voice commanded. *There is nothing to fear here.*

Rhoane inhaled through his nose, not quite trusting, yet wanting to believe. Air, not water, flooded his lungs and the panic receded. It didn't entirely go away, but enough he was in control of his actions.

They drifted deeper into the ocean, their bodies tangled as one, their hands exploring, tongues dancing. Taryn's ShantiMari surrounded them like a cocoon. The first opening he felt surprised him. It sounded like a *blop* to his oversensitive hearing. At first, he wasn't sure what had happened, until he spread his own power into Taryn and sensed her first energy store opening.

She was healing him. Just as he'd healed her in Ulla, she was performing the deed to him, here, now, drifting through the sea. And she'd somehow worked out how to heal herself as well.

No, my love, you are doing that. I cannot heal myself. Not yet, anyway.

Her legs wrapped around his waist and he entered her with a sigh captured by her mouth. So warm. So comforting. *Home*, he thought. *In her, he was home.* His heart, his body, his world belonged to her.

As everything I am, will be, desire, and accomplish is yours.

Their hair floated above and around them, a mix of silver and golden brown. Starlight and terrarae.

Their lovemaking was slow and sensual. With each new energy store opening, Rhoane heard the strange *blop*, then a wonderful warmth spread throughout his body. Each time, his strength renewed, his focus tightened.

He ground his pelvis against hers, driving himself deeper, needing to feel her completely. The warm water caressed their skin, washed away the turmoil of the past few days. The final energy store opened and Rhoane heard Taryn's gasp in his mind.

She arched again, her arms flung to the side like an offering to her god. He rammed his cock deeper still, his release building.

From his peripheral, he saw the darathi eneari approach, her tail swishing hard enough to cause a shift in the current. If Taryn heard, she didn't acknowledge the creature. Instead, she moaned and wrapped her arms around him, holding him tight. A flutter of anxiety cramped his desire.

Now, Rhoane. Please.

Desperation clung to her words and he tensed before releasing his seed into her, filling her womb. She shuddered with her own climax, a look of shattered relief on her face. Then, a small smile lifted her lips and she kissed him once more.

The water dragon snarled and swam closer, her fanged mouth open as if to consume them.

"You!" Excitement sounded in Taryn's voice, but a moment later, worry furrowed his love's brows.

The hornet's nest in his belly worked its way through his veins, stinging along the way. The darathi eneari circled them, her whisker-like tendrils furling and unfurling with the tide.

"You have returned," was all she said and Taryn looked to Rhoane for clarification.

"I have." Rhoane gave the mythical creature a pointed look. He hoped she wouldn't mention the episode with Faelara, or the dire prediction she'd made all those seasons ago.

"This is the creature that saved me. This is Xianqin," Taryn said, as if Rhoane should've known.

"You saved Taryn? Not one of the merfolk?" It was the inconvenient truth he didn't want to accept. A horrible sense of foreboding filled his heart. If Xianqin had rescued Taryn, what else had she done? He had to keep her from telling Taryn about his fate.

Sadness filled her eyes as her head shook from side to side, causing them to sway against the current.

"Look at yourselves," Xianqin instructed. "Look beyond the flesh and bones of who you are told to be. Remember who you are."

Taryn groaned and Rhoane suppressed a chuckle. She really hated riddles.

"Not that again." Taryn lifted her chin in Xianqin's direction. "There I am, practically dead, and this one starts in with the 'Remember who you are' business. It drove me insane."

Xianqin's tendrils wrapped around Taryn and Rhoane. "What else did you learn from the story?" Her eyes, as large as Baehlon was tall, regarded them with mischief in their depths. "You only remember part of the tale. Remember all of what you have learned. Remember who you are."

He had the sense she spoke to him alone, even though she looked at them both. What was the story he needed to remember?

"Take care of these shells. They are fragile and easily destroyed. Once you remember your purpose, you will no longer need them." Her head tilted and Rhoane swore he saw a tear squeeze from her eye. "Not all betrayals are bad."

Taryn sucked in a gasp and Rhoane's heart pounded against his rib cage.

Xianqin sped them to the shore, where she loosened her grip around their waists and slithered into the murky waters beneath the surf.

Taryn stood on the wet sand, her features a mixture of wonder and misgiving.

Rhoane took her hand and drew in a long breath. He let it out slowly, practicing the words in his mind before he spoke.

"Long ago, before you were born, I came to this very beach and met Xianqin. She told me many things, some of which I have forgotten and apparently need to remember." He chuckled to infuse lightness into his words. "She also told me I would betray you twice, then I wou—"

"You would kill me," Taryn finished. She squeezed his hand and turned to face him. Tears streaked to her chin. "I think she told me the same thing when she rescued me. The crone repeated the warning in Amdi's tents just before he struck her down. I think the old woman's main purpose was to make sure I recalled Xianqin's warning. Secondary was the Jansen Strait."

"You have known this whole time?"

Taryn nodded.

"You said nothing." Then again, neither did he. "I am sorry, Taryn. I do not want to hurt you. I never meant to betray you."

She put her hands to his cheeks and kissed his lips. "I know.

We'll get through this somehow. I suppose knowing my death will come from you makes it easier."

It didn't feel easier to him. He rested his head on Taryn's and held her tight. He'd fight his fate. It was his destiny to be the Surtentse to his Darennsai, but he'd be damned if he'd ever betray Taryn again. If he did, it would kill them both.

CHAPTER THIRTY-THREE

Taryn surveyed her hair in the mirror, startled once again by the elegance reflected back to her. This was not the woman who stumbled into the cavern over a season past. This woman Taryn hardly knew, but somehow suspected was hidden in the depths of her psyche all along.

Ellie was a gem. She'd taken Taryn's bedraggled, beach-tousled hair and performed miracles.

Taryn caught Darius's reflection and a pit sunk in her belly. He'd been avoiding her since the previous day and she couldn't blame him. Faelara had nursed him to consciousness, with no ill effects, and for that Taryn was grateful.

"Darius, come here. Please."

Ellie hid a worried frown, but not before Taryn saw.

"Yes, m'lady." Darius bowed at the waist, something he rarely did.

"I'm sorry for yesterday. I lost control and let emotions run rampant where they had no place being let loose." Taryn held her hand out for him to take. She noted a slight shake as he reached for her. "I'd like to make it up to you." She placed his hand over

Ellie's. "You have my blessing to court, even to marry should you so desire it."

Ellie blinked hard, her free hand going to her face to conceal her scar. Darius stammered something unintelligible, but sounded like a thanks.

"We'll have none of that, my sweet girl." Taryn removed Ellie's hand to reveal her entire face. She worked her ShantiMari into a mask, smoothing the slight crinkle tracing a crescent from the corner of Ellie's eye to her lips.

"What are you doing?" Ellie flinched from Taryn's touch.

Taryn ran her hands along the girl's face and traced a thumb across her jawline. "I made a mask of my power to hide your scar. This is permanent, my darling."

Ellie gasped as she brought her hand to her face, feeling along the old wound. She stared in the mirror, her mouth forming a wide *O*. "Your Highness, how can I ever repay you?"

Darius's hand was still clasped in Ellie's.

Taryn placed hers over theirs. "Be happy, always. Find joy in the little things and each other. That's all the payment I need."

Darius glanced from Ellie to Taryn, and a slow smile lifted his lips. It was the first time Taryn could remember him sharing a genuine smile and she was glad she could give that to him. To both of them.

"I'm expected at Sabina's soon, but I want the two of you to take Saeko and Lorilee for training." Taryn's voice trembled at the memory of her attack on Darius.

"It's forgotten, Your Highness," Darius said, as if reading her mind.

"Thank you. Truly." She squeezed his hand. "I've already spoken with Flik, to apologize, mostly, but he'll have what you need."

They didn't know it yet, but she planned to keep them here at the palace to train while she and Rhoane searched for Cashiel.

Kaldaar was getting stronger and she needed warriors beside her, not maids. By the time Flik was finished with them, they'd be as lethal as any assassin.

"Flik, my lady?" Darius asked, trepidation edging his words. "But he's the king's man. He trains only the best to become spies."

"Yes, and that's who you'll seek out. I won't yield, Darius. Not on this."

She left her rooms, with Ellie and Darius promising to take the others to see Flik. Taryn wished she could go with them, but she had an appointment with the bride. It was Sabina's wedding day and Taryn didn't want to keep her waiting.

Outside his rooms, Hayden intercepted her. His devilish grin made the butterflies in her belly flutter faster. She still wasn't sure how she and Rhoane would keep Kaldaar from using Hayden to make Sabina his vessel.

"And what is the groom doing today?"

His face paled. "I'm to see about my piercing. I have put it off as long as possible."

Taryn bit back a laugh and nodded. "You probably should've given yourself time to heal. On your wedding day, Hayden? Really?"

The squealing of a child's cry interrupted them and Taryn turned toward the sound. Her nephew thrashed in Armando's arms. She'd not seen much of him or Tarro since arriving at the palace, but then Sabina and Lliandra had kept the pair busy. It took everything in her not to grab little Percival. Instead, she asked politely to hold his child.

Once the baby was in her arms, he quieted down.

"Could you please visit more often?" Tarro begged. "He cries night and day. We cannot fathom how to comfort him."

Taryn sent her power through the tiny thing, finding nothing amiss. Then, she tickled his mind with her thoughts of love and safety. His was a violent birth and he held remnants of that night in his memories. She cautiously swept them away, hoping they would never return.

"He's a love. Perhaps you're feeding him the wrong milk?" she offered. "Ask Faelara what she recommends."

Taryn nuzzled her nephew's face and cooed like a fool, but she didn't care. She was one hundred percent in love with the boy.

"Armando…" Hayden began, his voice low, conspiratorial.

Taryn's senses went on alert. She was afraid he'd ask after the mother, but his query was personal. "I'm to see the royal piercer in a moment. Is there any advice you can give?"

Tarro's grin told her he knew she was in trouble.

"There's nothing to it." Armando propped his pierced ear so Hayden could see. "There's a pinch, but that's all. Of course, some men choose to pierce their cocks, sometimes a nipple, but with my profession, I felt an ear was best."

"An ear?" Incredulity dripped from those two words and Taryn suppressed the desire to run as far and as fast as she could. "You're wicked, dear cousin. I'll repay the favor someday, I promise you."

Despite the warning, she laughed. A full-bellied chortle that echoed down the hallway. It had been too much fun teasing him, but he was right—she'd been naughty to do it. Still, the look on his face every time she'd mentioned the piercing had been priceless.

"We must be going. I'm sorry to have to take Percival." Tarro gathered the now sleeping baby in his arms. "Please, come see us more often."

"I will." They started down the hallway and Taryn called after him, "How would you feel about staying on in Menurra?"

Both men's faces lit up and she promised to make the arrangements. With Percival in Menurra, he'd be protected from the schemers at the Crystal Court. And anyone else who might want to cause him harm.

"What are you planning, my wretched cousin?"

"Armando has family here, and I thought with the baby, they could use the help. Plus, it might get him to give up being a whore." She changed the subject and faced her cousin. "Are you ready for tonight?" She shoved Kaldaar's dire warning to the far recesses of her mind. This was a happy day. They'd thwart his plans.

"I've been ready since I first met Sabina in the gardens at Paderau."

"Yours will be a love story for the ages." Taryn stepped close and kissed him on the cheek. "I'm happy for you both. Truly." She squeezed his arm. "I'm off to see your bride. Have fun with the piercing." Her laughter mingled with his curses as she hurried down the corridor.

She stopped by Carina's room to check on her guard. The beating she received at the behest of Cashiel had left her partially paralyzed on the right side of her face. Faelara tended to her each day, and Taryn had stopped in to visit several times. Every time she saw her guard, guilt doubled. And now she was sending Darius and her maids to learn battle in case something like the attack on the ship ever happened again.

Taryn smiled and laughed through her short visit with Carina, never letting on how much she worried for her friends. She even joked that she'd send the woman to Ulla with Faelara and Baehlon. To Taryn's surprise, Carina didn't protest.

Sabina was in the midst of wedding preparations when Taryn arrived at her rooms. A dozen or so women fawned over her, and those were just the bridesmaids. Several servants bustled between them, filling glasses, or replacing food on elaborate silver trays. Sabina looked serene as she reclined on an overstuffed couch. Two women hunched over her hands, their paintbrushes making quick flicks against Sabina's skin. The colorful images reminded Taryn of her ghost tattoos and she peered closer to see if they were runes, but they weren't any design she recognized. Scrolls and curlicues twisted into intricate designs that looked like gilded ornamentation.

"Look." Sabina turned her right hand to show Taryn the small tattoo on the underside of her wrist. "It's a combination of my House's insignia, yours, and Hayden's."

Taryn studied the black ink, but couldn't make out any one thing. The skin around the tattoo was swollen and red from the needles. She traced her fingertip over the wound, healing the skin with her touch. The image settled into a coherent design that was, indeed, a mixture of the three Houses. "Why my House?"

"If not for you, Hayden and I wouldn't be together. We owe you our happiness." Tears shimmered in Sabina's eyes.

Taryn snuggled next to her on the couch.

"Without you, I would be Kaldaar's brood slave."

"You mean the world to me, Sabina. There's nothing I wouldn't do for you." She laid her head on Sabina's shoulder and wrapped her arm over the girl's bare midriff. "I'll even wear that ridiculous outfit that shows *everything*."

It was a semi-sheer beaded get-up Sabina had made especially for Taryn.

Her power swirled around them, a protective cocoon she wished would be enough to keep out harm for all of Sabina's life. Beneath Taryn's hand, she sensed the faintest thrumming and her heart jackhammered in her throat. Kaldaar immediately came to mind, that he'd somehow found a way to infect Sabina, but the force she sensed beneath her touch was gentle, full of innocence.

Keeping her breathing calm as best she could, Taryn sent a thread of her power into her friend, traveling along her veins, through her bones and marrow, to Sabina's heart and up to her brain, then back down. Taryn sensed nothing untoward. Then, just past Sabina's belly button, a strong tug pulled her attention to the tiny being inside her friend.

Taryn gasped, tears immediately filling her eyes. Her hand fluttered over Sabina's abdomen as giddiness bubbled inside her. She had to stay calm, to not give anything away, but she'd just discovered she needn't worry about Sabina.

She was already with child. Hayden's child.

Kaldaar couldn't impregnate her. Not tonight, not ever.

Taryn saw in her mind the day Rhoane and Faelara had struggled to bring Queen Prateeni's firstborn into the world. The queen had miscarried many times before, but with Rhoane and Faelara's assistance, she delivered a healthy boy. Once a child is born, the vessel is broken and Kaldaar can no longer claim her. A moment later, the image was gone.

Taryn wrapped her power through Sabina, making powerful wards of protection and nurturing. This child would survive. She reeled, overwhelmed with responsibility and love and a longing to keep those she cared for safe from, well, everything.

"Are you well?" Sabina took her hand in hers, rubbing it like she would an elder who was overly cold.

"I, uh, yeah. I'm good." Taryn took the cup of tea a servant offered and sipped it slowly. It was her favorite blend of cinnamon and spice.

"You aren't allowed to be sick on my wedding day. I forbid it." Sabina brushed her lips across Taryn's. Tears streaked down their cheeks—Taryn's, Sabina's, she couldn't tell.

Taryn's hand fluttered above the tiny fetus. He was no more than a week along, which meant Sabina had conceived in Menurra. A child born of love to a Summerlands princess and an Aelan lord. It was a start, but to what?

Tessa curled along her back, showing Taryn the markings on her hands. She and Eliahnna had the same temporary tattoos that were being applied to Sabina. When the artist was finished with Prateeni, who was seated with her ladies on the other side of the room, Taryn would have them applied to her hands. She snuggled closer into Sabina, her palm resting on her friend's belly.

Sabina didn't yet know she was pregnant and Taryn didn't want to take away from her wedding day with the news. She'd tell them in the morning, before she and Rhoane left for the Sitari.

With Tessa's warm body against hers, and Sabina's quiet conversation spoken above her head, Taryn drifted in a state of contented happiness. Her body stayed firmly on the couch with the others, but her awareness rose until she looked down on her sisters and best friend.

Eliahnna laughed, and Taryn saw true delight in her eyes. It had been so long since she recalled the serious girl enjoying herself. Beneath Eliahnna's dress rested Eoghan's gift. A small snippet of wood with Eleri words of commitment engraved upon the surface. He'd also infused the wood with a protection ward. Taryn sensed Rhoane's brother through the talisman.

Taryn's gaze roamed over the others. Maids, servants, Sabina's many sisters: they all crowded the princess's apartments. Queen Prateeni peered curiously in her direction, and Taryn felt a wave of warmth wash over her. Not just warmth, love. But Prateeni didn't look at Taryn's form on the couch, but where she drifted closer to the ceiling.

Then Taryn sensed another presence and glanced to her right. There, hovering beside her, was the spectral form of Julieta. The goddess's light didn't hurt Taryn in the way Nadra's had when she'd first seen the goddess in the cavern. In fact, seeing Julieta not as a woman, but in her divine light was softer on her eyes.

"She is protected, young one. Kaldaar cannot hurt her now."

"I placed several wards on her. She's my best friend, and her child will be of my blood. I cannot sit by and let Kaldaar destroy those I love."

"We are here to guide, Taryn. It is up to them to make their own choices."

"Sabina would never choose to be raped." A frisson of anger

snapped against Taryn's awareness and she cursed herself. "I'm sorry, Julieta. My words were callous."

Kaldaar, and Julieta's own father Rykoto, had both raped her.

"Please know I meant no harm by them," Taryn implored.

"I know, young one. You have much to learn, but your heart is pure. I sense in you the desire to punish those who sought to destroy me."

"Can you blame me?"

"You cannot defeat them as you are. You must lose this crude form that you now wear. Skin and bones can too easily be destroyed. Promise me you will wait to exact your vengeance."

"Until Rhoane betrays and kills me?"

"Not all betrayals are as destructive as what your sister did. Some are tiny in scope, but carry great importance. His betrayal is necessary to your future."

Necessary didn't make it any easier to accept.

"I never saw betrayal as a good thing."

"Sometimes, what we think is the worst thing to ever happen to us ends up being our saving grace."

This form of Julieta had no eyes, no face, no arms, but Taryn sensed she gazed on Sabina and Prateeni with the adoration of a mother to her children. Rays of her light stretched to the pair.

Julieta began to fade. "You will have much difficulty with the Sitari. They will not welcome your presence on their island, but Mallaqai holds the key to discovering how to defeat Kaldaar. Look for her there."

A flare of heat singed Taryn. She flinched from the burning fire of Rykoto's prison.

"Someone seeks to release the mad god. There are betrayers on every shore. Trust only those who prove worthy. The Sitari, should you gain their favor, will be the determining factor in the end."

Taryn came to in her own body, still snuggled against Sabina. Before Julieta left, she'd given Taryn an image of an island within an island, with a waterfall cascading between the two.

Once, long ago, when she'd sat upon a star with Nadra, Taryn saw the floating islands of the Sitari. Mallaqai was there. Somehow, she'd have to convince the Sitari she was an ally.

CHAPTER THIRTY-FOUR

The palace vibrated with expectant excitement. Trees twinkled with thousands of ShantiMari-enhanced lights and rose petals covered every walkway. Hayden worried the diamond stud he wore in his left ear, twisting it with barely controlled anxiety. Tonight, he and Sabina would be married. He should be thrilled, ecstatic, and he was, yet there was a tremor of fear beneath his joy.

The nightmares had started the day Taryn killed the Shadow Assassin. A force like he'd never known had spoken to him in his mind, making suggestions that had Hayden's guts twisting. The compulsion was difficult to ignore, but he had. So far. When he woke this morning, he'd had an overwhelming need to visit his bride and take her hard, demanding complete submission from Sabina. He'd fought off the desire and kept far from Sabina's rooms for the remainder of the day.

The rational part of himself told him to seek Taryn, that his cousin could help with the nightmares. Except, Hayden hated how everyone had begun expecting Taryn to solve their problems. He saw the strain on her lovely face, the tightness in her smile. No, he wouldn't add to her burden. Whoever or whatever this thing was, Hayden wouldn't let it control him. His and Sabina's futures depended on it.

A group of courtiers approached and Hayden tensed. He imagined all sorts of horrors as he strode to the garden where the ceremony was to take place. A hidden dagger, a poisonous dart, even the swing of a sword could end him. Except, somehow, he knew the entity haunting him wanted the wedding to take place, needed Hayden to bed his bride on *this* day. He just didn't know why. As far as he could recall, there was nothing special about the day, at least, not on any calendar he could find. But Aelinae had a long history and much of it was lived without records, timelines, or ages. Too much had been lost of Aelinae's first seasons.

Hayden smiled weakly to the courtiers, ignoring their salacious grins. Most of them thought Sabina was still a virgin and congratulated him on his accomplishment of winning the heart of one of Menurra's most sought-after princesses. Little did they know, he and Sabina had been sharing one another's beds for several moonturns.

A flutter of nerves stung his belly. If the entity thought Sabina still a virgin, perhaps that was why he felt compelled to take her brutally. And only one person would benefit from that— Kaldaar.

"You look like a lass who's drunk sour milk. Not having second thoughts, are you?" Baehlon's rich baritone startled Hayden.

"None at all."

"Then why the scowl?" Rhoane added to his right.

They'd managed to sneak up on him while he was lost in thought. Not good. He'd have to be more aware if he was going to keep Kaldaar from taking his mind.

"I want everything to be perfect tonight. For Sabina."

Rhoane placed a hand on his shoulder and Hayden felt the man's ShantiMari flow over him, calming his frazzled nerves.

"We are here. We will not let anything happen to you or Sabina."

The tone of his voice, the choice of his words, gave Hayden pause. He'd not said anything to Taryn, but she had always been attuned to his thoughts and emotions. Perhaps she'd picked up on his fear. Of course she'd share her concerns with her betrothed.

Hayden met Rhoane's steady gaze.

"I appreciate your support." More than they'd ever know, but he didn't voice what worried him. Instead, he buried his fear deep. It wouldn't do to have his bride apprehensive, not tonight. Not ever if he could help it.

Breathe, cousin, Taryn's soft voice said in his mind. *This is a night for joyful celebration.*

Hayden cut a glare to Rhoane, who smiled as if nothing untoward occurred. Damn the man and his meddling cousin.

Kaldaar can't harm you. He might try, Hayden heard the tightness of Taryn's emotions, but also heard laughter. Well, almost. *But he'll be sorely disappointed.* Now he did hear Taryn's laughter. *Actually, I hope he tries something. I have a surprise for him he won't like.*

At these words, Rhoane's grip on Hayden's shoulder tightened. His ShantiMari pierced through Hayden's wedding attire to warm his skin. Whatever Taryn had in mind, certainly Rhoane must know about it.

"All will be well," Hayden told Rhoane and Baehlon. For the first time in days, he dared hope it would be so.

"All will be well." Rhoane's grin matched the laughter Hayden heard in Taryn's thoughts.

"What have you got planned, old friend?" Hayden asked Rhoane, but the damned Eleri shook his head. Baehlon shrugged, his braids chiming.

They lived in a time of suppositions and guesses. No one really knew what Kaldaar was capable of, or if Sabina would always be the vessel, even after losing her virginity. Hayden didn't like uncertainties. He liked when life went according to plan, when everything made sense. This constant upheaval was unsettling, to say the least.

Rhoane gave a final, comforting squeeze then released Hayden. His ShantiMari remained.

"Ah! Look at you, my boy." Hayden's father met them at the entrance to the garden, his arms outstretched. "I couldn't be prouder of you."

Anje took him in his arms and gave Hayden a great bear hug, tapping his back with suppressed emotion.

Everyone's nerves were stretched, it seemed.

"Thank you, Father." Tears bit Hayden's eyes and he blinked them away.

His father also had tears, but he let them flow over his rosy cheeks before wiping them with a handkerchief.

"Can you feel that?" Anje whispered.

Hayden shook his head.

"The gods have blessed you this night. They're here, somewhere, watching, protecting."

Hayden's heart rammed in his chest. "All the gods?"

Rhoane nodded. "Even the younger ones. None of them want Kaldaar to claim Sabina any more than you do."

This gave Hayden pause. He searched his mind and found it lacking the presence that had haunted him of late. Had Kaldaar slipped from him? Or was he lurking, waiting? Hayden hated that the god could overwhelm him with such ease. Hayden wasn't a fledgling with the power, he could wield almost as much as his father, yet the banished god toyed with him as if he were as weak as a newborn.

A smile, genuine and heartfelt, lifted the frown he hadn't known he wore. Seeds of joy crept into the core of his being.

I told you so, Taryn teased. *Did you think I'd let anything happen to you?*

You're a brat.

I love you, too.

The men took their places and waited for the women to arrive. While they stood at the front of the gathered guests, Hayden did as his cousin bade—he breathed in and tasted the summer night. The sweet powdery scent of narcolis, mixed with sea air, settled on his tongue. He closed his eyes and listened to the murmuring of the crowd. His tension ebbed away, leaving him with a satisfied sense of purpose.

This was always supposed to happen. He didn't know how he knew, but something told him he and Sabina were meant for each other, just as Rhoane's destiny had always been linked with Taryn's. Hayden opened his eyes and saw what his father had felt —the presence of the gods. They hovered above the garden, not in Aelan form, but as their true selves, shimmering bursts of light. A sense of awe and wonder swept over him. To be graced with their presence on this night was humbling. He placed his hand over his heart and bowed his head, making a solemn promise to always uphold their honor.

Whatever came of him in the seasons ahead, he wouldn't forget this night, this moment.

Soft music played and Hayden pulled his gaze from the deities to see Tessa and Eliahnna approach the garden. They wore traditional Summerlands garments with Talathian tiaras on their heads. Behind them, Sabina's sisters stepped in time to the music, their pace painstakingly slow. In their hands, they held the edge of a veil that stretched from them to cover Sabina. His bride was completely shrouded by the thick fabric, but her step was steady and sure.

Hayden's heart beat in time to the music, although he would've preferred they sped it up. He was anxious to have her by his side.

Behind Sabina, Taryn marched in time with the others. She held the tasseled end of the veil, a place of high esteem within the wedding party. That Sabina chose Taryn for this role, over one of her sisters, had been a source of conflict within the family, but it was the queen who had given her blessing to Taryn and the conversation was closed.

At Taryn's entrance, a few faces pinched, lips pressed flat, eyes were not as joyful as they could be. What was it Taryn always said? *That was their issue, not his.* He refused to let family rivalry upset his night.

In stark contrast to Sabina's sisters, her brothers were boisterous and jovial, calling taunts to his bride as she walked through the garden. It was a strange custom of the Summerlands to tease the bride and groom on their wedding day. If the pair could withstand the torture without breaking out in laughter, then it was believed they would have a long and prosperous marriage. Hayden just shook his head and did his best not to let the words bother him. Mostly Sabina's brothers joked about the size of Hayden's manhood and whether he could satisfy her.

Hayden spied a smile beneath the veil. *Sabina was more than satisfied*, Hayden thought. At least, her moans and screams led him to believe so.

"You're almost grinning, dear man," Myrddin whispered. "You wouldn't want bad luck to fall upon your House, would you?"

Hayden schooled his features to a placid artifice.

"That's more like it," the mage said.

Hayden swallowed a chuckle. What an absurd tradition. But these were Sabina's people and he'd put up with whatever folly they concocted to be with her. Finally, his bride reached his side. Excited shivers raced over his body.

Her sisters lowered the veil until it pooled upon the ground. Taryn continued to hold her end of the fabric, a slight shake to her hands.

Taryn's power washed over him in waves, almost battering him with its intensity. She was scared. He glanced at her with what he hoped was reassurance, but she wasn't looking at him. Instead, she gazed at the gods above them. Her lips moved and he wondered what silent conversation they were having. When she finished, her power receded, but not completely. Nor did her features relax.

Hayden took Sabina's offered hand and drew his focus to the ceremony. Taryn wouldn't be thrilled if he spent his time worried for her instead of concentrating on his soon-to-be wife. *Wife.* The word vibrated through him with thrilling constancy. After everything they'd been through, in a few bells he would be able to call his beloved his wife for all time.

They recited the vows each had written and stood patiently while a troupe of dancers performed a dance erotic enough to make more than just the men squirm with heightened anticipation. Sabina had warned Hayden there would be surprises, but wouldn't elaborate. As the dancers shimmied and writhed, his blood heated and desire raced through his extremities. He snuck a glance at Sabina only to find her gazing at him, lust clear in her eyes.

I love you, she mouthed.

The temptation to lean in, to claim her lips with his own, was overpowering, but he held fast. The dance was meant as a test— to see if the couple could deny their passion until after the celebrations.

The music played on, the beat of drums a powerful aphrodisiac, the dancers doing their best to sway the couple. Despite his best efforts, Hayden's erection grew, stretching painfully against the tight fabric of his breeches. His joy receded and rage infused his every breath. *How could he be denied? Wasn't this his wedding night? Shouldn't he be able to take his bride any time he wished?*

The thoughts battered against his mind, causing searing pain behind his eyes. The thoughts weren't his. Hayden fought against the intrusion. The brutal emotions belonged to an entity not accustomed to gentility.

Light flared behind his eyes. Bright enough to blind, yet brimming with compassion. Taryn's presence filled him, taking over his thoughts, emotions, physical actions. For a brief moment, he *was* Taryn. He lived her entire life in that blink of an eye. Her pain was his; her strength, his. Gods, but she was powerful. More so than even she realized. Contained within her was the power of a god.

Hayden swayed against the battle being fought within his mind, body, and soul. Taryn hissed as she expanded, pushing Kaldaar out of him. The elder gods remained where they were, drifting above the guests. Their impartiality annoyed Hayden. This was their fault. Kaldaar should never have been allowed to return and yet here he was, infecting Hayden and how many others with his vile Telraicht-Noir?

The dancers began their final gyrations—the music drummed deeper, darker. Hayden's desire-stoked rage burned against Taryn's Light. Beads of perspiration broke out on his forehead and Sabina gave him a concerned glance. A slight shake of his head and pointed look at the dancers conveyed his thoughts. They had to remain unaffected. If she so much as reached out to hold his hand, the ceremony would be stopped, the wedding called off. His fingers flexed toward her, but he fisted his hands and kept them at his side.

To the left of Sabina, Taryn smiled without any outward sign of the struggle she endured. Another presence entered his being, rough, yet calming. Rhoane's Eleri ShantiMari snaked its way through Hayden, joining Taryn's to push out the entity's domination. When the two forces combined, a sharp pang tugged at Hayden's mind. He flinched, but stayed upright. Sweat rolled down his cheeks, his jaw tensed against the invasion.

Wedding guests chittered, about him, he supposed, but he didn't listen hard enough to know for sure. Heavy beats of music pounded his ears, and the dancers stretched toward the wedding couple, coming to within a few inches of them, tongues extended, fingers almost touching their privates. Hayden and Sabina remained impassive, but his cock twitched as if it had a will of its own and wanted nothing more than to be fondled by the nearest dancer.

Taryn and Rhoane's power twisted like a cyclone, pulling Kaldaar's brutality into it. His own ShantiMari flared bright against the entity, joining with his cousin's and the Eleri's. The three of them worked in tandem, cleansing Hayden of the god's filth.

A blinding flash snapped above the guests, spraying the calm night sky with colors of every hue. Only then did the elder gods swirl into the mix, creating a fantastical light show. The guests oohed and ahhed, thinking it an elaborate fireworks show.

With a heavy drumbeat, the music ended, the dancers crashed to the ground, their energy spent, their seduction complete.

A sucking sound popped in his ears, and then calm washed over Hayden. Kaldaar was gone. In place of his awful compulsion was an overwhelming sense of love and friendship. Taryn and Rhoane's ShantiMari lingered, but only as an afterthought. They were no longer inside Hayden.

He looked to his bride, who beamed at him. To the others, they'd passed the most difficult test, but what had truly transpired was far more important. Hayden was no longer under Kaldaar's control. Sabina was safe from the god. Forever, he hoped.

A light snow fell. Delicate flakes of chilled ice covered the guests before drifting to the ground, giving the warm summer night an ethereal glow. Most of the people gathered had never seen snow and opened their mouths to taste the foreign substance. Giddy with happiness, Hayden did the same.

As he stood with his head back, tongue extended like a child waiting for a treat, laughter bubbled up from deep inside. He let it come. Let it wrap around him until he shook with sheer joy. Others joined him, adding their boisterous laughing to his. Even Queen Prateeni chuckled, and her husband too.

Hayden's gaze swept the crowd, his love for those around him complete. Of everyone there to witness his and Sabina's wedding, only one person didn't marvel at the wonder of snow falling in the Summerlands. As his gaze locked to Myrddin's, a chill swept down Hayden's back.

Just as quickly, Taryn's ShantiMari warmed his cooled skin. Hayden blinked and the mage stood with his face lifted to the night air, laughing when flakes landed on his cheeks.

He doubted himself. Certainly Myrddin, a man who'd known Hayden all of his life, would wish him good health and good fortune. He'd been mistaken.

Yet there, just beyond the mage, out of reach and unseen, hovered a shadow. Faceless, formless, lacking substance, and filled with pure evil. Hayden's bones trembled beneath his skin.

Hayden's scream ripped through his thoughts, but didn't pass his lips.

Kaldaar.

CHAPTER THIRTY-FIVE

A wail interrupted Gwainne's thought and he paused, listening. Khrystina glanced at him, her short hair sticking up like little horns on her head. She was the strangest Eleri that he'd met. Most of the others were soft—in their speech, the way they walked, their dress—but everything about her was hard edges and crisp words.

"Did you hear something?" he asked, not quite sure if the scream had been in his mind, or someone in the temple had called out.

She shook her head, but he had the distinct impression she lied.

Gwainne frowned at the paper he'd been reading. Khrystina studied him as she usually did, but there was concern in her expression.

"I must be overtired." He stood and swung his arms to clear his thoughts and allow blood to flow freely through his limbs. He'd been sitting more than ever in his life and had yet to become accustomed to the sedentary lifestyle of an academic. He'd already found more than enough information to share with Taryn. He should leave the Narthvier, but stalled his departure.

Part of it was because he liked spending time with Carga and Khrystina, and a larger part was because he didn't enjoy the idea of traveling to Paderau and Talaith. What he'd discovered at the temple rocked his core beliefs far beyond his comfort zone. If a forest could do that, what would two major cities do? He wasn't sure he was ready to find out.

"You have been too long at the scrolls, Prince Gwainne. Perhaps a ride would do you good?"

Khrystina didn't ride, nor did she ever leave the library, at least not that he'd seen. Once, she told him the farthest she'd ever been was to the Weirren when she first became a novice. A grand ball was held for all the young women who would devote their lives to serving Verdaine and she'd been dazzled by the eloquence of the royal residence. Not much different than Gwainne had been. Yes, he was a prince, but his kingdom was lackluster compared to the Weirren. From what Carga told him, Paderau was similar in grandeur to the forest court, but Talaith, and the Crystal Palace, were leagues above them both.

He was afraid. Plain and simple. He'd been raised sheltered from the outside world and he feared he would lose himself in the city. Emotionally, physically, spiritually. He'd already been challenged by meeting Verdaine, and several of the novices had been only too happy to "study" lovemaking with him during his visit. While not complaining, their expertise had startled him. He'd always been told the Eleri mated for life, but novices weren't bound by the constraints of Eleri law in this regard. What the novices had taught him would make even his brother Loghan blush.

If young Eleri women could surprise him, what would happen when he ventured south to where crime lived beside wealth, gods of many names were revered, and morals were subject to personal opinion?

Perhaps this was what Verdaine had wanted him to experience. The free flowing of ideas and prejudices found in other parts of Aelinae. He ran a hand through his hair, needing air like Khrystina had suggested, but not wanting to leave his scrolls. Despite all he'd learned, he was close to uncovering something, yet it eluded him the more he grasped for it.

It didn't have to do with the Jansen Strait, or even the Eirielle, and yet he couldn't shake the feeling that it did. While reading through the myths surrounding the Jansen Strait, he'd found an obscure entry scribbled in the margin that read, "Heed ye not to where travels are borne, but to the place where worlds are torn." Then, farther down the page were the lines, "Travelers be warned, the witch queen be scorned. Only the one who is and who is not shall straddle the line." It was the last line that caught his attention most.

He'd heard the phrase before, perhaps from his father, or even at the Weirren. He couldn't place the exact time or setting, but the emotions surrounding the words stayed with him. Danger. Fear. Whoever had spoken them knew who the phrase applied to, and didn't trust the person.

And now Gwainne heard someone screaming in his mind. No one else seemed to hear it. This place was driving him mad. That was the only logical answer.

"I think you are right," Gwainne said at last. "A ride would do me good. But only if you accompany me."

The look of surprise on her face was charming. She would say no, but still he persisted. Of all the novices he'd bedded in the short time he'd spent at the temple, Khrystina was the only one who hadn't asked, and the only one he wished would.

"I do not think it would be wise. I am not fond of horses."

"Then let us go for a walk. Surely you are not opposed to stretching your legs? I am leaving in the morning and would like to spend some time with you away from these papers." Even as he said the words, he committed to the plan of leaving the temple. It was time. Verdaine had told him to be in Ulla within three moonturns and he'd already pissed away a fortnight.

It was his turn to be surprised. Khrystina stood and stretched her lithe limbs. He spied peeks of naked skin beneath the shawl she always wore. The novices wore simple garments depending on their role in the temple. For Khrystina, this meant a short tunic worn under a tight vest, and a long skirt that hid soft boots. Most of the novices wore silken nets to contain their hair, but not her. She flaunted her short tresses. Everything about her begged to be challenged and despite his best efforts, Gwainne had come no closer to discovering why she'd agreed to live her life as a priestess to Verdaine when she so obviously rebelled against their rules.

"I need to tell my superior I am escorting you outside the temple. Meet me in the foyer of the grand room in a quarter bell."

A small thrill that she'd said yes warmed him. Once outside the confines of the library, he hoped her tongue would loosen. Of course, he meant in conversation, but he wouldn't eschew the other meaning either.

As he rounded the corner to the room she'd directed, Carga raced toward him, her face an array of concern and rage.

"You must leave at once," she sputtered when she was several paces away.

Gwainne's heart seized at the harsh tone. Never had he heard her so much as raise her voice, but now, she demanded he get out of the temple.

"Is this because of my indiscretions with the novices? They assured me it was acceptable, even preferred."

"The novices? No. They are allowed to bed others while in the temple. If you were to bed them outside these walls, they would be sheanna and need to be purified, but this is sacred space."

Her explanation was rushed, almost an afterthought, but he caught a tremor in her words, nonetheless.

"Then why must I leave?"

"I heard," her features pinched in frustration, "something has happened. I know not, but I fear for my brother and his betrothed. They are too far for my reach and while I sense they are not in danger, well, any more than usual, there is a darkness surrounding them. It is impenetrable and vile. I wish for you to travel to Talaith, meet them upon their return and see for yourself if what I sense has come to pass."

"Why not go yourself?"

He knew Carga once lived in Paderau, but not the circumstances of her being outside the vier, or for how long. It was a subject she made clear she didn't wish to discuss.

"I am High Priestess now. I cannot leave the temple unguarded."

It was a flimsy excuse. Verdaine had three high priestesses, any one of them skilled enough to handle their duties.

"Then I will leave at once for Talaith."

Despite the timing, Gwainne suspected no other ulterior motives from Carga. Still, he hated to leave before saying farewell to Khrystina. As if reading his mind, Carga said, "I will convey your apologies to Novice Khrystina. I am sure she will be saddened by your early departure. If there are any scrolls you wish to have copied and sent to Talaith, please let us know."

He'd already left a list with Khrystina and made extensive notes that he had secured in his bag. "I will. Thank you."

He turned away from the foyer and hurried to his rooms. If Carga sensed danger, he would not question her. In the short time he'd gotten to know her, he understood she wasn't one for dramatics. She spoke her mind, was fair, honest, and passionately devoted to the novices and her duties in instructing them.

It wasn't until he was far from the temple and past several veils that he realized Carga had said she heard something. It couldn't have been the same wailing that had startled him. And if it was, what did that mean?

CHAPTER THIRTY-SIX

Taryn heard Hayden's scream, but not aloud, only in her head. She searched for the source of terror, but saw nothing untoward. The wedding guests were dazzled by the appearance of snow, something most of them had never encountered before. They stood with their heads back, mouths open to receive the tiny cold flakes. It was a ridiculous display, but she couldn't help herself. There was something pure about snow, cleansing.

After what she and Rhoane had just accomplished, more than just Hayden needed the respite. Kaldaar had clung to her cousin, stubbornly insinuating himself in Hayden's thoughts and actions. It had been a true test of their combined strength to banish him, but she and Rhoane had done it. The elder gods were there as a precaution, willing to step in if needed, but Taryn understood if she failed this test, more than just Hayden's soul was at stake.

Her limbs trembled from the sheer adrenaline rush needed to combat Kaldaar. Despite wanting nothing more than to curl on a sofa and sleep, she stood tall, clapping and laughing with the others as Hayden and Sabina performed their marital dance. Thankfully, it was nowhere near as sultry as the other dancers' had been. How the couple had kept from moving while being sexually taunted, Taryn didn't know. Several guests were squirming by the time the dance ended. She most likely would've been among them had it not been for the focus needed to rid her cousin of the entity.

How Kaldaar managed to insinuate himself so fully in someone strong in ShantiMari was a question that terrified her. If Hayden had succumbed to him, how many others not as powerful would? There could be legions of followers waiting for their moment. Dread swept down her back and she shivered against it.

"Cold?"

"No, frightened. You saw how tenacious that thing inside Hayden was. How many others do you think he's corrupted?"

Rhoane took her hand in his and immediately her worries faded; her heartbeat slowed. "I do not think he can compel more than one person at a time. At least, not until he is fully restored. We have excised him from Hayden. He and his bride can enjoy their marriage night without fear of reprisal."

Taryn knew Sabina wasn't in danger, but what she hadn't told Rhoane or anyone else was her fear that Kaldaar would compel Hayden to bed other women, impregnating them with the god's seed. At least that wouldn't happen now. Still, her concern lingered.

"Smile. It is my wedding night," Sabina whispered in her ear. "Have you shown Rhoane the tattoo?"

Taryn instinctively hid her wrist in the folds of fabric of her nearly see-through pants. "No. I will later." Rhoane wouldn't mind, of course, but she'd had the tattooist ink her skin on impulse and since in the Summerlands it was considered a marriage tradition, she didn't want anyone getting the wrong idea. She and Rhoane didn't need a ceremony. They were bonded by the gods.

And yet, every so often a little dip of disappointment would sour Taryn's belly. Even though to the world they were more than married, it would be nice to be asked.

Hayden swooped his bride into his arms and spun her around the garden. It was then Taryn realized the ceremony had turned into a free-for-all of guests dancing, laughing, and drinking wine from elaborate goblets. The party spilled over into the palace and raucous laughter could be heard from every corner. By the sounds of it, the entire kingdom celebrated Sabina's wedding.

Taryn shut off the part of her mind that fretted over every little thing and allowed herself to be swept into the dance, a pair of strong arms embracing her. She glanced into Rhoane's eyes and the breath was stolen from her lungs. The love and desire she saw reflected back at her was nothing short of the most erotic thing she'd ever witnessed. And after the dance meant to tempt the wedding couple, that was saying something.

"Taryn ap Galendrin," Rhoane started, his voice lighter than usual, joyful, "would you consent to being my wife? I do not have much to offer in terms of coin or kingdom, but if you say yes, you will always have my heart, my loyalty, and my sword."

A huge grin broke out on her face. "I thought you'd never ask. Yes, I consent to being your wife, your lover, and your friend for as long as we both shall exist. In whatever form that may be." She tilted her head, the grin growing even larger. "Your sword? As in Claidholm Solais, or, um, your *love sword*?"

"What is a love sword?"

The sincerity of his question had her doubling over in laughter. Of course he wouldn't understand. "I'll explain it later," she choked out between hiccups and giggles.

It wasn't until the sun's rays stretched across the ocean to the west that the party showed any signs of slowing. Too exhausted to remain upright, Taryn excused herself from the festivities to seek out Sabina. She and Rhoane were leaving on the morning tide and she needed to say her goodbyes. She hugged her friend tight, not wanting to let go, but knowing she must. Before parting, she whispered, "Take care of my cousins."

Always alert, Sabina glanced sharply at Taryn, who nodded with a wide smile. "Do you mean—?" Sabina's hand went to her belly. "When? How?"

"If you need me to explain how, then perhaps you shouldn't be having babies."

"I thought we were careful. Who else knows?"

Taryn was taken aback by the harsh tone in her friend's voice, then understanding dawned. "No one. I've not even told Rhoane. We'll be here for the birth, and I've set a protective ward around your womb. Nothing and no one can harm you or your child."

Sabina's arms tightened around Taryn, squeezing the breath from her. "Thank you. You are truly a wonder."

They spoke for a few minutes more, then Taryn made her way through the other guests until each one of her friends and family had been hugged, kissed, and told how much they'd be missed. Every word she spoke was true. Leaving them was much harder than she ever guessed it could be. She and Rhoane were headed to a hostile environment, with no clue as to the outcome.

Despite the early hour, her guards and maids waited for her in her rooms. They'd already discussed plans for each of them. All that was left was to grab her bags and be on her way, yet Taryn lingered. These weren't just her servants—they were friends. Carina and Timor were going to return to Talaith, but Darius and Taryn's maids would stay in Menurra for several moonturns, training with Flik. By the time Taryn saw them again, she hoped they'd be better prepared to face whatever challenges came their way.

Of course, Lliandra wasn't happy with Taryn's decision, but she had no say in what her daughter did with her maids. Something Taryn had to remind the empress of several times. They'd survived the Shadow Assassin and Cashiel, but Taryn couldn't risk their lives any more without the kind of training Flik would provide.

In Talaith, the girls and Darius would be under the watchful eye of Lliandra's captain of the guard, and there was no telling if they'd get the instruction needed to protect not only her, but themselves. It was best they stayed in Menurra, where the queen and king supported Taryn's radical idea.

Taryn left her rooms with tears swimming in her eyes. This sort of melancholy wasn't like her and it unnerved her to be so emotional. She'd left family and friends plenty of times. Why this one in particular was hitting her so hard, she hadn't a clue. Kaida padded silently beside her and Taryn stretched her fingers into the grierbas's silky fur. That simple touch was enough to calm the fluttering of her heart, to ease the strain tugging at her gut.

Taryn asked that they stop by the stables to give their horses a treat. They'd been sorely neglected during their stay, and Taryn promised to make it up to them when she returned to Talaith. By the time they reached the harbor, the ship was ready to set sail. She sent a silent prayer to the gods to please let this trip be drama-free.

Her gaze swept up to the masts and a chill snaked down her spine. Rhoane's hand pressed against her lower back and she took a tenuous step onto the gangplank. Kaida nosed her palm and she stroked Kaida from snout to ruff. This wasn't the ship Cashiel had overtaken. That ship was in Menurra's shipyard, being repaired. This ship was similar in size and build, but it wasn't where she'd been brutally beaten. Still, the sight of the deck, scrubbed and ready for sea, paralyzed her.

It had been far too easy for Cashiel to overtake the ship. Not for the first time, Taryn wondered if he'd had help of a divine nature. Or had Zakael been lending assistance? She wouldn't put it past her half-brother to try something so brazen. He'd made no secret that he desired Taryn for his own purposes and her power had everything to do with his disgusting needs.

She forced herself to take one step, then two, then snap her shoulders back and face the reality of the ship. If she let what Cashiel had done to her stop her from ever traveling on a ship, then he continued to hold power over her, and that was something she couldn't allow.

"I am here, Darennsai." Rhoane's soft words were spoken just for her and she leaned in until her shoulder touched his. "You are safe."

Hearing the words spoken aloud diminished much of her apprehension, but they were a lie. She would never be safe. As long as Kaldaar and Rykoto continued to plot against her, she was a target for every misbegotten soul on Aelinae. Her two half-brothers included. She'd all but forgotten Cashiel was related to her by blood. Some days, she really wished she was an only child.

Rhoane's hand slipped into hers and she squeezed a little too hard. "Thank you."

He lifted their hands to kiss her wrist and paused. She glanced nervously at him, but the small half smile that crooked up his lips made the anxiety disappear. In its place, desire tickled and expanded until her girly parts grew warm.

"What is this, my love? Have you gone and gotten married so soon after I proposed?"

A furious blush stained her cheeks and she swallowed the giggle that sprang to her lips. Gods, but he made her feel giddy and young and alive. "I had that done yesterday morning while Sabina was getting ready for her wedding."

He turned her wrist to examine the design she'd chosen. It was the symbol for ShantiMari, three intersecting lines with an upside-down heart linked between them. Surrounding the symbol were flourishes and leaves. It reminded her of the Weirren, where they'd first made love. But she wasn't about to admit that to Rhoane onboard ship with a dozen sailors within hearing.

"It is perfect," he said at last. "It is us."

"That's what I thought, too."

He lifted his wrist and placed it against hers. A swirl of his ShantiMari circled their hands and cut into her skin. She sucked in a breath, but kept her hand still. With a snap, the pain ended and his power faded to nothing. Their runes shimmered, but the tattoo was unaltered.

"What did you do?"

His grin grew and a saucy wink was her answer.

"No, seriously, what just happened?"

"I will show you later."

"Tease."

"Of the highest order." His arms circled her and they stood close to the rail, swaying with the movement of the ship. His erection pressed against her and she tilted her ass slightly to increase their contact. "Now who is teasing whom?"

The captain shouted orders and the men scurried around them, tying sails, and setting rigging. Kaida panted at her side, uncomfortable in the heat, most likely. The Summerlands weather was muggier and warmer than Taryn liked. It left her feeling sticky all the time. King Faisal and Queen Prateeni kept the palace as cool as they could, but outside of the palace walls, the full force of summer was evident. She hoped the Sitari Islands weren't as humid and hot as the Summerlands. She was already cranky about the trip. Adding discomfort to their meeting wouldn't bode well for anyone.

As they pulled away from the dock, Taryn scanned the city for threats. Finding none, her gaze shifted to the palace high upon a hill. There, lining the walls and waving frantically, were her family and friends. Her heart seized at the sight.

She and Rhoane waved back, calling out names and farewells. Echoes returned to them, of their voices and the others, which sounded like a discordant loop of gibberish. Taryn didn't care. She continued to shout to her friends until they were little more than specks in the distance. When her arm ached from being held aloft, she lowered it and gazed into Rhoane's eyes.

"I think it's time you tell me about that tattoo thing."

"And I think it is time you tell me what a love sword is."

Taryn burst out laughing. She'd forgotten about her promise the night before. They raced to their stateroom, with Kaida loping not far behind. The grierbas stationed herself outside their door while Taryn and Rhoane took advantage of the oversized bed. Taryn had refused to take one of Lliandra's ships, but had acquiesced to allowing King Faisal to lend her one of his. She worried if she traveled with the royal emblem on the flags, it would make her a target, so the ship had been stripped of all decals or icons signifying who traveled aboard. In fact, the crew had gone a step further and painted images that could easily be mistaken for pirate markings.

As Taryn tumbled into bed with Rhoane, she jerked on his tunic, lifting it above his head. His shirt followed close behind. She halted midway, gasping at the sight before her. There, covering his right shoulder and extending down his chest to dip below his arm, was her tattoo, elongated and utterly sexy.

"Oh. My. Holy. Hell." She traced the lines with her fingertips, growing warmer by the minute. They had four days at sea and she had no desire to set foot outside her cabin in that time.

Rhoane tossed his shirt aside and began untying his breeches. The look he gave her said he wouldn't mind the seclusion either, not one little bit.

CHAPTER THIRTY-SEVEN

The gates of Gaarendahl were bolted shut, allowing no one in or out, just as Zakael had ordered. Torches burned brightly along the parapet, showing several guards making their rounds. All was as it should be. He circled the castle several times, his beady little eyes able to track movements, but not discern one form from another. Whether it was a man or woman carrying a basket to the barracks, he couldn't say. Levons were known for their speed, not eyesight.

Once he had Taryn's dragon, he'd no longer need birds.

As it always did, the thought of his sister warmed his blood, grew his excitement. Soon. Much sooner than Kaldaar had planned. But Zakael was done taking orders from the shapeless creature at Caer Idris. That's why he'd left the northwest for Gaarendahl. That, and he desired to see Cashiel again. *Rykoto's balls—Kane.* He had to remember he was vexed with Kane, but the memory of his sweet mouth and tempting body had dissolved some of Zakael's bloodlust.

Being away from Kaldaar's influence had helped curb his desire to murder the lad, too. Although, when Kane had written to Zakael about visitors, people Kane was excited for him to meet, that's when he'd ordered the castle on lockdown. Whoever these people were who caused Kane to break Zakael's rules had to be important. Otherwise, he knew the punishment and even he wasn't stupid enough to tempt Zakael's wrath.

On the sixth circuit around the towers, Zakael dipped low, aiming for an open window on the third floor. All of the other windows were closed, with the drapes drawn tight. This room would have to do. If memory served, it was to a guest room that rarely saw inhabitants.

He angled into the room, narrowly missing the flames of several lit candles. Immediately, his senses piqued, his feathers ruffled with suppressed anger. How dare Kane act like the lord of the castle. How dare he invite others to Gaarendahl without Zakael's permission. He swooped toward the ceiling, away from the light, to settle in a darkened corner. It took his levon eyes a moment to adjust, but when they did, he saw the most remarkable sight—on the bed, fornicating like common whores, were a man and woman. She, fair of face, hair like summer straw, petite and lithe; he taller, with the dark coloring of a Summerlander.

They writhed on the bed, naked as the day they were born, making no attempt to keep their illicit activity secret. Zakael should stop them, should transform into a man and demand an explanation, but a movement caught his eye and he averted his gaze from the couple to a chair not more than two paces from the bed. There, his face covered in bandages, his ruined hands gripping the armrests, sat Kane.

His Kane. The man sworn to be his and only his. Even though Kane only watched, jealous fury ripped through Zakael. His lover wasn't allowed any sexual relief unless the king commanded it.

"Harder, Adesh," the girl cried out. "By the gods, you are too weak." The last was said under her breath, but Zakael heard the sentiment clearly. A levon's eyes might not be sharp in the darkness, but their hearing was exceptional.

A few muttered words, followed by a drawn-out grunt, and it was done. The man flopped to his back and Zakael recognized him as the spice merchant from Talaith. The one Cashiel, né Kane, had contracted to supply him with a ship. It had been a rather involved, laborious plan, that in the end didn't beget Zakael his sister's dragon. His rage flared anew.

If it wasn't for Kane's presence, and the fact the girl lay on the bed picking at a cuticle, clearly unsatisfied and bored, he would've killed the man on the spot. Instead, his mind reeled with other ways Adesh might be useful. First, he had to punish his errant lover and see about the girl's needs.

His night just became far more interesting than he'd imagined.

A shudder came from where Kane sat and the scent of his release drifted to Zakael's beak. The traitor had soiled himself watching the two lovers. Punishment wouldn't be enough to satisfy the king's ire. Images of feeding Kane to the runyon tree played out in his mind, calming the fire that burned within.

"Is that a bird in our room?"

Kane followed the girl's outstretched finger. When he saw Zakael perched in the corner, he visibly shook. Immediately he went to his knees, babbling apologies and asking for forgiveness. The pair on the bed looked mildly amused at his antics.

Zakael swept down to land beside his lover and transformed into a man. The pair's expressions turned to horror at the sight of him. Adesh scrambled from the bed, taking the sheet with him, which left the girl exposed. While Adesh dressed, Zakael studied the pretty thing on the bed. A slow smile made its way from her lips to her eyes and she adjusted herself on the mattress, displaying her wares.

"My lord." One hand trailed from her collarbone to between her legs, the other cupping a breast. "It's a pleasure to make your acquaintance."

Zakael's depravity was held in check, until her wicked fingers pinched her ripe nipple and she let out a moan. His cock surged against his trousers, seeking release.

"Your Highness, if it pleases you, take the girl," Adesh offered.

Zakael glanced to where he knelt, his clothes haphazardly buttoned, his hair a mess. Until that moment, Zakael was willing to offer the man forgiveness, for a price, but his words sealed his fate. There would be no forgiveness for him. Only pain and, eventually, death.

"May I?" Zakael said sweetly. "That's so kind of you, sir."

Either Adesh was an idiot and didn't hear the mocking tone of Zakael's words, or he thought he could outsmart the king. "Anything for you, Your Majesty."

"Anything?" Zakael cocked his head to the side. "You say this as if you ever had a choice. What's yours is mine. I don't need your permission to take this girl, or your life."

At that, Adesh paled, his dark Summerlands skin turning a sick shade of ash. "Please, sir, I meant no harm."

"Yes, well, you meant no harm, but you see I, I enjoy harming people." He snapped his fingers and Kane sprang forward, head bowed. "Remove this man's clothing and see that he is bound to that chair. You know how I like it."

Adesh's whimpering was ignored as Kane did as told. Zakael's gaze never left the girl's as Kane stripped Adesh, then tied him to a chair, his ass lifted high in the air, his legs and arms spread wide. Her expression turned from one of confidence to fear and finally to excitement. For that moment, Zakael had waited.

"What is your name?" Zakael rasped, his own excitement reaching painful levels.

"Amanda, sir." She scooted to the edge of the bed and knelt before him. "How would you command me?"

Sweeter words were never spoken. Zakael began untying his breeches, his cock anxious to spring free. Amanda reached out to help and a slight whine came from behind him. He motioned Kane forward and inspected the bandages he wore.

"These will not do." He ran a finger down the length of fabric, searing it with his power. Then, gently, he lifted the bandage from Kane's face. The damage wasn't as bad as he'd feared. The healer he'd sent to Gaarendahl was better than he'd thought. Welts and some scarring covered the lad's once handsome face, but it wasn't ghastly or horrifying to gaze upon.

In fact, there was beauty in his deformity.

Amanda pushed Zakael's trousers over his hips and gasped. "My lord. I've never seen a cock decorated." She touched the gold ring he wore over his cock and balls, her eyes wide, a pink tongue lapping around her lips. "Does it hurt?"

"Pleasantly so."

He ordered Kane to strip and Amanda to continue undressing him. When all four were naked, Zakael stood in the center of the room, his power a controlled tempest in his chest. These three were his playthings, to command as he saw fit. By the time the sun rose, he'd make sure they understood who was in control, and that their lives were no longer their own. Every moan, each release, would be allowed only if Zakael desired it be so. And he would start where Adesh had ended—with the girl.

Two days later, when neither Kane nor Amanda could take much more, and Adesh lay sobbing and bleeding, only then did Zakael stop their play. He'd used them in ways better suited for the torture chambers. Made them scream his name over and over again until it became a melody to his ears. A soothing lullaby by which he was able to block out the sneering rasp of the dark creature at Caer Idris. Zakael made certain to never say or think the name of the god, for when he did, the thing slithered into his psyche, compelling him to do things Zakael didn't wish to do. Like, return to the Temple of Ardyn.

The creature wanted Zakael to release Rykoto, but to do so he needed all thirteen seals. What the god didn't realize was—Zakael had no idea where the seals were, nor did he intend to release Rykoto until such a time that he'd be dependent upon Zakael. Among his father's papers, Zakael found many obscure codices, two of which he could use to his advantage. One foretold of the return of dragons to Aelinae.

Kaldaar be damned, but Zakael had to focus on Taryn and her dragon soul. He'd wasted too much time and resources planning the attack on Lliandra's ships. This time, he'd make Taryn come to him. Mallaqai's ruins were in his kingdom. Sooner, rather than later, Taryn would seek answers there. All he had to do was wait.

First, he'd go to the temple. Not for Kaldaar, but for his own reasons. A carefully worded request to Rykoto would spur Taryn's arrival at the ruins. Kaldaar had underestimated Zakael. A mistake he'd exploit with perfection. If Zakael knew anything, it was how to find someone's weakness and use it to his advantage. Gods included.

Zakael lay among his dutiful worshippers, arms and legs tangled in a mass of flesh. The stink of rutting filled the air. Their soiled bodies warmed his skin; their lust, freely given, filled that part of himself that wanted more, always more.

This is what it is to be a god.

Someone stirred on the bed and Zakael grimaced. Just once more before they left, then he'd be satisfied. He lifted his hand and let it fall. Whoever it landed upon would be his morning fuck. With a soft thud, his hand plopped onto Amanda's buttock. Lucky her.

He rolled atop her and spread her legs with his knees. Her eyes opened, a look of surprised fear in them. Zakael placed a hand over her mouth and another at her neck, squeezing the life from her. She fought back, thrashing against him, but he was too strong for her petite body to overpower. The harder she fought, the greater his desire became and he thrust his cock into her, gritting against a moan that threatened to ruin the moment.

Her body went rigid, then, with each rock into her, she relaxed, even started grinding against him. He squeezed her throat tighter until she was gasping for air. Her movements stopped and her eyes bulged. Zakael released his seed with a full-body shiver.

"Bathe, then get dressed. We leave within the bell."

King Zakael strutted from the room, his mind planning their travels, plotting how best to overthrow a god.

CHAPTER THIRTY-EIGHT

Taryn stood at the bow of the ship studying the topography of the Sitari island. Rough seas delayed their arrival by two days, making it a total of six tumultuous days at sea. Most of that time was spent in their cabin, naked. She didn't have any complaints. Her cheeks hurt from the near-constant grin she wore. The only odd occurrence that happened was a strange dream she had of a blue-haired woman and faeries. As much as she tried to put the dream into context of their quest, she couldn't. Even Rhoane had been perplexed by the very real, but definitely not, vision. In the end, they'd chalked it up to the stress Taryn was under. Which was tremendous and sex was a definite stress reliever. Especially since they'd discovered how to open energy stores from the Ullan healers. When they weren't making love, they strategized and planned.

The Sitari were warriors, but approaching them defensively could be catastrophic. Yet the rumors they'd heard about their attitude toward Taryn left little in the way of compromise. If she attempted submission, they would see her as weak. If she demanded control, they would rebel. Rhoane didn't see a course that led to a positive outcome, but Taryn insisted they had to visit the islands. Not just to investigate Adesh's movements, but to search for Mallaqai.

Taryn believed she resided somewhere with the Sitari and while Rhoane had expressed serious doubts the witch still lived, he'd agreed to at least try. Taryn sensed his animosity at being near the Sitari, not least of which because he was a man, but also because the Sitari shared a difficult history with the Eleri.

In her research, she'd discovered before the Sitari settled on the southernmost islands of Aelinae, they made their home on the plains west of the Spine of Ohlin in the no-man's-land between Danuri and Caer Idris. Mallaqai had been their unofficial leader and when the Great War broke out, they sided with Rykoto. It was after they lost the war Mallaqai had cursed them. Forever after, their female children were born with skin the color of twilight—a dusky hue of blue that marked them as outcasts.

The Eleri ruler of the time, Queen Clennais, offered them sanctuary within the borders of the Narthvier. Some Sitari took refuge with the Eleri, but most eschewed the offer. The war had not made enemies of the two races—pride had.

As Taryn regarded the island, she hoped that same pride wouldn't prevent the Sitari from listening to them. She had little doubt they would kill her if given a chance—she had to make certain they never were. If they could win the Sitari's trust, perhaps more than answers could be gained from this trip. An old wound might be healed and new alliances formed.

"It looks peaceful." Taryn slid her arms around Rhoane's waist and rested her chin on his shoulder.

"Aye, it does. But I have learned to never let appearances deceive me."

The captain shouted orders to his crew and the ship was brought round to a small cove. To the casual observer, the place was deserted, but Taryn knew better. Over the sounds of the ship, her Eleri hearing picked up movement in the trees. Several dozen women stalked across fallen leaves to the edge of the jungle. This forest was much like those on the Summerlands—thick with vines and wide-leafed plants. Varying shades of green made a canopy over the land, which provided adequate shelter from prying eyes, from land, sea, or sky.

"Do you hear them as well?" Taryn asked.

"Aye. They are waiting for us twenty paces from the clearing." He faced her fully. "Are you sure about this?"

"It's a little late to turn back. I can't shake the feeling that Mallaqai's here." Her gaze drifted above his shoulder. "If not her, then someone else. Look there."

To the west was one of the wonders of Aelinae—an island floating above the others. And above that, a smaller island. Both had waterfalls streaming from one to the next. A figure stepped to the side of the middle island, yet even with her enhanced Eleri vision, the figure was nothing more than a hazy outline.

"Do you think that's her?" Taryn's voice held resignation.

"Why does she shroud herself?"

"Shy, maybe?" Taryn tried to joke, but the seriousness of their trip weighed heavy on her.

The anchor jerked the ship to a halt and they bumped against the railing. Taryn swore under her breath and gave him a kiss on the cheek. "I really hate sea travel. Have I mentioned that before?"

"Once or twice. Definitely not more than a dozen times."

"Good, then you won't mind if I say it again. Hate. Sea. Travel." She adjusted the strap across her chest and inched her sword higher. She wore it on her back instead of at her side like Flik had suggested, but wasn't convinced it would be better for fighting.

Without a dock, they had to leave the ship in the harbor, which didn't sit well with her. But knowing the reputation of the Sitari, Taryn didn't want to risk the crew's lives if their meeting didn't go well.

She lowered herself to the rope ladder, regretting her choice of leather pants. Despite her hope that the Sitari islands wouldn't be as hot and muggy as the Summerlands, the sweat pooling in every nook and cranny would suggest these islands were even hotter.

She dropped the last few rungs into the small boat and steadied herself. "Kaida, come. I'll catch you." Taryn held out her arms for the grierbas and Kaida scrambled to the edge of the opening where the rope ladder dangled.

Rhoane joined Taryn and stretched his arms wide. "Come on, girl. We are here for you."

The grierbas crouched on her belly and inched forward until her forelegs were braced against the side of the ship. With more of a lunge than a leap, she shuttled forward into their arms. The boat lurched to the side and they all almost went overboard. Taryn's ShantiMari whipped around the boat, steadying it.

Rhoane set a snarling Kaida between them and planted his feet to the boards. Taryn suppressed a chuckle. At least she wasn't alone in her contempt for sea travel. The deckhand who rowed them to shore kept one eye on the beast, and another on Taryn. Poor man. Neither of them would do him any harm, but Taryn wasn't about to tell him that. Let the deckhand think they were lethal. She'd found, it was best if people feared you just a little.

They rowed as close to shore as possible, but still had to jump into the waves at waist level. Taryn griped about wearing leather pants and chafing while Kaida sprang from the boat. She paddled through the water to shore, shaking water from her long fur with several barks.

"Show off." Taryn grumbled.

"You do not have to wear wet breeches," Rhoane suggested as they trudged through the water. "I think sometimes you forget you have power." The chuckle in his tone lightened her mood.

"Thanks for thinking of me." The smile she wore was heart-felt and meant just for him. Her comfort and her protection were never far from his thoughts. Even now, as they shook out their hair and squeezed water from their clothing, she sensed his apprehension. Could feel his unease as if it were her own. Neither wanted to be on this island, but there was no other way.

Once they reached the shore, Kaida took off at a sprint. Taryn called after her, but the grierbas didn't respond. After several minutes ticked by, they had no alternative but to chase after her into the lush jungle. Memories of the Hben Firn near Menurra brushed her mind, but she pushed them aside. If the gods were on their side, this jungle wouldn't try to kill them. She just wished she could say the same for the Sitari.

They stumbled through the thick overgrowth, following Kaida's path, but soon lost her amid all the green. Every so often they'd see a flash of white, but even her soft padding couldn't be heard.

Taryn glared at the surrounding trees and paced a small circle. "What now?"

"We wait." Rhoane found a log and sat down, scuffing sand from his pants and boots.

Taryn walked a tight ring, wearing a path in the dirt the diameter of her outstretched arms. After perhaps a bell, footsteps sounded not far from where they were. Taryn reached behind her to touch the hilt of her sword.

"You'll not be needing that, Taryn ap Galendrin," a low voice said.

"Show yourself," Taryn demanded.

A chuckle answered. This wasn't a good beginning.

She held her hands at her side, to show she held no weapons and said, "We mean you no harm. I come here seeking answers, that's all."

"If you mean us no harm, why are you armed?"

"I have read stories and heard tales of the Sitari warriors. I come armed with Ynyd Eirathnacht as a show of respect."

"Kill her," another voice whispered, loud enough for all to hear.

"Quiet, Beilis." Then, to Taryn, she said, "You bring with you a man. Is he an offering?"

"He is my betrothed and not to be touched." Taryn reached for Rhoane's hand and gripped it in hers. They couldn't have him.

A collective sigh of disappointment rippled through the jungle.

"Ask your questions, then be gone from here."

Taryn bent to one knee, head bowed, hands steepled in front of her face. She'd recited the phrase many times over the past sennight, but now it had to be perfect. Hers and Rhoane's lives depended on it. Rhoane joined her on one knee, his hands clasped before him.

"Of kings and queens, I have no need." She paused, timing the cadence just right. "My kingdom lies beneath a cage of bone." Taryn breathed with the final syllable.

Rhoane's surprise flowed through her cynfar. He didn't know she'd studied the Sitari customs in her research, first in Talaith nearly a season past, and again in Faisal's library in Menurra.

A gasp came from not far away. The Sitari had them surrounded. From her peripheral, she saw his fingers inch toward his sword, but she gave a slight shake of her head, warning him off doing anything rash.

Leaves rustled with the approach of several Sitari and Taryn remained kneeling, wary.

A slender woman stepped from the trees, her skin a muted blue, her hair as white as the moon. On her brow rested a simple crown of feathers, but there was no mistaking this was the Sitari leader.

"I am Shandris, chieftess of the Sitari. Rise, Rhoane al Glennwoods ap Narthvier and Taryn ap Galendrin."

They stood, Taryn a pace from Shandris, Rhoane a step behind. They'd not said their names, but somehow, she knew. Taryn's senses went on high alert. If Shandris knew their names, then Adesh most certainly had passed through. Or, he was still on the island.

"Come with me," Shandris commanded. Her gaze raked over Rhoane and Taryn bristled. This wasn't a woman to cross, but if she thought Taryn would leave Rhoane, she was sorely mistaken. "You, as well."

Taryn reached for his hand, needing his strength. They'd passed the first hurdle, but she suspected there were many more to overcome. Shandris noted their entwined fingers and Taryn thought she saw a small smile lift the chieftess's lips. Beneath her right eye, a tattoo of two wavy lines caught Taryn's attention. Several more tattoos marked the woman's skin. Their significance was unknown, but what intrigued Taryn most were the leader's elongated ears. They came to sharp points, reaching nearly to the back of her head. Shandris wore no jewelry or ornamentation, save for the silver thread of her outfit. What there was of it, anyway.

If Taryn thought the Summerlands' dress was scandalous, the Sitari made Summerlands women appear demure. The top Shandris wore barely covered her breasts, and her skirt left far too much leg exposed.

"Why do you wear skirts in a thick jungle?" Taryn asked, genuinely curious. "Wouldn't pants be more comfortable?"

One of the Sitari glared at Taryn and grunted.

"And are you comfortable, *Darennsai?*"

Taryn's gait was uneven, her legs bowed. "Not really. But then, I jumped in the water."

"Stay in these jungles long enough, it will be like swimming in the sea."

Taryn wished she'd changed her attire like Rhoane had suggested, but with Kaida running off, she'd lost the thought to other concerns. With her leather pants chafing, she regretted not taking a moment to think of her own comfort. If she altered her attire now, the Sitari might be offended and she didn't need to give them any further reasons to distrust her.

Perhaps two dozen Sitari escorted them through the dense jungle until they came to a set of stairs spiraling around a thick trunk. Kaida bound toward them, tongue lolling to the side. Taryn stretched her fingers toward the grierbas and Kaida went to her side.

Does something amuse you? Taryn asked Kaida.

Yes. You.

Care to explain? But the grierbas didn't reply. She loped up the stairs until she was out of sight.

One by one, they followed, winding their way up the stairs, their boots echoing on the wood. Up and up they went until Taryn was dizzy from the climb. Unlike in the Weirren, these stairs were tightly packed beside the tree, making the journey claustrophobic and uncomfortable. Taryn kept her focus on the next step in front of her and ignored the tilting of her vision.

At the top, she steadied herself a minute before surveying several bridges that spanned across the treetops. Rhoane emerged from the stairs looking like he'd been through a tornado. Hair askew, he shuffled with a distinct lean to his gait. Shandris led them to a bridge on the right, her footing sure on the wobbly structure.

Taryn hung back with Rhoane, noting each time he almost lost his step and careened to the side. He walked as if he were drunk on a boat.

Are you well? Taryn's concerned voice penetrated his mind.

Yes. I…just…this place is strange. I do not feel myself.

Taryn took his hand in her own. She wrapped her ShantiMari around him, but instead of giving comfort, he flinched from her touch.

"What are you doing to him?" Worry dripped from her words.

Shandris spun around, her deep-blue eyes alight. "What do you mean?"

"Something is making him ill. Is it you?"

The chieftess scanned the others, a question clear upon her face. "No, it is not us. Quick, bring him inside."

They entered a high-ceilinged room, or rather, more of a series of rooms that spread out across the tree tops. Tree trunks pierced the floor and disappeared through the ceiling. Any other time Taryn might've paused to marvel at the fascinating interior, but her attention was focused on Rhoane.

"Put him over there," Shandris ordered.

Taryn led Rhoane to a pile of blankets and pillows and lowered him slowly. He sank to the floor like a sack of rice. Sweat beaded his forehead. He clung to her hand, his grip shaky.

"Do not leave me. Not here. Not alone." Rhoane pleaded.

Taryn knelt beside him, her thoughts scattered fragments of fear, confusion, and horror. "I'll be right here the whole time."

Rhoane's eyes darted across the room as if he spun on a wheel and Taryn placed a hand over his eyes. His skin burned beneath her touch. Her insides quivered with each passing moment that he suffered. She'd gladly take the pain from him if she could. Tears stung the backs of her eyes, but she wouldn't allow them to fall. Not in front of the Sitari. If she showed any kind of weakness, surely they'd kill her.

She smoothed his hair and whispered words of comfort. "Stay with me, Rhoane." Was this how he'd felt upon finding her in Ulla? If so, she regretted him the anguish her battered body had brought. For certainly, seeing him like this was worse than any suffering she'd encountered thus far.

Rhoane thrashed and moaned, his lips turning an ominous shade of grey.

"Who is your most skilled healer?" Taryn asked Shandris.

Two women slunk to the shadows, one the Sitari who challenged Taryn in the forest. Taller than the others, she couldn't hide from Taryn's glare.

"What's your name?"

The Sitari stiffened, a haughty look crossing her features. "I do not answer to you, Offlander."

Taryn ignored the slight and said again, "What is your name? Tell me, or I'll rip it from your mind."

This caught the woman's attention. "I am Sitari Beilis."

Taryn's fingers wrapped around Rhoane's wrist and she closed her eyes. Her power infused with his and she knew his torment as if it was her own. Then, she reached a hand toward the Sitari named Beilis and grabbed the woman's wrist. Taryn felt a jerk of power, then a slow chill crept through her veins. She needed the Sitari's strength to fend off his fever.

"You cannot do this." The woman hissed, her face scrunched, her teeth bared. "I will not help you."

Taryn sensed rather than felt Rhoane's body lighten, as if he drifted in a sea of in-between. She saw through his mind the darkness that sought his embrace.

"Please," Taryn begged. "Please help. I won't force you, but if you help me save him, I will be in your debt."

From the look of distress on the chieftess's features, Taryn didn't think the Sitari were responsible for what ailed Rhoane. But if not them, who? And why now?

CHAPTER THIRTY-NINE

The answer to her unasked questions battered against her psyche with unyielding force. Her enemies were also Rhoane's. Those that wished Taryn dead would benefit from his demise as well. A sob caught in her throat and tears bit the backs of her eyes. She let them flow. Let her weakness show. If the Sitari thought her unworthy, she no longer cared. All that mattered was Rhoane.

Her heart rebelled that this was happening. Not now, not to Rhoane. He'd fought hard to save her in Ulla, it wasn't fair. Taryn pressed her ear close to Rhoane's lips and heard the uneven, ragged breathing. His pulse slowed to dangerous levels and his clammy skin was hot beneath her touch.

"Is this Mallaqai's doing?" Taryn asked Shandris.

Her look of surprise confused Taryn.

"Mallaqai? Why would you ask about her?"

"She lives here." Taryn didn't say, "you dolt," but her tone implied she wouldn't suffer fools. Not on this day.

"Mallaqai is dead. She was killed after the Great War. Once she cursed us, our forefathers exiled us to these islands, taking all the male children with them. Mallaqai lived here for a time, but the others blamed her for their fate and stoned her to death."

Riddles. Always more riddles.

"Then her spirit resides here. We don't have time to argue. Where are your healers? We need to bring Rhoane's fever down. Is this some sort of jungle disease?"

The Sitari called Beilis stared at Rhoane, her eyes huge with fear. Taryn looked to see what horrified her. Dark-red splotches covered his exposed skin. Taryn strangled a cry. Several Sitari took a step back, their hands resting on sword hilts.

Her sword. Taryn drew Ynyd Eirathnacht from its scabbard and held it over Rhoane's prone body. It glowed softly as Taryn sent her power through the blade. She would either kill him or heal him, but she had to take the chance. She dipped the metal toward his skin and flinched when it came into contact. Nothing happened. Not a burn, nor a healing. Nothing. She tapped the blade against the tops of his hands, then lay the sword across his body and still nothing.

"Well, shit. I thought maybe that would work."

"Why would a sword heal him?" Beilis asked, confusion mixed with derision in her tone.

"It healed me once, and I was hoping it could help now." Taryn set her sword back into the scabbard and removed Rhoane's sword from his side. Again, nothing happened when she touched the blade to his blistered skin.

Taryn searched frantically for an answer. Faelara's potions might help, but she didn't have any and Faelara was on a ship in the middle of the ocean. She could try the Ullan method of healing through sex magic, but she hesitated. The blisters covered Rhoane's exposed skin, if he had them everywhere, it might be more painful than healing.

Tears tracked over her cheeks to drip from her chin. She placed her hand on Rhoane's chest and sent her power into his bloodstream. An oily presence fought against her and she gasped. Poison. Rhoane had been poisoned. Her heart thrummed with the realization. Questions flung across her mind, when, and by whom? And why wasn't she poisoned as well? They hadn't been apart the entire journey from Menurra, and they'd eaten the same food. One face hovered in her thoughts. Cashiel. He'd come back to finish what he started, but instead of poisoning Taryn, he'd tried to kill Rhoane. It had to be him. For all she knew, he'd been in Menurra the entire time. Might even have been on the ship that brought them here. She'd been distracted and hadn't paid attention to the crew. Stupid, stupid, stupid.

"This is beyond my skills." She whispered. A tremor of anxiety wrapped itself around her heart. If Cashiel had discovered another way to steal Rhoane's darathi vorsi, she had to stop him.

"I will help," a young woman said from the back of the room. She moved forward, but Shandris held out her hand.

"No, Nikki. I cannot let you do this. We don't know what this man has, or what destruction he might cause to our island." She turned her azure gaze to Taryn. "It would be best if you took him on your ship and left."

Taryn was gobsmacked. She was turning them out! Although, Taryn understood her reasoning. If Rhoane had contracted something aboard ship, their immune systems couldn't handle the infection. It might wipe out the entire Sitari population. But he hadn't come down with an illness. Before she could tell Shandris Rhoane was poisoned, another Sitari rushed in and spoke to Shandris in low, hurried tones. Taryn heard every word she said, each one deepening the pit in her stomach.

"Your ship has raised anchor and is heading for open water," Shandris said matter-of-factly.

If the captain was abandoning them, it could only mean one thing. Except, Taryn argued with herself, Faisal had chosen him. His fealty belonged to the king. Unless someone else had paid him to desert them. Taryn wouldn't believe the king could betray her this way, but if he did, she'd deal with him later. For now, she needed to stop the ship and heal Rhoane.

"He stays here. You," Taryn pointed to the young healer woman, "do what you can until I return. I believe he's been poisoned. I don't know with what, or when, but I'll find out." Her gaze swept over the room, landing on Beilis. "If he isn't alive when I return, there won't be a Sitari left on Aelinae, am I understood?"

Beilis glared at Taryn, her eyes hard agate in her tanned face. "You do not command me."

Several choice words came to Taryn's lips, but she ignored the Sitari and held Kaida's face between her shaking hands. "Stay with him. If anyone tries to harm Rhoane, kill them." Kaida barked her response, certain everyone in the room heard.

"There is no need for threats, *Darennsai*. Despite what you think, we are on your side." Shandris's tone was authorial, yet full of compassion.

"From where I'm sitting, I don't know who's on my side any more. It's getting harder to tell friend from foe, but I do know if we don't act fast, the *Surtentse* will die and that will leave Aelinae more unbalanced than it already is. Now, unless you desire a world ruled by Kaldaar and his Telraicht practitioners, I suggest you do what you can to make sure Rhoane is alive when I return."

Shandris shared a look with the tall Sitari and something passed between them.

Beilis swallowed hard, but nodded. "We will care for him like he is one of our own."

"I'd appreciate that." Taryn said with genuine gratitude. She didn't want to leave Rhoane, but had to stop the ship.

She touched her forehead to Kaida's. *I am scared*, she admitted.

Kaida whined and scratched at the floor. *Remember who you are, Darennsai.*

Taryn would've laughed if not for the tears that choked her speech. She let go of Kaida's fur and transported herself to the deck of the escaping ship. Several sailors swore at her appearance and made the sign to ward off evil above their heads. She ignored them and stormed toward the captain, who manned the ship's wheel.

"Stop this ship at once." Taryn shouted as she ran up the steps to the quarterdeck.

Surprise flickered across his face and he faltered. She took advantage of the pause to send a thread of ShantiMari over the ship's wheel, giving her control. She wrenched on the thread and the ship lurched. A heavy grinding came from below them and the captain sputtered curses.

"Who gave you permission to leave us?" Taryn asked, her heart beating hard enough she could barely hear her own thoughts.

"I was told to bring you to Sitari and return to Menurra at once. I'm only following orders."

"Whose? King Faisal wouldn't let you abandon us."

By the sweat rolling down his face, Taryn suspected there was more to his deceit. A gnawing started in her stomach, burning with vicious intensity.

"Tell me who paid you to desert us, or I'll feed you to King Baldev." She withdrew her sword and held it to just below his chin. The blade cut into his skin, leaving a thin line of blood.

A commotion on the deck below them alerted Taryn to a possible flaw in her plan. Of course the sailors would take up arms to defend their captain. With her sword at his neck, they'd keep a distance, but for how long, she couldn't guess. A movement above them gave her a clue—not long. A wily sailor dangled from a rope, a dagger between his teeth.

"Fuck it." Taryn pushed her power into the captain's mind and shuffled through his thoughts. The betrayer was male, cloaked to hide his identity, and with too much coin to be a hired mercenary. As far as she could determine, the captain didn't know who he was, but had felt a compulsion to obey him.

Taryn stumbled backward with the realization. She'd assumed Cashiel was behind this. A shiver forced its way down her back. Kaldaar had found a way to bribe the captain. Most likely by controlling another in much the way he'd tried with Hayden. Someone weak in the power, even weaker of mind. *Fuck.*

Then, just as she pulled her ShantiMari from the captain's thoughts, she saw an image of a small vial. Ochre in color, like a sunset across the ocean. *Poison.* The captain himself had poisoned Rhoane.

"Why?" she demanded, although she knew his answer would be that he had to. Kaldaar didn't give his victims a choice. "Why did you poison him? And with what?"

The sailor inched closer to them and, using her power, Taryn burned through the rope holding him. The stink of burnt hemp and the sound of the sailor thumping to the deck caused a stir with the others. Taryn kept her eye trained on the captain, her sword at his neck.

"Tell me now, or your ship, and all your men, will be destroyed."

"I don't know. I swear to you, I don't know what the poison is. The vial was given to me by the man who commanded me to leave you here. I was told to give it to the Eleri prince once we arrived. No sooner."

"This morning?" Taryn's eyes narrowed as she fought off the need to sort through their actions since waking. It didn't matter how he'd accomplished the task. It was done and Rhoane was dying.

The captain met her glare, his eyes soft now, full of remorse. "The crew didn't know."

"Do not leave this harbor, do you understand? I don't care who compels you, or how much they offer. If you sail without us, I'll hunt you down. Are we clear?"

His swallow shifted the blade, cutting further into his skin.

"Yes, Your Highness. I—" His words croaked out, "I'm sorry."

The sailors' bravado crumbled. Swords hung loose at their sides, daggers were sheathed. Taryn drew a breath, relief flooding through her, but she didn't trust the captain or his men. Remembering Cashiel's attack on Lliandra's ship, Taryn summoned a heavy fog, tying her power around it to keep the ship safely anchored. The captain might be foolish enough to try to escape, but she also placed a ward on the rudder, preventing it from moving. If they managed to raise the anchor, and leave the fog, they'd sail in a wide circle, but no further.

"Show me the vial." Taryn released her sword from his neck and motioned him forward.

"I don't have it. Once you left, I threw it overboard."

"And here I thought we were making progress." Taryn squeezed his elbow hard. Her power wrapped up his arm toward his chest, where it penetrated his skin to clamp around his rapidly beating heart.

"Fine. I have it here." He fished in his pocket for the vial, his breathing wheezy. "Take it. Please, leave us be. We have families."

"So do I," Taryn gritted through clenched teeth. She grabbed the vial and transported herself back to the Sitari.

Marissa's words haunted her. She'd brazenly told Taryn they were alike, but Taryn had denied it. Now, after casually threatening not only the captain and sailors, but the Sitari too, Taryn wondered. Her actions were out of desperation, but what if Marissa had believed she was doing what needed to be done for the greater good? What if all along Marissa had been right, and the others wrong?

No. Taryn shook the treacherous thoughts from her mind. She wouldn't believe anything Marissa did was for anyone but herself. Even though Taryn worked toward the betterment of all

Aelinaens, did that make it any less repulsive? Would she really destroy a ship over a vial of poison?

"*Darennsai?*" Shandris's voice held a note of panic.

Taryn blinked at her surroundings, not recalling leaving the ship. She stared at the Sitari as if seeing them for the first time. They were warriors, yes, but they were women trying to keep their race alive. Shandris stood before her, blue skinned and tattooed, her spiky white hair pulled into a long ponytail, her dress nothing more than a bikini and skirt. They did the best they could with what they had. Wasn't that what Taryn was doing? She didn't know anymore.

Didn't know if any of this was worth the trouble or the cost.

"It was poison. The captain was paid to kill Rhoane once we arrived here." Taryn held the vial up for Shandris to see. "I don't know anything about poisons. Do you?"

What did it matter? Rhoane would die and the prophecies said without him she would fail. He was already a ghostly shade of grey. His once luxurious hair lay limp against the pillows. The blisters had burst and left weeping wounds in their place. Kaida rested her head against his chest, her low whimpers hurting Taryn's heart.

She knelt beside Rhoane and brushed her lips to his. "Come back to me, mi carae."

His thoughts were muddied and indecipherable, but she clearly understood he continued to fight.

"This is beyond my skill. I'm sorry." Nikki touched Taryn's shoulder.

She glanced up at the pretty girl.

"We are rarely sick here. This island is home to many poisons, but I do not recognize this one."

"It would be rare, I imagine. Not one easily known, or cured." Kaldaar was cunning, Taryn had to give him that much credit.

"Do you have healers where you come from?" Distress clouded Nikki's eyes.

Taryn's heart faltered. Faelara was skilled in potions and would know how to counteract the poison. But Faelara was somewhere on the ocean between Talaith and the Summerlands. It could take Taryn days to find her. She gripped Rhoane's hand, careful not to touch the open sores. They didn't have days. Or even more than a few bells. She needed someone powerful. Then, like a curtain opening to reveal an actor upon the stage, Loghan's image came to her.

"I know of someone. A man. If I bring him here, you must promise you won't take advantage of him."

Shandris's laughter was guttural and harsh. "I see our reputation has remained secure on the mainland."

The others chuckled with their chieftess.

"He'll be safe. You have my word." Shandris placed her fist over her heart and bowed her head.

Taryn bent low and whispered in Rhoane's ear, "I promised not to leave you, but I must. I'll be back before you know it. Kaida's here to keep you company until I return." She stood and squared her shoulders. "There's a reason Rhoane was meant to be ill on your island. I think the cure might be found in one of the plants that grow here. Gather as many as you can."

Shandris nodded, her lips tight. "Despite our reputation, we are simple folk. Warriors, yes, when needs be, but this is foreign to us." Her eyes opened wide and she shared a glance with Beilis. "Perhaps one of the others might have knowledge we can use."

"Others?" Taryn cocked her head.

"A man came through here, perhaps a moonturn ago. He stayed only a few days, drinking our wine, satisfying our women, then left without saying farewell. With him were several women, most of whom he abandoned."

"Adesh came here. Asshole." Taryn would question the women he left behind later. Right now Rhoane was her priority.

"See if they can offer assistance, but don't let them touch Rhoane. Do you understand?"

"They are being guarded in a house far from here. We'll bring them closer, but not disclose why."

"Thank you." Taryn reached to embrace the chieftess, not at all surprised by her stiffness. "Where I come from, close contact doesn't always involve violence or lovemaking. Nor does it make you appear weak."

"I will take your word for it, *Darennsai*."

Taryn chuckled and gave Kaida one last pat before she cleared her mind of everything but a tent in the Ullan desert.

CHAPTER FORTY

Loghan reclined on the bedding Taryn had shared with Rhoane little more than a fortnight past. Her smell no longer lingered on the pillows, but he recalled the delicate floral scent. Eyes closed, he pictured her as she was healed, not as his nightmares would have him remember her—bloodied and bruised, close to death.

In his dreams, he was always too late to save her. Too inexperienced to be of much help. No matter what he tried, his nightmare always ended with her death. Despite his efforts, he was always the cause. Each time he awoke with a sense of dread overshadowed by shame. His love had caused her death. As much as he wished to honor Verdaine, he couldn't stop loving Taryn.

A breeze tickled his skin and he opened one eye to see who had entered the tent, even though he'd not heard anyone approach. Unless his daydreams were playing tricks on him, Taryn stood in the center of the room. A sharp thrill pierced his heart.

This was no dream. Taryn was dressed not in the white gown he always imagined, but in dark leather pants and blue tunic. A sword stuck out from behind her, and a look of fury set her features.

"Thank the gods. I have need of you." She stepped toward him.

Loghan scrambled to stand, catching his foot and tripping into her.

He gripped her arms hard until she grunted against the pain. "Are you here? Now? In the flesh?"

"I've come from the Sitari Islands, where Rhoane lays dying." Tension roiled along her words. "I need your help to save him." She glanced around the tent, a frown marring her beauty. "Where is your mother?"

"She is with Father. Let me bring her here. It would upset the laird too much to see you now. He's not been the same since Gwainne left."

"Gwainne's gone? Where? Why?"

"You didn't meet him in the Narthvier?" A sense of dread filled Loghan's belly.

Verdaine had said he'd meet Taryn and Rhoane at her temple, but if Taryn hadn't gone there, where was his brother?

"Our plans changed. I'm sure he's fine. Please, can you send for your mother?"

Loghan wavered. Verdaine had said he should love Rhoane most of all, did that mean she expected him to heal the Eleri prince? What cruel gods must they be to ask this of him.

"Loghan," Taryn placed a hand on his forearm, her eyes like the night sky. "I know what I'm asking and what it will cost you. Please."

She couldn't know the toll her request would take, but how could he deny the woman he loved? Even if it meant saving the man she loved, he had to help. He was a healer.

He sprinted through the encampment, skidding to a halt at his father's tents. Inside, too many braziers were lit, making the interior akin to a steam bath. Sweat dotted his forehead and rivulets of moisture traveled the length of his spine. His father insisted on the heat, claiming it helped keep his thoughts sharp. His mental decline increased with each passing day, with nothing Loghan or his mother could do to prevent it.

His mother sat with the laird talking softly when Loghan approached. She regarded him with curiosity. He whispered in her ear that she was needed elsewhere. After a moment's hesitation, she rose and stroked his father's brow. She conferred with one of the servants briefly, then he and his mother left Amdi's tents. They didn't speak as they hurried to where Loghan had left Taryn, but when Kaleigh entered the tent and saw the Darennsai standing alone, the questions came rapid-fire. Most of them centered around Gwainne and his quest.

"I don't know where Gwainne is, or what's happened to him, but I promise I'll find out. For now," Taryn glanced at Loghan first, then Kaleigh, "I need your help. Rhoane's been poisoned and will die if we don't act quickly. I had hoped Loghan could come with me."

"Come with you? How? I see no horse, and we are too far for sea travel." Kaleigh gripped her robe until her knuckles were white.

Loghan wrapped an arm around his mother and she sank against his body. She was exhausted from caring for his father. What Taryn asked was too much of a burden.

"Don't worry about the how." Taryn waved away the concern. "What do you know about poisons? Can an antidote be made if the exact poison is unknown?"

His mother slipped from his embrace and paced long enough to consider Taryn's questions. He could almost see her shift from concerned mother to healer in that short space of time.

"Yes, I believe so. Although, any antidote you make might be just as lethal as the original poison. Do you have any idea what was used?"

Taryn produced a vial from a pocket in her breeches. "I don't know what's in here, but it worked fast. No more than a bell from inception."

Kaleigh took the vial and sniffed the contents. Her nose wrinkled against the acrid scent. Next, she tilted the near empty bottle upon her finger and cautiously tasted the oily, yellowish substance. With a nod, she replaced the stopper and handed the vial to Loghan.

He repeated what his mother had done, grimacing at the smell. This was not a poison he knew.

"If I am not mistaken, Prince Rhoane is covered in boils, his skin a deathly shade." His mother turned to him. "You must go with Taryn. I will write out what you need."

Loghan's heart tripled its beating. The thought of accompanying Taryn to the Sitari islands would've been enough to entice him, but the healer in him was curious about the poison, and Rhoane's symptoms. This was a healing opportunity for him as well as a chance to be closer to Taryn. Despite his reservations about the Eleri prince, he couldn't let the man die.

His mother grabbed a piece of paper from a nearby table and scratched out a list. Every so often, she'd make a clucking sound with her tongue, shake her head, then continue scribbling. "Loghan, go to the healer's tents and get these items. Some you might need from the Sitari, but most we will have here."

Loghan jogged to the healer's tents and sped through the rooms, gathering items on his mother's list. A healing plan formulated in his mind with each new ingredient he found. Even though the poison was unknown to him, he understood his mother's wishes. It came with working beside her day after day in the healer's tents. He knew her habits as well as his own.

Every so often he interrupted a healing in progress and mumbled an apology before moving to the next room. If it had been him healing a patient, he would've been furious, but he didn't have time to spare on feelings. Not if he had a chance to help Taryn.

When he returned to where he'd left the women, they were seated on the bed, heads close together. Tears stained both of their cheeks and Loghan steadied his pace. Whatever they'd been discussing, neither mentioned as they stood. Taryn embraced Kaleigh and whispered in her ear, words too low for Loghan to hear. His mother nodded once, her eyes downcast. A pit of jealously lodged in his throat. Just below that, anger bubbled. He hated that his mother shared a private moment with Taryn, but also hated that whatever the Darennsai said had upset his mother. Flummoxed, he stood impotent in the middle of the room.

"Are you ready?" Taryn asked.

Loghan searched his mother's face for a sign, anything to tell him that she was all right, but she avoided looking at him.

"Yes," he said at last.

"Hold my hand, and whatever you do, don't let go." Taryn gripped his hand hard, her face set in a fierce grimace.

Before Loghan could answer, the room darkened and a whooshing sound drowned out anything he might've said. In a blink, they were not in Ulla, but in a round room with several dozen blue-skinned women looking at him. Curiosity illuminated their eyes.

The Sitari.

Two things crashed in his thoughts simultaneously—somehow Taryn had transported them here and by "here," he meant an island where women were notoriously known for using men and killing them. And he saw the strain Taryn's use of power had caused. She swayed where she stood, her face pale from exertion.

"This is Loghan," Taryn told the others, a slight tremor in her voice. "He's an Ullan healer, one of the best. His mother gave us instructions for making an antidote for Rhoane, but we might need a few ingredients from here. Do you have any eggs?"

"Eggs?" Loghan didn't recall seeing eggs on the list.

One of the women darted through the group, her long ponytail bobbing out of sight.

"Kaleigh said we need to give him egg whites. That should stabilize him until we get the potion mixed." Taryn spoke to him, but her eyes never left the prone figure lying at their feet.

Loghan took in the sight of the prince and shuddered. It was worse than he'd imagined. Blood oozed from open wounds on his exposed skin, and his clothing was stained. "You need to remove his clothing. The sores need to breathe."

A Sitari stepped forward, but Taryn stopped her. "I'll do it."

"I meant no harm, *Darennsai.*"

"I'm sure you didn't," Taryn muttered.

Loghan turned away from her to speak to the Sitari he believed to be their leader. "Where are your cooking facilities?" She led him to the next room, where a heavy brick stove took up an entire wall of the structure. "How do you keep from burning your house down?"

"We're careful in our work."

Her answer was sincere, but there was a slight mocking tone he caught. "I am sorry. I come from the desert where fire is difficult to sustain, and even harder to contain." He thought of the braziers in his father's tents. With one strong wind, the whole tent could be in flames before anyone could help.

"I've heard of the Ullan healers. How you use the body to restore health. Is it true this makes healing easier?" The taller of the two Sitari asked.

"Not easier, more complete." Loghan set out the items he'd gathered from the healer's tents, arranging them in the order his mother had listed.

"I'm Beilis. Shandris is our leader, but I am her second. If there is anything you need, please ask." An invitation lingered on her words and Loghan smiled to himself.

"I am here to heal, Sitari Beilis. If, after the prince is restored, you have anything you need to be addressed, I would be happy to assist. You should know, however, healers do not take their charge lightly. We heal. We do not make love."

"Pity."

Yes, it was. He tried to ignore her presence, but at the height of a man, and dressed in clothing that left little to the imagination, it was difficult. Several times she drifted from the front room back to where he worked, never speaking, just observing. As it turned out, he needed three items from the jungle, but since Taryn had the foresight to request the Sitari gather as much flora and fauna as they could, the ingredients were readily available.

He mashed herbs with flower petals, then simmered the mixture over an open flame. All the while, he sensed Taryn's desperation, her anxiety at how long it was taking. Her fear enveloped him, almost suffocating him in its intensity. While the antidote cooled, he went to kneel beside the prince. Taryn remained where she sat, her hands over Rhoane's heart, her head bent close to his lips.

Across from him, a huge white beast glared with golden eyes. One of her giant paws rested on the prince's arm, her stance protective, possessive. Next to her, a young woman held a towel beside the Eleri's head. He'd vomited the egg whites, which wasn't a good sign. His body would reject anything administered through the mouth. He'd have to think of another way to give him the antidote.

"Why is he still clothed?"

"The fabric stuck to the wounds. If we tried to remove his clothes, we'd take skin with it."

Loghan understood the reasoning, but was unaccustomed to working around fabric. Nothing about this was a regular healing, so he might as well get used to change. "It will not be much longer, Darennsai." He spoke in Eleri, hoping if Taryn heard the familiar language it might bring her cheer.

"Thank you."

She reached her hand to grasp his and for a brief moment,

the enormity of her love for Rhoane wrapped around his heart. What he thought of as his own great love for her was nothing compared to this. What a foolish boy he'd been to think she would love him in return. Foolish and selfish.

"He's my life, Loghan. I can't lose him."

Tears shimmered in her eyes and he felt the wet sting in his own. He'd heard a near identical plea from the prince when he discovered Taryn lying naked on the table in the healing tents. Rhoane had saved her then, not Loghan.

Rhoane's love. Yes, the prince's love had mended Taryn's broken bones, and knit together her torn skin. Had it really been so short a time past? He glanced at Taryn, at the turn of her lips, the healthy glow in her cheeks. He'd been certain she would die the first time he saw her, but she'd not only recovered, she'd fought one of his father's beasts in the arena.

Because of Rhoane's healing and love. As much as it pained him, he knew what he had to do.

"Taryn, I can only make the potion. It is you who must heal him."

She turned red-rimmed eyes on him. They were bluer than he remembered and full of despair. With each passing moment, she was losing hope.

"I can't. I've tried. My touch is torture to him. He isn't strong enough to handle it."

"Not…" he started, but the words were like sandpaper on his tongue. "Not Ullan healing. There is another way." By giving her this knowledge, he was breaking the oath he'd taken as a Healer. He was also doing what he must to save the prince's life. As much as he loved Taryn, and wanted her as his own, the pain and desperation in her eyes convinced him this is what must be done. She was never meant to be his. Verdaine had said as much, but he'd wished beyond all reason the goddess was wrong.

Loghan retrieved the cooled antidote from the kitchen and poured it into a wineskin.

"You must drink this first, then administer it to the prince."

Taryn took the wineskin, her lips flatlined. "Thank you."

"There is more." He hesitated, not sure he could let her go through this alone, but knowing he must. "You must be inside the prince when you give him the antidote, or he will reject it."

"Inside him? As in, I have to go inside his mouth?"

"His mouth, his pores, every orifice."

"Every orifice," she repeated. "Great."

"You must consume the antidote, then through you, he will absorb it."

"Yeah, I got that part. I'm just not sure how to get inside him without killing him in the process."

"Well, our usual methods will not work in this case."

"No kidding." Taryn's gaze roamed over the festering wounds on Rhoane's skin.

Beneath his clothing, nothing of the prince's natural body remained. He was a pile of bones and oozing flesh.

Loghan leaned forward to touch her shoulder. "You can do this, Darennsai. He needs you as you needed him in Ulla. Do not think, just act."

She took a deep breath and squared her shoulders. With one long gulp, she emptied the wineskin and tossed it aside. "That," she sputtered, "was revolting." She wiped her mouth and grimaced. "Here goes nothing."

Taryn bent lower until her lips met Rhoane's, then, slower than the sun rises, she slipped into the prince. What Loghan hadn't told the princess was that this was forbidden. Claiming another's body, even for healing, was against everything he held as true and right. He knew if he told Taryn these things, or what she might experience once inside, she would've faltered. If she hesitated at all, she and Rhoane would both be dead. What waited for her on the other side wasn't just Rhoane's cure, but her deepest fear.

CHAPTER FORTY-ONE

Taryn had half-expected to find herself miniaturized inside of Rhoane's body, clinging to a blood cell as a life preserver as she rushed through his bloodstream, past his beating heart and pulsating lungs. Instead, she was surrounded by nothing but darkness.

A tremor of recognition tickled her mind. This was eerily similar to the void.

"Hello, Taryn," a voice she knew all too well said from behind her. Or in front of her—there was no way to tell.

"Kaldaar." The long-honed fear she had for the god asserted itself and her shaky confidence faltered even more. She didn't need him undermining her attempt to heal Rhoane.

"Were you expecting someone else?"

The way he said "expecting" triggered warning bells, as if he'd been expecting her. The past day's events scanned through her memory. This was a trap. An elaborate, perfectly planned, trap. And she'd played right into it. Anger burned through her fear. Although, how was he to know she'd seek out Loghan's help and not Faelara's? Something told her if she'd tried to bring her friend or even Kaleigh, Kaldaar would've found a way to divert her to Loghan.

He'd known Loghan would suggest this as the only way to save Rhoane.

"Is Loghan working for you?"

Kaldaar laughed, but there was no merriment, no joy in the heartless echo. "Not hardly. He's too in love with you for me to have much influence."

In love with her? Loghan? She pushed aside the ridiculous idea. "What do you want?"

"You really have to ask? You are much stronger than when you first arrived, but not able yet to defeat me." A slight pause, as if he needed the break from talking or moving, as if the sheer energy it must be taking to be here, with her now, was taxing. Then, "I want you, Taryn ap Galendrin. On my side, by my side, with me for all eternity. We would rule many worlds, you and I."

Taryn shifted against the dead air of the in-between. "Is that why you've tried to kill Rhoane? So I can be free to make that commitment?"

"The *Surtentse* is as good as dead. There is nothing you can do to save him. The poison I used has no antidote."

His voice rasped harder now, his energy almost spent. The darkness surrounding her wavered and she saw something in the distance. It was hazy, but she thought it was a tree—dark and solemn against a stormy grey sky.

"They will never stop their quest to claim you, girl. The others. They think with your power, they will rule Aelinae. Their dreams are simple."

"While yours are far-reaching. You hate them, don't you?"

A hacking cough served for his laughter. "Hate is such a strange word. I love them for fearing me, but yes, I hate that they want to take away what is rightfully mine."

"I don't belong to you or anyone else."

"Not you, stupid girl. My divinity. The others think by killing me they will become gods themselves. But to do so, they need you."

"Who are the others?"

"Why should I tell you? The enemy of my enemy is my friend and all that."

Taryn knew the quote well. Who were Kaldaar's enemies? Zakael, certainly. Valterys was at one time, perhaps. Rykoto? Would a god destroy his own brother? She scoffed at the question. Of course he would. That's what started all of this—Kaldaar raped Rykoto's daughter, then applauded the god when he took a turn with Julieta. Gods could be just as cruel as the lesser beings, and equally petty.

A breeze raised the hairs around her face and she lifted a hand to smooth them back. She touched something solid and flinched. Kaldaar's rank breath assaulted her nostrils. He was close enough to touch. She froze. Unable to move, unable to think. Her head pounded and mouth went dry. Kaldaar could kill her. He would kill her. She should reach for her sword, but was paralyzed by fear. He'd always been able to kill her. Keeping her alive was part of the game.

Fighting past her inertia, she brought her knee up, hoping to connect with his groin, but there was nothing there. At least, nothing solid. His cackling laughter drifted away and the dank smell evaporated.

"Not today, girl. When you're strong enough to defeat me, then we shall see about a battle. It isn't fun when your opponent is unqualified."

Again, a tree wavered in the distance and this time, Taryn recognized it. The runyon tree at Caer Idris. She inched her way toward it, half surprised when it came into view. This wasn't the void she remembered from when she'd first arrived on Aelinae. That expanse of nothingness didn't have sound, or air, or anything to indicate movement, but it had a presence. Something sinister that had tried to seduce her. If it was Kaldaar, that was his first attempt to woo her to his side. She'd denied him then, and would again. He would never have her, even if it meant killing herself to keep him from gaining control over her power.

The tree came closer still, and now she could see a form in the thorn-ridden bark. The outline of a man, his face contorted in agony, his hands curled as if ready to strike. If Kaldaar was allowing her to see this, there had to be a reason why. The next minute, she understood.

The man trapped in the tree was familiar.

Rhoane.

Her heart chilled at the sight. Rage burned like ice through her veins. Kaldaar had poisoned Rhoane with sap from the runyon tree. No wonder he said there was no cure. The tree trunk shifted and more faces protruded from the bark, more victims of Kaldaar's vileness. Rhoane was crowded to the back of the tree and Taryn called out, begging him to come forward again.

Kaldaar's rasp sounded just behind her. "I told you he was as good as dead. Those souls feed this tree. Their fear sustains it."

"They'll never truly die. You've trapped them in hell."

"Isn't it lovely?"

The void was gone now and she stood on the clifftop near her father's castle. Slowly, she turned to face her nemesis. Instead of a man, or ball of flickering light, there was a shadowy form without face, or features, or limbs.

She took Ynyd Eirathnacht from its scabbard and held the sword in front of her. Kaldaar hissed and the shadow slithered a pace backward. Interesting. She brought the blade down until it was waist high, pointing toward Kaldaar. A deep-red glow came from the sword, something Taryn had never witnessed. White, yes, but never crimson. Blood. The color reminded her of blood.

Yes, the blood of his victims. She turned toward the tree. The thorns wept with a sticky substance the same color as her blade. She pulled her arm back and swung forward, impaling the trunk with the sharp tip. Screams from inside the tree rent the air and Taryn jerked her sword free. Kaldaar wheezed a chuckle. He'd expected this of her. *Damn.*

She paced the area, cursing Kaldaar, herself, and that fucking runyon tree. Kaldaar seemed to know every step she'd take before she even knew. What wouldn't he expect? What did she herself not even know she was capable of? She glared at the tree, thinking, her mind spinning like a top that never topples.

Shit. Fuck. Goddamn bastard. Fire. Yes, she'd burn the tree and to hell with those trapped inside. But wait, that's what he'd expect. The runyon tree oozed a sticky ochre substance and Taryn shivered. Fire would feed the tree—knowing her luck, it would make it bigger. She needed the opposite of fire—ice.

But how? She ran a hand through her hair, jerking several strands free of her braid. Once, long ago, the morning after her coronation in fact, she'd made fire and ice, but had never been able to duplicate it. Taryn stared up at the churning sky. A storm brewed over the sea and would soon cover Caer Idris. An ice storm? No, nothing that dramatic. Although, as the heir to the Crystal Throne, she had the capability to control weather. Except, she wasn't the heir any more. She'd given the mantle to Eliahnna. Yet she'd summoned fog to hold the ship captive in the harbor.

Her thoughts continued to spin out at random tangents, never landing on one long enough to focus.

"Time's wasting. Admit defeat. Join me."

"This is a test?" Of course it was. Everything the gods did was a fucking test.

"It's time you realize you need me. You can't save Rhoane without my help."

Taryn scoffed. "As if you were ever going to let him out."

She whirled around and stabbed at the shadow but it dissipated, only to reappear closer to the runyon tree. It was what she expected. Kaldaar was always a step ahead of her. Bastard.

Taryn studied the tree carefully, as if it were an artifact found on a dig. She analyzed and mentally sorted each pointed thorn and every crag of the bark.

"What do you hope to find?"

"None of your business."

"Be quick about it. We don't have all day."

"Actually, I do." Something in the way he hurried her made her think he expended huge amounts of energy just making the projection of the shadow. If she could wait him out, then perhaps she could find a solution to her problem without him hovering over her.

"Rhoane is dying, Taryn. If you don't think of something soon, he'll join the other lost souls for all eternity."

Terror coursed through her blood. He was right. She didn't have time to dick around. She returned her attention to the tree, a sense of urgency scattering her thoughts. After a minute of staring at the tree with unabashed worry, she leaned back and drew in a long breath. This was what Kaldaar wanted—for her to panic and make a mistake. He was waiting for something, but what?

Despair. For her to give up. Kaldaar fed on fear and misery. The more she panicked and worried, the stronger he became. That was why he distracted her from studying the tree. When she was analyzing, she wasn't fretting. The more control Taryn displayed, the less power he had—over her, the tree, and the souls locked inside.

The question was, then, how did she maintain control and destroy the tree?

"Has Rhoane told you of his path?" Kaldaar floated near the tree, black tendrils of smoke curling around the thorns.

Taryn shrugged off his question. It was more distraction and she was close to sorting out how to free Rhoane.

"Did he ever tell you how you came to be?"

"I'm not a child, Kaldaar. I know how making babies works."

His chuckle was like the clomping of horses' hooves. "Yes, but has he ever told you what *he* did to assure your birth?"

Annoyed with the game, Taryn turned her attention to the specter. "No. What did Rhoane do? You want to tell me, so go ahead."

The shadow drifted closer, but not too near she could reach him with Ynyd Eirathnacht.

"You don't know him at all, do you?" Kaldaar's voice dropped to a whisper. "He's a murderer."

Taryn's legs wobbled and the throbbing in her head sped up. She didn't want to know. When Rhoane's memories became hers, she'd blocked most of them. Some of the horrors she relived as if they were her own had brought fresh nightmares. She put her hands over her ears to block out Kaldaar's voice.

"He's a murderer." Kaldaar repeated in a sing-song voice. "He murdered Zakael's mother."

"No." Taryn shook her head. "Stop it."

"Killed her while she slept. An innocent woman. Murdered her without any remorse." Kaldaar's rank breath burned her nostrils. "He'll kill you just as easily. Without guilt. With pleasure."

"No," Taryn sobbed and sank to her knees. Ynyd Eirathnacht clambered to the ground, useless.

Kaldaar drifted toward the tree, his mocking laughter worming through her heart.

She scraped her nails over the hard dirt. Dust choked her sobs and she curled to her side, defeated. The truth of Kaldaar's words destroyed the last shred of hope she'd harbored. Rhoane's destiny was to kill her. As much as she wished they could control their fate, it was just that—a wish.

The last of her will drained into the terrarae. Her anguish and horror and love and hatred, all pooled around her in the dirt. A small rivulet of something dark traveled across the ground toward the runyon tree. Taryn watched it for a moment. Fresh terror ripped through her psyche.

She was feeding the tree.

That asshole god had tricked her. He was stealing her power to feed his own deficiencies.

Taryn scrambled to her feet and wiped her face with the backs of her hands. The agony and despair she'd felt lingered, but she shoved it deep. Past her insecurities and anxiety, down far enough she could focus on what needed to be done. Rhoane. Murderer or not, she had to free him.

Like a flash, she knew how to destroy the runyon tree. Her darathi vorsi. Her dragon breathed fire—why not ice? She was made of Light and Dark, sun and moon, fire and ice.

She took a step back and lifted her arms.

"What are you doing?" Kaldaar's voice came out as little more than a croak.

"Freeing them." Her body elongated into her darathi vorsi form. She glittered like silver jewels as scales replaced skin.

"Stop it! You'll destroy them!" But his words lacked truth. As she'd hoped, this was what Kaldaar feared more than her sword. He couldn't control her dragon.

Her vision and hearing sharpened and she turned her azure eyes on the shadowy form of Kaldaar. "You have no power over me, banished god." Taryn raised her snout toward the sky and sucked in air. She then aimed at Kaldaar's shadow and blew a freezing breath. The shadow cracked and for a split second, Taryn thought she saw the glint of a glass orb before black shards splintered and fell to the ground.

She twisted to face the runyon tree, uncertainty rippled through her. If this failed, she'd either condemn the souls to hell, or worse, kill them for good. She couldn't let them linger in purgatory any longer. Not if there was a chance of freeing them.

Once more, she lifted her snout to the sky and breathed in the raging storm clouds. Lightning cracked in the distance, startling her. It wouldn't do to lose her nerve now, not when she'd committed to her purpose. With a puff, she blew frigid air on the tree, spanning from the tips of each branch, to beneath the ground where roots twisted and furled under her talons.

Ice formed on the surface of the tree, causing it to crackle under the weight. She took in another gulp of cool air and blew a second round onto the frozen tree. More cracking sounded, echoing off the cliffs and castle far behind her. First one, then another, and yet another branch tore from the trunk of the runyon tree. Crash after crash, they fell, shattering as Kaldaar's shadow had. Taryn held her breath, hopeful the souls weren't trapped inside. Then, after a few moments, ghostly shapes drifted from the pile of rubble, drifting upward before dispersing into a million tiny lights. Her hope renewed with every spark.

It took five more tries to destroy the tree. Each one, more souls were released, but she didn't see Rhoane's corporeal form. The joy of freeing the others twisted to desperation. Rhoane had to be freed. What was the purpose otherwise?

When finally she panted against her efforts, the tree lay in ruins, the roots nothing more than crumbled bits of ash. She blew one last breath and the runyon tree was no more. Parts of it scattered over the ocean while more floated to the clouds. A mournful wail could be heard over the countryside. Kaldaar, she assumed, but had no idea where to find him. For now, her war with him had ended. His power was limited without his supply of fuel.

Taryn rested on all four legs, gazing at the expanse of water. She'd lost count of how many spirits were trapped in the tree, but the only one that mattered wasn't there. Kaldaar had tricked her again, in the cruelest way imaginable. He'd taken Rhoane.

Heavy tears dripped from her snout to *plop* upon the ground. She curled her talons around each one, burying them deep in the dirt. If she had to travel to Dal Ferran to find Rhoane, she would. She'd not stop searching until he was by her side.

She lifted from the cliff and soared over the dark sea. A bolt of lightning flashed to her left and she veered right, cutting her turn so sharp she stared into the tumultuous water. A long shape wove beneath the white caps and Taryn's dragon heart beat faster. She dove straight for the water, transforming into a woman the moment her snout touched the cold waves. The speed with which she'd been traveling propelled her deep beneath the surface, exactly as she'd hoped.

Xianqin's face appeared from the darkness. Long whiskers furled around her, and a blue-scaled muzzle stopped an inch from her face.

"He's gone. Rhoane's gone." Taryn said by way of greeting. She stroked one of Xianqin's whiskers—the closest thing she had to a hug.

"Not every death is in vain."

"Please, no riddles. Not right now. Kaldaar took Rhoane and I had hoped you'd help me find him." Taryn kicked to swim away, but the water dragon stopped her.

Xianqin shook her head, making the long whiskers snap and snarl. "Your faith is limiting. The prince is no longer in danger. Your antidote worked, but so did Kaldaar's plan to separate you."

"I'm going to kill him," Taryn muttered, more to herself then Xianqin.

"Only a god can destroy another god."

"Then I'll find a god strong enough. He has to be stopped." Taryn would search every realm if she had to. "But wait, I thought gods weren't really destroyed, only banished. Is it truly possible to kill a god?"

"Everyone has a weakness. Kaldaar knows yours. You must discover his."

Gods had weaknesses. It never occurred to her.

"If I didn't know better, I'd say you're following me," Taryn ran a hand along Xianqin's snout.

"Someone has to watch over you." The water dragon

motioned toward the surface. "You are far too reckless, young Darennsai."

"I know. I feel bad about that." Taryn continued to stroke the darathi eneari's muzzle. "Thank you. For saving me."

"You will save us all in time. It is the least I could do." Xianqin nudged her hand. "They are waiting for you and the prince. It is time."

"Time for what?"

"For their return."

Taryn looked at Xianqin's aquamarine eyes, not quite understanding. Her thoughts were still with Rhoane and the runyon tree. "Whose return?"

"The darathi vorsi. They have waited a long time for you. But first, you must travel to your beloved. He is anxious for your touch."

"Where is he?" Even as she asked, she saw Rhoane in the treehouse of the Sitari. He was weak, but alive. "Thank you," Taryn said. "For everything."

"When you remember who you are, then you may thank me. Now, my darling, sleep." Xianqin opened her mouth wide, displaying huge white fangs and sharp teeth that stretched to the far reaches of her mouth. A pink tongue unfurled and Taryn felt herself slide onto its softness. *Sleep. Sleep now, my darling.*

Taryn fought as hard as she could, but her eyelids drooped and her body relaxed against her will. The darathi eneari sang to her as she fell into a web of darkness. Taryn recognized the song —it was one her sword often sang. She held onto the melody, letting the words cover her like a warm blanket.

CHAPTER FORTY-TWO

Bright sunlight stung her eyes and water flooded her open mouth. She was on a beach, but where? Taryn rolled to her back, immediately regretting the movement. Her sword's scabbard pressed against her back, making her arch uncomfortably. She flung a hand over her eyes to block the persistent sun and slid to her side. Birds chirped in nearby trees, stirring a memory. Warm water splashed on her cheek and she lifted her head to gaze into a thick forest.

She was either on a Summerlands or Sitari island. Gods, but she ached all over. She pulled the scabbard's strap over her head and flopped to her back. She should get out of the water, but movement of any kind didn't sound alluring. She turned her ankles, groaning against the stiffness found there. Next, she bent her knees and flexed her legs one at a time. Her wrists were followed by her arms and shoulders. Everything was in working order, but sore as hell. Rolling onto all fours, she arched like a cat, feeling the strain of her muscles. She dipped her belly low and stretched her chest, her head reaching toward her bum.

A shadow fell over her and she looked up, surprised and a little pissed she hadn't heard someone approach. Her sword was within hand's reach, but she sensed no danger from whoever stood a few paces away. With the sun angled behind him, he was a dark silhouette.

"Your Highness, I found her," he called over his shoulder.

Taryn recognized Loghan's deep timbre.

He stepped forward, a hand extended. "We were worried about you."

She took his hand and groaned as she was lifted. "I was worried about me, too. What the hell am I doing out here?" She turned and scanned the shore, seeing several Sitari emerge from the lush vegetation. "Where's Rhoane?"

"He is well, Darennsai. Just after you entered his body, his breathing leveled, and the blisters healed. What happened?"

She scooped her sword from the shallow waves and shook her head. "I'm not really sure."

A crashing sound came from the jungle and she stepped around Loghan. Rhoane burst through the trees, looking healthy and relieved. He sprinted across the sand to swoop her into a hug.

She gripped him as forcefully as he her. "I thought I had lost you."

"And I you."

"How long was I gone?"

"Two days." He set her down and inspected every inch of her, starting at her face, then making his way down to her toes, and up to her face again. "What happened?"

"I met up with an old friend. I'll tell you about it later."

The Sitari emerged from the jungle, and Kaida with them. The grierbas bound to Taryn's side and nuzzled her hip. She bent and rested her forehead against Kaida's. It was good to be with her and Rhoane again. Her heart beat stronger in their presence.

Two days. The last she remembered, Xianqin told her to sleep. Yet exhaustion tugged at her like a soaking wet wool blanket. Scratchy and sodden. Something wasn't right. With the timeline, and elsewhere, elusive. Xianqin had wanted her reunited with Rhoane too badly. Had even warned her that Kaldaar's plan was to separate them. But why?

"I'm starving. You wouldn't happen to have food in your wonderful tree houses, would you?"

Rhoane took her hand in his, igniting their runes with his touch. "You have no idea what a relief it is to see them glow."

"What do you mean?"

"During your absence, they turned a nasty shade of grey."

"And they were flaking," Loghan added.

"Flaking? Like they were peeling off?" Taryn turned her wrist where the small tattoo rested within her ghostly runes. Kaldaar was trying to sever their bond. After everything they'd been through, he sought to break her spirit. That was the key to taking her power. Make her believe she'd lost everything. Exploit her weakness.

"Exactly. But I never lost hope."

"Hope." Taryn smiled. "That's what I always say. We need to have hope."

She'd forgotten that on the clifftop. Hope had eluded her when she saw Rhoane trapped in the runyon tree. What a fool she'd been.

"And do you, Darennsai? Do you still hope?" Rhoane asked, his eyes misty.

Taryn lifted her face to the sun to feel its warmth. She'd been too long in the cold of Kaldaar's shadow.

"Yes. I do." She gripped Rhoane's hand. "With you by my side, and friends like Loghan, how could I not?"

"We owe this man much, my love." Rhoane's lips brushed against her temple. His power flooded through her.

"That we do. He's been instrumental in saving both of our lives." A flutter of insecurity upset her good mood. "Were you in my thoughts while I was gone?"

"I am not sure. I have strange recollections."

They climbed the endless stairs leading to the tree houses in silence. Rhoane might've been in her thoughts, or in the tree—she wasn't sure. At least he was safe for now.

A meal had been prepared and they sat at a long table to dine. A hearty stew was served in thick trenches of bread and Taryn swooned over the smell. Rough chunks of meat swam in a glorious gravy with root vegetables. She sopped her bread in the juices and savored the taste. The conversation during their meal centered on harvesting times and planting schedules, something Taryn never would've associated with the warriors.

As she sat between Loghan and Rhoane, she listened carefully to the banter between the women. This was a society built on respect. Shandris was clearly their leader, but each woman had the opportunity to speak and when they did, the others listened respectfully. Twice Taryn spied Beilis slipping scraps of beef to Kaida, who had sat beside the Sitari during the meal.

"You know," Taryn offered when there was a lull in the conversation, "there's a ship in your harbor with several sailors who might not mind a night in a warm bed."

The women chattered among themselves, each looking to Shandris with eyes filled with desire.

"To uphold your reputation and all that." Taryn added.

"Will you be staying, then?" Shandris inquired. She held a dagger in her hand, a chunk of beef dripping from the tip.

"A few days at least. I still need to see Mallaqai."

"Mallaqai is dead." Shandris shoved the meat into her mouth.

Taryn swirled a hunk of bread around her bowl, sopping up gravy. "It's been my experience that death doesn't make someone unavailable."

Shandris's brow rose, but she didn't correct Taryn. "I suppose if the men would like to come ashore, we could see to some comfort for them."

"What are your plans for Adesh's women?" Rhoane asked.

"I was hoping you'd take them with you when you leave."

"Do any of them want to stay?" Taryn sipped her drink, grimacing at the sourness of the wine.

A gasp went around the room.

"They are not Sitari," Beilis protested.

"So? You would deny a woman residence because her skin isn't blue? That's ridiculous."

"You do not understand the Sitari." Shandris warned.

"What I don't understand is forbidding someone something just because they aren't like you." Taryn took a deep breath. "I don't want to start an argument. I was just asking if any of the women had expressed a desire to remain on your island. The mainland can be tough for women like them." Taryn hoped they understood her meaning. Whores like Armando were well paid and taken care of, but street whores risked their lives every moment of every day.

Shandris set down her knife and scrubbed a hand over her face. She pulled on the tips of her ponytail. "We'll discuss this and make a decision before you leave."

"That's all I'm asking for." Taryn plucked a spiky orange fruit from a tray and held it up. "I've never seen one of these. What is it?"

"A grumlil."

Taryn hoped it tasted better than the name implied. She cut it in half with a dagger and took a dainty bite. The sour-sweet taste tickled her tongue. It was like nothing she'd had before.

"Interesting." A lingering sweetness coated her tongue, reminding her of a candy she used to buy at the corner store in London. The memory triggered an involuntary homesickness. She hadn't thought of London or Earth in a long time.

Rhoane wrapped an arm around her shoulders and pulled her against him. She snuggled into his warmth, grateful she didn't have to defend or explain her feelings.

After the meal, Taryn, Loghan, and Rhoane were led to where Adesh's women were kept and she had to endure several minutes of gawking and rude comments made about her betrothed. After the women finally settled down, Rhoane handled the interrogation while Taryn leaned against a far wall, observing. Loghan, clearly uncomfortable with the attention the women paid, stood behind Rhoane, using the Eleri as a buffer.

Several times she caught him glancing her way, concern lacing his features. When their eyes met, he'd look away, guilt cutting through the concern. He was a strange one, to be sure. After nearly a quarter bell of asking the women questions, without getting any real answers, Rhoane excused himself and left the room. Loghan followed, which left Taryn alone with the whores.

The women regarded her with skepticism. Their seasons of betrayal and brutality etched on their features. Taryn remained still, her heart quickening with the prolonged silence. Except for a few, these women looked as if they'd prefer her dead. Their ratty hair and dirty clothes weren't from living in the cramped room, but from neglect on the women's part.

One of the younger of the group lifted her chin and met Taryn's gaze. "You're promised to the prince, aren't you?"

If she was looking for permission to bed Rhoane, she'd be sorely disappointed. "I am."

"They say you'll bring a new age to Aelinae. More prosperity, better crops, a new way of life."

Several of the women scoffed and one spat on the floor.

"Who are 'they'?" Taryn asked the young girl. She couldn't have been more than seventeen seasons. The same age as Eliahnna.

"People on the streets. Customers." The girl shrugged. "Ain't nothin' to me, is it?"

Taryn studied each face, the hopelessness in them tugging on her heartstrings. "If you could choose a different life, would you?"

A bout of laughter answered.

"We ain't never had a choice." One of the older whores spoke out. "Not like you lot. Wearing yer fancy clothes an' sipping yer rich wines." She hawked a glob of sputum at Taryn's feet.

Fury blazed along her skin. These women had no idea. She was never given a choice, either. Instead of lashing out, Taryn drew in a long breath.

"What happened to Adesh and Amanda?"

Blank stares met her glare.

"If you don't want to tell me, that's fine. But seeing as I'm the only person who can get you off this island, you might want to rethink your choices."

"They enjoy this line of work. I don't." The young girl blurted. Her eyes widened and the fear in their depths was like a punch to Taryn's gut. "Please don't make me go back to the streets. Take me with you. I can be your maid or fetch you water, whatever it takes. I can't spend another moment beneath a man I hate."

Her words chilled Taryn. "I can promise you passage to Talaith, but that's all."

The older whore grunted and spat another glob to the floor.

"Your boss sent men to kill me. So, you'll forgive me if my trust is a little low right now."

"He what?" The younger girl trembled and bit her cuticle. "We didn't know. Adesh said it was his usual voyage to Menurra. When we were boarded, we were told to pleasure the men and not ask questions. But there was something odd about the whole thing. A few of us were sent to the other ship." She looked to the others for corroboration, but they wouldn't meet her eyes.

Taryn watched the interplay with interest. Some of the whores had known what was going to happen. "Who was on the other ship?"

"He wouldn't say, but we had the feeling he was powerful. A lord, certainly by the way he carried himself."

"With dark hair and storm cloud eyes?" Taryn's insides roiled.

"How did you know?" The girl leaned forward and whispered. "He liked it rough and he wore a gold ring around his cock. Have you ever?"

Yes, she had. Fucking Zakael *had* been there. "How did you end up here? Why didn't Adesh stay with his ship?"

"Oh, that." Her thumb made its way back to her greedy teeth. "Adesh sold his ship. Said he made enough to settle on his own island and live out his days like a lord. A third ship came a few days after the lordship's and the women were loaded aboard. Next thing I know, I'm tossed ashore and told to find my own way home."

The other whores squirmed and clucked, clearly uncomfortable with the admission.

"Did you meet another man who goes by the name Cashiel?"

Several whores looked away—at their feet, at the walls, anywhere but at Taryn or the young girl.

"No, never saw him. Heard that name, though." The girl said, her thumb forgotten. "The men feared him something fierce. Truth be told, I'm glad to be rid of the lot."

"What about you?" Taryn asked the older whore. "Are you glad to be rid of Adesh? Or are you waiting for another ship to arrive and take you back to Talaith?"

Several heads swiveled in the old whore's direction.

"I don't know what ye mean. I 'ate it just as much as the others."

Taryn didn't believe her for a second. She could shove her power into the woman's mind, but Taryn didn't relish what she'd find there.

"I'm sure you do." Taryn left it at that and excused herself.

Something wasn't right. Why did Adesh bring the women here and leave them? She retraced her steps to the main tree house and paused in the entryway. Kaida lay sprawled on her side, head in Beilis's lap, enjoying a good tummy rub.

The Sitari glanced up and caught Taryn watching her.

Instead of making a fuss, Taryn gave a brief smile and turned to head down the stairs. They might be feared warriors, but beneath their tattooed blue skin, the Sitari were like everyone else.

Rhoane and Loghan sat on a driftwood log, their heads bent in conversation.

"Am I interrupting?" she asked as she came out of the jungle.

"We were just trying to determine what caused the fog around your ship." Loghan pointed to the swirling grey mist in the harbor.

Taryn scrunched her nose. "That might be my doing." With a flick of her wrist, she released the fog. Rhoane chuckled and Loghan gaped at her.

"What? I am the daughter of the Lady of Light, who, as you know, has weather capabilities. I might've learned a few tricks from her."

"Well met on this day," Loghan joked as he stood.

Taryn cocked her head, eyes narrowed. "Where have you heard that phrase?"

Loghan shrugged, his lips pursed. "I do not know. From Father, perhaps. Did I say it wrong?"

"No," Taryn began, "it's just that I've not heard it before and was surprised."

Rhoane studied her, his expression cautious. She shook her head and in his mind, promised to explain later.

"I suppose one of us should tell the captain they are welcome onshore." Loghan stood.

Before they could stop him, Loghan shouted to the ship, waving his arms to get their attention. In short order, a dingy lowered and the captain rowed ashore. While they waited, Taryn told the men about her chat with the captain before she went to find Loghan. Rhoane's jaw twitched with suppressed anger and his fists clenched, but he said nothing. She knew him well enough to know when to stay silent, but Loghan didn't. He roared his disapproval and threatened to poison the captain if he didn't make amends.

When he moved to storm across the sand, Taryn stopped him. "Loghan, men will do many things for money. This wasn't personal for the captain or his crew."

"So now you trust them? Just like that?" He snapped his fingers.

"Of course not, but there's something much bigger happening here. We don't have time to waste on one man. Question him if you will, hell, interrogate his entire crew, but I doubt you'll find any more information than the whores supplied." Taryn watched his retreating back and sat with a heavy sigh beside Rhoane.

"He is in love with you, you know."

"Loghan?" Taryn snorted. "I seriously doubt that."

Rhoane took her hand in his, smiling when their runes lit up. "Just as I believed Marissa was not in love with me."

"Ouch." She traced a rune with her fingertip. It resembled a castle on a crag. "I don't return his affection, if you're worried."

"I know you do not." He tipped her chin until she was looking at him. Fear lurked in his moss-green eyes—not for Loghan, she hoped. "I am in your thoughts, remember? I know you see him only as a friend. And now that you are in my thoughts, you know I never intentionally led Marissa on, but people are curious creatures. They will believe what they wish to be true."

"Don't I know it. A girl in the room up there told me Zakael was on a second ship. Most likely he orchestrated the whole thing."

More words were on her lips. Questions about what happened in the two days she was absent, what Kaldaar meant about Rhoane murdering Zakael's mother, and more. But she bit her cheek to keep from asking. When they were alone, she'd get her answers.

Shandris and several other Sitari emerged from the jungle, their blue skin painted with ash. Each held a spear in their hand, with several daggers folded into thick belts. Taryn and Rhoane stayed where they were. This was Sitari land. It was Shandris's law the captain and his men would have to follow. The group spoke low, but not too low Taryn couldn't hear. Shandris was upset with the captain's betrayal and ordered him and his men to stay on the shore. If they set foot in the jungle without a Sitari guide, they would be killed on the spot.

Taryn raised an eyebrow, curious why she wasn't more upset at the captain. He'd tried to kill Rhoane—she should be livid, but empathy won out. She felt bad for him. The captain was lured here, the same as them. For different purposes, but by the same man, no doubt.

"If Kaldaar wanted us here so badly, there must be something he wants us to discover." Taryn stood, bringing Rhoane up with her. "Come on. While they're busy negotiating, let's do some exploring."

They strolled to the edge of the jungle and took one last look at the others before slipping behind the thick foliage. For several minutes, they trekked over tree trunks and beneath thick leaves until they came to a small opening. Taryn gripped Rhoane's hand tighter. "Hold on."

In a flash, she'd transported them to the middle island. \

"I will never get used to that." Rhoane placed a hand over his stomach.

"You might want to work on that. It's a wicked fast way to travel. Now," Taryn said, glancing around, "what are we supposed to find?"

They scoured the island, finding nothing more than a large lake that was fed by a smaller island above. No dwellings, no signs of life save for the plants that grew on the island. They both used their ShantiMari to aid in their search, and still they found nothing.

"I think we need to go higher." Taryn took Rhoane's hand. "Think your tummy can handle it?"

"It is nice to see you have not lost your sense of humor."

She grinned and made the leap to the smaller island. There, shimmering like he'd just stepped out of the pool of water to his left, was Brandt.

CHAPTER FORTY-THREE

Taryn's belly fluttered and a sob caught in her chest. What she saw couldn't be real. It had been too long since his last visit. Too much had happened since she'd seen her grandfather. There was so much she wanted to share, but words failed her. She stumbled forward and embraced him, surprised by his solidity.

"Baba." She snuffled back tears and breathed in his scent of tobacco and cologne. "What are you doing here? How is this possible?"

"I'm breaking all the rules." His gaze took in Rhoane. "I see you survived the poisoning. I was hoping Loghan would be beneficial."

"You sent me to Loghan? But I thought Kaldaar had planned everything."

"He was getting stronger, as you know, so I felt it necessary to step in. I'm sure Nadra and Ohlin won't be pleased with me, but I couldn't let you be destroyed by that vile creature. He doesn't play fair, so why should I?" Brandt looped her arm in his and strolled along the edge of the pool.

"You led us here?" Taryn's head spun. Birds chirped in nearby trees, and the gentle sound of a waterfall brought a sense of serenity to the area. "What about Mallaqai?"

"Oh, she's still hanging about. That was truly her who gave you the warning through Saeko. I just haven't figured out whose side she's on." Brandt patted her hand, his brows furrowed.

How she'd missed him. Taryn leaned in and breathed deep. If she closed her eyes, she could picture them in London, in their flat above the pub. Happy. Unaware of Aelinae or all the troubles they'd encounter. Except, Brandt had always known about Aelinae, and London was nothing more than a place for them to hide.

"In the Great War, she fought for Rykoto." Rhoane drew her out of her memories. By his tone, it was clear who's side he thought Mallaqai was on.

"Yes, she did, which makes one wonder if her allegiance is so easily turned." Brandt countered.

"But her warning helped us."

"Did it?"

Taryn traveled with Rhoane's thoughts to the day Cashiel attacked her mother's ship.

"Mallaqai spoke through Saeko. She said Taryn was in the ocean, being guided by an old friend. She also said Taryn sought her death." Rhoane tugged at a braid, his face set in a scowl. "Two truths and one lie. Did she mean to say she'd told me two truths and one lie? Or, something else? I found Taryn in the desert, not the ocean. But Xianqin *had* rescued Taryn."

Brandt rubbed a thumb over his lips and nodded absently. "That she did. But as for the witch, we shall see."

"If Mallaqai was not trying to help that day, then why seek me out? Why pretend to give assistance and claim to be allies?"

"A changeling does not give without getting something in return. What was your payment, Rhoane?"

Taryn watched him, wary of his answer. His thoughts tumbled the same as hers, his confusion just as debilitating.

"A kiss."

Taryn raised an eyebrow. "A kiss, kiss? Or just a peck on the lips?"

"A peck. I would not debase myself with that witch more than necessary." His affront came through with every syllable, which made Taryn happy for selfish reasons.

They stopped beside the waterfall and the crashing water echoed the beating of her heart. "Then what's the problem? It's not like he's sheanna or anything."

"Witches know the ways of the mind, Taryn. If Rhoane was distracted enough, she could've plucked any number of memories from his thoughts."

Rhoane's shock reflected her own. "You think she meant to steal from me?"

Brandt shrugged and raised his hands, palms up. "What do you know about the ruins where Mallaqai once lived?"

Taryn looked out toward the Spine of Ohlin on the mainland. The ruins were to the west of them, on the plains. She'd flown over them once, but couldn't recall learning much about the ruins in her research.

"Only what legend says. Mallaqai lived there. She fought on the side of Rykoto during the Great War. When they lost, she cursed the women of her village, giving them their blue skin and marking them as outcasts." Taryn recited the scant information she knew.

Brandt turned and strolled toward the far edge of the pool. "In here, you'll find some answers. Not all, but enough to aid in your journey." He gazed toward Dal Tara, a pinch to his brow. "I've said more than I should." He reached for Taryn, and she wrapped her arms around him. "I don't think they'll be letting me loose any time soon. I'll do what I can, but Nadra believes this must be your path, yours to succeed or fail. Both of yours."

"Understood."

Rhoane embraced the both of them, but a moment later, Brandt was gone.

"Do you think they'll be pissed at Grandfather?"

"I would not worry overmuch about Brandt." Rhoane stripped off his clothes. "We have a mystery to solve."

Taryn tossed her garments atop his and stood with her toes hanging over the rock. "Ready?"

They dove into the pool together, swimming to the depths. They searched along the rocky bottom before turning their attention to the sides. Clear water made their search easier, but with each passing minute, Taryn's frustration grew. She had no idea what they were looking for, or why, yet she continued to scan the pool for something, anything.

Rhoane discovered a small tunnel hidden behind a thick tuft of weeds. He swam into it first, using his power to light the way. It was short, perhaps ten paces or so, but cramped, making it hard for Taryn and Rhoane to edge their way through. At the end, the tunnel turned upward and opened to a large cavern.

With two strokes she broke the water's surface. Rhoane tread water beside her, his gaze scanning the area.

Glittering crystals studded the walls and Taryn gasped at the similarities of this cavern to the one on Mount Nadrene. Unlike Nadra's cavern, this one had been lived in at one time. There were crude furnishings: a bed, a desk, even a kitchen of sorts. There were no windows, but the crystals provided adequate light by which to see. They explored the area, turning over linens that still smelled fresh, shuffling through papers that could've been written the previous day.

"Everything's so clean. You'd think there would be dust, or mold, or something." Taryn flipped through a stack of vellum sheets, taking one from the pile. "Rhoane, read this."

He scanned the page, his brows making a deep V in his forehead. "If this is true," his eyes held fresh terror when he looked at her, "then I gave Mallaqai exactly what she wanted."

"The kiss?" Taryn pawed through more papers, her irritation at Rhoane kissing Saeko for Mallaqai's sake lessening with each page she uncovered.

"No," Rhoane mumbled, his eyes scanning the page. "Something far more valuable." He set the paper down and breathed out long and slow.

Taryn heard him, but her attention was drawn to the papers in her hands. The notes and scribblings hit a familiar chord and Taryn re-read a few pages to sort out her thoughts. These weren't ramblings of a mad witch. On several pages detailed instructions were written in a scrawl Taryn didn't recognize. The purpose of them, she did.

"Oh my God, Rhoane," She handed him two more pages. "This tells how to open portals and this one gives their locations on Aelinae."

She picked up the final page and her gaze flicked over it. Dread oozed down her spine with each word she read. Other worlds, and the creatures found there, were listed in alphabetical order. Not in Elennish, but English. Old English, to be exact.

Taryn's heart rammed beneath her ribs and her breath came in short drags. She glanced at the table and froze.

Tucked into the corner, a velvet cloth draped over something round in shape. Taryn knew what was hidden beneath—a glass sphere the size of a bowling ball. She knew of only one person on Aelinae who possessed such a thing. Even as the thought tumbled through her mind, she fought against it. Myrddin was her friend. He'd been one of Brandt's closest friends.

Myrddin was older than anyone else on Aelinae. Certainly old enough to learn about portals and other worlds and archaic languages.

Myrddin wouldn't betray Brandt. Couldn't betray Lliandra. Could he?

Rhoane opened his mouth to speak, but she put a finger to his lips and with her other hand pointed to the looking glass.

I've seen something like this before, in Celyn Eryri. It was in Myrddin's tower. I found it when I was looking for him after Ellie was attacked.

What is it? Rhoane crept closer to inspect the velvet covering.

I think he uses it to spy on people. I didn't really think much of it. I mean, everyone has spies at the Crystal Palace. Hell, even we have our own pair of spies.

What is it doing here?

Good question. I think these might give us a clue. She handed the pages to Rhoane and watched the play of emotion across his face as he read. He was equally as horrified as she.

Taryn slipped her hand beneath the cloth, unsure if Myrddin knew they'd been there or not, but not wanting to leave anything to chance. She pulsed her power into the glass, filling it until it burst into thousands of tiny shards. Several cut her hand and she winced. Another pulse of ShantiMari and the remnants of glass turned to ash. The velvet, too.

Rhoane cocked his head, "Did you hear that?"

Taryn listened, but only the sound of her head pounding filled her ears. "No, what is it?"

"I believe whoever these belong to, they know we destroyed them." He indicated the pile of rubbish on the table.

"Take the papers and let's get out of here." She headed for the tunnel and stopped. "Um, how do you suppose we should carry them?" She indicated her naked body.

"Perhaps you could do that thing you do?" Rhoane's grin and slight shake of his head brought levity to the situation.

"Let's make sure we have everything we'll need. I don't want to come back." She eyed the pile of ash and shuddered. "Why would he come to this place?"

"No one would think to look here. I doubt we would have found it without Brandt's help."

"True." Brandt and Myrddin were close before Taryn was born. Like brothers. Her grandfather had to have known it was

Myrddin using the place, and not Mallaqai. He wouldn't have risked the anger of gods if not. "What if it wasn't really Mallaqai that spoke through Saeko?"

Rhoane gave her a guarded look. "Who do you think it was?"

"I don't know, but things are getting weird. It's hard to believe what I see, or trust anything I hear."

He reached for her and placed his palm against hers, runes to runes. "We can trust this." He stood with his legs on either side of hers, their bodies pressed together. "Our hearts beat as one, have you noticed?"

She closed her eyes and listened to the rhythm of their hearts. It was true—they beat in unison. Hers tripped with the realization and his copied the hiccup. "Does that mean we're one person? Just, in two bodies?"

"I am not sure what it means. But I do know I will not betray you, Taryn ap Galendrin. I do not care what Xianqin or Mallaqai say. I will not be the cause of your death."

Hearing him make the promise sent a spiral of relief through her. She knew he'd never willingly hurt her. Somewhere, in the depths of her soul, she knew he spoke true. She also knew what it felt like to lose all hope and to lose faith in not only him, but herself.

"I believe you. I vow to never lose faith in us. We have to have hope, always." She stood on tiptoe to kiss him, savoring his scent and taste. "You always smell so damn good." A flicker caught her attention and she glanced to her left, where the runes lifted from their skin. "Um, Rhoane?"

He followed her gaze and sucked in a breath. As soon as he removed his hand from hers, the runes settled into their skin. When he pressed his palm to hers, they lifted again, floating on the air, looking eerily similar to ancient Egyptian markings on a tomb. Taryn studied the pattern of runes, making mental notes of what came from her hand versus his. Not all of the runes danced in the air. Several remained ghost tattoos on their skin.

"We should copy these down for future reference."

"My love," Rhoane chuckled, "there is no need." He pulled his hand away and the runes settled into place. "We have them already."

It was true, but having a single sheet with the images would be easier than sorting the individual runes from their respective hands. Instead of arguing, she nodded agreement. They still stood naked in the strange cavern and she wasn't entirely sure Myrddin's destroyed looking glass couldn't see or hear them. It wouldn't do to feed him information, not when they weren't sure what the information was or if it would cause harm.

"Gather what you can. I'd like to study the papers further before heading back to Talaith. I figure we'll leave day after next." Taryn's mind whirled with plans.

The two days would give the crew and Sitari ample time to play, and by then hopefully Shandris would bend her will enough to allow some of the women to stay on the island. Adesh might not have realized it, but by bringing the women here, he might have saved their lives. If only the whores would see it that way.

They returned to the tree houses and set up in a spare hut far from the main living area. Taryn and Rhoane placed several wards around the small room, deterring anyone from entering while they were away. Sprawled across a table were the papers they'd taken from Mallaqai's rooms.

All, except for the two lists in English, were written in an old text. Rhoane knew enough of the archaic language to translate most of the writing. It sounded like gibberish, the ramblings of a mad person, but Taryn had a gut feeling there was something more, the meaning escaping them.

Mallaqai, or Myrddin, or whoever had used that room, had marked thirteen places on a crude map of Aelinae. Taryn peered closer at the markings, and the page of runes she'd made for her benefit, matching several of the shapes.

"I think I know where I've seen these. They were on the seals at the Temple of Ardyn. I put wards on all the seals and columns, sort of an alarm system to alert me if anyone tried taking them. I remember each one, but some were missing." She pointed at the paper. "I'll bet these are them. What does it mean?"

Rhoane studied the runes, his face intent, lips pursed.

"Perhaps we should visit the temple, to make sure none of the seals have been tampered with. We might uncover the meaning there." He leaned forward, inspecting a single image. "Why is Mount Nadrene with these other runes? Surely that was not on one of the seals?"

Taryn recounted the seals at the temple, and he was right. Mount Nadrene hadn't been on any of them. But she had seen it before—on the seal Brandt had smuggled in her backpack. "It's from the seal we brought from, um, where we were living."

Rhoane turned to her, brows lifted, questions dancing in his eyes. "Truly? I do not recall seeing an image, only words scrolling across the surface."

"Beneath the words, there was always an image. It took me some time to see it, but once I did, I couldn't not see it. Does that make sense?" Excitement edged her words. They were close, she could feel it. Close to discovering what the images meant.

He scrunched his face, contemplating.

"Do you suppose these are a road map?" Taryn continued, her voice rising with her enthusiasm. "Like, to other worlds? Think about it. The seal Brandt had in his possession showed Mount Nadrene, where the portal is. These other pictures could be where more portals are."

"It does make a certain amount of sense." He poked an image with his fingertip. "Show me your location," he commanded, but the rune stubbornly remained unaffected. "It was worth a try."

Taryn grinned at his attempt. She was about to try the same thing. They were complete opposites in many respects, but remarkably similar in others. Two halves of the same whole. Yin and yang.

Rhoane lowered his face close to the papers, almost as if he were sniffing them. "What do you see here?" he said against the grainy sheets of parchment.

"You kissing the paper?" She meant it as a joke, but Rhoane's merriment had vanished with his inspection. "Let me see."

He moved aside and she squinted at the papers, trying to focus on minute details. One image in particular sent ice through her veins. It showed a ruined castle, half hidden by a slash, as if fabric had been torn, and above that, a dragon.

CHAPTER FORTY-FOUR

Rhoane pushed away from the table, away from the awful image he saw within the image, but it wasn't enough. The scene continued to unfold in his mind—of Mallaqai standing before a great rift in time and space, her staff held aloft, her chanted words swirling with the wind. She called forth the darathi vorsi, and they obeyed. They came in flocks of hundreds. They came to their damnation.

The witch Mallaqai had always resented the Eleri. It was well known how she'd tried to seduce not one, but three Eleri kings, each time being rebuffed for her efforts. After the Great War, she'd cursed the women of her village with long, pointed ears, and blue skin to mock the gentility of all Eleri. Then, once she'd maimed her kin, she set about destroying the bond the Eleri had with Aelinae's darathi.

The winged beasts flew to her for reasons Rhoane couldn't comprehend. One by one, they dove into the vortex, never to be seen again. In the macabre vision, he watched them soar to their deaths, impotent to save them.

"No," Taryn interrupted the horrible illusion, "there was nothing you could do then. We can save them now." She took his face between her warm hands. "You wear the Crown of Awakening. It is time. Now we know where Mallaqai's portal is, we can go through it and reclaim the darathi."

It was risky, but she was right. Nadra had placed the crown upon his head at Dal Tara. Was it truly just a moonturn past? He flexed his marked hand, recalling the roots and leaves he'd witnessed growing from his arm that night. Taryn's skin had glistened with an abundance of stars. Nadra had called her Daughter of the Sky, and he Son of the Terrarae.

He should've known then he, too, was destined for divinity, but his focus had been solely on Taryn. It was time he remembered who he was. He was an Eleri prince, betrothed to Taryn ap Galendrin, Darennsai of his people, and he their Surtentse. Together, they would bring life to new worlds. They would shape and mold them into fantastical universes where mortals would live and breathe, would love and hate, would live and die.

Species would come and go, yet he and Taryn would remain. Ever watchful, ever vigilant, ever aloof.

Taryn gasped and he saw in her eyes the realization she never saw this future for herself. Never knew she was to become a goddess.

"I'm just a girl," she said without conviction.

"You are so much more than that, mi carae."

She squinted and a slow smile curled her lips. "What a remarkable thing." Her gaze drifted beyond the rough-hewn walls of the Sitari treehouse. "They are waiting. It's time, Rhoane."

"How do we find them?" For thousands of seasons, the Eleri believed the darathi to be extinct.

"They aren't extinct, Rhoane. They're banished to a world not their own. They long to return and only you can do that. It's part of your path." She pointed to the rune glowing softly on his wrist. It was the same one he'd been studying on the parchment. His rune. Not Taryn's—his.

"Then we shall leave at once."

Except, it wasn't that simple. They gathered their papers and secured them with a leather tie before they made arrangements with the captain to take Loghan to Talaith, as well as any women who wanted to return to the capital city.

Before Rhoane left the men, he turned to the captain. "If anything happens to your passengers, the Eirielle and I will be most displeased." He still hadn't forgiven the man for poisoning him, and despite Taryn's wishes Rhoane not punish the man, he swore to one day find vengeance.

"No harm will come to us, Your Highness," Loghan assured him. "When I reach Talaith, how will I find my way to Ulla?"

In the two days Taryn had disappeared from the Sitari, Loghan didn't leave Rhoane's side. The Ullan had used all of his healing skills, albeit without sharing his body, to bring Rhoane back from the edge of death. Rhoane owed the man a great debt and had set aside his irritation with the young Ullan to form a friendship of sorts. They both loved Taryn, yes, but Loghan assured Rhoane he understood her path was with the Eleri.

"Lady Faelara and Sir Baehlon were planning an extended trip to your kingdom. They will act as escort." Rhoane handed Loghan a sealed letter he'd penned to his friends. "Give this to them. There will be no questions asked. And Loghan, if you happen to meet a smallish man, goes by Ebus, do not trust him with anything of physical value, but your life and your secrets, those he will defend, by my honor."

"Where shall I say you have gone?"

"To right a wrong. I expect to return before Harvest."

"But that is more than two moonturns hence. Surely your quest will not be so taxing?"

Rhoane studied the Ullan healer for a long moment. "I know you love her, Loghan, as do I. Believe me when I say her safety is ever at the forefront of my mind. I appreciate everything you have done for us, pray we not have need of your services again, but if the time comes, I should hope you will not forsake us."

"Never, my lord." Loghan kissed his thumb before touching it to first his forehead, then his heart. "When next we meet, may it be in sweetness and not sorrow."

"When next we meet." Rhoane placed his brow against his Ullan cousin's, more than a little surprised he knew the Eleri saying. But then, of course Kaleigh would've taught it to her sons. She was Eleri, despite her pretense of being an Ullan queen.

After his conversation with Loghan, Taryn went to speak with the whores and Rhoane roamed the forest. Mentally, he played out what he hoped to find at Mallaqai's ruins. The darathi were somewhere beyond Aelinae's veils, and he would find them.

"Your Highness, a word." Shandris said by way of greeting.

Startled, Rhoane glanced at his surroundings, unaware how he'd found his way to the treehouses. The chieftess stood with one hand resting on a spear, the other on her hip. A playful smile teased her lips.

"How may I be of service?" As with Loghan, Rhoane owed the Sitari a debt. They'd been instrumental in his recovery, too.

"The women." Her posture shifted, the smile dipped. "I do not wish to let them remain, yet I am loathe to return them to their past lives."

"A conundrum, to be sure." Rhoane glanced at the trees and breathed in the scent of forest.

Unlike the Narthvier, the smells here were vibrant with citrus and berries. Huge fronds blocked the sun from burning their heads and sand shifted beneath their feet. It wasn't a terrible place to call home.

"You have made a good life for yourselves. Have you ever thought about returning to the mainland?"

Shandris sucked in a breath. "Never. Our place is here."

Rhoane understood her reticence. Long ago, he'd fought against leaving the security of the Weirren. "I will not force you to allow the women to stay."

"I appreciate that. The other Sitari, they do not agree with me. They wish to open our hearths to the whores. They believe in redemption. I do not."

Shandris would hone her bitterness until something caused her to reevaluate her position. Nothing he said could change her mind. Rhoane sighed and turned to ascend the stairs.

"We do not want your Darennsai dead."

Rhoane paused mid-step. "I know you do not. Just as I know you are not the monsters you would otherwise have us believe."

The smile returned to Shandris's face. "We keep the rumors alive to dissuade anyone from coming to our islands."

Whether she realized it or not, the Sitari made it possible for Myrddin to work here without anyone suspecting the mage of betrayal.

"I will be certain to inform the captain. No one shall be the wiser that the Sitari are genteel women with good hearts."

Shandris scoffed and shook out her white hair. "You Eleri."

He chuckled as he made his way up the never-ending stairs. What was Taryn always saying? *It was a start.* The Sitari had their place in Aelinae's future, too.

Rhoane found Taryn in the main room, talking to the Sitari Beilis. The warrior knelt beside Kaida, her hand stroking the grierbas' soft fur. He hung back, not wanting to interrupt, but wary of the distress on each woman's face. A moment later, Beilis rose and hugged Taryn. The rare display of affection surprised Rhoane, and by the look on Taryn's face, her as well. She kissed Beilis's cheek and murmured a few words before stepping away, Kaida at her side.

"She wants me to leave Kaida, but I have a feeling we'll be needing her."

Rhoane didn't need to be reminded the last time Kaida was separated from her, Cashiel had attacked Lliandra's ship. The guilt he'd felt that day, and every one since, was still raw. He'd supported Lliandra's decision to have Kaida sail with him.

"Kaida should be with you."

"I can't transport us there since I don't know where we're going, so we'll have to fly." She scratched Kaida's ruff. "You might not like this, but it's the best I can do for now."

They wove their way through myriad huts until they came to the farthest one. Along the perimeter was a wide deck with a sturdy rail from which they could leap into the air. Rhoane held Kaida aloft while Taryn situated herself atop the bamboo rails. She grasped Kaida by the scruff and dove forward, transforming into her great silver darathi vorsi in mid-air. The sight stole his breath just as it had the first time he saw her flying over the ocean, her scales glinting like diamonds in the moonlight.

She was the most remarkable creature he'd ever known. Woman or dragon, there was no one like Taryn.

He followed his beloved and dove toward the canopy, his wings unfurling to beat hard against the warm air. It was heavier here in the jungle, uncomfortable too. He hadn't noticed the humidity on the ground, but up here, where birds flocked and nested, where monkeys swung from thick vines, the air crushed his lungs the smallest bit.

Is the air difficult for you to breathe?

No, why?

Rhoane beat his wings harder, clearing the top layer of foliage and springing toward the clear blue sky. *I had a hard time sucking in air beneath the canopy. But I am fine now, I believe.*

Weird. Maybe it's a lingering effect of the poison? You know, you were close to death just a few days ago.

Perhaps.

He didn't want to linger on the poisoning, or what had occurred after, when Taryn went to Caer Idris. Rhoane had been there, in the tree, and saw everything that happened. Not saw, exactly, but experienced it. He heard Kaldaar's taunts, knew the god wanted Taryn to use her power on the tree, but Taryn hadn't. Rhoane had screamed when her sword pierced the rough bark of the tree—not out of pain, but as a warning. Kaldaar coveted her power and her sword, needed both of them to become fully realized. And one other thing—the tear of Aelinae.

Nadra's tear, to be exact. Rhoane had no idea what that meant or how he could find it, but he'd sworn an oath as he was trapped in the runyon tree—he would find it and prevent Kaldaar from ever fully returning to Aelinae.

But first, he had a promise to keep. One he made when he was a lad and barely understood the significance.

He had to find the darathi vorsi and return them to Aelinae.

To do that, he needed Mallaqai's vortex.

CHAPTER FORTY-FIVE

They flew over the Summer Seas, high enough to avoid being seen, but not so high they couldn't land immediately if necessary. Taryn banked to the east past Haversham, avoiding the fires of the mountain Artagh. They soared past the island of Ankae and over Gaarendahl, where the castle loomed dark and vengeful on the high crags. At last they came to the plains where Mallaqai once lived and an entire village thrived. All that remained were ruins.

Over there. Rhoane directed Taryn to what was once Mallaqai's tower, a large stone structure that stood higher than any at Caer Idris or the Crystal Palace. It was often said Mallaqai could see all of Aelinae from her great tower. Now, it was a pile of rubble, with stairs leading to roofless floors.

As they circled the ruins, Rhoane saw movement within the tower. A moment later, his heart beat a rapid staccato, his breath edged in flames.

Taryn, be wary.

Taryn's dragon snout dipped low and he heard a sharp gasp. *What is he doing here?*

Her irritation rippled over his scales, pinching with its intensity. Zakael stalked the lower floor of the castle, his ShantiMari a dark whirl around his body. The timing of their arrival at the ruins and Zakael's presence couldn't be a coincidence. Yet they hadn't told anyone where they were going.

Kaldaar could be manipulating us again. Taryn's thought brushed his.

Then we shall be forewarned and ready.

They ghosted to the top floor of Mallaqai's tower and transformed into flesh and blood. Kaida shook her fur, a low rumble in her chest.

"She's not a fan of air travel," Taryn jested. "We need a plan," she added, her tone serious.

Rhoane cocked his head to the side, listening. "He is not alone. Two—no, three others accompany him." He listened further. "He knows about the vortex, knows how to open it."

"How? We don't even know that. Do you think he has the seal?" Consternation twisted her features. "I'm sure my wards are solid, but with him, you never know."

"Only one way to find out." Rhoane led them down the crumbling steps, being extra careful not to make a sound.

Halfway down, a scream reverberated through the stairwell, echoing cries following close behind. Rhoane held up two fingers, but Taryn nudged his back to keep moving. More screams, higher pitched than the first, battered his sensitive ears. Shouts sounded and Rhoane took advantage of the disruption to move swiftly down the stairs, Taryn right on his heels, and Kaida behind her. With each step his heartbeat quickened, the blood rushed through his veins. Anxiety pooled in his gut.

At the bottom step, he paused to take in the room. A huge mirror stood in the center of a cavernous area, its reflection turned away from the stairs, facing an altar that looked hastily constructed. Adesh lay prone upon the blood-soaked stones. Bones protruded from his open chest to stick out at painful angles.

Rhoane swallowed bile and willed his heart to slow, focused his mind on the task at hand. He slipped into his assassin mentality to remove any personal feelings from his actions. It was a cloak too easily donned.

The scent of Taryn's perspiration stung his nostrils and her heavy breathing tickled the hairs on his neck.

Is Mallaqai here? Can you sense her? Then, Taryn whispered in his mind, *Is this another trap?*

Rhoane gripped Claidholm Solais's hilt tighter. Coincidences be damned. *Trap or not, we must be prepared.*

A pace from the altar, Zakael held a dripping red blob in one hand, and a dagger in the other. Amanda cowered at his feet, her body smeared crimson. What the bloody hell was happening here? His heart screamed at him to take action while his mind cautioned patience.

Holy hell. He took out Adesh's heart. Disgust dripped from Taryn's words in his mind.

Taryn was right. The organ continued beating despite being torn from the man's body. A figure stepped around the mirror, a smug grin on his damaged face. Taryn's hiss blew against Rhoane's cheek.

"Cashiel."

Blind fury overrode prudence and Rhoane strode from his hiding place toward the villain. This man had beaten Taryn near to death. Rhoane's vision narrowed until he saw only Cashiel and nothing else mattered but this man's death. Slow, brutal, without mercy.

Cashiel looked at him, surprise on his once handsome features. His eyes widened and a flicker of fear lit from their depths. Claidholm Solais sang a song of redemption, but Rhoane ignored it. This was no time for forgiveness, not for this man. He clenched the hilt hard, ready to impale Cashiel upon it.

Voices rose on the other side of the room—Taryn and Zakael, but Rhoane ignored them. His pace increased with purpose.

A blow of ShantiMari slowed his step, but not by much. He continued his advance, reaching striking distance in a few strides. Cashiel backed away, his hands covering his face, his lips mumbling apologies or asking for forgiveness or blaming Zakael. Rhoane didn't care. He shuttled all emotions to the pit of his core. Reason left him as he glared at the man who almost killed Taryn. A reassuring coolness swept through his blood, giving him calm. Clarity.

Instead of impaling the man, Rhoane swung hard with his fist, connecting to Cashiel's chin with a resounding crack. The man's head snapped to the side. His hair flung up with the sharp movement.

Sounds of fighting rumbled in Rhoane's mind and he held a tiny thread of conscious awareness to it, but kept his focus on Cashiel, who scrambled away from him.

"Please, my lord, I was coerced. Forced, you might say. I didn't want to harm her, I swear to you!" With each falsehood, Cashiel's voice rose an octave higher, until his timbre could break glass.

Rhoane didn't bother answering.

Somewhere behind him, Kaida barked.

In that moment of distraction, Cashiel's disposition changed. Gone was the sniveling lord, in his place was a confident killer. The air shifted with unspent energy. Tension coiled through Rhoane's muscles.

Cashiel came at him hard and fast, a black blade whirling in his hands. Rhoane swung his sword and met steel with steel. An awful clang rang out and Cashiel stumbled backward. Confidence slipped from his features.

Again, Cashiel came at him, and again Rhoane deflected his attack. Of the two, it was clear who was the better swordsman. With each defeat, Cashiel's consternation grew until his face was a riot of frustration and fury. Rhoane parried a clumsy attack and sent Cashiel's inky blade clattering to the ground.

Green sparks lit from his dark eyes and spittle formed at the corners of his mouth. A swirl of ShantiMari stung Rhoane and he sliced through it with his sword. Cashiel cried out and cowered against a wall, his hands clasped over his face.

A hush fell over the room.

Rhoane dared not look away from Cashiel to check on Taryn.

Her half-brother chuckled. "Worried about your slag?" He licked his lips with a smacking sound. "That's one sweet morsel, to be sure."

Rhoane let Claidholm Solais speak for him. He lunged forward, his sword aimed at Cashiel's heart. A wall of ShantiMari sprang up, blocking Rhoane's path. He struggled forward, using his own power to fight through the barrier. His boots skidded on the slate floor. Wave after wave of immense power pushed against him.

Sweat slicked his palms and his grip loosened on his sword hilt. His muscles ached and his breathing became labored. Behind the wall, Cashiel grinned.

The power wasn't coming from Cashiel, but somewhere else. Rhoane shifted his body and renewed his grip on Claidholm Solais. The threads came from behind Cashiel. The man was being used as a puppet and didn't even realize it.

His body shook with the effort to keep the wall of Shanti-Mari from falling on him. Another few moments and he'd succumb. Rhoane closed his eyes and let the power sweep past him. He imagined it as a breeze, nothing more. Cashiel's gasp popped like a bubble in the torrent of power.

Rhoane's own ShantiMari flowed to his sword. In one swift movement, he plunged it into Cashiel's chest.

A wild cry, unlike any Rhoane had heard before, tore at his eardrums. Someone other than Cashiel wailed in the distance and Rhoane paused, listening. The sound was not from Taryn. He blocked out the keening, directing his focus to Cashiel. Even mortally injured, the man begged forgiveness, swearing upon everyone and everything that it wasn't his fault.

Rhoane withdrew his sword and plunged it into the man's soft body thrice more. Blood gurgled from his blistered lips, and his eyes took on a faraway look, then finally a deathly veil covered Cashiel's deep grey orbs. Satisfied he would never harm Taryn again, Rhoane turned with a grunt of disgust.

Taryn held Zakael by the throat, her stance rigid, her feet planted to give her leverage. At her neck, Zakael held a dagger. They were at an impasse.

Rhoane's ragged breathing stalled. Seeing the blade at Taryn's neck incited new fury, but he held himself in check. One wrong move on either side would mean death.

"Rhoane!" Amanda cried, "Thank the gods. Please, Zakael has me here under duress. He's threatened to kill me like he did Adesh and use the sacrifice to open a vortex."

"Shut up, stupid whore." Zakael kicked out, missing Amanda.

Taryn spun away from the blade and brought Zakael's arm around to his back. The dagger clattered to the stone floor. Rhoane raced to Taryn's side, his sword held at chest level. He bent and snatched the dagger before Amanda's greedy hands reached it.

"You'll never get the vortex open," Zakael taunted.

Taryn shoved Zakael's arm higher, eliciting a cry from her half-brother.

"Rhoane, please," Amanda held her bound wrists out for him to see.

A collar wrapped around her neck, with a silver leash leading to Zakael's pocket.

"I trusted you." Rhoane stalked toward her, his pace slow, deliberate. "You and Adesh. And now you want my help?"

"I was forced. You have to believe me."

Taryn watched the interplay between him and Amanda, her

gaze narrowed, her lips a tight line. Zakael's features remained placid, as if he were bored by the proceedings, yet the way he cocked his head to hear better belied that farce. He was being too quiet, too complacent. For Zakael to be this passive, there had to be a reason.

Keep her talking. Zakael's distracted by what she might say. I'm sifting through his thoughts, which is so gross, but I need to know why he's really here. Taryn's thought was wrapped with her power and Rhoane drew on it for strength.

"Do I have to believe you? Because Matilde has another version of events." Rhoane began.

"Matilde? She's dead." Amanda's flippant reply held no emotion.

Kaida slunk toward Amanda, a snarl coming from deep in her throat.

"Please, make it go away."

"*It* has a name. And she isn't fond of liars and cheats. Kaida, stand down," Taryn commanded. "Let Rhoane handle this."

Kaida sat on her haunches, her eyes trained on the shuddering young woman.

"I saw Matilde on the Sitari Islands." Rhoane knelt until he was eye to eye with her.

Amanda's eyes grew huge and filled with tears. "You went to see the Sitari?" Her gaze went to Zakael, who shrugged. "Wh-what did you find there?"

Rhoane had the feeling Amanda wasn't worried about the other women, but something far more valuable. This could be the reason for Zakael's silence.

"What was there to find?"

"Nothing. I mean, just Sitari and the women Adesh left." Her shuddering was a full-on tremble now. Her teeth chattered together.

"You would not be this frightened over a few dozen warriors and whores. What were you searching for?"

Amanda glanced at Taryn, then at the ground. Her mouth worked, but nothing came out.

"Say nothing, you little cunt." Zakael kicked out, but Taryn's power stopped his movements.

The brilliant strands of Taryn's ShantiMari whirled through the room, encompassing not just Zakael, but the rest of them, too.

"He has your crown. He means to bring the dragons back to Aelinae and be their lord." Amanda blurted.

"I told Adesh you were worthless. We should've killed you first. At least he knew how to hold his tongue." The venom in Zakael's words singed against the tension in the room.

Amanda cowered, tears streaked down her face, and she bit her bottom lip. Whatever their relationship, she feared Zakael. Yet she'd told him about the crown.

"Where is my crown?" Rhoane addressed Zakael.

"Fuck you." Zakael's flint colored eyes were full of hatred.

Rhoane struck hard, hitting Zakael in the solar plexus. He doubled over, huffing against the pain.

"Where. Is. My. Crown?" With each word, Rhoane struck Zakael.

"I'm King of the West," Zakael wheezed, "I do not answer to you."

He's waiting for something. Taryn brushed Rhoane's thoughts.

Is Kaldaar here?

I'm not sure. He thinks he's outwitted the god, but I sense… something.

"He's not going to tell us anything." Taryn said between clenched teeth.

Zakael struggled against her hold. Dark threads of his power fought against Taryn's and beads of sweat dotted her brow.

Rhoane added his power to hers and pinned Zakael's free arm at his side.

"A threesome, how charming." Zakael's leer churned Rhoane's stomach.

"Where's the fucking crown, Zakael? Don't make me rip you apart to find it." Taryn threatened.

Zakael's lecherous grin grew larger. "There's nothing I'd like better. Especially if the Eleri is there to watch."

Rhoane had had enough. He sent several threads of Shanti-Mari into Zakael and filled him with Eleri power. Zakael's Dark—and Telraicht-Noir—ShantiMari fought against Rhoane's, but he shoved past the resistance to flood Zakael. The king gasped and shuddered, his eyes wild.

A slip of Zakael's power spun out to snatch Cashiel's fallen sword and flung it toward him, but Rhoane was quicker than the hobbled king. He grabbed the blade in mid-air and drove it forward, into Zakael's chest, then pulled it free. A surprised gasp gurgled from his open mouth, and his eyes glared at Rhoane.

"You can't," he muttered as his legs buckled. "I'm a king. Would be a god."

"Yeah, well, now you'll just be dead," Taryn jerked him around to face her. She held his cloak with her left hand and brought her right fist hard against his temple. "Prick."

Zakael slumped to the ground, his wheezing the only sound in the room.

CHAPTER FORTY-SIX

Damn, that felt good. Like, way too good. She should've punched Zakael ages ago, but her damn bleeding heart always got the better of her. She shook out her hand, shocked at the amount of pain zinging up her fingers to her shoulder. She'd put every ounce of anger into that punch and now she'd be sore for her efforts.

The girl huddled against the side of the altar cried openly now, her sobs more of an annoyance than source of pity. Rhoane paced a circle, his grip on his sword firm, his jaw tight. She turned her attention back to Amanda, disgusted by the snot running from her nose, and the way her doe eyes followed Rhoane's movements. She had yet to address Taryn, perhaps out of fear, or because she thought she could seduce Rhoane into letting her go free.

Fuck that.

Taryn spun on her heel, kicking Zakael in the process. Bloody bastard stole Rhoane's crown and was going take command of the dragons. *Ha! As if he could.* Taryn knelt and fished in Zakael's pockets, not finding the crown, but coming away with several scrolls written in the same archaic language as the pages they found in Mallaqai's secret room. She knew these scrolls. They were the missing pages from the library at Caer Idris. Zakael must've found them in Valterys's rooms once he became king.

"Rhoane." Taryn handed him the parchment and returned to searching Zakael's clothing. Finding nothing, she addressed Amanda. "Where's the crown?"

"Why should I tell you?" Her chin lifted in defiance and Taryn sent a thread of her power around the girl's neck.

Her eyes bugged with the increased pressure and her hands flailed at her throat, trying to pull free of Taryn's ShantiMari.

"Because if you don't, you'll die."

"You're worse than him, you know." The words croaked from the girl, each a gasp of wasted air.

"That's not very nice." Taryn tightened her grip, sending a second thread to Amanda's heart.

"Cashiel," Amanda said at last, her face a purplish shade of red.

"That's better." She released the pressure and jogged to Cashiel. She knew Rhoane had killed him, but the savagery she saw gave her pause. This was what Flik had trained him to be—a killer. But she'd never seen this side of Rhoane. It was one she didn't wish to encounter too often.

And yet, a little voice said in the back of her mind, *look how easily you murdered your own sister and would've killed Amanda just now.*

Two halves of the same whole.

Taryn shook off the dark thoughts and rummaged through Cashiel's pockets. She found the crown tucked into the back of his breeches, a little dinged from his fall. She used her power to straighten out the ridges and buff the tarnish.

How the hell had Zakael found it? She and Rhoane had hidden it far in the depths of the Narthvier, where no one would think to look. Unless Cashiel had stolen the location from her thoughts when he was torturing her. It was possible.

She studied his burned face and neck, hoping the scars had caused him great amounts of pain before Rhoane ended his life.

Oh, God, what was wrong with her? This wasn't her. She didn't condone killing, did she? Not normally, but when someone tried to kill her, certainly the rules could bend? She hated that she'd been put in this predicament. Again.

"Taryn," Rhoane called her over and showed her two pages that outlined exactly how to open the vortex. "It does not say anything here about sacrifices or blood exchange."

"Well, we knew Zakael was a sick bastard. He probably did it for kicks."

"Or another reason." His low tone held an ominous edge.

An image of Rykoto eating the heart of his sacrifices scalded her memory. Rhoane flinched as if he saw it, too. Taryn glanced at the altar, at Adesh's mutilated body and the heart resting beside his face. Blood ran in rivulets to the stone floor, some of it congealed into thick puddles.

"We should cleanse this place." Rhoane rolled the scrolls and tucked them into an inner pocket of his coat.

"No," Taryn said, surprising herself. It's exactly what she'd been thinking. "Not this time."

She kissed the gold band on her right ring finger, the one Carga's message had come wrapped in, and whispered a few words. The ring slipped off her finger with ease and she placed it atop Adesh's heart where it wouldn't be missed.

"What should we do with her?" Taryn said, ignoring Rhoane's curious look.

Amanda sobbed anew, her face a splotchy mess. "Don't kill me, please. I promise to be good. I told you about the crown. I'm on your side, see?"

Rhoane snorted, surprising Taryn with the ungenteel-like sound. "Hardly. You are, as ever, on *your* side. I have granted immunity to the whores with the Sitari, and I shall do the same for you."

He knelt in front of her and reached out to touch her temple. She flinched as if burned, but he continued. Taryn sensed him placing a ward in Amanda's mind, but couldn't distinguish its purpose.

"This is a chance for you to make better choices. I hope you do not squander it."

Then he suggested she sleep and the girl slumped over, nestled atop Zakael's body.

Taryn raised a brow.

He shrugged. "It would not do to have her see where we are going, or how we got there."

She handed him the crown. "You know, I don't think you actually need this. The darathi vorsi know who you are, have known since your birth. They wouldn't follow someone just because they wore this."

Rhoane rubbed his thumb over the three jewels of the crown. "I am not so sure. These are not just any gems, Taryn. They are darathi eggs."

"Xianqin," Taryn whispered. "She won't have to be alone anymore."

Rhoane's face softened. "You have a good heart, mi carae."

She forced herself not to look at Zakael or Cashiel, and to let Rhoane's compliment settle in her thoughts. "I gave it to a good caretaker."

He took her hand and kissed her knuckles. "Are you ready?"

"Are we ever?" Her nerves frayed.

His chuckle slid over her, calming the stinging in her blood.

"Take my hand." He placed the crown squarely on his head and stood before the mirror, his hand out for her to hold. When her fingers slipped into his, he chanted the words that would open the vortex.

"Kaida," Taryn extended her other hand for the grierbas. "You're coming, too."

Kaida loped over to them, her tongue lolling to the side. At least she wasn't nervous about stepping into the unknown.

When she had a firm hold of Kaida's fur, she said to Rhoane, "We're ready."

The air buzzed, gaining speed like a tempest in a bottle, then blew upward through the open roof. Tornado-like winds whipped their hair and clothes as the mirror stretched into a gaping maw. Blackness edged with lightning beckoned them forth. Rhoane took a tentative step and Taryn followed. Then they moved as one, the pair and Kaida, into the vortex.

Before the void swallowed them, Taryn sent a thought to Hayden. *There's something we need to take care of. We'll be back soon. Give everyone my love.*

Taryn gripped Kaida's fur and Rhoane's hand as if her life depended on it. In a way, it did. Aelinae's future rested on what they found on the other side of the vortex. The Darathi Vorsi Prince wore the Crown of Awakening. She just hoped there were still darathi living to return.

She turned to take a last look at the ruins of Mallaqai and saw in the shadows someone creeping through the rubble. The cloaked figure stood before the mirror and chuckled, a deep-throated snarl that curdled her blood. Before she could cry out, the vortex closed in on itself, the sound of shattering glass echoing through the darkness.

CHAPTER FORTY-SEVEN

Kaldaar walked through the ruined castle, keeping to the shadows until the others were through the vortex. Things had gone better than planned. The Eleri prince had provided him with a selection of assassins. He only had to choose which one would benefit his needs most.

He stepped around the altar, inhaling the stink of blood and death as if it were a rose in summer. Later he would luxuriate in the scent, but first he had to make certain the Eirielle and her mate never returned to Aelinae. It had taken him too long to get them here, but at last he'd found a way to make certain they would find the opening to where Mallaqai had banished the dragons.

They were almost to the tipping point when he stood before the mirror and said the words that would collapse the vortex around them. If that didn't kill them, an endless nightmare awaited them in the void. Oh, yes, he'd planned well for this day.

It was her fault. He'd given the Eirielle plenty of chances to join him, but she insisted on being his adversary instead of his ally. So be it.

Aelinae was his to claim now that she was no more. And how simple it had been, too. Of all his convoluted plans, this one turned out to be the least unique, but with the sweetest reward.

He pressed a hand to the mirror and it shattered, slicing his palm in a dozen places. *Bitch.* This, too, was her fault. Everything that had happened in the past season was her fault, but he didn't have to worry about that anymore. He'd waited season after season for her birth, and finally he could celebrate her death.

A moan brought his attention back to the moment and he scanned the bodies lying along the floor. The one named Kane, but who called himself Cashiel, showed no signs of life. There was no pulse beneath his fingertips, no breath from the dead man's lips.

He would make a fine Shadow Assassin. Noble born, he understood the ways of warfare and espionage. Betrayal was second nature to this one. He'd served Kaldaar well when alive, dead he would be even more lethal. And without ambitions of his own. Yes, this one would more than suffice.

Kaldaar bent low and touched his lips to the dead man's, breathing new life into him. After several minutes, he stirred, his arms jerking upward, legs scrambling for footing.

"Shhh, shhh, my son. Quiet now. You are safe." He placed a hand on Cashiel's forehead and the lad calmed.

"I was dead."

"Yes, but you are not now." To his right, another moan drew his attention. He told Cashiel to rest and scuttled to where Zakael lay slumped against the floor. Gently, he rolled the man over, surveying the bruise at his temple, the gash in his chest. Zakael's eyes fluttered open and he stared at the ceiling.

"Kaldaar," he whispered. Then, his gaze lowered to the god. "Where am I?"

"Mallaqai's ruins."

"Taryn…is she gone?"

"Yes, my son. She is gone for good." He pushed his hood back to better see to Zakael's wounds.

Zakael gasped in a breath and stuttered, "My-my—"

He put a finger to his lips and shushed him. "I will heal you and you will serve me."

With a sigh, Zakael nodded. "Yes, my Master."

"What should we do with this one?" He indicated the girl to his right.

"Does it matter? We're all dead now, aren't we?"

"Not yet, my son. Not quite yet."

Kaldaar closed Zakael's eyes and sent him to sleep, to heal. When he woke, they'd discuss his betrayal, but for the moment, he'd ignore the brat's temperament. It was a boon to find him living. Although he would've made an excellent Shadow Assassin, Zakael was far more valuable to him alive. The girl, however, served little purpose.

He turned her face to the side, admiring her delicate beauty. Perhaps she did hold some charm after all. He would let her live, for now.

His laughter echoed through the empty rooms. How long had he waited to live? To fully embrace life as a whole entity and not the half shell he'd paraded as for season upon season? It was time to reclaim what was rightfully his. After depositing his new children at Caer Idris, he'd pay a visit to his brother Rykoto. They had an old score to settle and he needed the mad god freed from his prison.

His laughter grew louder, shaking the timbers of the ruins. The elder gods were fools. They'd placed all their hopes on a girl. A stupid Aelan girl who'd fallen in love with an Eleri prince. Now they would all suffer.

He stood beside the altar and inhaled the dead man's scent. A glint of gold caught his eye and he spied the little gold band resting on the heart Zakael had ripped from the man's chest. Kaldaar bent low, wary. It was nothing more than a ring. He prodded it with a finger. When nothing happened, he picked it up.

At his touch, the ring spoke.

"Kaldaar," Taryn's voice filled the ruined castle. "You have not won."

The god hissed and threw the ring to the floor. He stormed across the stones to the shattered mirror and raised his fist at the empty air.

"You are nothing but a stupid Aelan girl," he shouted.

He paced and swore and tugged on a beard that was not there.

Then he returned to the ring and snatched it from the cold floor.

"You cannot defeat me. I know you." Taryn's voice grew stronger. "I know your weakness. I also know you'll try to prevent me from returning, but I'll be back. Of that be assured."

Kaldaar glared at the broken pieces of glass as if they could provide answers to her riddle. He alone ruled the edge of nothingness. Only he knew the vastness of the void.

Kaldaar laughed, a jubilant hiss that frightened sleeping birds from the rafters. Taryn was nothing. She was born of flesh and therefore could be destroyed. He held the ring in front of his face and glared at the simple gold band.

"You can never return. I forbid it."

"I will return," Taryn insisted. "For you see, I remember who I am." Taryn's hushed voice held no fear.

It could not be. He would not allow it. Taryn was nothing. Her words, nothing. She could not return. Her words were empty threats meant to frighten him, but he was no squabbling child. He was not to be trifled with and she would understand sooner, rather than later.

The ring melted with his rising anger. The molten gold dripped over his fingers, singing his rotted flesh. Kaldaar breathed in the scent and pulled his lips back in a grin that showed his pointed teeth.

"I am Kaldaar," he said to the empty air. "I too remember who I am. I am a god and Aelinae my kingdom."

Soft as a breeze, he heard Taryn's voice whisper, "We shall see."

CAST OF CHARACTERS

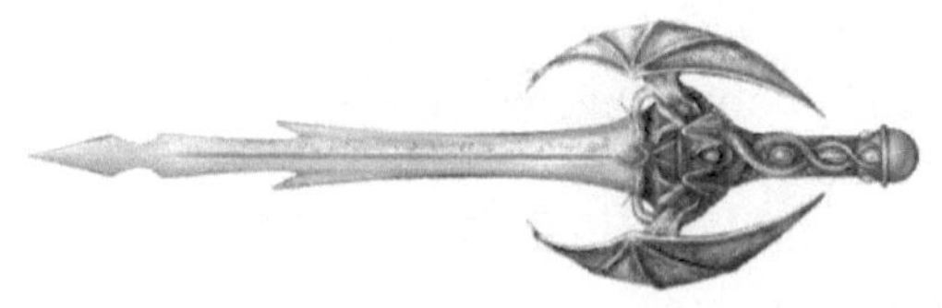

Adesh ~ Summerlander. A spice merchant in Talaith. Tabul's brother.

Ahmbra (Amm-brah) ~ A golden darathi vorsi living in exile. Conceived on Aelinae, she was born in exile and is the last of her kind.

Aislinn al Glennwoods ap Narthvier (Ay-s-lynn) ~ Queen of the Eleri. Aislinn perished in a ShantiMari accident when Rhoane was a young man.

Alasdair (Alice-dare) ~ A faerie servant in the service of Rhoane. Brother to Illanr and Carld.

Alswyth Myrddin (Alls-with Mere-din) ~ Mage with exceedingly long life. Myrddin is the advisor to Empress Lliandra and is often far from court on assignments from the crown. No known children or spouses. No known House.

Amanda ~ Aelan. A young woman living in Talaith with dubious ties to Adesh the spice merchant.

Amdi Agnar ~ Laird of the Ullan tribes. He claimed Kaleigh as his consort and has two sons with her. Descendent of House Agnar.

Anje ap Paderau (Ann-jee ap Pah-der-oo) ~ Duke of

Paderau, father to Hayden, husband to Gwyneira (now deceased). Anje is cousin to the Lord of Darkness, and third in line for the Obsidian Throne. His father was brother to Valterys's father. A prince in his own right, Anje renounced his Dark heritage to live with his wife in the Light. Descendant of House Djeba.

Aomori di Monsenti (A-more-ee di Mon-scent-ee) ~ A young Danuri lord fostering with Tinsley in Paderau. Descendant of House Monsenti.

Armando ~ Summerlander. Lover of Tarro. Whore in Nena's house. Marissa's favorite.

Ashanni (A-shawn-ee) ~ A mare Duke Anje gives to Taryn.

Baehlon de Monteferron (Bay-lohn de Mont-fair-on) ~ Danuri and Geigan knight employed by Empress Lliandra, sworn to protect Taryn and her House. Descendant of House Monteferron.

Baldev de Deistra (Ball-dev de Des-tra) ~ King of the Seas. Baldev lives within a vast complex at the bottom of the ocean. Merfolk are believed to be legends as they are not often seen. Once a year, on their naming day, merfolk have the option to walk among the other races on Aelinae. It is unknown if Baldev has ever honored the tradition. Married to Salaria. Father to several daughters and sons. Descendent of House Deistra.

Beary ~ {Master} Unseen character in book one. Advisor to Taryn on household matters.

Beilis (Bay-leesh) ~ Sitari. Second in command to the Chieftess Shandris. Does not trust outsiders.

Bornu (Bore-new) ~ Summerlander. A young boy who works for Adesh.

Brandt Kaj Endion (Brant) ~ Aelan. High Priest of Talaith and advisor to Empress Lliandra, Brandt was commissioned with Taryn's safety when she was born. After his death, Nadra took Brandt to Dal Tara, (home of the gods), which allows Brandt to communicate with Taryn. House Arran.

Bressal ap Narthvier (Bress-all) ~ Eleri. Second Son to King Stephan and Queen Aislinn (now passed beyond the veils).

Carga ap Narthvier ~ Eleri. Daughter to King Stephan and Queen Aislinn (now passed beyond the veils).

Carina (Ka-reen-a) ~ Aelan. A member of Taryn's personal guard.

Carld (Car-uld) ~ A faerie maid in the service of King Stephan. Sister to Illanr and Alasdair.

Cashiel (Cash-eel) ~ Second son to Lliandra, fathered by Esna fei Garrith. Given name is Kane, but now goes by Cashiel.

Celia ~ Aelan. Minor noble and Marissa's favorite until she perished at the Stones of Kaldaar. Descendant of House Deltanna.

Cora ~ Aelan. A maid in the service of Empress Lliandra assigned to Taryn upon her arrival in Talaith.

Crone ~ Ulla woman who gives warning to Taryn in Amdi's tents. She is killed for her efforts.

Cynda (Sin-dah) ~ A mare Rhoane provides for Taryn.

Daknys (Dak-niss) ~ Elder Goddess. Daughter of Nadra and Ohlin, she is worshipped by the Light and Dark in the central area of Aelinae.

Darius (Dare-ee-us) ~ Artagh, Eleri and Aelan. A page at Celyn Eryri who joins Taryn's guard.

Darrew (Dare-oo) ~ Danuri lord, Chief Councilor to the Steward of Danuri.

Denzil de Monteferron (Den-zell) ~ Danuri and Geigan. A mercenary hired by Lliandra to patrol Talaith's docks. Brother to Baehlon.

Deshan Agnar (Day-shawn Ag-nar) ~ Ullan. Deceased laird of the Ullans. Brother to Amdi Agnar.

Ebus (Ee-bus) ~ Race unknown. Spy employed by Taryn and Rhoane. Can see the Shadow Assassin.

Eiric (Err-ic) ~ Danuri. Lover of Zakael.

Eliahnna Tjaru (Ee-lahn-ah Shar-U) ~ Aelan. Daughter of

Lliandra. Her heritage is much debated since Lliandra has never publicly named her father. She is third in line to the Light Throne. Descendant of House Nadrene.

Ellie ~ Aelan. A maid in the service of Taryn.

Enghor (Ain-gore) ~ Beast forced to fight Taryn in the Ullan arena. With the legs of a man, chest of an ape, and head of a goat, he is not a creature from Aelinae.

Eoghan ap Narthvier (Eee-gan) ~ Eleri. Third Son to King Stephan and Queen Aislinn (now passed beyond the veils).

Esna fei Garrith (Ez-nah fay Gare-eth) ~ Danurian. Minor noble who attracted Lliandra's attention. Fathered a son with the empress and Marissa, the crown princess. Was executed for trying to poison the empress. Descendent of House Garrith.

Faelara Dal Arran (Fay-lara) ~ Aelan. Daughter of Brandt, Faelara is currently a lady-in-waiting to Empress Lliandra. Her Healing skills are legendary, as were her father's. House Arran.

Faisal dei Tarnovo (Fay-sal) ~ Summerlander. Sabina's father and the king of the Summerlands. House Tarnov.

Fayngaar (Fain-gar) ~ Rhoane's stallion.

Gameson ~ {Master} Aelan. Head tutor in the service of Empress Lliandra.

Gayvn ~ Taryn's twin. See 'Shadow Assassin'.

Gian ap Brenbold (Jawn) ~ A faerie found in Valterys's dungeon.

Gilchrist (Gill-krisst) ~ Elder darathi vorsi living in exile. Mate to Jinnipher.

Gris ~ Aelan. A kitchen boy in the service of Duke Anje.

Gwainne Agnar (Gw-ayn) ~ First son to Amdi Agnar and his Eleri wife Kaleigh. Heir to the Ullan Laird.

Gwyneira Tjaru ap Paderau (Gwin-eera ap Shar-U) ~ Aelan. Sister to Empress Lliandra, wife of Duke Anje, mother to Hayden. Gwyneira died after childbirth when Hayden was a young man. Houses Nadrene and Djeba.

Hanan ~ A Summerlands spice merchant living in Menurra.

Hayden ap Valen ~ Aelan. Lord Valen, Marquis of the province Valen, son of Anje and Gwyneira. Hayden is cousin to the heirs of the Light Throne and the Obsidian Throne. Descendant of House Djeba.

Herbret ~ Aelan. A minor noble in Talaith's court and one of Marissa's favorites until he perished at the Stones of Kaldaar. Descendant of House Gilfroy.

Illanr (Ill-an-or) ~ A faerie maid in the service of King Stephan. Sister to Carld and Alasdair.

Iselt (Ee-selt) ~ A blacksmith at Celyn Eryri with secrets and a past he's trying to hide. He is half Artagh and half Eleri.

Janeira (Juh-nair-a) ~ An Eleri warrior of great standing, excellent skill, and deadly capabilities.

Jayved dei Tarnovo (Jay-ved) ~ Summerlands prince. Heir to Faisal and Prateeni. Brother to Sabina.

Jinnipher (Gin-i-fur) ~ A darathi vorsi living in exile. Mate to Gilchrist.

Julieta ~ Younger Goddess. Daughter of Rykoto and Daknys.

Kaida (Kay-da) ~ A grierbas Taryn rescued in the Narthvier. Companion to Taryn ~ they have the ability to speak with each other in their minds. Kaida can track the Shadow Assassin.

Kaldaar (Cal-dar) ~ Elder God. Son of Nadra and Ohlin, worshipped by inhabitants of the Southeast until his banishment after the Great War. Kaldaar hasn't been seen in Aelinae in over five thousand seasons.

Kaleigh al Fyrnwood ap Agnar (Kay-lee) ~ Eleri. Sheanna living among the Ullans. The sworn concubine to Laird Amdi. Kaleigh has two sons with the laird.

Khrystina (Christina) ~ An Eleri novice studying at Verdaine's temple in the Narthvier.

Kragor (Kray-gore) ~ Geigan. A brutish man Rhoane fights in the arena.

Lliandra Tjaru (Lee-on-dra Shar-U) ~ Aelan. Empress of

Talaith, Lady of Light. Mother to Marissa, Taryn, Eliahnna, and Tessa. Lliandra is directly descended from the goddess Nadra. She is thought to be a just ruler who thinks of her subjects in all matters. House Nadrene.

Loghan Agnar (Logan) ~ Ullan prince. Second son to Amdi Agnar and his Eleri wife Kaleigh. Acclaimed healer. His entire body is covered in tattoes that are meant to aid in his healing.

Lorilee ~ Aelan. A maid in the service of Taryn. Sister to Mayla.

Lucitan (Loose-eh-tahn) ~ Rhoane's Ullan stallion, given to him by Amdi Agnar.

Marissa Tjaru (Shar-U) ~ Aelan. Crown Princess of Talaith, heir to the Light Throne, daughter of Lliandra and Esna (not named in books one or two). Descendant of House Nadrene.

Mayla ~ Aelan. A maid in the service of Duke Anje. Sister to Lorilee.

Margaret Tan ~ Geigan. Seamstress to Empress Lliandra, she often travels with the court. Her tailoring skills are said to be admired in all the kingdoms.

Marina ~ Summerlander. A maid in the service of Marissa.

Matilde ~ Aelan. Amanda's mother. Lives in Talaith with dubious ties to Adesh the spice merchant.

Micha Askell (Mike-uh Ask-elle) ~ Aelan. Baehlon's intended wife. Daughter of Lord Askell. House Askell.

Michel (Michael) ~ Ullan. Young boy who found Taryn on the shores of the Jansen Strait.

Nadra ~ Mother of Aelinae, Great Mother of all Creation. Along with Ohlin, Nadra created Aelinae. Mother to Daknys, Rykoto, Kaldaar, and Verdaine.

Nena ~ Race unknown. Owner of a house of prostitution in Talaith.

Nikki ~ Sitari. Companion and beloved to Shandris, Chieftess of the Sitari. Healer.

Nikosana ~ Black and tan Ullan stallion given to Taryn at the Light Celebrations by Duke Anje.

Ohlin (O-lynn) ~ Father of Aelinae, Great Father of all Creation. Along with Nadra, Ohlin created Aelinae. Father to to Daknys, Rykoto, Kaldaar, and Verdaine.

Oliver ~ Aelan. A servant in the service of Hayden, Lord Valen.

Percival ~ Marissa and Armando's child. He was born in secret and only a few know of his existence. Since male heirs are unwelcome at the Crystal Court, Taryn gave him to Armando to raise.

Phantom ~ An unknown entity manipulating Celia, Herbret, and Marissa. The phantom is thought to be an agent of Kaldaar.

Prateeni dei Tarnovo (Pruh-teen-ee) ~ Summerlander. Sabina's mother and the Queen of the Summerlands. House Tarnov.

Rhoane al Glennwoods ap Narthvier (Rone) ~ Eleri. First Son of Stephan, King of the Eleri, and Aislinn, Queen of the Eleri (now passed beyond the veils). At birth Rhoane was prophesied to be the Eirielle's protector. When he was old enough, he took an oath forsaking all others and devoting his life to upholding Verdaine's prophecy.

Rykoto (Ree-ko-toe) ~ Elder God. Son of Nadra and Ohlin, worshipped by inhabitants of the Northwest and of the Dark. Rykoto was imprisoned in the Temple of Ardyn after the Great War.

Sabina dei Tarnovo ~ Summerlander. Daughter of King Faisal and Queen Prateeni. Currently fostering with Empress Lliandra in Talaith. Sabina's ShantiMari was unlocked after the ordeal at the Stones of Kaldaar. Descendant of House Tarnov.

Saeko (Say-koh) ~ A maid in the service of Taryn.

Shadow Assassin ~ Taryn's twin brother. Stillborn, he was stolen from the Crystal Palace the night Taryn was born. His master raised him to hunt Taryn. He is used as an anchor to the god Kaldaar.

Shandris (Shawn-driss) ~ Sitari. Chieftess to the Sitari. Skilled warrior and benevolent leader.

Stephan ap Narthvier ~ King of the Eleri. Direct descendant from Verdaine. Married to Aislinn. Father to Rhoane, Bressal, Carga, and Eoghan. Stephan firmly believes the Eleri are stronger on their own, away from the other races of Aelinae. He opposes the Verdaine's prophecy regarding his son, Rhoane.

Sulein ap Lorn (Sue-lain) ~ An Artagh living in Talaith.

Tabul (Tah-buhl) ~ Summerlander. Spice merchant from Paderau.

Tarro (Tare-O) ~ Danuri. Assistant to Margaret Tan. Lover of Armando.

Taryn Rose Galendrin (Tare-in) ~ Daughter of Lliandra, Empress of Talaith, Lady of Light and Valterys, Overlord of the West, Lord of the Dark. Raised on Earth, Taryn grew up unaware of Aelinae, believing Brandt was her grandfather and only family. House Galendrin.

Tessa Tjaru (Shar-U) ~ Aelan. Daughter of Lliandra and Razlog (not named in books one or two). She is fourth in line to the Light Throne. Descendant of House Nadrene.

Timor (Tim-or) ~ Aelan. A member of Taryn's personal guard.

Tinsley Alcath (Tins-lee All-koth) ~ Aelan. A young lord with business ties to Duke Anje and is often at Paderau Palace. Descendant of House Alcath.

Troyanna Djeba ~ Aelan. Deceased. Wife to Valterys Djeba, mother to Zakael. House Djeba.

Tudyk (Too-dic) ~ Aelan. Sword Master in the service of Empress Lliandra.

Valterys Djeba (Val-terr-iss D-jj-ay-ba) ~ Aelan. Deceased. Was Overlord of the West, Lord of the Dark. Father to Taryn and Zakael. Valterys is directly descended from the god Ohlin. He ruled his kingdom with a tight grasp on its economy and trade. His subjects thought of him favorably. House Djeba.

Verdaine (Vare-dane) ~ Elder Goddess. Daughter of Nadra and Ohlin, she is worshipped by the Eleri in the Narthvier.

Zakael Djeba (Zah-K-ay-el D-jj-ay-ba) ~ Aelan. King of the West. Son of Valterys and Troyanna. Descendant of House Djeba.

GLOSSARY OF TERMS

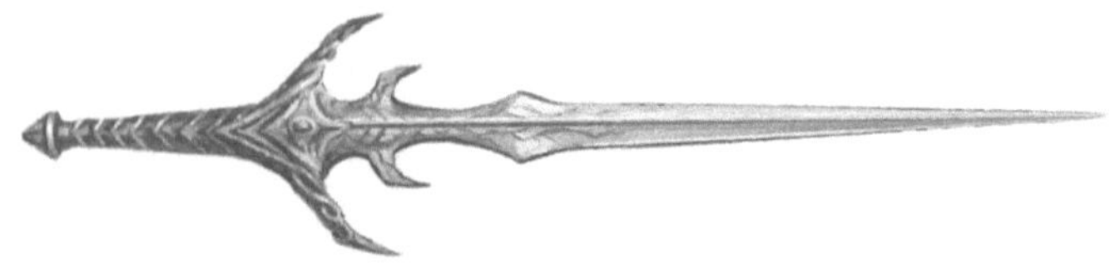

Aelan (Ay-lan) Any person born of Aelinaen descent. These are usually men and women descended from the Elder Gods: Nadra, Ohlin, Daknys, Rykoto, and Kaldaar. In modern times, Aelan refers to those not of another race.

Aelinae (Ay-lynn-ay) A world created by Nadra and Ohlin. It is disk-shaped with waterfalls at the edge of the world, and volcanoes beneath it.

Aelinaen(s) (Ay-lynn-ee-an) Of or having to do with Aelan culture.

Aergan (Air-gahn) An ancient, valuable ore found in only a few places on Aelinae.

Air Faerie Winged Faeries who call on the elements of air for power.

Anklam (Ahnk-lahm) A city on the coast, south of Talaith.

Artagh (R-tah-g) Related to the Eleri, Artaghs lack the Eleri Glamour, as well as the sophistication of the ancient race. They are rumored to be the best at making weapons and working with metals, especially the fabled Godsteel found only in the Haver-sham Mountains. Outsiders are often distrusted and it's rare to find Artaghs far from their caves.

Bells Aelinae's form of time telling. One bell is one Aelinean hour.

Caer Idris (Care Ee-dris) The ancestral home of The Overlord of the West. Currently, Valterys, Lord of the Dark sits on the Obsidian Throne.

Carlix A sleek, winged feline who makes her home in the mountains known as the Spine of Ohlin. One of the first creatures to inhabit the planet of Aelinae. Often referred to for their flexibility and quick responses, the number of people who have actually seen a carlix is few.

Celyn Eryri (See-lynn Air-ee) The mountain home of the Empress of Talaith. It is here the Light Celebrations take place every Wintertide.

Chantain Summerland's game. Played with six to eight players, it's a board game played where players are directed to act out what's given to them on a card.

Claidholm Solais (Kleeve Solish) ~ Sword of Light. Ohlin had this sword made for his daughter Verdaine during the Great War, but she refused to use it.

Cockleberry A yellowish fruit that grows in glens and meadows throughout Aelinae. With a taste similar to blackberries, cockleberries are often used in pies and tasty treats.

Crystal Court The accepted nickname for the court of the Empress of Talaith.

Crystal Palace The accepted nickname for the palace in Talaith where the Empress rules. It's fabled walls are made from a thin layer of rock clear enough to see through, yet unable to be penetrated by weapons or ShantiMari. No one knows who built the great palace, or where the stone came from.

Cynfar (Sin-far) The Eleri name for a talisman given to someone. Usually a pendant, it can also be a bracelet, earrings, or even a small stone. It must be kept close to the recipient for maximum benefit, hence the use of jewelry.

Dal Ferran (Dahl Fair-en) The fiery pits of hell beneath Aelinae's surface.

Dal Tara (Dahl Tar-a) A celestial resting place for the Gods and those they deem worthy. It is located in the second quadrant of the Meirdia Nebula.

Danuri A Province located in the West. The second largest city to Caer Idris, Danuri is widely known for their wine and ale making skills.

Danurian Anyone of Danuri descent.

Darennsai (Dar-en-sigh) An ancient title given to Taryn by the Eleri. Most don't know the true meaning of the word, thinking of it as nothing more than an honorific bestowed upon her by the Goddess Verdaine. Only a few know the word means, Daughter of the Sky. Less an oath than a promise that one day Taryn will sit at the side of Verdaine, as a goddess in her own right. The Eleri reject this idea.

Dark The part of ShantiMari that is derived from the sun. Only men are skilled in the ways of the Dark, except for the anomaly. To have Dark powers does not automatically make one bad, or evil. There are many men who use their Dark Shanti for good.

Dark Master A highly skilled practitioner of Dark ShantiMari.

Dark Shanti The male side of ShantiMari.

Darathi Vorsi (Dah-rahth-ee Vor-see) Aside from the carlix, *darathi vorsi* are the oldest creatures on Aelinae. Several thousand seasons ago they disappeared from the planet, but the Eleri hold the belief that one day they will return.

Delante (Day-lan-t) A dance performed with a group of people.

Dhur Ullan slur. It's the most offensive word you could call someone.

Dreem A whisky-like drink that ladies don't usually partake of.

Drerfox Cousin to the fox, a drerfox is bigger, with fangs coated with poison. Their coats shimmer in the sunlight, blending them into the background, making them difficult to see during the day.

The East A geographical location on the map indicating all lands, properties, kingdoms, etc east of the Spine of Ohlin. Includes the Narthvier, Ulla, Talaith, and the marshes near Kaldaar's Stones.

Eirielle (Air-ee-elle) The one of prophecy. Said to be the destroyer or the savior of Aelinae, depending on which prophecy you read. Only one Eirielle is ever said to be created, but that doesn't stop those of the Light and Dark from trying to make one. The Eirielle is rumored to possess all the strands of Shanti-Mari: Light, Dark, Eleri, and Telraicht-Noir. Although, the last is only known to the Brotherhood.

Eiriellean Prophecy A collection of prophecies that record various oracles' visions and ramblings about the Eirielle. Throughout history, there have been those that decried the prophecies, and those that touted them as truth. Nearly everyone fears either version coming to pass.

Elennish (Elle-enn-ish) The oldest language on Aelinae still spoken in the East and West.

Eleri (Ee-ler-ee) A mysterious clan of elf-like men and women who live in the Narthvier. They stay within the borders of their forest and don't like outsiders coming on their land. The Eleri share a collective conscious, in that they can call on the wisdom of past and future Eleri in times of duress. The oldest race on Aelinae, they and the *darathi vorsi* share a common bond. Thought to be caretakers of the beasts, when the *darathi vorsi* disappeared, it was a time of great mourning for the Eleri.

Fadair (Fah-d-air) The name Eleri have given to anyone not Eleri. It is meant to be used as a way to signify someone not of Eleri descent, but often it is used as a disparaging slur against non-Eleri.

Faerie Cakes Small cakes light in texture, but filling. Made with sponge cake and jam, these are Taryn's favorite. Don't ever leave a plate sitting around or she'll eat them all.

Feiche (Fee-ch) A large black bird similar to a raven, but faster and a bit bigger. They hunt in packs and are capable of taking down a small horse if so inclined.

Frost End The time between Wintertide and Summer. On Earth, it would occur around April.

Gaarendahl (Gare-en-doll) An older castle located between the Spine of Ohlin and the Summer Sea. It belongs to Valterys's family, but Zakael uses it most often.

Geigan (Guy-gan) A warrior race of people. Dark in coloring, they are rumored to be the source of mating with the Sitari.

Genari (Gen-ar-ee) ~ The Summerlands term for midwife.

Glamour A slight shimmering beneath the skin. Found only on Eleri.

Godsteel A metal forged by the Artagh of Haversham. Stronger than any other metal, godsteel is unbreakable. Long ago, only the gods could wield weapons made of godsteel (hence, the name), but at least two swords have made their way into mortal's hands. Rhoane's and Taryn's. But there are rumors that a few other swords have been tainted by Telraicht-Noir ShantiMari. Their owners are unknown at this time.

Grhom (Gr-om) A spiced drink made by the Eleri. It has healing properties and gives strength through the many ingredients used to make it. Taryn likens the taste to a thick chocolate mixed with chai. Occasionally, the Eleri will add alcohol to the drink.

Grierbas (Greer-bah) A large, wolf-like animal that makes its home in the Narthvier. Wild and territorial, grierbas keep away from civilizations, even avoiding the Eleri.

Grumlil Small orange fruit found on the Sitari islands. Tastes sweet and sour with a slight fizz.

Gyota (Gee-o-tah) In Eleri, *gyota* means 'destroyer'.

Harvest The months during the season between Summer and Wintertide. On Earth, this time is referred to as Fall.

Haversham A mountainous region where Artagh mine for gems, minerals, and the necessary metals to make weapons. Highly guarded, outsiders are not welcome in Haversham.

Hben Firn Jungle forest on the outskirts of Menurra in the Summerlands. Usually a peaceful place full of blooming flowers and luscious plants.

Hildgelt (Hill-d-gel-t) A Danurian ornamentation made from thin layers of blown glass.

House The family name by which most Aelans associate themselves. Every House has their own color and insignia. It is by these outward displays members of nobility and the court can recognize another's importance.

House Galendrin Ohlin created this House for Taryn on her crowning day. This is the highest honor anyone could hope to achieve and has only been granted once.

Kalaith The art of communicating with only a fan. Summerlanders have perfected this archaic language. It is often used as a form of seduction in the Summerlands.

Kidaris An ancient Eleri curse that's forbidden in modern Aelinae.

Kiltern River A river that runs north of Paderau to Ulla.

Lan Gyllarelle (Lahn Gill-a-rell) A vast lake located in the Narthvier. Its waters are rumored to hold healing properties. The Eleri often hold ceremonies on the banks of the lake.

Lake Oster Located between Talaith and Paderau, Lake Oster is often used as a stopping point for travelers. Fresh water and an abundance of fish refresh stores between the two great cities.

Levon (Le-von) A sleek black bird. Faster than any other birds, the levon is a favorite form of transportation for those competent in transformation.

Light A strain of ShantiMari found in females born on Aelinae. Not all women exhibit traits of the power, but are able to pass on Light ShantiMari to their daughters. Eleri females have Light ShantiMari, but their powers will differ from the Fadair's in that they use nature as a catalyst and Fadair use the air and sky. The Lady of Light is able to manipulate weather and has slight control over the sea.

Light Celebrations A week long event featuring competitions of physical prowess. The celebrations began as a way to offset the dreariness of Wintertide.

Light Throne The ancestral court of The Lady of Light, otherwise known as the Empress of Talaith. Also referred to as the Crystal Court. The actual throne is made of ancient oak from the Narthvier. Woven into the planks of wood is a thin layer of crystal.

Mari (Mar-ee) The female side of ShantiMari. Also referred to as Light.

Mind-Speak A form of communication used between two people within their minds.

Mount Nadrene (Mount Nay-dreen) The holiest place on Aelinae, Mount Nadrene is where Nadra sent Taryn through a portal to Earth. It is also a cavern filled with glittering crystals and a large lake. Some believe the cavern is the birthplace of all the gods and goddesses of Aelinae.

Mowbat A Summerland creature resembling a tiny winged squirrel.

Nadra (Nah-d-rah) The Mother Goddess, she and Ohlin created Aelinae.

Narcolis Flower found in the Summerlands. Has a sweet, powdery scent. Small white petals surround a vibrant pink center.

Narthvier (Narth-veer) A vast forest covering the northeast portion of Aelinae. The Eleri make their home in the Narthvier, or vier as some call it. The Eleri are protective of the forest and use veils to dissuade unwelcome visitors. Only the Eleri know how to raise the fabled veils.

Obsidian Throne The ancestral home of the Lord of the Dark. The actual throne is made of the same oak planks as the Light Throne. Within the wood fibers is woven obsidian granite.

Offlander Any person raised outside of the courtesies of court. The term is an insult of the highest order.

Ohlin (Oh-lynn) The Great Father, he and Nadra created Aelinae.

Paderau (Pah-der-oo) A vast city ruled by Duke Anje. Paderau sits between the Narthvier and Talaith, which makes it a busy port city for trading goods.

Paderau Palace The home of Duke Anje and his family.

Plenta ~ An Eleri pastry filled with sausage and cheese.

Privy Council A body of advisers to the Empress of Talaith. The council is made up of senior members of the highest Houses. On occasion, as with Hayden and Duke Anje, a junior member can represent their House in council. Also included in the privy council are the High Priest, and captains of the guard or military.

Ransthip Ullan medication used to ease the passing of one's life. Strong poison that works within minutes of ingestion. Leaves behind a rank smell like burning bark.

Ravenwood The less formal home of the Duke of Anje. When in residence, he oversees the local businesses.

Runyon Tree A black, gnarled tree with sharp thorns embedded in its trunk and branches.

Sargot (Sar-go) An orange-like fruit that tastes similar to a mango.

Scremp A leech-like worm used for bloodletting.

Seal of Ardyn Seals created by the Elder Gods to keep Rykoto imprisoned in the Temple of Ardyn.

Shanti (Shahn-tee) The male side of ShantiMari. Also referred to as Dark.

ShantiMari (Shahn-tee Mar-ee) Two halves of the same whole. ShantiMari is a power found in all things on Aelinae. Within men and women, it manifests itself in varying degrees from no visible signs, to extremely powerful. Those in positions of great power will have more ShantiMari than those born to the lesser clans or Houses. ShantiMari is often referred to as Light and Dark, or female and male. Within the confines of Shanti-Mari are rules, or etiquette. The power can be culled from the smallest pebble to the stars themselves. Wielding more power than one is capable of controlling often leads to a painful death.

Shadow Assassin Neither alive nor dead, Shadow Assassins were the elite force of Kaldaar's army. Only a powerful Master can create the demons.

Shadow Spawn, Shadow Soul Nicknames given to the Shadow Assassin.

Sheanna (Shee-ahn-a) An exiled Eleri. When an Eleri is *sheanna*, they are required to cut their hair and live outside the borders of the Narthvier until a certain amount of time has passed. Once they return to the Narthvier, they must complete the purification ceremony before they are considered to be Eleri once more.

Silden River This river runs south from Paderau to Lake Oster.

Sitari (Sit-ar-ee) Blue skinned warrior women who live in a community devoid of men. Their island sits at the southernmost edge of Aelinae. It is rumored their preferred mates are Geigan males. Sitari women can be found in other kingdoms of Aelinae, usually scouting for the strongest to procreate with. Once coupling has been achieved, the Sitari return to their island. Male offspring are said to be sacrificed to their goddess.

Skirm (Sk-ur-m) A banana-like fruit. The leaves of the skirm tree are broad and often used in cooking roasted meats.

Skirth A slim weapon favored by the Ullans. A cross between a pike and an arrow, Ullans can throw skirths with deadly accuracy.

Smelting Day An annual celebration of Artagh to honor their god. The fires of Haversham burn brightest on Smelting

Day, but no actual forging is done. Instead, the Artagh participate in dances and rousing songs around the flames.

Spine of Ohlin The range of mountains stretching from the Temple of Ardyn in the far north to the Summer Seas in the south.

Summerlands An island kingdom located south of Talaith in the Summer Seas.

Summer Seas The body of water covering the entire southern area of Aelinae.

Surtentse (Sir-tants) An ancient title meaning 'Son of the Terrarae'. Verdaine gives this honorific to Rhoane.

Sword of Ohlin Also known as Ynyd Eirathnacht. Ohlin had the sword made out of godsteel for his daughter, Daknys. The bearer of the sword must be pure of heart and worthy of the weapon.

Sylthan Age (Sil-than Age) The fourth century of Aelinae's time clock.

Talaith (Tal - eth) The capital city of the East. Ruled by the empress, also known as The Lady of Light.

Telraicht Arts (Tell-rah-ckt) A twisted version of ShantiMari that binds one's soul forever to the banished god, Kaldaar. Practitioners can be either male or female, but females become barren once they invoke the Oath of Fealty. Because of this, they are viewed as Brothers alongside the men.

Telraicht Brotherhood (Tell-rah-ckt) The oldest, most secret religion in Aelinae's history. Much of the Brotherhood is unknown to any except those who are counted among the members. Once a practitioner is invited to join the Brotherhood, they are challenged to a series of tests, many of which require virginal sacrifices. See also Vessel. Membership is often passed from one family member to another, but the terms must be satisfied before being accepted. Those who do not satisfy the requirements, or are not deemed worthy are destroyed.

Telraicht-Noir Shanti and **Telraicht-Noir ShantiMari**

(Tell-rah-ckt Nwaarh) Also called simply Noir. See also Telraicht Arts. This form of ShantiMari uses chaos to fuel its power. External and internal sources give practitioners their strength. They pull their power from the world around them, or the inner conflict people try to conceal. The use of Telraicht-Noir Shanti-Mari is shunned by the Light and Dark, but there are those who have found a way to manipulate the strands of light and shadow into a woven tapestry of devastation that cannot be traced. These are Masters that even the Telraicht Brotherhood fear.

Temple of Ardyn (Ar-din) Rykoto's temple and source of power. He was imprisoned here by Daknys and the Elder Gods after his defeat in the Great War.

Terrarae ~ Aelinean name for earth, or ground. The substance upon which life is built.

Treplar (Treh-p-lar) Round apple-like, spiky fruits from the Summerlands.

Trisp A thick alcoholic drink.

Ulla (Oo-la) A kingdom located in the far East of Aelinae. The Ullans are a tribal people, following their herds throughout the season. Ullan horses are of the finest stock.

Verdaine (Vehr-d-ane) Daughter of Nadra and Ohlin, goddess of the Eleri.

Verdaine's Prophecy When Rhoane was born, Verdaine prophesied that he would be exiled from his people until the *gyota* returned. His fate would be tied to the one who is and who is not for all time.

Veil A mysterious barrier preventing outsiders from entering the Narthvier.

Vier ~ Nickname of the Narthvier.

Vorlock A huge, lizard-like creature with heavy scales and a wide frill around its head. Vorlocks contain a poison that can kill a man or woman instantly.

Weirren (Weer-en) The ancestral home of the Eleri King and Queen.

Weirren Court The gathered nobility of the Eleri live among the many buildings interwoven through the ancient tree that makes up the Weirren.

Weirren Throne Built into the oldest tree on Aelinae, the Weirren Throne is a living, breathing seat.

The West Geographical area located to the west of Ohlin's Spine. Includes the kingdom of the Overlord of the West (now called King of the West), Danuri Province, and Haversham.

Western Seas The body of water located off the Western Coast of Aelinae.

Woodland Faerie Faerie folk who make their home in the forests Aelinae, most commonly found in the Narthvier. Woodland faeries grow to be around three feet in height, although some are taller. They are the exception. Woodland faeries share a special bond with nature and can cultivate new species of living plants or animals.

Ynyd Eirathnacht (Inid Air-ath-nack-t) The name of Ohlin's sword, currently in the possession of Taryn Rose Galendrin.

Zaff Animal found in the Narthvier. Extremely good at climbing trees. They make their home in the treetops and canopy of forests.

AUTHOR NOTES

It is an honor for me to be able to bring my stories to the world. There are many people who help make that happen. From my first Beta readers to the final proof, I couldn't do this without their assistance. First, to my Dazzling Dragons. You are a blessing to my life! Thank you for being such a fantastic reader group. Thank you to Carly O'Donoghue, Abel Fetter, Lynn Trahan, Karol Inskeep, Caprice Whitmire for your notes, insight, and suggestions on making this book better.

Last, but as always not least – to my husband and kids—you inspire me every single day. Love you to the moon and back—to infinity.

ABOUT THE AUTHOR

Tameri Etherton is a *USA Today* Bestselling and award-winning author of fierce scorching fantasy and paranormal romance. She grew up inventing fictional worlds where the impossible was possible.

It's been said she leaves a trail of glitter in her wake as she creates new adventures for her kickass heroines, and the rogues who steal their hearts.

She lives an enchanted life traveling the world with her very own prince charming and their mischievous dragon, Lady Dazzleton.

Read More from Tameri Etherton and explore the Aetherverse at
www.TameriEtherton.com

9 781941 955222